"Winn, this isn't the time to be shy," Asher said from the base of the ladder. "Toss down your dress."

She blushed to the roots of her hair. Unfortunately, even turning crimson wasn't enough to warm her frozen fingers and stop her teeth from chattering.

"I'm n-not b-being shy," she stammered, fumbling with the fastenings. "Y-you've already s-seen me w-without the dress."

"You're quite right. Therefore, there's no reason to stand upon ceremony."

Before she could ask what he meant by that, the top of his head emerged over the edge of the loft. She might have gasped at his audacity, but then the rest of him came into view and her mind whirred to a sudden stop.

Asher Holt was naked.

Well, mostly. His bare, broad shoulders and sinewy arms appeared first, muscles shifting and bunching beneath his skin as he navigated the final rungs—and far more adeptly than she had done. Then he unfolded from a crouch, and stood.

Her greedy eyes skimmed the length of him, taking in every . . . blessed . . . inch.

By Vivienne Lorret

Lord Holt Takes a Bride

The Mating Habits of Scoundrels

VIVIENNE LORRET

AVONBOOKS

An Imprint of HarperCollinsPublishers

LORD HOLT TAKES A BRIDE. Copyright © 2020 by Vivienne Lorret. All rights reserved. Printed in the United States of America. No part of this book may be used or reproduced in any manner whatsoever without written permission except in the case of brief quotations embodied in critical articles and reviews. For information, address HarperCollins Publishers, 195 Broadway, New York, NY 10007.

First Avon Books mass market printing: April 2020

Print Edition ISBN: 978-0-06-297659-8
Digital Edition ISBN: 978-0-06-297657-4

Cover design by Amy Halperin
Cover illustration © Jon Paul Ferrara

Avon, Avon & logo, and Avon Books & logo are registered trademarks of HarperCollins Publishers in the United States of America and other countries.

HarperCollins is a registered trademark of HarperCollins Publishers in the United States of America and other countries.

FIRST EDITION

20 21 22 23 24   QGM   10 9 8 7 6 5 4 3 2 1

*For my mother,
who insisted that this story needed
a horse named Victor
instead of a rabid badger.*

Acknowledgments

This book would never have been possible if not for the readers who wrote numerous emails, demanding that Asher Holt have a story of his own. So, with heartfelt gratitude, I want to thank each and every one of you for sending me emails for weeks, months, and even years after Asher Holt made his first appearance in the novella, *Just Another Viscount in Love*.

This book was a simple *kidnapping an heiress* story in the beginning, but one that needed to evolve. And so, next, I would like to thank Cathy and Jan for our brainstorming session at *Buns & Roses* that helped me work out the important details of consent in a kidnapping story.

I'd also like to thank my editor, Nicole, for reading the synopsis and being just as excited about this book as I was to write it. And another thank-you goes out to my agent, Stephanie, for all her hard work and for being a great sounding board.

I'm also grateful to my sisters for understanding when I disappear inside my cave for weeks, but are there to greet me when I step out for a breath of air. And special thanks go to Cyndi for being my second set of eyes and for her abundance of encouragement.

Last but not least, I would like to thank the woman

who laughed at my idea to put a rabid badger in the story. Even after I explained how many hours I'd spent watching terrifying YouTube videos for research, she insisted that the book needed a horse named Victor instead. And, in the end, I think she was right. So, thank you, Mom.

Lord Holt
Takes a Bride

Prologue

Asher Holt jolted awake as a woman's soft, warm body landed hard against his hips. Grunting from near castration, he shifted her lush figure to the left. "Easy now, sweets, or my Thoroughbred will never leave his stall."

He blinked groggily up at a pair of wide hazel eyes, studying the peridot green irises rimmed with a rich penumbra of cinnamon, and tried to recall her name. Nothing came to him. Brushing aside the disheveled mane of sweetly fragrant reddish-blond hair, he took a closer look at her heart-shaped face, gently rounded chin and carnation-pink lips. A tiny constellation of freckles emerged through a fine dusting of face powder, her cheeks red and blotchy beneath. Absently, he wondered if she used lemon juice to diminish blemishes like so many women did.

Such a pity. He'd always been partial to freckles.

Though, with such a complexion, society would never declare her a great beauty. And yet . . . there was *something* about her.

But not enough to spark his memory.

Then again, his skull was about to crack open like a desiccated milkweed pod and he could hardly put two thoughts together. His brain seemed caught in a mire of fuzz and fluff that even coated the back of his tongue.

"You're foxed," the lush creature accused, wrinkling her nose. "And you smell like a rum pot."

That would explain things. "Peculiar. I never imbibe to excess."

"Well, you certainly picked a fine time to begin. We don't have an instant to waste."

She pushed herself clear of him with a huff, affording him the view of a four-strand pearl necklace and heaps of cream-colored taffeta, enswathed by silver netting and bespeckled with even more pearls.

The mystery woman looked like she'd exploded straight from an oyster bed . . . or a treasure chest.

A dull buzz of alertness niggled at the back of his mind. Though at the current trudging pace of his thoughts, it would take days for any information to breach the thick fleece threatening to burst through his eye sockets and ears.

Head spinning, he maneuvered into a more upright position. Only then did he realize he was still clad in yesterday's riding clothes, greatcoat, and weathered top boots. He also recognized the aged burgundy interior of the carriage surrounding him, the familiar upholstery worn thin to an apricot hue over the squabs.

The girl in pearls tugged on the sparse, uneven tassel strings at the ends of the shades. He hoped she was careful. He was almost certain that this decrepit conveyance was held together by nothing more than a few boards and some clever stitching. Pull on the wrong thread and the walls might very well crash down onto the street.

The tassel broke off in her gloved hand and he braced himself, just in case. Thankfully, the walls remained intact.

Unconcerned, she merely flicked it from her fingertips, then peeled back the brittle fabric from the window. A dull wash of gray light entered the cabin and opened another crag in his skull. Grimacing, he recoiled into the corner of the bench as she peered outside toward a fine mist collecting on the church steps.

Apparently, she didn't like the view either, for she turned back to him, worrying her plump bottom lip between her teeth. Her gaze met his, beseeching him with some unknown plea.

All at once, he felt a strange sense of recognition . . . while still having no idea who she was. Though it was becoming clear that they must have met before.

"Well?" Her hand impatiently stirred the air between them, her lips parting on panted breaths of . . . anticipation? Disquiet?

Either way, he felt compelled to take in a lungful of air for her. "*Well*, what?"

"Shouldn't we be . . . getting on by now?"

Ah. At once he understood.

His appreciative gaze drifted over her voluptuous form, then focused on those strands of pearls above the rapid rising and falling of her lush bosom. Clearly, she was a young courtesan. Perhaps she'd been looking for a new protector and, drunk out of his gourd, he'd invited her into his carriage.

A pity, really. "My apologies, sweets. I wish I had the coin to afford you. Alas, I do not. Nor do I ever mix business with pleasure. In my opinion, carnal delights should be uninhibited and unconstrained by the obligations of monetary transactions."

Her tawny brows furrowed and a tiny rosebud of wrinkles formed above her nose. "*Whot* are you—"

Abruptly, her cheeks flushed to crimson. Then her mouth formed a small round O.

She swallowed and shifted back on the bench with a crunch of taffeta. Surrounded by voluminous netting, she looked like a fuzzy-headed caterpillar in the midst of slipping into a chrysalis for an overdue nap.

A grumpy caterpillar, who started to wag her finger at him.

"You should be ashamed of yourself. I'm not going to become a harlot or a street . . . strumpet. Jane said you were slow-witted but, honestly, I didn't realize she'd left me in the hands of a proper buffoon." She darted another glance through the carriage window. "Oh, this was a mistake. I knew it all along, and yet there was no other way. And now, there's no going back either. I just made certain of that."

Asher ignored the *buffoon* remark for the moment. "Jane?"

"Your cousin, of course!"

He was fairly positive he didn't have a cousin named Jane. But there was the off chance that he'd merely lost her in the opaque quagmire between his ears.

The courtesan speared him with an impatient glare as if she'd expected him to say something in response. When he didn't, she groused, "*Honestly.* Do you think it possible for us to continue this . . . introduction *en route* since my father is doubtless discovering my absence and bound to burst upon us at any moment?"

The threat of her father's wrath—or any father, really—spurred Asher into motion. He called out to the driver and, with a crack of the whip, the carriage jolted. And so did the contents of his skull.

Squinting, he took another long look at his companion. When she was perturbed, the outer cinnamon band of her irises seemed more like a ring of fire encircling molten green pools. And as he stared into them, his head cleared bit by bit.

Stretching out his legs, he kicked an empty bottle that coggled a few memories into place. "Your father a tyrant, is he?"

"Not entirely. He isn't one to shout or to raise his hand when an opposing argument is set before him. However"—she hesitated, pursing those pink lips thoughtfully—"he has a knack for turning conversations into mazes and, before you know it, you've agreed to whatever he wanted in the first place."

He nodded in commiseration, having been sired by a master manipulator as well.

In fact, come to think of it, *he* was the reason Asher was here. If it wasn't for his dear old pater, then he wouldn't have heaps of debt waiting to bury him alive. Asher even recalled forming a desperate plan to finally liberate himself from the Luciferian tyranny.

But what *was* that plan, precisely?

He had no idea. Though he seemed to recall being disgusted by his own actions. Enough to drink an entire pint of rum. Enough to take a carriage to the church last night. Enough to wait outside until morning for his chance to . . . to . . .

No.

Asher sat forward as realization dawned, and he winced at the shaft of silver light lancing through the center of the carriage.

Lowering his face into the cup of his hands, he mumbled, "Just so we're perfectly clear, your name is . . ."

"Miss Winnifred Humphries."

"Yes, of course." Now he recalled everything.

She was the heiress he intended to kidnap.

Chapter 1

The week before

Winnifred Humphries never imagined that the sum of her existence would dwindle down to corsets and cakes. Cinched laces and afternoon teas. Whalebone and wedding plans.

Betrothed at the beginning of her second Season, she'd hoped for waltzes and even warm lemonade. Glittering chandeliers and moonlit terraces. Shared secrets and stolen kisses.

But those things didn't happen to plump, freckled heiresses.

Resigned, she dutifully watched her fiancé dash off to his new barouche, the silver trim gleaming in the midday light like a freshly minted coin. Mr. Woodbine bade her no more than an absent wave, and his steps were far lighter in leaving the stately townhouse than in entering it.

Her own steps might have been nimble as well if she could breathe. But Mother—in her unending quest to have a slender and graceful daughter—ordered Winnifred's laces drawn tighter for the special occasion of having Mr. Woodbine for tea.

Not that it mattered. He'd grimaced each time a morsel of cake had passed her lips. And because of him, she'd eaten the whole blasted slice. She hadn't even been hungry.

Combined with tea, that last spiteful bite was expanding to continental proportions. The country of Plumcakia and all its inhabitants now dwelled inside her, some holding hand-hewn spears and waging war on her lungs.

Placing a hand over her midriff, she hoped for peace between nations. Then she returned to the parlor, prepared to beg her friends to loosen her laces.

Unfortunately, Mother was still lingering in the gold-chintz-papered room, fussing with red and pink roses in a cobalt meiping vase. Her keen gaze cut to Winnifred and she clucked her tongue. "I warned you against the plum cake, dear."

Winnifred exchanged wry glances with Jane Pickerington and Elodie Parrish, who were sitting primly on the camelback settee. Her friends were well-acquainted with Lady Waldenfield's ongoing and, frankly, futile pursuit of perfection.

Sinking down onto the edge of an upholstered chair, Winnifred was careful not to bend at the waist. She couldn't risk a corset eruption, after all. Because of Mr. Woodbine and the troubling letter that arrived before him, the afternoon was already dreadful enough without the possibility of impaling her friends with shooting spears of whalebone.

On a brighter note, if she fainted and her head lolled onto the lofted expanse of her own bosom, she would surely smother herself to death and wouldn't have to marry Mr. Woodbine. In addition to that boon, Mother could order her daughter's corpse fitted into the newer fashions of narrow dropped waists and puffed sleeves without any complaint whatsoever.

Inhaling a sip of flesh-pinching air, she said to her mother, "As I recall . . . the words . . . 'Try the cake, dear. It's simply divine' fell from your lips."

"Yes, but I raised my brows as I spoke," she said, turning to demonstrate.

A master of her craft, the subtle arch revealed a refined degree of censure and only a trace of wrinkles on her still-youthful countenance. Imogene Humphries certainly did not appear old enough to have a child of two and twenty. Ever-stylish in her violet checked silk tobine, she might have stepped from the pages of *La Belle Assemblée*. Her willowy figure hardly required the aid of a corset, and her golden hair was always artfully coiffed—unlike Winnifred's unholy tangle of reddish-blond curls.

Thankfully, Mother had given up on taming it ages ago.

"With your wedding scarcely a week hence," Mother continued, "you should be mindful of Mr. Woodbine's moods. Surely you noticed the way he eyed your every forkful of cake with grim disapproval. He never does that with Lady Stanton. In fact, just last night, I saw them at a dinner party. And, *by the by*, she was wearing the most elegant gown of—"

"You do realize you're admiring my fiancé's mistress, do you not?" Winnifred interjected.

Her cheeks heated with embarrassment and her stomach roiled in suppressed umbrage. A volcano erupted on Plumcakia, killing all the natives and scorching the tender lining of her throat. She swallowed, too ashamed to look past the gold-inlaid edge of the low table and toward her friends.

"*Pish tosh*. That's simply the way of things in our circle. Mr. Woodbine has had Lady Stanton's companionship long before you came along. She was a poor, childless widow and his family forbade him from marrying her. It's positively pointless to imagine that he would abandon her simply because he's marrying a young woman whose dowry is too appealing to resist."

Winnifred felt as desirable as the burlap sack a highwayman might fill with gold sovereigns. A lovely reminder that she was merely the vessel that transferred a fortune from one hand to another.

Of course, she wasn't stupid enough to believe that he was marrying her out of affection. From the beginning, Mr. Woodbine could scarcely stand to linger in the same room with her.

It was her father who'd arranged the union. Paying no attention to Winnifred's unwavering objections, Viscount Waldenfield had mulishly chosen Mr. Woodbine because he was third in line for a dukedom and poor enough to manipulate.

Among other disappointments, life had taught her that marriage was nothing more than an obligation to one's family. So then why did her foolish heart still yearn for love? To find a man who might want her without condition or fortune?

"Now, now. There's no need to turn all prickly," Mother said, coming to her side to fuss over her chrome-yellow gigot sleeves, puffing up the left to match the right. Then she lifted a rosewater-scented hand to Winnifred's cheek, her expression soft and solemn. "I'm only trying to save you from any romantic inclinations. I was once a young, wealthy bride, too, you know. Believe me when I tell you that it's far better to have a firm understanding now, rather than to suffer disenchantment for the years ahead of you."

For an instant, Winnifred could have sworn she saw the reflection of her own longing in her mother's eyes.

Then Imogene Humphries stood tall and flitted an elegant hand in the air toward Jane and Ellie. "Now then, girls. Don't let my Winnifred talk you into loosening her laces. She's been attempting to bribe her maid with comfits all day. But I'm determined that she will make the ideal portrait of a bride by next week."

Then, with a wink, she turned on her heel and sashayed from the room.

The instant the doorway was vacant, Winnifred slouched back onto the chair, her bustle crumpling like crushed dreams. "I can only hope that the world will erupt in fire in the next seven days. Do you think there are any volcanoes beneath London?"

Ellie sat forward on a huff, blowing her inky dark fringe from her forehead. Ever-quick to show her emotions, her amber eyes were fierce and her porcelain complexion hosted two spots of pink on the apples of her cheeks. "Winnie, you cannot possibly marry Mr. Woodbine."

"Actually, she is *capable* of marrying him," Jane added in her usual logical fashion, her topknot of wispy brown curls slightly askew. "Regardless of how it isn't the sensible thing to do *and* will guarantee her misery for years to come."

"Thank you for that," Winnifred said dryly. "Lovely to know I can trust my friends to have a care for my tender feelings."

"Prue will say the same once she arrives. Though it seems her trademark tardiness has gone beyond the pale today."

"But Prue isn't coming. Haven't you heard?" Winnifred looked from one friend to the other. "Oh my, then it's worse than I thought."

"Whatever do you mean?" Jane's sable lashes clustered around a pair of inquisitive blue eyes.

Beside her, Ellie choked on a whimper of distress and her complexion lost its luminescence, fading to pasty white. "Something terrible has happened. I sense it now. Yes . . . there's a dark presence among us."

Ellie had a knack for seeing Death around every corner. In fact, her fear of the great beyond rivaled Mother's horror at the thought of letting out Winn's laces.

"Prue merely"—Winnifred hesitated, trying to sound cheerful and not reveal any of her own qualms until she knew for certain—"embarked on an unplanned holiday."

"*Saints preserve us!* My aunts said the same thing when I was young and my canary went missing. Days later, the gardener's dog dug up Goldie's corpse beneath the cabbage roses."

Winnifred wasted a precious breath on a sigh. "That wasn't a euphemism for Prue having passed away in her sleep."

"Winnie should hardly have served us tea first if that were the case," Jane tutted. "She would have told us at the door and had footmen and smelling salts on hand if we happened to faint. Which reminds me . . ."

Reaching down to the carpet, Jane hefted a red paisley reticule of epic proportions onto her tiny lap and began to sift through the mysterious contents. She was famously—or *infamously*, depending on the parties involved—prepared for any situation.

"Ah. Here we are," Jane announced, holding out a small brown vial like a prize cup. Removing the stopper, she waved it under Ellie's nose. "Now take a deep breath of this vinaigrette. I've infused it with lavender. It's bracing but with a pleasant finish. What do you think?"

Ellie issued a cough and noncommittal murmur. Jane's inventions weren't always raving successes.

While her friends were somewhat distracted, Winnifred decided to retrieve the letter from the escritoire on the far wall. Standing, she clenched every part of her that she could and heard a series of creaks that either foretold impending doom to her seams or announced that the oak-sized busk running down the center had suddenly sprouted a limb. Somehow, she managed an erect posture without incident and crossed the room.

Retrieving the missive, Winnifred unfolded it as she returned to her friends.

"This arrived only moments before you did, so I haven't had time to fully digest it." *Much like the plum cake*, she thought as she carefully sat down again. "Prudence writes, 'Dearest Winnie, Please forgive my dreadful scrawl. I am penning this note in great haste before I must away this very morning! I doubt I shall return in time for your wedding breakfast and it is all due to a complete misunderstanding. You see, last night my father discovered me in the gardens at Sutherfield Terrace . . . and not quite as alone as I ought to have been.'"

Ellie gasped. "Dear heavens! She had to have been with a man."

"Clearly," Jane said. "But the important question is, who was he and in what state was *she* found?"

"Well, one thing is for certain—he could not have been a gentleman," Ellie answered. "Or else there would be no reason to send her away."

"And yet, who other than a gentleman would have been invited to Sutherfield Terrace?"

Winnifred cleared her throat. "The two of you could continue to speculate, or *I* could simply read the letter, using what little air I possess at the moment."

Sitting forward, Jane gestured with an impatient roll of her hand. "Merely forming a hypothesis. You may proceed."

Winnifred skimmed the slanted scrawl, finding her place. "Let's see . . . *great haste* . . . *wedding break-fast* . . . *gardens at Sutherfield* . . . Ah yes, here we are. 'And now my father threatens to send me to a convent. Thankfully my mother persuaded him—just this morning—to pack me off to my stodgy aunt and uncle instead. I, however, am not certain my circumstance will fare any better. I shall be in a convent all the same. And yet, I tell you, dearest Winnie, that nothing of great import transpired between myself and Lord F—. I do not fancy myself in love with him. At all. Oh, bother, I hear Mother calling for me. I shall write again when we've reached the coaching inn. Yours affectionately, Prudence Thorogood.'"

"Poor Prue!" Ellie lamented. "To be sent away at the height of the Season. Do you think she was seduced by this . . . Lord F—?"

Jane pursed her lips in speculation. "If she was not, then it was near enough that it gave her parents reason to fear that it would only be a matter of time. This Lord F— is unquestionably a scoundrel if her parents do not anticipate a proposal of marriage."

Winnifred thought of her own experience, and how she was informed of her betrothal at dinner. Over calf's brains. Not quite as thrilling as a scandal in the garden.

Just once, she'd like to get caught unawares in a garden. To have a man go completely mad for her. To gaze at her with desire instead of with disgust.

Mr. Woodbine would never look at her that way. There wasn't an ounce of passion between them. Yet in a week's time, she was doomed to marry him.

She stood again, away from the chair's confinement. But she still felt trapped. Utterly suffocated.

Fanning herself with the letter, she focused on something more agreeable. "But what if this man genuinely liked Prue? Perhaps so much that he'd—*oh, I don't know*—forgotten they were likely to be discovered. And perhaps after his night with her, he was willing to relinquish his status as a scoundrel and marry her without delay."

Jane arched her brows, a sly smile glinting in the upward tilt of her eyes. "Quite the fancy, Winnie."

"Not really. After all, how could Prue, or any of us for that matter, have known his intentions? It isn't as if debutantes are taught about the ways of the marriage-minded gentleman in finishing school."

"Now that would have made a grand primer—*The Marriage Habits of the Native Aristocrat*," Ellie said with a laugh.

"It isn't a terrible idea, actually." Winnifred felt tingles race over her skin, raising gooseflesh. "Jane is forever talking about writing a book."

"I am. *And?*"

"Well, this should be it! Why, simply imagine all the women you could help. How to recognize the signs for when a gentleman is trying to catch a wife . . . *and* when he is trying to avoid being caught."

"You may not have noticed, but my wallflower status keeps me from being much acquainted with gentlemen, or scoundrels, for that matter."

"Well, perhaps we should be. All of us."

"Winnie, you are scandalous!" Ellie grinned, excitement brimming in her expression.

Jane tapped her fingertip against her mouth. "There have been a number of other debutantes sent away like our dear Prue."

Winnifred nodded with breathless encouragement. "It's practically an epidemic. There must be dozens who've mistakenly believed they were being courted with honest intent."

"Or more," Jane agreed. "And if we did uncover the mystery between an honorable gentleman's pursuit and a scoundrel's seductive charm . . . Why, just think of how much more prepared it would make us."

"If *you* were any more prepared, you'd be a fortune-teller." Ellie laughed. "But how do you propose to come by this information, oh scholar of the ages?"

"It will have to be the three of us. Or rather, just the

two of us, since Winnie will be married in a week and then on her wedding trip."

"I'm not taking a wedding trip," she announced, feeling another suffocating pinch inside her lungs. Only this time, it wasn't from the corset. "Mr. Woodbine wishes to buy a grand house as soon as my dowry fills his coffers. Therefore, you can certainly rely on me to do my part for the primer."

Jane tilted her head in speculation. "Doesn't he already own a townhouse?"

"Yes, but we both agree that keeping separate residences is more the thing. After all, my parents live on completely separate floors, so it's as if they are in different houses. The practice works swimmingly for them."

Trying to appear unaffected, she turned away and made a show of taking the letter back to the escritoire.

"Is that truly the life *you* want?" Ellie asked.

"Well, I'm hardly inclined to hang on Mr. Woodbine's waistcoat like a golden watch fob. Let him keep his house and his mistress while I enjoy freedom for the first time in my life."

"*Freedom* is the key word in your little speech," Jane said as she rose from the settee.

Then, in a blur of sprigged muslin, her sprite-like form darted across the room to the open doorway. After a quick peek into the hall, she closed the pair of white glazed doors, then went about rummaging through her reticule once more.

Confused, Winnifred looked to Ellie, who shrugged but quickly averted her gaze as if there were certain goings-on that they didn't want to tell her.

"Ah-ha!" Jane said with triumph. Pulling out a metronome, she placed it on the floor and set it to a quick meter.

"Do you have a sudden urge to sing to us?" Winnifred asked.

Jane took her hand and led her back to the chair. "We can't risk anyone overhearing us."

"You're quite right," Ellie agreed with a stern nod. "Our plan is too important to risk being thwarted by eavesdroppers."

Winnifred looked from one friend to the other, suddenly wary. "Plan? What plan?"

Jane absently sat on the table, her expression set. Resolute. "To free you from marrying Mr. Woodbine. He—"

"Doesn't deserve you," Ellie interjected, her fist raised.

"—has proven himself to be deaf to any desire of yours. Do you truly want to marry—"

"A pompous stuffed shirt who cannot see past your fortune?"

"Ellie, please," Jane said with a pointed stare. "I have practiced this speech all morning. We'll never get past page one at this rate."

"Then, just skip to the page where Winnifred dashes out of the church on the morning of her wedding and escapes in your cousin's carriage."

"*Whot?*"

"Now you've done it. Winnie needs to be eased into these things and you've skipped directly to page three." Demonstrating, Jane withdrew folded papers from the infamous reticule, shuffling past the first and second pages before pointing to a sketch on the third.

It depicted a rudimentary drawing of a figure in a bell-shaped gown, slipping through a church window that was engulfed in . . . "Are those flames coming out of the window? Surely your plan isn't to set the church on fire?"

Jane squinted at the drawing. "Those are pigeons, of course."

Winnifred looked again, unconvinced. "And on top of my head?"

"Well, that's your hair, obviously. I planned your escape to follow the release of two dozen pigeons into the church. The chaos that would ensue afterward would give you time to shimmy through the window. You see, I've broken down each component into stages . . ."

"I cannot run away from my own wedding."

"Actually, you are capable of doing anything you choose," Jane said firmly, then continued in a softer tone. "And it is your choice to make. This is the nineteenth century, after all."

"Winnie, I cannot bear the thought of you marrying a man who frowns with disapproval over everything you say and do, *and* who refuses to take you on a wedding trip even though you've been waiting your entire life to travel abroad." After her speech, Ellie drew in an enviably large breath.

The truth was, Mr. Woodbine didn't see merit in many things that interested Winnifred. He didn't even want to tour Hyde Park with her.

She looked down at the drawing again. "But imagine the embarrassment my parents would suffer. I've disappointed them every day of my entire life, first by being born a girl and then by being not quite right in every other way. The least I could do as my final duty to them is to enter into my marriage without a scandal."

Ellie huffed. "But *they* aren't marrying the odious Mr. Woodbine. You are."

"But to run away from my own wedding . . ."

"I have considered the possible ramifications. Page four," Jane added, tapping the blunt end of a stubby black pencil to the papers. "And from what I've determined, the worst possible outcome would be going through with the wedding. After all, since your father frowns upon unnecessary travels and never ventures farther from London than his country estate, I highly doubt he would send you away like Prue's parents did her."

"No, they have other methods of showing disapproval, the primary one being silence. To give you an example, my father hasn't spoken to his own sister in ten years. He barely speaks to my mother. I imagine he wouldn't think twice about completely cutting me out of his life."

"If you ask me, your parents don't deserve you," Jane said. "They certainly don't appreciate you enough. I'd like to have my parents adopt you. With eleven of us romping through the halls, it isn't likely they'd even realize someone new had been added to the brood."

Ellie reached out and clasped her hand. "And my

aunts love you, as well. You could live with us whenever Jane wanders off and loses herself in a pile of books for days."

Winnifred laughed softly, feeling tears prick her eyes. She was inordinately grateful to have such friends.

Even so, the list of ramifications on page four terrified her. Her actions would wreak so much havoc in their lives. And, honestly, she couldn't guarantee that the outcome would grant her a better life. Or a chance at love.

She might go through all this only to discover that a man could never love her without the promise of a fortune. The last thing she wanted was proof of this suspicion.

Shaking her head, she relinquished the pages. "I cannot—or rather—I *will not* do this."

There. She'd said it. A firm declaration.

She waited for a sense of rightness to overtake her. A weight to lift. But that feeling never came.

Instead, she felt suffocated again. In that instant, she wished her seams would rip. Her lungs needed to fill with air, to be unrestrained. But Mother had ordered her dresses made with double stitching and stomachers for additional confinement. Like a cage.

"I understand," Jane said solemnly. "We will always support you in whatever you choose."

Ellie wiped a tear from the corner of her own eye and forced a smile. "Well then, we'll simply focus on our primer."

Tucking *the plan* into the depths of her reticule, Jane then withdrew a palm-sized ledger. "We'll start off by listing the names of all the men we know and what we know of them. That will give us a splendid foundation from which to begin. Each of us will take on specific tasks and write chapters on the information gathered."

"I volunteer to ferret out whoever this wholly contemptible Lord F— could be. In addition to whatever else is needed." Ellie sniffed.

"Winnie, I should think you'll be able to offer insight into what awaits a young woman on her wedding night," Jane said with a scholar's interest and not the barest blush.

But Ellie's cheeks flamed bright pink. "Jane! You cannot ask her about . . . *that*."

As far as complexions went, Winnifred sensed hers had turned decidedly chartreuse.

"I'm sure it will be nothing but awkwardness," she said. "Mother told me that the first night in the marriage bed is much like that time our carriage wheel broke and we were forced to crowd ourselves into a passing mail coach until we reached the country house—rather jostling, sweaty, and with someone breathing directly into your face."

Ellie cringed.

Jane wrote furiously.

And Winnifred . . . well, she didn't want to think about it until she had to.

"For my share of research, I shall ask the married set what drove them to the altar," she offered.

Yet she already knew what she'd find—an abundance of gentlemen willing to do anything for money.

Chapter 2

Asher Holt would sell his soul for money . . . if he still had one. But that ethereal core of hope and morality had abandoned him years ago. Right around the time he'd started donning his signature black cravats.

He wore the length of black silk tied around his neck to mourn the eventual death of his father. Regrettably, the Marquess of Shettlemane was still quite hale and doubtless infused with a fresh surge of vitality each time he practiced beggaring his only son.

At this rate, he would be immortal.

Yet Asher's days of agonizing over a future in Fleet Prison for his father's debts and schemes would soon be at an end.

The chimes on the clock tolled the eleventh hour. He expelled a breath of relief when the man in the burgundy coat appeared at the threshold of the billiards room at White's. The horse-toothed Lord Berryhill cast a skittish glance past the men calculating their angles with cue sticks in hand, and the ones hunched over chess and backgammon boards, until alighting on Asher near the fireplace.

Berryhill bobbled his head in a nod and trotted over. Sinking with stiff trepidation onto the opposite chair, he nudged a newspaper across the polished table and whispered, "It's all there."

Like any worthy Captain Sharp, Asher surreptitiously slipped two fingers into the folds and tucked the money up his sleeve.

"Aren't you going to count it?" Berryhill gulped and tugged at his snowy cravat, his knee bouncing like a piston in a Watt condensing engine at full boil. The man was a veritable cornucopia of twitches.

Asher could have won a fortune from him if they'd played cards.

He offered a half shrug in his usual aloof manner, smoothing the newspaper to read it. "I trust it's there."

Though, in truth, Asher *had* counted the money. While some lads were taught philosophy and religion at their father's knee, he had learned gambling and greed. A lifetime of training had taught him how to discern one note from the next with a mere flick of his thumb. Even with a folded stack.

And by the jaded age of six, he knew never to trust another soul when money was on the line. Especially not his father.

Berryhill joggled to the edge of his chair and mopped his brow, looking more eager to bolt than the horses on the paddock earlier. "You're a good man, Holt. Better than I thought, at any rate. I'd never wagered before and when my rider lost, I'd worried that you'd try to extort more money by threatening to tell my mother, or something of that sort. Indeed, everyone knows that your father's a cheat and a charlatan and never honors his . . . um . . . well . . ."

As he spoke, Asher coolly appraised the chinless lord over the top of the paper until his words sputtered to a halt. Berryhill's cheeks suddenly infused with the eponymous colors of purple and green. Then he stood, anxiously wiping his palms down his coat.

His comments were accurate, if not understated. Nothing compared to having firsthand experience with the Marquess of Shettlemane at his most greedy and depraved.

Even so, it was bad form to go around insulting another man's father.

"If I could offer a bit of advice," Holt said before this pompous little pony could dash away.

Berryhill's eyes widened with alarm. "I meant no slight."

"Then perhaps, when you hear a nervous ramble spewing from your own lips, simply excuse yourself from the table. It will save you any future regrets."

Berryhill swallowed, making a slurping sound through his overbite. With a shaky hand, he tipped his hat. Then he set off at a trot toward the nearest exit.

Asher expelled a hard breath of irritation and self-loathing. He didn't like to dole out threats—that was too much like something his father would do.

Yet if everything went to plan, he'd never need to wager or demean himself for money again.

If everything went to plan, he and his two associates were going to be as rich as Croesus. But only if he fulfilled his part of the bargain. And he was cutting it close because the ship sailed tomorrow.

Winning the wager against Berryhill had finally

given him the money he required. Asher had made other wagers as well, keeping his gaming even more secret than usual. He couldn't risk word spreading.

His father had a knack for sniffing out every last farthing in his vicinity, then spending it on any passing fancy. Shettlemane would lie, cheat and steal to satisfy his insatiable greed. Concoct elaborate stories to excuse his behavior. Destroy lives without a backward glance. And whenever he found himself facing the consequences of his maniacal spending, he'd throw Asher into the fire, forcing him to make things right again.

Not any longer, Asher thought, a kindling of hope sparking for the first time since he was a child.

Tomorrow, he was sailing away from his father and toward the grandest opportunity he'd ever encountered. This venture would gain Asher a fortune enough for ten lifetimes, and ensure that he'd never again concede to his father's unrelenting demands.

Of course, when he'd first learned of the scheme, Asher had laughed at his friends. The Hollander twins—or One and Two, as they were known—were immature dunderpolls of the first order. Therefore, it couldn't have been possible that they'd stumbled upon a bona fide treasure map, hidden in the walls of the hunting lodge they'd purchased.

Asher had reluctantly agreed to help research the validity of a tiny seal-shaped island on the outer reaches of the Caribbean Sea. He was ready to call it an elaborate farce. After all, only children believed in tales of buried treasure. He ought to know, since he'd been one of them.

Someday, Asher, his mother had often whispered as

she tucked him in at night. *Someday, the two of us are going to sail away on a treasure ship and start a whole new life, full of adventure.*

Yet after months of pouring over maps and charts and letters and logs with a cynical eye, he made an uncanny discovery. The Hollanders' new hunting lodge had once belonged to an infamous privateer, Roderick Devine. Rumor had it that Devine's spoils on the high seas were so prodigious—and seldom shared with the crown—that his letter of marque was revoked. Then, before he could be hanged for his offenses, he'd disappeared. And that was the last anyone had heard from him until his reported death.

As much as Asher wanted to refute his findings, he couldn't. Astonishingly enough, the existence of the treasure was entirely plausible.

At the news, the twins were full of gunpowder, ready to set off that instant and hire a crew to sail to the West Indies. They'd begged him to join the expedition.

Asher knew too well how money could destroy the closest of bonds between people. Aside from those two and Viscount Ellery, Asher didn't have many true friends he could rely upon. While One and Two might very well possess the mental acuity of a mayfly, they had loyalty in abundance—a commodity too precious to risk losing.

Yet, thinking of how impulsive they were, imagining them trusting the wrong sort and ending up with their throats cut by an unruly crew of miscreants, Asher had agreed. But he would put up an equal share for the venture. In his mind, an equal partnership was the only way to ensure their friendship remained intact.

That decision had led him here.

Easing into the wingback chair, Asher snapped the paper wide, listening to the muted rattle of dice, the clack of billiard balls, and low murmurs of conversation. Since this would be the last day he'd spend at White's—or on land—for some time, he felt like savoring the moment.

Skimming over the latest society gossip in black and white, his attention was snared by the words *heiress* and *vulgar dowry*. Apparently, there was to be a wedding in three days and a certain Mr. W— was about to become inordinately wealthy.

Asher had tried the occupation of the heiress-marrying noble, but it hadn't come to fruition. The heiresses he'd met had never possessed dowries vulgar enough to rid him of the burden that would befall him upon his father's death. The Shettlemane title was nothing more than a heap of debt and shame, growing larger by the hour.

But one day soon, he would return as a man who could hold his head high.

Yes, indeed. It finally looked like his life was on the right—

Suddenly, a shadow fell across his shoulder, blotting out the light on the page. The flesh on his scalp tightened and a shiver snaked down his spine.

Damn it all to hell.

A long-fingered hand bearing the Marquess of Shettlemane's signet ring smacked down on the table. "There's my boy, the ole devil's spawn himself."

"Father." The sound of bone grinding against bone

filled Asher's ears. He made a concerted effort to loosen his jaw as he continued to study the paper.

The marquess took the silence as an invitation to occupy the spot that Berryhill had vacated and made himself comfortable.

The years had been kinder to him than he deserved. Such a degenerate, compulsive liar and cheat ought to look the part, at least. But instead, he presented a fine figure—still trim and straight-backed into his sixty-third year—and with a head full of black hair liberally woven with silver. His appearance was even respectable in his starched white cravat and tailored blue coat. Yet if one peered closely, beyond the distinguished angular features, then one would see a hunched, gnarled and soulless creature with keen, greedy eyes lurking in the shadows.

"Hmm . . ." his father murmured, fingers steepled. "Chair's still warm."

Asher turned the page over. "Likely due to its proximity to the fireplace."

"Or you had a visitor. A chat with a wealthy friend, perhaps? Come to think of it, I saw you wearing a sly grin when I first entered the room. A man only looks like that for two reasons—women and money. And since I haven't heard of you strutting about with any heiresses of late, I'd say you've got a bit of shine in your pocket."

"Though the concept may be unfamiliar to you, men often smile when they find something amusing. Perhaps even when reading it in the paper."

"Do you know what I find amusing?"

"Titled nobility with money in the vault? Accounting ledgers with more credits than deficits?"

The marquess snorted in derision. "What about a black-cravat-wearing son who thinks he can fool his father?"

Knowing how much the marquess detested the garment tied around his neck, Asher made sure to lift his chin, providing him a better view.

"So, if the seat's still warm," Shettlemane continued like a bloodhound at a fox den, "and the only one leaving the club when I was coming in was that rich fop Berryhill, then I speculate he was the one sitting here. Had a nervous look about him, too. And considering what I heard about a race against a Cheshire stallion and one of Knightswold's Thoroughbreds, I imagine you've won about a hundred pounds. Perhaps even two."

With practiced calm, Asher met his father's gaze. "There couldn't have been a wager because no one is fool enough to put their coin against Knightswold's stock."

Except for the pigeon Berryhill, of course. It was what Asher had been counting on.

"I can smell the money on you, boy," his father said with a bark of laughter, earning a few coughs and sideways glances from the other gentlemen in the room.

Asher lowered the paper and said *sotto voce*, "You're making a spectacle."

The marquess flashed his famous smile around. "Simply having a chat with my ne'er-do-well. A father's duty is never done."

But when he turned back to Asher, the smile twisted at the corners. A wild gleam pulsed in his gaze. "Come now, give it over. I'm to dine with Lord and Lady Fenquist this evening. There'll be cards afterward and I could use a spotter."

Pretending he hadn't heard, Asher laid down the paper and pointed to a notice. "It says here that Lord Englebright finds himself at Fleet. Perhaps you could pay him a visit. After all, it was your last wager that laid him flat and set the creditors on his heels."

"Couldn't be helped. The truth is, I'm in a bit of a bind," he said with frank solemnity, doubtless hoping for an understanding ear. "Had to borrow a small sum—insignificant, really—from Lord Seabrooke. In return for all our years of friendship, the blighter threatened to set a couple of lads on me. Doesn't believe I'm good for the debt."

"Imagine that."

"Well, I said to him, 'I pay my debts, and if I can't, then my boy will make it right. He always does.' After that, Seabrooke agreed that the loan would change hands to your name if I am unable to pay him by Wednesday. And since you won't spot me . . . Well then, it'll be on your head, won't it?"

Asher glared at him, incredulous. This wasn't the first time he'd been embroiled in one of his father's outrageous cockups. Not even close.

Splaying his hands on the table, he stood and leaned in, growling beneath his breath, "I cannot come to your aid this time. There's nothing left of mine, or my late mother's, to sell—you've made sure of that."

"There's still Ashbrook Cottage."

Asher's only home. His father had been trying to manipulate the trustees to release the deed of the property, which had been part of his mother's dowry, for as long as Asher could remember. Clearly, he wouldn't be satisfied until every last remnant of her was gone.

"Isn't it enough that you've already looted the cottage, stripped every room bare of her cherished heirlooms and furnishings? Or do you feel compelled to put her final resting place in the hands of strangers over a game of cards? At least I can be grateful that my grandfather saw fit to put the estate in trust before you married. He knew what you were. I only wish she had seen the truth as well."

The marquess sneered. "Then you wouldn't be here at all, my boy."

Asher took that as an invitation. He walked away, glad he'd be leaving this nightmare in the morning.

Thankfully, his father wasn't desperate enough to chase after him. Likely he was already moving on to someone else to charm a pound or two out of.

It felt good to step out of White's and onto the pavement. He took a deep breath of London's fetid night air, the rain-slicked streets clamoring with rabble-rousers and partygoers. Already his steps felt lighter as he headed in the direction of the Hollander townhouse.

Until recently, Asher had kept his own flat of rooms on Brook Street, but he'd given it up to save funds for his journey abroad. And he was looking forward to a change of scenery. To a new life.

Great opportunities came once in a man's lifetime. He wasn't about to squander his.

A carriage rolled up beside him and a dainty hand flitted out the window, hailing him with a wave of a lace kerchief.

Speaking of opportunity . . .

He paused his stride as they rolled to a stop, thinking that he wouldn't mind spending a few hours of oblivion between the thighs of a comely woman. A proper send-off.

"My good sir, would you consider yourself more of a gentleman or a scoundrel?" a feminine voice asked from within the shadowed interior.

Interest piqued, he grinned and strolled closer. "Under the proper circumstances, any man can admit to being a bit of both."

A soft laugh answered, and a different voice spoke. "I think only a scoundrel would make such a claim. And there is something in those devilishly dark eyes of his. Don't you think so, Jane?"

Two women in the carriage, then? His night was looking better and better.

"Hush now. There's no need for names when we only require him for our study."

A pair of bluestockings, apparently. This could be interesting. "The last scholar who'd *required me for study* took me to her flat above a bookstore in order to research a private collection of erotic etchings. A fine week spent, as I recall."

Gasps answered from within and he playfully arched his brow, taking another step closer to stand in front of the door. All he required was an invitation inside the carriage.

Then a low chuckle—decidedly *not* feminine—gave him pause. Proper send-off or not, even he drew the line somewhere.

"Cousin, I wish you wouldn't laugh. This is serious. As I explained before, we need him for our book."

Squinting to peer inside, he saw the silhouettes of two slender forms on one side and the hulking figure of a man on the other. "What's all this about, then?"

A plain, fresh-faced young debutante peered out the lowered window. "You see, we are writing a primer—"

"On the marriage habits of the native aristocrat," the dark-haired young woman interrupted, leaning forward.

"—and we need a scoundrel's point of view."

Asher jerked a nod toward the man on the bench across from them. "Why not ask him?"

"My cousin is neither gentleman nor scoundrel and, as far as I'm aware, has no intention of marrying."

At the mention of marriage and seeing the naivety in their countenances, Asher wanted nothing more to do with them. He would find his amusements elsewhere this evening.

"Alas, I have another engagement at present. My best wishes on the future success of your book, ladies." He touched two fingers to the brim of his hat.

"*Drat!* He's truly leaving us. Jane, do something."

"Cousin, I know you are expected by your employer, but will you not come to our aid and persuade this gentleman to linger a moment longer?"

There was no answer from within. And no warning either.

The carriage door opened before Asher could move out of the way and he was knocked aside, as if a ham-sized fist had connected with his jaw.

Then everything went dark.

Chapter 3

⌒

The instant Winnifred's hackney arrived at the mysterious Southwark address, she felt an ominous shiver. In the chary glimmer of a single streetlamp, the narrow house seemed to lurch toward the street. Windows listed to the side in slanted frames, the wooden exterior buckling in the places where it hadn't yet rotted, and the whole of it was the unsettling color of creosote.

Surely this couldn't be correct.

But then a familiar face emerged through the opened door. Holding on to the hood of her cloak, Ellie looked left and then right before waving her hand impatiently. "Come quick, Winnie."

Both alarmed and curious by all the subterfuge, she did just that. Hopping down to the pavement without the step, she bade the driver to wait.

Entering the dim interior of the house behind Ellie, she saw Jane in the small musty foyer, holding a lit taper in a tarnished brass chamberstick. "I wasn't certain you'd come. It was, after all, your parents' dinner party."

"Of course I came. You wrote that it was a matter

of *great urgency*. I stole away after whispering to Father that I had a headache. And I'm certain Mother was glad that I excused myself before the syllabub was served. But tell me why the two of you never arrived, and why we're all standing inside this ruin, of all places?"

Winnifred took in her surroundings. The meager light flickered over the rubble of fallen horsehair plaster on the floor, great fissures in the wall exposing the lath, and tilted doorways that seemed an instant away from collapsing like a fan snapping shut in dismissal. The vision did nothing to ease her disquiet.

"We were on our way, if that makes a difference," Ellie said with a nervous glance back toward a darkened doorway.

Jane cleared her throat. "Before I explain, allow me to preface it by telling you that I never intended for this to happen."

"You said that the time you attempted to make your own gunpowder," Winnifred added, feeling the continuous wave of dread that had been rolling through her since she'd first received the missive. As they started to walk toward the next room, she carefully studied the flame wavering over Jane's countenance. "Well, I'm grateful that your eyebrows are still intact this time."

"I didn't incinerate anything."

"It's much worse," Ellie lamented, shaking her head. "A small explosion would be lovely compared to this."

"What could possibly be worse than—"

Winnifred stopped short on a gasp as they entered

the dingy parlor, her gaze alighting on a solitary figure. Tied to a chair!

"Tell me you found him that way and are in the process of a grand rescue."

A trio of thick ropes bound his lean torso to the spindleback. With his arms behind him, his gray herringbone coat parted to reveal a tailored silver satin waistcoat that drew into tight horizontal furrows each time he took a breath. He sat with his trouser-clad legs sprawled scandalously wide, though it was likely to accommodate their length as they were long, tautly muscled, and bound at the ankle. And though he didn't utter a sound, he emanated a keen alertness—and likely fury—in the rigid set of his broad shoulders.

"In my own defense, I only wanted to speak with him," Jane said in a rush, nearly guttering the candle.

Ellie nodded in agreement and wrung her hands. "The rest was simply an accident."

"Oh? He just happened to fall backward onto a chair *and* a pile of rope that tangled his hands behind his back? And, let me guess, the wind blew that sack over his head and neck?"

"Well, that took a bit of doing actually," Jane offered, then proceeded to gesture from the chair to the door as if she intended to explain it all in detail. "You see . . ."

Winnifred stopped her before she could. "Who is he?"

"Haven't a clue." Ellie shrugged.

"It was dark," Jane said. "Besides, we weren't interested in his name, only his information. One minute we were speaking with this man and the next—"

"Flat on the pavement." Ellie added a single clap of her gloved hands for effect.

"When he started to walk away, I only asked my cousin to intervene. I never imagined a carriage door, opened without even a modicum of malicious intent, could cause such calamity. Of course, I blame the lamppost that struck him the second time. But when I saw him lying there, and with our book still turning in my thoughts—"

"You know how single-minded Jane can be."

"—a sudden brilliant notion overtook me. I mean, there we were with a scoundrel at our disposal. We couldn't just waste an opportunity and leave him to the elements."

Winnifred wondered if she was the only sane one among her friends. "You're speaking as though you expected insects to carry him away, or for the rain to dissolve him. He's a man, not marzipan!"

"Precisely why I summoned you. Now that we have him, I don't know how to get rid of him."

"Can we not simply . . . put him back where you found him?"

"I'd thought of that," Jane said, then pointed an accusatory finger at Ellie. "But *she* refuses to permit me to give him laudanum so that he'll be asleep when we remove the ligatures. It is, after all, the obvious solution."

"You've already kidnapped him . . . and you were hoping to drug him as well?" Winnifred huffed. In fact, she was starting to hyperventilate. Light-headed, she imagined that it would be just her luck to die as a disappointment to her parents, suffocated by her own corset, dropping dead at the feet of the strange man tied to a chair in Southwark. "I cannot . . . afford to be . . . embroiled in a scandal. For heaven's sake, I'm getting . . . married. Wednesday! The contracts have already been signed."

"It isn't too late," Jane said, matter of fact. "You don't have to tether yourself to a boorish man you will never love, simply because your father has arranged it."

"I am obligated all the same."

Ellie frowned. "Surely you wish for something more than to merely endure the rest of your life. What about joy and laughter and—"

"Stop," Winnifred warned with a wag of her finger at both of them. She took in a steadying breath. "We are not venturing down this fruitless path again. I haven't slept a wink ever since you mentioned your plan."

Jane's eyes caught the candle flame, glimmering with midnight blue triumph. "Because you're tempted by it. I knew you would be! And I have faith that you'll come to your senses and run away from disaster."

Winnifred set her hands on her hips. "Well, if that isn't the pot calling the kettle black. At least my disaster won't land me in irons."

"No. Yours will be worse," Ellie said with a sniff. "You'll be shackled in misery for the rest of your life."

"Again. *Thank you* for your support."

Jane laid her free hand over Winnifred's shoulder. "Our support will be the carriage, waiting to abscond with you outside the church."

"But you'll be glad to know that she's abandoned the pigeon aspect of the plan."

"My brothers set them free," Jane said with an exhausted sigh. "I cannot begin to tell you how many of my experiments they've ruined."

Winnifred snapped her fingers. "Shall we focus on our current dilemma, ladies?"

"Oh, yes, right."

The three of them stared at the accidental hostage. The way he cocked his head to the side, he seemed to stare back.

Winnifred felt a chill skitter down her spine. "Are you certain he cannot see us?"

"Yes," Jane offered with authority. "I had two sacks in my reticule and tried it myself. Couldn't see anything more than shadows."

A harsh exhale puffed the sack out over his mouth. Almost as if he were laughing at them.

"And you're certain he's fully conscious? Not injured or impaired? After all, he isn't speaking."

"He's merely being stubborn. You should have heard him curse at us when he awoke to find himself in this . . . situation."

Winnifred could just imagine. Her father had quite the colorful vocabulary when merely inconvenienced by traffic. The only thing that might pacify him during those moments would be if all the other carriages disappeared and he was left alone on the road.

Hmm . . . she thought, an idea sparking to life. Then she drew her friends out of the room. "I think I've got a plan."

ASHER SLIPPED free of the wrist bindings his captors had so *helpfully* loosened. Jerking the hood from his aching head, he made quick work of the other ropes. He could still hear the crunch of their carriage wheels on cobblestones. But it was fading quickly.

In the dark room it was difficult to get his bearings. Yet there was a sliver of light bleeding in through a rip in the dusty drapes and he found his way to the window, then peered out onto the lamp-lit street. Not a soul in sight. Turning back to the room, he glimpsed the shadow of the doorway.

Determined to catch them, he rushed through the foyer, the front door, and then burst outside with a growl in his throat.

But there was nothing to bark at when he reached the wet pavement. There was no carriage on the narrow, winding street. And no assistance to be had from the surrounding houses either. They were nothing more than ruins, crumbling into misshapen piles of rubble.

He cursed, wondering what time it was. The air felt damp and cool against his skin, the sky graying around the edges. He patted his waistcoat, forgetting for a moment that the engraved watch his grandfather had once given to him had been filched by Shettlemane and lost in a game of hazard years ago.

With the reminder, Asher searched his pockets to ensure that everything was as it should be.

A solitary cheroot—broken in half, damn it all. A bent calling card. A silk handkerchief.

Hmm . . . nothing was missing. Apparently, those girls truly had abducted him for the purpose of answering their odd questions.

Would you say that you're more gentleman than

scoundrel or vice versa? Do you live your life flitting from one act of debauchery to another? Have you recently attended a party at Sutherfield Terrace? Ever been in love?

Idiots, the lot of them.

Considering the misfortune debutantes could inflict upon an unsuspecting male, was it any wonder that he'd never been induced to marry? Never been stricken by the poetic impulses of the romantics? As far as he was concerned, a man susceptible to falling in love deserved his fate.

Agitated, Asher straightened his coat with a tug. Now that it was over, he was even more overjoyed by the fact that he would soon be sailing away from all this utter *non—*

Wait a moment . . . something wasn't right. He shifted, stretching out his arms.

At once he was quite aware that he didn't feel anything up his sleeve. He began patting again, furiously. Fishing inside, he tore off his coat and jerked up his shirtsleeves, hard enough to rend seams. Nothing.

He'd been robbed!

"They're worse than idiots. They're thieves!"

He supposed he'd been a fool to have the £1,000 he'd collected over the weeks tucked up his sleeve and ready to deliver. Yet prior lessons from his father had taught him how easy it was to filch a man's pockets or rob his home. And the henchmen that were set on him from time to time to collect one of Shettlemane's debts never thought to look for a money clip hooked in a cuff buttonhole.

Apparently, the same could not be said for bluestockings.

Rushing back into the house, he found a three-legged table with a lamp resting on top and flint and steel in the drawer beneath. He lit the taper, but his search was fruitless.

The money for his share of the expedition and his only chance for a new life were gone.

❧❧❧

BY THE time Asher had made his way to the Hollander townhouse, the sun had risen. So had his fury. In fact, he wasn't entirely sure if there were crimson bands of clouds on the horizon or if he was seeing everything through a murderous red haze.

Staring out the morning room window, he recounted his tale of unfortunate events to One and Two.

"Rotten luck," Lord Avery Hollander—the aforementioned One—said, ruffling a hand through a widow's peak of sandy brown hair as he slumped down onto an overstuffed chair by the hearth.

Lord Bates Hollander—Two—launched a rust-colored pillow at his head. "Close your banyan, brother. Want me to maw-wallop on the rug? No one wants a gander at your bits and pieces."

One rolled his jade-green eyes, adjusting the blue silk robe. "We're identical twins, idiot. We've got the same bits."

"Fat lot you know. My *piece* happens to be much larger. Lady Clarksdale couldn't stop her roving eye at dinner last night."

"Because you had your shirt bunched in your trousers like you were still in nappies." He fired the pillow back at his brother. "Honestly, Holt, I cannot wait until the ship sails, just so I can push this inferior spare overboard."

"Well, we won't be sailing until Wednesday next," Two said, launching the pillow back with enough force to earn a grunt out of the other.

Prophesizing that he was about to become embroiled in another infantile Hollander battle, Asher stepped between the chairs and snatched the pillow from the air, ready to smother the pair of them. "And what, precisely, is the reason for the delay?"

"The captain said he's superstitious," Two answered with a disgruntled shrug. "Saw a black cat yesterday or something of the sort. Not only that but everyone knows you don't set sail when the sky's red. Looks like a storm's headed our way."

Asher looked again to the window. "Then I've got a week to get the money."

"Not that I have my doubts or anything, but that's a tall order. Even for you," One said, not unkindly.

"It's a shame those girls kidnapped you just to rob you. I'd have wanted them to have their way with me first."

As a matter of principle, Asher fired the pillow at Bates's head. Then, out of the corner of his eye, he saw yesterday's newspaper, lying open on the mahogany Pembroke table. Precisely to the page announcing the wedding of the heiress and her vulgar dowry.

With a sudden burst of recollection, the conversation between the two nitwits who'd abducted him and their late-arriving cohort played through his pia mater like the echoes of a mockingbird. And a plan started to form out of the ruins they'd left him in.

Sometimes there was only one way to deal with a thief . . . and that was to become one.

Asher was going to get his money back one way or the other.

Chapter 4

Winnifred didn't think anything could make her wedding day worse than the dismal imminence of marrying Bertram Woodbine. Until she looked at her dress.

Apparently, Mother had commissioned the dressmaker to sew a few last-minute alterations to a ball gown Winnifred hadn't had the chance to wear this Season. The yards of ivory taffeta with puffed sleeves and tiers of batting-stuffed rouleau at the hem were now enshrouded in an overlay of scratchy silver tulle and applique flowers dotted with pearls.

"I look like a meringue left in the confectionary shop window too long and covered in cobwebs."

"Nonsense," her mother said, coming up behind her in the oval standing mirror. "You look lovely in it."

Winnifred might have gasped if not for the additional whalebone in her corset and stomacher reinforcement. Instead, all she managed was a silent pantomime of openmouthed surprise. It wasn't like her mother to dole out compliments. Well, not without adding something derogatory.

"I do, truly?" she asked, her reflection lighting with a hopeful smile.

"Of course. This gown is so exquisite that it will draw all the attention away from that unruly nest of hair atop your head."

Ah, of course. She should have known.

They'd had a similar near-tender exchange earlier. Before Winnifred was dressed, Mother had come into her bedchamber with a gift—a pair of new silk stockings, embroidered with a row of tiny silver-threaded shells on either side.

"Your grandmother gave me a pair of stockings like these on my wedding day, as well. She'd spent weeks ensuring that every embellishment was just perfect."

"And you stitched these for me?" Winnifred had asked and received a modest smile in response.

"I suppose it's my way of being with you as you take your steps into your new life."

Touched by the tender gesture, she sniffed. "They're simply beautiful, Mother."

A moment had passed between them, giving Winnifred hope that she was being seen and loved for the person she was.

But then Mother added, "I've always found that vertical stripes offer a comely, narrow appearance."

Winnifred had made no comment. She'd simply sunk down onto the tufted bench at the foot of her bed and slipped on her stockings and garter ribbons, choosing to focus on the thought behind the gift. At least Mother had been trying. In her own way.

Besides, Winnifred had much larger worries on her mind. *Even larger than my calves*, she thought dryly as she stared at her doomsday dress again.

In a matter of hours, she would be Mrs. Bertram

Woodbine. The wedding breakfast would follow, along with scowls from her new husband. After that, she'd discover what new lodgings her dowry had purchased. And then . . . the wedding night.

She swallowed down a rise of bile, thinking about being crowded and jostled and breathed upon in Mr. Woodbine's *nuptial carriage*.

"You're looking rather green, dear," Mother said absently before her reflection left the looking glass and began to bustle about the room. "Try not to be ill, for it makes your freckles noticeable. As it is, we'll have to apply lemon juice before we go."

A bitter taste lingered on the back of Winnifred's tongue. "I feel ill because I'm about to marry a man I don't even like, let alone love. I don't think lemon juice will alter the fact."

"Consider it a blessing in disguise. I'd made the mistake of falling in love with your father"—she expelled a harsh, impatient breath—"and just look how that turned out. We can barely stand to be in the same house together. No, you and Mr. Woodbine are starting off with indifference and that is much more agreeable."

"It would be even *more* agreeable if I didn't have to marry him at all," she said bravely into the looking glass, waiting for a response.

Ever since hearing Jane and Ellie's plot to help her run away, she hadn't stopped thinking about it. The certainty that she didn't want a life with Mr. Woodbine grew larger by every passing second. And now, an urgent need to be heard welled inside her.

"We are speaking of the rest of *my* life, after all," she persisted after a nervous gulp of air. "I don't want to spend it in misery. Perhaps that sounds dramatic and even maudlin, but it's true. I am certain that any hope for my own happiness will die a quick death if I stand beside him in the church."

Again, silence was her only response. She didn't even hear her mother's footsteps.

Her shoulders slumped in defeat. Apparently, Mother had stepped out and Winnifred had been emptying the contents of her soul to a vacant room.

Issuing a self-derisive laugh, she began to turn away. "So, I think I'll simply refuse to marry him. Surely, you and Father don't care about appearances so much that you'd force me—*eeeeee!*"

Mother hadn't left the room at all. She was standing behind her. Frowning.

"Have I taught you nothing?" she asked, tapping her foot beneath the hem of an exquisite lavender gown. "Appearances are all we have. Women in society are *never* happy. When we converse, we keep to trivial topics—where we went on holiday and what new baubles and fabrics we've purchased. We brag on the skills of our dressmakers while concealing the fact that we can't breathe and we're always hungry and our breasts are sagging. We sip from teacups while monotonously gulping down rumors. Day after day. We complain about the heat, the cold, and our husbands with equal fervor while never revealing our deepest fears. And we do this because we're *all* miserable and we need each other."

"Mother . . ." Winnifred said, stunned. "I never knew you felt that way."

"Then, clearly, I've failed." She threw up her

hands, moisture glistening in her eyes. "And to think of all the years I've wasted trying to prepare you for the disappointments you'll face when I'm not around. A mother's love is never appreciated."

Turning away, Mother began to storm out, only to stop abruptly at the sight of Father standing in the doorway.

The viscountess sniffed and issued a cursory nod. "Julian."

"Imogene," he responded in turn, standing tall and broad-chested in his maroon coat, his russet brows knitted together as his gaze drifted from her to his daughter and back again. "Something amiss?"

"If I thought it would make a difference, I might bother to tell you."

His wife straightened her regal shoulders, then pushed past him, storming off. And he watched her go, his square jaw clenched all the while.

By way of greeting Winnifred, he said, "The carriage is waiting. And this"—he lifted a brown paper parcel and took three long strides into the chamber— "arrived from Mr. Woodbine a moment ago. Well, don't just gape at it. Take it."

She did, but was more puzzled than ever. "Are you certain it's from Mr. Woodbine?"

Her father merely arched a superior brow in response. She'd categorized these subtle forms of expression years ago, deciding that the higher the arch, the more she'd stepped over the line. They went from *I've sired an idiot*—and this was usually accompanied by a roll of the eyes—to *how dare you question me, peasant?*

This one was somewhere in the middle. The *I know everything* arch.

Tentatively, she took the parcel, wondering what Mr. Woodbine could possibly have sent her. A book itemizing all the foods he forbade her to eat? A wilted corsage? A dead rat?

Yet, as she pushed aside the paper and carefully opened the lid of the carved wooden casket, her breath caught.

It wasn't something terrible after all.

On a bed of red velvet lay the most beautiful, lustrous pearls she'd ever seen. The perfect ivory spheres formed a necklace, four strands high and held together by a silver clasp. She dared to brush her fingertips over them.

No matter how she felt about him, this was certainly a nice gesture. "I never expected something like this, and from Mr. Woodbine of all people."

Her father issued a grunt that she interpreted as him sharing a similar sentiment. Then he reached down and took them, holding the necklace aloft and bidding her to turn around with an impatient shooing motion.

When she did, she saw the card lying underneath. Reaching for it, she flicked it open as her father fastened the strands.

My dearest Ophelia,

Let this token of my love be your companion. Let each perfect pearl kiss your neck in my absence.

*After I've married that cow and performed my
dreaded duty for this one day apart, I shall be
yours forever more.*

                    With undying ardor,
                              B

Winnifred's eyes blurred. She wasn't sure if the
tears stinging her eyes were from disappointment or
from fury.

"Wait," she managed on a choked whisper. "I need
to send this back."

Her father clucked in disapproval, continuing to fuss
with the clasp. "Nonsense. Refusing your husband's
gift is no way to begin a marriage. If he wants to spoil
you, then let him."

A hot tear slipped from the corner of her eye and
rolled down her cheek as she issued a papery laugh.
"They're not for me."

And before her father could say a word, she showed
him the card.

His hands went still, and he said nothing for a
moment.

Then he continued his task and gruffly stated, "Your
dowry paid for these all the same. It will serve him
right to see them on you. And in the future, he will
learn to be more discreet."

He fastened the pearls to her neck. The prettiest
shackle one could ever imagine.

Winnifred felt another tear slide down her cheek
as she tossed the card into the box and closed the lid.
Wiping the tracks away, she made three decisions.

One—those would be the last tears she would ever shed over Mr. Woodbine.

Two—she refused to live the rest of her life being treated like a sack of money.

And three—she was going to run away from her wedding.

Chapter 5

Hands full of skirts and lungs collapsing from strain, Winnifred rushed down the church steps. The light drizzle made her mad dash even more perilous. And she wished that she'd agreed to Jane's original plan. A pigeon distraction might have afforded her more time. As it was, she only hoped that her ruse of needing a moment to *cast up her accounts* would keep her parents waiting near the vestry long enough for her to escape.

Seeing the promised carriage beside the pavement, Winnifred jerked open the door and leapt inside.

She never expected to find Jane's cousin asleep, sprawled out and taking up half the carriage. Tripping over his foot, she fell forward in a crunch of taffeta and tulle, her curls tumbling over her face.

"Easy now, sweets, or my Thoroughbred will never leave his stall," he murmured in a low, drowsy drawl that caused a peculiar heated shiver to race through her.

She wasn't even sure what he meant. Though Jane had remarked on a number of occasions that her cousin, Mr. Pickerington, wasn't the brightest candle in the chandelier. So, it was likely nonsense.

Winnifred might have asked him to repeat himself,

but then his eyes opened. They were dark and warm as an August midnight. And her heart began a queer rhythm, tripping hard and fast along the inner wall of her ribcage, while the outer wall strained against her corset lacings.

For an instant, she couldn't breathe at all. Couldn't seem to move away from the hard, lean body beneath her, not even when she felt his hand at the curve of her waist.

He lifted his other hand to brush the hair from her face. Never in her life had a handsome man gazed at her with this foreign, half-lidded intensity. A pointed frown, perhaps. A passing glance, certainly. But not this.

At their close proximity, she could count every one of his minky lashes as well as the dark whisker stubble emerging along the angular cut of his jawline and the shallow cleft in his chin. Beneath the straight slope of his nose, his broad mouth appeared firm and smooth like a sculpture of a Greek warrior. Yet a slightly dusky hue gave his lips warmth. And she had a surprisingly wayward notion to test what they would feel like against her own.

He is Jane's cousin, she reminded herself, mentally wagging her finger.

With musings like these racing through her mind, she supposed it was fortunate that no other man had scrutinized her so thoroughly or she might have ended up like Prue.

How did pretty women bear these types of gazes on a daily basis? And was it any wonder that so many of them succumbed to a scoundrel's charm?

Of course, Jane never said anything about her cousin being a rake, so she shouldn't worry about that. But when he expelled a heavy liquor-soaked breath, she started to question if Jane knew everything about Mr. Pickerington.

"You're foxed," she accused. "And you smell like a rum pot."

Taking his state into account, Winnifred came to the immediate conclusion that inebriation was the likely reason for his slow perusal. On a huff of abashment, she wiggled back to her own side of the carriage.

"Peculiar. I never imbibe to excess." He frowned, the flesh above his nose puckering to a V between his dark brows.

"Well, you certainly picked a fine time to begin. We don't have an instant to waste."

Of course, I wasn't in a terrible rush while sprawled on top of him, she thought wryly. Hiding a guilty blush on her cheeks, she turned to the window facing the church.

View impeded by the blind, she went to lift it, only to have the crusty tassel come apart in her hand. As she flicked it to the floor, she hoped the rest of the carriage was in better condition.

So far, no one was rushing down after her. At least . . . not yet. And when she looked back toward Mr. Pickerington, he didn't seem to be compelled to make haste. "Well?"

"*Well*, what?"

"Shouldn't we be . . . getting on by now?"

His lips curved in a slow grin and, this time, his thorough hedonistic gaze drifted over more than just her face. The pulse beneath the flesh of her throat rabbited with a shameful degree of wanton excitement.

Then he shook his head. "My apologies, sweets. I wish I had the coin to afford you. Alas, I do not. Nor do I ever mix business with pleasure. In my opinion, carnal delights should be uninhibited and unconstrained by the obligations of monetary transactions."

"*Whot* are you—"

Oh. Understanding dawned at once and her heated pulse turned decidedly cool. Apparently, Mr. Pickerington imagined that the only recourse for a young woman who'd just cut ties with her parents was solicitation, of all things!

Outraged, Winnifred sat up straighter and wagged her finger at him. "You should be ashamed of yourself. I'm not going to become a harlot or a street . . . strumpet. Jane said you were slow-witted but, honestly, I didn't realize she'd left me in the hands of a proper buffoon."

She darted another glance through the carriage window. Any moment now, her father would be red-faced and dashing down the stairs.

He'd never forgive her.

"Oh, this was a mistake," she lamented. "I knew it all along, and yet there was no other way. And no going back either. I just made certain of that."

"Jane?" her carriage companion asked with a slow blink as if he'd never heard the name before.

"Your cousin, of course! *Honestly.*" He was about as sharp as a wooden sword. She knew she should be patient with someone clearly mentally deficient, but panic was starting to set in. "Do you think it possible for us to continue this . . . introduction *en route* since my father is doubtless discovering my absence and bound to burst upon us at any moment?"

That seemed to spark some life into him and he called to the driver.

Then, at last, they were off.

Winnifred tried to calm her nerves by taking in a deep breath, but was forestalled by her damnable corset and the busk threatening to crack apart her ribs. So she tried to stretch out her legs, only to nudge something with the toe of her slipper. Looking down, she saw that it was an empty bottle.

Had he consumed the entire contents this morning while waiting for her? Well, that was certainly alarming. Jane likely didn't know about this either.

Strangely, he didn't appear the drunkard. Just to be sure, however, she indulged in another perusal.

Lifting her eyes slowly, she took in his lean form, noting the appealing way his leg muscles bunched beneath a pair of buttery buckskin breeches as he stretched out. Then he lifted his arm to scrub a hand through layers of dark, wavy hair and his coat parted over a maroon waistcoat, tailored to his flat middle and broad chest.

He likely wasn't one of those gentlemen who required the aid of a corset to diminish a paunch. And beneath her gloves, her fingertips tingled with the desire to discover the answer for herself. Would he look like a Greek statue there as well?

She'd touched one of those once in a museum. Jane, Ellie and Prue had all taken turns while the others kept watch. And Winnifred had marveled at the rippled bands of muscle.

She'd had scandalous dreams of that statue for a fortnight. And now she was having positively brazen thoughts about Jane's cousin, wondering if he would feel the same. *Shameless!*

"Your father a tyrant, is he?"

Guilty, her gaze jerked up to his face. She hoped the meager light in the carriage would conceal her blush.

"Not entirely," she answered quickly, pretending their thoughts were in tandem. "He isn't one to shout or to raise his hand when an opposing argument is set before him. However, he has a knack for turning conversations into mazes, and, before you know it, you've agreed to whatever he wanted in the first place."

At first, her companion nodded in understanding. But, suddenly, he sat forward, his expression marked with—what she could only describe as—startled disbelief, as if she'd given him most unwelcome news. Then he lowered his face into his hands.

"Just so we're perfectly clear, your name is . . ."

She resisted the urge to roll her eyes. Poor addle-brained man. Clearly, she'd confused him with too many words at once. For his sake, she would do better to keep her sentences shorter. "Miss Winnifred Humphries."

"Yes, of course." He lifted his head and eased back against the squabs. The drowsiness had abruptly left his gaze and he studied her with a fresh, sober intensity as the carriage bumped along the cobblestone streets. "And to where am I escorting you on this fine morning, Miss Humphries?"

She glanced to the window, beaded and blurry from rain. All the color seemed to be washing away from

London, leaving behind charcoal sketches of brick buildings and box windows that crowded the streets to a suffocating degree.

This was not what she would consider a *fine morning* at all. Especially considering what she'd just done. "Surely Jane told you."

"Afraid not."

Feeling a pinch in her side, she shifted on the bench and thought back to the parlor a week ago, and mentally skimmed through the pages. "Come to think of it, I didn't read that far into the plan. I suppose we ought to drive to your aunt and uncle's house and discuss the rest with Jane."

"Mmm . . . perhaps," he said, thoughtfully grazing a thumb over his bottom lip. "But wouldn't that be the first place your father would look?"

A surprisingly sound argument for a simpleton. She was ashamed that she hadn't thought of it first. Then again, she'd been momentarily distracted by that thumb of his.

All his fingers were long and lean like the rest of him. Elegant, even. Yet that thumb was slightly rounded toward the top as if it had a purpose, like playing an instrument or holding a paintbrush. She was strangely intrigued by that thumb and those lazy sweeps across his mouth. And, once more, her own lips tingled.

Jane's cousin, she reminded herself in a singsong voice inside her head.

Winnifred cleared her throat. "Perhaps you're right. Yet that would rule out Ellie's home as well. Besides, it wouldn't be good to involve my friends, regardless."

"You could always return home."

She shook her head, adamant. The motion caused the necklace to snag the fine tendrils at the back of her nape and she winced. This was the third time it had pulled her hair since she'd put it on. *Hateful necklace.*

"No. My father would only force me to marry Mr. Woodbine."

"Woodbine, you say? Brown hair, big ears? Always brags about inheriting a dukedom the minute his great-uncles kick off?"

She offered three succinct nods, thinking of the current Duke of Tuttlesby and his two younger brothers, each of them octogenarians separated by two years. One would imagine that a dukedom would soon be in hand for Mr. Woodbine and he'd be able to ignore his family's wishes and marry Lady Stanton. Yet, after having survived wars and fever when most of their family had not, the uncles' proven longevity and vigorous constitutions left no guarantees. In the meantime, the third usurper had a mistress he wanted to lavish with riches. Which brought Mr. Woodbine to his current position and she to hers.

Irritated, she lifted her arms to unfasten the necklace—a near impossible feat when she could scarcely move in this dress.

"Well, I'm sure he isn't all that bad. Here," Jane's cousin said, moving lithely to the bench beside her.

His hands were already lifting, his fingertips skimming lightly over the susceptible flesh at the back of her nape before she could utter a protest. An instant later, the weight of the necklace slithered down her breasts and fell in a succinct patter to her lap. The corner of his mouth curled in a scoundrel's grin. Then he resumed his position on the opposite side.

"Thank you," she said as if asking a question, her voice somewhat confused and breathless. She wasn't quite sure if she should be alarmed by the deftness of his hands or if she should take notes for the primer.

Those thumbs were certainly capable. A man with such skills might take other liberties if she wasn't careful.

Then again, she was plump Winnifred Humphries. And it had been proven that the only thing appealing about her was her father's fortune. So she needn't worry.

She scowled down at the pearls and thought about the missive from Mr. Woodbine. What might have been a lovely necklace now only reminded her of his cruel *cow* remark. "Believe me, my betrothed is even worse once you get to know him. Which is why I am here in this carriage instead of at the church."

"But the question is, to *where* are you going?"

"Oh, how am I supposed to know?" she asked crossly, shaking the strands at him. "I didn't know I was running away from my wedding until this morning. So you'll simply have to give me a moment to think this through."

He eased back against the squabs again and smirked at her as if he believed *she* was the simpleton. "Make up your mind quickly, sweets. After all, the carriage driver will demand payment, and I don't have any coin."

"You don't?"

He shook his head.

Drat. Winnifred didn't either. Whenever she went somewhere it was with her family's drivers. She never carried money with her—she charged what she needed to her father's accounts. Rather than giving her pin money, he preferred an itemized account of what she purchased from week to week. It had never been an inconvenience . . . until now.

"Seems to me, the only sensible thing would be for you to go home. Your parents will likely worry otherwise."

Spoken like a man who didn't know her parents a wit.

She skewered him with a glare. "As I said before, I closed that door today. And why are you peculiarly eager to send me home, hmm? Have another bottle of rum under the bench that needs a quick guzzling?"

"I was just thinking that it would be a pity if the driver decided to hie us back to the church, that's all." His lips curved in a cold smile that only enhanced his attractiveness with appealing creases bracketing his broad mouth. Even squinting at her didn't lessen the effect. When his lashes crowded together, his eyes glinted like onyx.

Winnifred decided then and there to be rid of him, and the sooner the better. She didn't need the distraction.

Rolling the strands methodically through her fingers, she came up with a plan. "Money won't be a problem. I'll simply offer the driver this necklace."

"You can't do that," he said, and with more force than was warranted. But on the bright side, his smugness disappeared behind a frown.

With a flick of her wrist she twirled the pearls, catching his attention. "I can do whatever I like. They're *my* pearls."

"Are you so spoiled, so determined to have your own way, that you'd give a family heirloom to a stranger?"

"Believe me, I have no sentimental attachment to this shackle. It was a gift from my betrothed—"

"Then you should definitely keep—"

"—to his mistress," she said, relishing the sight of his mouth snapping shut, even if her pride was sorely wounded. "The parcel arrived at my father's townhouse by mistake this morning."

"But how did you know . . ."

"There was a card." She didn't elaborate further. Torture wouldn't make her reveal the humiliating words she'd read. "Regardless, I shall be more than happy to make use of them. So, if you wouldn't mind hopping out at your earliest convenience, I have a journey ahead of me."

He looked out at the rain and then back at her— or her necklace, rather. His jaw was clenched and a muscle twitched beneath the unshaven scruff of his whiskers.

"I have a better idea," he said. "I know a jeweler who'll give you a fair price. Then you'll have coin enough to take you anywhere you choose to go, and some to spare, I'd warrant."

Hmm . . . that *was* a better idea. And surprising, too, coming from a simpleton.

"Very well. Take me to your jeweler."

Chapter 6

The instant Asher saw the two henchmen through the jeweler's box window, he knew trouble was headed directly for him. He'd never met the lanky man in the sagging Wellington hat, but he recognized the hulking bruiser in the brown coat with a pale scar bisecting his brow. He'd had dealings with Mr. Lum before, over one of his father's loans from Lord Seabrooke. And, if he recalled correctly, Mr. Lum preferred the *violence first, request payment later* method of collecting debts.

Stepping to the heiress's side, Asher bent his head to whisper, "We need to leave."

"But we haven't concluded our—"

"*Now*, Miss Humphries." He took hold of her gloved hand and tugged her past an older man with curling gray mustachios and a broad feathered hat, who'd come in shortly after they had arrived.

She resisted, slipping free. "What about my necklace?"

Without so much as a backward glance, he snatched the necklace out of Mr. Windle's grasp and headed out the door, taking her with him.

"Wait just one moment. You've no right to manhandle me."

The shop bell chimed above their heads as he slid an arm around her waist, pulling her close. "Turn your head. See those two men crossing the street and staring at us? See the one with the scar who's reaching inside his coat and tearing into a packet of powder with his teeth?"

"Is that a . . . a . . . *pistol*?" she asked in incredulous disbelief.

"A blunderbuss to be precise."

"I do believe he's aiming at us. Surely he isn't actually intending to shoot at—"

Before she could finish, Asher jerked open the carriage door and stuffed her *and* her voluminous skirts inside. Bloody hell. She was wearing enough silk to decimate an entire population of worms. He barely had time to climb in and close the door before the driver cracked the whip.

Then they were off, hell-bent for leather through the narrow London streets.

A shot blasted through the air and Asher tucked her against him. Holding his breath, he kept her close, long enough to ensure they were both unharmed.

Glancing out the window, he saw that the mustachioed patron left Mr. Windle's shop and had apparently bumped into Mr. Lum, causing the shot to go up instead of straight. What a stroke of luck!

"Don't worry," Asher said as he set her apart from him. "Mr. Portman has been my driver for years and knows his way around these streets. He'll have us out of town in no time at all."

Absently, he watched Mr. Lum and his cohort run toward a black curricle, hitched to a sleek pair. When he turned his attention back to her, he noted that her face was ghostly white under a smattering of amber freckles on her cheeks and nose.

She stared off, unblinking. "They shot at us."

"More noise than anything, and not with any precision. I'm sure it was used more as a scare tactic," he said, hoping it was the truth.

All his life, he'd learned valuable lessons about the hazards of owing money to the wrong people. They'd do anything to get what they were due, usually stopping just short of murder. After all, dead men could not pay their debts. Then again, there was a limit to everyone's patience.

Asher wondered how much money his father had borrowed this time.

"It suc-cee-ded," Miss Humphries said, taking a short, stuttered breath between each syllable. The hand gripping the necklace splayed over her bosom, her lips parting on tiny gulps of air.

He cursed under his breath. She was going to faint if she didn't take a fortifying breath. The last thing he needed was to have a collapsed heiress on his hands.

Yet before he could offer assistance, the carriage careened around a corner.

With a startled yelp, she toppled forward.

He caught her against him, all soft and warm and . . . scared. He could feel it in the tremors rolling through her body. See it in her hazel eyes. This close, the evocative color in the center was no longer vibrant, but stark and cloudy. It was like looking at absinthe through a frosted glass. And the surrounding band wasn't a fiery cinnamon but a cold brown instead.

"I . . . can't . . . breathe . . ."

With his hands in the dip of her waist, he could already discern the culprit. "It's this bloody corset. I've never encountered so much whalebone in all my life." And, considering all the laces he'd undone, that was saying something.

"Mother demanded . . . double . . . reinforcement," she panted. Then she frowned down at him. "*Whot* are you doing?"

He followed the ribbing lines like a map. "Nothing untoward. Simply fishing through this netting to unbutton your gown."

"You most . . . certainly . . . are . . . not."

She was breathing like a fish at the bottom of a boat, and now she was wiggling like one, too, pushing up from his chest. And though he withdrew immediately, she slapped at his hands for good measure.

"Very well, but if you keep taking those rapid shallow breaths, you're going to faint. And once you're unconscious, I'll have to do *something* to revive you or else you're likely to get hurt inside this carriage."

"You . . . wouldn't . . . dare." And yet, within the belligerent glare she cast down at him, a flash of understanding returned a trace of rosy color to her cheeks. "Jane never warned me . . . that you were . . . a scoundrel."

"I'm sure Jane wouldn't know," he said, tucking a lock of silken hair behind her ear. Then, settling his hands on her shoulders, he eased her to an upright position on the opposite bench. "If you don't wish me to loosen your laces—"

"Absolutely not."

"—then you'll need to slow your breathing."

She huffed harder than before, her brow furrowed with incredulity. "They . . . *shot* . . . at . . . us!"

"Try not to think about that just now."

Of course, as he said it, the carriage jerked into another sharp turn. Her gasp was consumed by the sounds of hoofbeats echoing along the snug streets. But Asher kept her safely perched. Bracing her legs with his own, he swept his hands in soothing, methodical strokes from her shoulders to her elbows.

"And instead of casting nervous glances out the window, keep your gaze on mine." He smiled reassuringly as she complied. More color rose to her cheeks. "There, that's better. You're doing swimmingly, Miss Humphries. Hmm . . . under the circumstances, it would be better to abandon formality. I'll address you by your given name as if we're old friends simply taking a tour about the park."

"Why would you . . . wish to call me . . . Winnifred?"

"I see your point." He nodded sagely, considering. "Winnifred is still quite a mouthful. And far too many suffocating syllables in Miss Winnifred Humphries, if you ask me. So, I think I'll just call you Winn. Yes. I like the sound of that. It's almost like *wind*. And there, you're already breathing better, aren't you?"

She drew in a much deeper breath and her eyes widened with surprise. "You're quite good at this. Even if you are being a bit forward."

"It's all a matter of context, really. Perhaps if we had just met at a ball or during a tour of a museum, then my actions might be considered . . . overly familiar. But in this instance, it's more of an essential obligation. After all, neither of us wants you to faint."

He was already feeling the uncomfortably sharp spurrings of guilt. Being shot at wasn't part of the plan. Then again, being kidnapped by her friends hadn't been part of his either. The memory of it helped him tuck those *spurrings* away.

A moment later, the last of the tremors left her on a series of slow, even inhales and exhales. Her eyes cleared on a few blinks, returning to that stunning peridot green and circlet of warm cinnamon.

Dropping his hands, he eased back into his own seat. The carriage was on a straighter path now and, with a glance, he saw that they were leaving London behind. Even better news, no one appeared to have followed them down all the winding streets that brought them here.

Unfortunately, that didn't mean the danger had passed.

Once the henchmen couldn't find him in town, they'd broaden their search. None of the debt collectors had ever simply given up. They'd always found him.

The heiress looked out the window, a riot of softly tumbled curls shielding her face. "I suppose I've crossed the line. There really is no going back."

The quiet resignation in her voice was understandable, considering everything that had happened, but there was a lot she didn't understand. Even so, it wasn't in his best interest to explain the whole of it.

All he wanted was to return her to Lord and Lady Waldenfield and collect the money her friends stole.

He had a chance for a new life awaiting him and he wasn't about to squander an opportunity.

"Nonsense," he said. "I'll have you home in time for afternoon tea."

"Oh, please don't mention food. You've no idea how long it's been since I've—"

Her stomach chose at that moment to emit a loud and forlorn yowl, clearly discernable above the clatter and jangle of the carriage. She turned back, her cheeks flushing crimson as she covered her midriff. But it wasn't enough to muffle the next growl, this one even more insistent than the first.

He chuckled. "Sounds as though you've been fasting for days."

"An eternity. Mother is determined that I make a good showing in society, much like a horse at Tattersall's," Winn said with chagrin, sinking back against the squabs on a sigh. "Though, as of this morning, I will be forever out to pasture."

"Not likely," he said, knowing that her father's type of money earned all sorts of forgiveness in society. That greedy little Woodbine would still have her, and so would any other man for that matter.

"Oh, you don't know my father. Once he's reached his limit of tolerance, he'll cut a person from his life as cleanly and as permanently as a severed limb."

"Happy thought," Asher muttered wryly.

She was quiet for a while, staring vacantly at the mottled carriage roof. "Yet I cannot understand why he sent those threatening men after me."

"What makes you think *your* father had anything to do with this?"

"Well . . ." She hesitated, pulling her bottom lip through her teeth. "When you'd excused yourself to visit the back room of the jeweler's shop when we'd first arrived, I wrote a missive to my father. Mr. Windle scrawled a hasty note of his own and kindly offered to send mine out with his errand boy."

"Oh, he did, did he?" Asher scowled. Damn it all, couldn't a man take a piss without the world turning ends over apple carts?

So that was the reason the henchmen knew where he was. Not to mention the reason for Mr. Windle's incessant bartering.

Asher had known something was amiss when they couldn't reach a bargain after a quarter hour had passed. Regardless, he'd been determined that Winn would at least get a fair price, especially after learning how the necklace had come into her possession. It must have been quite a blow to have a mistress's gift arrive on her wedding day.

Another quarter hour had passed when he first spotted Mr. Lum and his cohort. Clearly, Windle sent a missive either to Lord Seabrooke or to his father. Though the last he knew, the jeweler had refused to do business with the Marquess of Shettlemane at all. Because of that, Asher had thought Windle's shop was his best place to go, without his father being any the wiser.

Apparently, he'd been wrong. And now there was even more at stake than merely recuperating his money to set sail.

Winn was involved, whether she realized it or not.

After all, Mr. Windle was a sharp old bird. He'd never have missed the Waldenfield title on the letter she'd sent. And whether the jeweler was on speaking terms with Shettlemane or throwing a bone to Seabrooke, he wouldn't hesitate to share the news that Asher Holt had run off with an immensely wealthy young woman.

"That changes things a bit," he said gravely. This wasn't going to plan at all. He'd have to think of something else. And quick. "Taking you home may be more difficult than I'd imagined."

She lifted her head. "I've already explained that I cannot return. The only option left for me is to sell my necklace and travel to my aunt's."

A fine proposal, indeed. He wished it was that simple.

Damn it all. He'd only wanted his money back. Was that too much to ask?

Yet even last night, he'd had his doubts.

Waiting in the carriage and keeping company with a bottle of rum, he'd started to wonder if his brilliant scheme was a bit too much like something his father would do. And now, with a pair of henchmen after them, the element of danger changed everything. And she only knew half the story.

Perhaps it was time to tell her who he was.

Then again, a full confession might only complicate the situation.

A handful of minutes passed while he deliberated. The ancient coach creaked and swayed. The horses charged ahead. And Asher knew what he had to do.

Tension slipped out on a tight breath and he scrubbed a hand over his face. "I want you to know that it wasn't supposed to be like this."

"Can anyone truly plan running away from a wedding? Well . . . no one other than Jane, of course. Your cousin had a marvelous plan. Though, I'm not sure even she could have accounted for blunderbuss-bearing men."

"You don't understand. She isn't my cousin."

Winn issued a papery laugh, her gaze lit with humor and a touch of pity as if she imagined him to be daft. "Jane would know her own cousin, I assure you. Why else would she have asked you to wait outside the church?"

Asher didn't want to alarm her by revealing everything in one cataclysmic statement. The last thing he needed was for her to faint. Nor did he want to see her expression turn stark again and the fire to vanish from her eyes.

So he proceeded with caution. "If I recall correctly, you mentioned that her cousin is a simpleton. Perhaps this Mr. Pickerington was waiting outside the wrong church."

"Well that's a silly notion. It would mean you're a perfect stranger."

He held her gaze and nodded.

She shook her head. "No, you are most definitely Jane's cousin. After all, what interest would a man I've never met have in helping me escape my wedding?"

Hmm . . . this wasn't going to plan either. Perhaps the direct approach would be best, regardless of consequence.

"Oh, I don't know," he said. "About as much as a man who'd been accosted on the street, only to awaken later to find himself tied to a chair and robbed by a pair of debutantes, I suppose."

Her grin slipped. "You have a dry sense of humor, Mr. Pickerington. This is certainly a strange tale you've concocted."

"Stranger still to have lived it, I should think. And my name is Asher Holt."

"That isn't possible. Everyone knows that he always . . . wears . . . a . . ." She glanced down to his black cravat. Her eyes turned round as celadon-glazed saucers as if she'd only now noticed his signature garment. Then her gaze snapped back to his. "I do not find this amusing in the least."

"Stubborn one, aren't you?"

"Now wait just one moment," she blustered, sitting forward to wag her finger at him. "That's going too far, Mr. Pic—"

"Asher Holt," he repeated, keeping his tone easy and conversational to avoid any hysterics. "A courtesy title of viscount makes me *Lord Holt*, heir to the Marquess of Shettlemane. Though I doubt I shall ever inherit. It's been my experience that evil people—particularly Luciferian fathers—never die. They feast on the misery they bring, getting stronger year by year. Which means, my father will likely outlive me. Hence the reason I'm in mourning now. No sense in wasting an opportunity."

She blinked. *Twice.* Her lips parted and closed and parted again. "Then you . . . really . . . aren't . . . Jane's . . ."

"Winn, you're looking like a fish again." He leaned forward and, as before, spoke in a soothing voice, brushing his hands up and down her arms. "Remember to breathe slowly. Inhale and exhale. Yes, that's better. Soon you'll be out in the world, able to do this on your own without allowing every trifling news to upset you."

"Trifling?" She sputtered. "You kidnapped me!"

"That's not exactly the way I recall the events of this morning."

Her eyes flared with unbanked fire and she shrugged free, batting away his hands. "Stop this carriage at once! I'm leaving."

"On foot?"

"It's none of your concern, I'm sure, *Lord Holt.*"

He crossed his arms and sat back, refusing her request. Yet in the same moment, he realized that Portman had slowed the horses. With a glance out the window, he saw they were traveling on a narrow, shady lane. And gradually they came to a full stop.

"Beggin' your pardon, my lord," Portman said, lifting the hood flap, "but I don't want any part of all this shooting and kidnapping business."

Bloody hell. This was the last thing he needed.

Chapter 7

Winnifred had made her choice. There was no going back. No getting married. And absolutely no going forward with a scoundrel like Asher Holt.

She only wished her dress would cooperate. This voluminous, impossible-to-manage *meringue* was not designed to enter or to leave—as she was attempting now—these narrow carriage doorways with any haste whatsoever.

Of course, it would be simpler if she could gather up her skirts to get them out of the way. But the dishonest, dark-haired devil had slipped out the other door and was now standing on the sloped ground. Directly in her path.

"Winn, will you please stop this nonsense? You're filling Portman's head with the wrong notion."

"Right, because this is *my* fault entirely. The men shooting at us had *nothing* to do with it, I'm sure."

He had the nerve to hiss through his teeth with impatience. "Let's talk this over before it starts to rain again."

"A deluge wouldn't entice me to linger in your company."

Yet even as she spoke, she cast a quick glance up to

the clouds. Surveying them, she decided they appeared more like the pale lavender color of freshly squeezed clouds, rather than the dark bloated gray of imminent rain.

Not that it would matter either way. She'd made her decision. And the sooner she started, the better.

Turning around, she tried to descend backward. At least that way, she wouldn't have to worry about exposing her undergarments to the viscount. Not only that, but her corset was pinching again, the busk digging into her navel, and she didn't want him to see her wince.

Folding the thick hem around one wrist, she took a hasty sip of air, and clutched the meager strip of framing on either side of the door. Then, clenching every muscle inside her body, she lowered her bottom through the opening.

A pair of strong hands settled over her hips and she squeaked with surprise.

"As much as I enjoy this view," the blackguard said in a low drawl, "I will not stand by while you hurt yourself."

Winnifred paid no attention to the warm tingles spreading down her limbs and up her torso. And didn't give a passing notice to the quick flutters low in her midriff.

Or at least, she tried not to.

Momentarily breathless, she said, "I will manage perfectly fine . . . on my own. Kindly remove your . . . hands from my person."

He growled but obeyed, stepping aside.

She lowered one foot to the ground, then the other,

and planted her slippers securely beneath her. Proud of her accomplishment, she cast him a smug look over her shoulder and took a step back . . . but without realizing that a portion of her dress refused to leave the carriage.

A tug. A rip. And before she knew it, she was flat on her rump, her teeth clacking together, her hands full of rocks and dirt and grass.

Angry, she batted down the cloud of tulle and taffeta and blew the mass of fallen hair from her forehead. "I despise this dress!"

"Oh, I don't know. I think the lace is quite nice."

"There isn't any lace on—"

She gasped. With a glance, she saw that the hem had risen above her knees, exposing the two rows of Belgian Point de Gaze that edged her sheer white linen drawers. Squeezing her legs shut, she hastily shoved down her skirts.

"Cad," she muttered. He had the nerve to flash a grin that made heat climb to her cheeks. And when he extended his hand to help her up, she glared at him. "Don't you think you've taken enough liberties today?"

"It's still early," he teased with an impatient waggle of his fingers.

She shooed his hand away and awkwardly stood on her own, brushing off her skirts the best she could. "If I didn't find you so utterly reprehensible, you would make the ideal subject to study."

"If that's a reference to the book your insane friends mentioned, then I want no part of it."

"You needn't worry, regardless. A man like you would only deserve a small mention in the chapter 'How to Spot a Scoundrel.'"

She was sure that Jane and Ellie would understand that she could no longer offer insight into the reasons that gentlemen marry. But she had to contribute something. She may as well use the horrid man at her disposal.

He scoffed. "You didn't even know who I was until I told you."

"Perhaps." She shrugged, pursing her lips. "But I knew you were a scoundrel right off with the way you . . . And then how you . . ." She waved a hand toward the carriage and arched her brows with meaning, recalling every improper touch. Her cheeks caught fire, flushing crimson, and she cleared her throat. "Well, you know what you did."

The rascal had the nerve to chuckle.

Without warning, the sound touched a raw wound inside her. The one that reminded her of every disappointed sigh from her mother. Every grunt from her maid tying up her laces. Every look of disgust from Mr. Woodbine.

And suddenly she realized that she'd been intimating that the excessively handsome Asher Holt had been attempting to seduce *her*—freckled Winnifred Humphries with the impossible hair and plump figure.

That chuckle told her she was a fool, and it reminded her that a man could only be interested in her father's money.

"What was your aim in kidnapping me, hmm?"

He shook his head and glanced up to his driver. "There was no kidnapping, Portman. I merely aided in her escape."

"By deceiving me!"

He returned his attention back to her with a frown. "If that was true, then I'd hardly have told you my name, or revealed that I was the one your friends accosted. All I wanted was to get back the money they stole from me."

"Jane and Ellie may have used less than sound judgment the other night, but they never would have robbed you." She set her hands on her hips and eyed him shrewdly. "The truth of the matter is, you thought to ransom Lord Waldenfield's daughter to gain a fortune."

He scowled back at her.

"I dunna want any part of this, my lord," Mr. Portman interjected from his perch, his brow knitted beneath a brown beaver hat. He clutched the reins so tightly that the horses shifted nervously on the rain-softened path. "My wife is about to have our first babe. I canna go to gaol! And, if you'll permit me to say it, you canna either."

"No one is going to gaol," Asher said with the steady assurance that only a blackguard—far too familiar with such episodes—could summon. "We're simply going to step back into the carriage and figure out a way to return Miss Humphries to her father before any permanent damage has been done to her reputation. After all, I don't want to end up married to a willful, spoiled little heiress for the rest of my life."

"*Ha!* My father would sooner sell me to a shopkeeper than a profligate like you. At least then he'd gain something of worth in return," Winnifred hissed. "And for your information, I would have paid handsomely for you to escort me to my aunt's. Far more than you claim to have lost. Oh, and by the by"—she narrowed her eyes—"just how were you intending to recuperate your money, kidnap my friends as well?"

"Are you admitting that your friends stole my money, then?" he asked, his tone gaining volume as their argument progressed.

"Absolutely not! Though you were certainly quick to suggest selling my necklace to a jeweler and, I imagine, eager to take your share of it."

"We'll never know, will we?" He sneered. "And *this* is the gratitude I receive for having saved you from a pair of ruffians!"

"For all I know, they were after you!"

He arched a brow. "As far as I am aware, *you* are the only one of us who has recently absconded from her own wedding. Moreover, if not for my assistance, you would likely be married to that philandering Mr. Woodbine this instant. Do you think he planned to share a bed with you *and* his mistress this evening?"

Winnifred gasped. He'd crossed a line. By the ever-so-slight widening of his eyes, she could tell he knew it, too.

"You. Are. Despicable." She'd had enough. "I'm leaving! You can go to my father if you like. Or, better yet, go to the devil. All I know is that I never, *ever*, want to see you again. Now, hand over my necklace."

"I don't have it. You probably left it in the . . ."

They both turned toward the carriage. But it wasn't there.

Apparently, at some point during all their shouting, the driver had pulled away. And worse, *with* her necklace.

Chapter 8

They stared down the tree-lined lane, catching a fleeting glimpse of the carriage. But Mr. Portman had spurred the horses, driving far too fast for them to reach. Then he vanished like flaming brandy-soaked currants in a game of snapdragon at a Twelfth Night party.

"*Splendid.* You've scared away your own driver," Winnifred accused, throwing her hands up in the air. "He's likely heading back to London to fetch a fine price for my necklace and will soon be gorging himself on tea and toast."

And *oh*, what she wouldn't give for a spot of tea and even a crumb of warm, crusty bread. More than a day had passed since her last morsel, and now the pebbles beneath her feet were starting to look appetizing.

"Say what you will about me, but leave Portman out of it," Lord Holt said darkly. "He's an honest man. If it wasn't for all your accusations about kidnapping, then we wouldn't be in this predicament."

She turned on him, unwilling to concede one iota. "Pardon me, but *I* wasn't the one who kept my identity a *secret*. You knew precisely who I was. And if I had known who you were, I . . ."

"Yes? You would have done *what*, exactly?" He arched his infuriatingly smug brows and blinked with false owl-eyed innocence. "Skipped gladly back inside the church to marry your beloved?"

Winnifred hated Asher Holt. She didn't bother to say it, but believed her feral growl spoke volumes as she stormed off toward a wooden signpost at the end of the lane.

He kept pace beside her. "You and I both know you would've chosen to stay with me. There's a sensible woman lurking somewhere inside you. The same one who talked her friend out of drugging me with laudanum the other night. And I firmly believe that, after you learned about the money they—"

She speared him with a glare.

"—about the money that went missing," he amended through gritted teeth, "then you would have concluded that I am merely an innocent man caught up in a situation not of my making. At that point, you would have sold your necklace and paid me, before setting off on your merry way."

"Perhaps I would have stayed in the carriage *if* you'd told me the truth. We'll never know, will we?" she spat, firing back his own words. "Your actions—and yours alone—have brought us here, stranded and without another conveyance in sight."

She marched onward. Ire helped her to ignore the sharp rocks beneath her slippers and the pinch in her side. She only wished it would help the light-headedness that made her head ache and her vision wobble. Her stomach gave another mournful wail. Thankfully, this time she didn't think he heard it.

"Portman wouldn't have gone far," he said with conviction. "Most likely, he's already turned the horses around and is heading back for us."

Hmph. "You certainly put high stock in his devotion to you over the needs of his family."

"And just what do you mean by that?"

Unconcerned by the edge his voice acquired, she lifted her shoulders in an offhand shrug. "Only that I noticed the dilapidated state of your carriage. Not to mention his weather-beaten hat and the mended patches on his coat. I only have to wonder how long it has been since he's earned a decent wage. After all, he does have a family to consider. A child on the way . . ."

And now, a four-strand pearl necklace in his possession.

As if she'd said her last thought aloud, he leveled her with a dark look. "Contrary to what someone like you would know—you, with pearls on your dress and your father's fortune to cement your friendships— there is a far more valuable commodity than money, Miss Humphries. It's *loyalty.* And Portman has that in abundance."

He stalked ahead of her, leaving her to stew in his wake.

Of all the nerve! She didn't have to purchase her friends. Having learned ages ago how people treated her once they discovered who her father was, she knew how to spot those who merely pretended to like her.

As for Jane and Ellie and Prue, they had become her friends before they ever knew about her dowry or her father's many bank accounts and landholdings.

She would do anything for them and, in turn, they would do anything for her. So, contrary to what this presumptive jackanapes thought of her, she knew all about loyalty. Far more than a man like him could ever know.

Squinting furious thoughts at his profile, she stopped beside him at the fork in the road. She didn't miss the uncertainty tightening the flesh around his eyes when there was no sign of a carriage of any sort.

"As I recall, there's a tavern not far from here," he said with a jerk of his chin toward the road to the left. "That's likely the only place to turn a coach around without getting stuck in a trench."

Winnifred reserved comment. Her opinion of the man who abandoned them was not nearly as elevated.

"Once we find him there," Holt continued tightly, practically daring her to contradict him, "we'll settle up our account and I'll see you safely home to London. What you choose to do after I deliver you to your father's house is none of my concern."

"Lord Holt, I release you from any sense of obligation that the guilt over deceiving and kidnapping me has incurred. And even when we don't find your driver waiting"—she had to get one more dig in for good measure, and quite enjoyed the thunderclap of irritation in his dark eyes and the way the muscle pulsed on the side of his arrogantly chiseled jaw—"that is where you and I will part ways. After all, I imagine that one of the pearls on my dress will garner me a delightful meal and transportation far, far away from you."

Then she turned on her heel and headed down the road, careful to avoid the deep wheel ruts. She didn't want to twist an ankle, after all.

"And how do you think you'll fare without me?"

"Trust me. My day will only get better without you in it."

The instant the words fell from her lips, it started to rain. A veritable monsoon flooded down through the canopy of trees.

He had the nerve to laugh as he walked toward her, shrugging out of his caped greatcoat. "You were saying?"

❧❦❧

FROM A distance down the road, Asher glimpsed the familiar mottled brick facade of the Spotted Hen through the downpour.

For the past half hour, he and Winn had kept to the tree line, his greatcoat serving as a makeshift umbrella. They'd done their best not to touch each other, maintaining their mutual animosity. The weather, however, conspired against them. With his arms lifted to hold his coat aloft, it forced a more intimate proximity. Therefore, the duty of maintaining the sliver of space between them fell upon her. And she did it well, for the most part.

She walked stiffly by his side, one arm wrapped tightly around her middle, the other gripping a handful of skirts away from wet grasses and mud. But there were occasions when she'd misstep, over a root or a stone, and bump against him.

These errant collisions only lasted a fraction of a second. Yet every touch left a disturbing imprint on him, lingering warmly on his skin long after, like a burn that refused to heal.

"The inn's just up the way," he said on a murmur, still feeling the heat of the last impact—the soft crush of breasts, her small hand splayed on his waistcoat, her quiet breath of surprise.

She darted a glance at him, a blush on her cheeks as if she was thinking about it, too. "And soon we'll be rid of each other."

Underneath this canopy, the scarlet strands woven through her wild curls seemed darker, turning a ripe, lush red. And in each breath, he caught a temptingly sweet fragrance that rose from her skin, making him think of sun-ripened berries.

In fact, *she* reminded him of a strawberry, with freckles for seeds and the netting of her dress like the scratchy leaves that needed to be plucked away before a man could sink his teeth into the succulent fruit.

Though, if Winnifred Humphries were any type of berry, she'd likely cost too much and turn out to be poisonous.

Keeping that thought in mind, he paused beneath a brace of evergreens and directed his attention to the Spotted Hen on the other side of the rutted road.

He'd only stopped here once, years ago, before the former owner had died, leaving the place to his brother. And now, the tavern showed signs of neglect. Weathered shingles on either side of a second story window hung at an odd angle. The gabled roof bowed inward like a soldier's tent. And the black-painted front door flared at the bottom, where it had been warped by age and rain.

So it surprised him to see two well-sprung carriages, fixed with high steppers near the stables. Clearly, this off-the-beaten-path location drew in clientele of means. And yet, as he peered closer, Asher's keener senses became alert, tightening the bands of muscle across his neck and shoulders.

Something wasn't quite right with this picture.

The men loitering in the yard, with their uneasy pacing and quick, shifty glances, seemed more like common variety highwaymen than drivers of fine landaus.

Turning to Winn, he leaned closer to position his coat over her head. "Wait here. I'll return in five minutes."

A pair of hazel eyes narrowed beneath an arch of rain-darkened leather. "Absolutely not. I'm wet. I'm cold. I'm hungry. And I'm not going to wait here while you find your driver, then flee for London with my necklace."

Stubborn, spoiled baggage!

He gritted his teeth. "I only want to have a look around to ensure that we don't step into another ordeal like before."

The last thing he wanted was to alarm her, or to see fear glance across her countenance. But he had to keep her safe. They were in this mess because of his brilliant notion to take her to the jeweler's instead of directly home.

"I'll return shortly. Then we'll make sure you're dry and warm and fed, hmm?"

And he intended to ensure all of those things once he delivered her to her father and regained the money that was stolen.

Receiving a nod in response, he left her to stand beneath the fragrant pine boughs with a dry cushion of fallen needles underfoot. At least here, he could trust that she was out of sight, protected from the elements and, most importantly, not in any sort of danger.

✣✣✣✣

WINNIFRED WAITED beneath the greatcoat for ages. So long, in fact, that her stomach started mewling a requiem for the dead. She'd never been so hungry in her life. Or cold. Or wet.

If she were still in London, she'd be eating her wedding breakfast. Then again, likely not. Instead, she'd be staring at a plate of sumptuous pastries and other foodstuffs, unable to eat any of it—both from being sickened by the marriage altogether and from wanting to avoid censure. And she'd do this for the rest of her life.

At least now she had the freedom to be hungry and to complain about it. And all it took was severing ties with everyone and everything she'd ever known. Happy thought, indeed.

Poised above her head, her arms started to ache. When would Asher return? She was beginning to wonder what tree bark might taste like.

Across the road, she spotted two elegantly dressed women in ermine-trimmed pelisses and broad-brimmed hats adorned with mountains of ribbons. They were leaving the inn, chatting and laughing together beneath the shelter of actual umbrellas.

The men she'd seen a few moments ago had gone off in a fine carriage. And surely, if the inn hosted clientele such as they, there was nothing to fear.

With her decision made in a snap, she hurried out from under the trees and dashed across the road as fast as her slippers would carry her.

"Pardon me," she hailed, repeating herself until she drew their attention. Umbrellas tilted and hats turned inquiringly in her direction. "Do you happen to know when the next stagecoach will stop?"

"Sadly, we don't know a thing about the next stage," the one in the lovely red pelisse said. Her gaze scrutinized Winnifred's cobweb-covered meringue. "But I must say that your dress is simply divine. You must tell me the name of your modiste!"

The one in the peacock blue agreed with an eager nod. "So elegant. Quality simply oozes from every stitch."

Even though she felt a bit worse for wear at the moment, Winnifred thanked them with a gracious smile. "I should much prefer to wear something dry instead. Though I shall persevere until the next coach arrives."

Inclining her head, she turned toward the inn, prepared to wait inside and see if she could find Asher or perhaps a sympathetic owner with a complimentary tea tray.

The women rushed around to block her path, shielding her with their umbrellas. It was only then that she spied the peculiar silken kerchiefs they wore beneath their collars, like loosely tied cravats. Perhaps it was a country fashion Winnifred knew nothing about.

"Surely you're not traveling alone."

"No, I'm with . . ." Winnifred hesitated, not wishing to say anything that would embroil her in scandal. Then again, she was wearing a man's greatcoat, so it seemed reasonable that she should mention something to explain it. "My driver, of course. Although he . . . stayed behind with the carriage."

The two women exchanged a look, then turned their attention back to Winnifred.

"Your driver wouldn't happen to be a man about"— the woman in red stretched out a hand just beyond reach of her hat's brim and lifted it by varying degree—"this tall?"

Well, since her hand wavered anywhere between an inch and a foot, Winnifred nodded.

"And wearing a pair of muddy boots?" the woman in peacock blue asked.

Again, Winnifred nodded.

"With . . . um . . . breeches? And a dark coat?"

A sense of dread washed over Winnifred, leaving her light-headed. "Actually, yes."

The women exchanged another look, then clucked their tongues with pity. "I hate to be the bearer of bad news, but we just saw him leave in a carriage that was waiting along the road toward the back of the inn."

"I believe he was headed to London."

Asher Holt had abandoned her? Of all the underhanded, lowdown, despicable nerve! First he kidnapped her and then he just simply left her standing in the rain while he jaunted merrily back to London?

What a fool she was. All that talk of kidnapping must have alarmed him enough to think she would call upon the authorities. As far as she was concerned, that man deserved to go to gaol, and with his driver!

"Oh, dear. You've had quite the shock, haven't you?" Red pelisse put her arm around Winnifred and began to walk toward their landau. "And we cannot possibly leave you here to suffer because of some dreadful man. No, you must come with us. We'll take you anywhere you wish to go."

"After all," peacock blue added, "a woman in need should always be able to depend upon the kindness of other women."

"Oh, and be sure to lift your hem a bit higher, dear. Wouldn't want the mud to climb up on any of those pearls. They're all real, aren't they?"

Winnifred absently nodded and stepped up into the carriage, following Red. "My mother prefers embellishments."

"What a coincidence," peacock blue said as she closed the carriage door. "So do we."

Her lips curved in a peculiar smile that made Winnifred wonder if she'd neglected to catch a joke. But the instant her gaze fell on the point of the blade being brandished by the woman in red, she realized that she'd missed a good deal more.

"Hand over the dress, Miss Pearls."

⊰✺⊱

WHAT ASHER discovered when he crossed the road did not ease his mind. The men standing by the stables were armed. And instead of cravats around their necks, the garments looked more like the kerchiefs worn by highwaymen.

He kept to the side of the Spotted Hen to avoid notice and made his way to the back, where a narrow lane wove in an arc toward London. He was sure he'd find Portman waiting for him, or turning the horses around.

Regrettably, he didn't. What he saw was much worse.

Asher stopped short, spotting the same henchmen from outside the jewelry shop, having a row inside their curricle.

"What are you doing, idiot? Holt isn't here," Mr. Lum railed, trying to take the reins from his wiry cohort, whose long-limbed reach outspanned the barrel-chested man's. "They could be all the way back to London by now. And Shettlemane won't be none too happy with us for letting him slip through our fingers either. Especially now that he's got that heiress."

Shettlemane? Asher felt a shock jolt through him. So his own father had sent Seabrooke's henchmen after him? They must be working together. Honestly, he didn't know why he was surprised by this news. His father would do anything to remain friends of those with money—even throw his own son to the wolves.

"But how do you know Holt's going back?" the younger man with the pockmarked face asked. "I'd wager he's taking her all the way to Gretna Green. That's what I'd do. Make sure I've got her fortune, right and proper."

"Proper." Lum scoffed. "Jamey, you'd have nicked

her maidenhead in the carriage, afeared she'd get away."

Sneering, Jamey puffed out his sunken chest. "Wouldn't have needed to, would I? Everyone knows the bloke at the Spotted Hen will turn a blind eye to whatever might happen in the room upstairs. I've heard tale of all sorts of doings there."

"If that's true, then Holt could have done the deed before taking her back to her rich father to demand a king's ransom. Mark my words, Holt's standing in Waldenfield's study right this moment."

"You say London, but I still say Gretna Green."

Lum spat into his palm and held out his hand. "I'll take that wager."

Asher felt a chill roll through him as he watched the curricle turn around toward London. Then he headed back to Winn.

He wasn't sure how he'd tell her, but there wasn't any way they could go back now. Not with her father's house being watched.

The Marquess of Shettlemane would have dozens of men on the lookout for any sign of his return. More than likely, he'd tell half the ton about the kidnapping, thereby forcing a wedding between Winn and Asher. And then Shettlemane would have half of Waldenfield's fortune spent before the ink was dry on the marriage license. Within a year, he'd be in over his head and the wheel of gambling, debt and manipulation would keep turning. For years and years to come.

No, Asher thought. He refused to let that happen. This time he was going to do whatever it took to free himself of this constant burden once and for all.

Both he and Winn would have to forge a careful plan to proceed, of course. He just hoped she wouldn't prove to be too stubborn.

Yet as he stepped across the road and through the line of trees, he realized her willfulness was the last thing he needed to worry about.

Because she was gone.

Chapter 9

Asher was going out of his bloody mind. Half an hour had come and gone since he'd begun his search, but it had been longer since they'd parted ways. And for the time being, Winn was his responsibility. So where the devil was she?

He rubbed his fist against the unfamiliar tightness in his chest and knew he never should have left her alone.

Wondering if she might have gone back the way they'd come, he retraced their steps, racing down the road like a wild dog. But she was nowhere in sight.

Dimly, it occurred to him that one of those highwaymen he'd seen in the stable yard could have taken her . . . carried her into the room upstairs and . . .

At once, he was plunged into panic. But the feeling wasn't like being submerged in a frozen lake. It was like being bathed in volcanic fire. Boiling fury coursed through his veins as he sprinted back, ready to rage through the inn and tear the place apart.

Yet as he neared the Spotted Hen once more, voices from inside a departing carriage caught his attention and he stopped in his tracks.

". . . pearls on her dress, too. We've never nicked

anything so fancy from those posh coaches we've robbed."

A cackle of laughter cracked through the air. "And she made it too easy, the poor lamb. Believing us about having been left alone to fend for herself."

"We did her a service leaving her in the cooper's shack instead of tossing her into the stables with the lads. And she didn't even thank us." They laughed again.

As the carriage rolled away, Asher squinted off in the distance and spied a little sloped-roof shack that looked one breeze away from toppling down. He didn't waste another moment.

Out of breath, pulse hammering at his throat, blood rushing in his ears, he arrived at the door and shoved it wide, the bottom digging into dirt floor. "Winn?"

He didn't see anything at first, only the dark interior. And for an endless minute, there wasn't any response. He didn't know what other fate had befallen her.

But then he heard a sniff, and a soft voice say, "Asher?"

A wave of relief washed through him so powerful that he staggered from it and gripped the door for support. She may be a spoiled, pampered bit of baggage, but she was *his* spoiled, pampered bit of baggage.

At least, for the time being. "Aye. It's me, sweets."

"I . . . thought you'd left me."

"I wouldn't do that to you," he said, meaning every word as he peered toward the far corner, seeing only barrels and shadows. "Are you hurt?"

She hesitated. "Only my pride and . . . well . . . my slippers have seen better days."

"That doesn't matter. We'll get you new slippers as

soon as we're far away from here. Come on, then. We need to get a good foot under us."

"I . . . I can't."

"What do you mean? If your slippers are ruined, then I'll carry you out of here. Hell, I'll even let you wear my boots."

"That's quite gallant," she said without a drop of venom. "But I couldn't leave you stocking-footed after they took your greatcoat."

Damn. He'd liked that coat. And that meant they wouldn't have any protection from the rain. "Rotten luck, but we'll make do without it."

"Well, you see . . . they took something else, too."

Asher waited for her to continue. He didn't expect her to emerge from the shadows, her eyes downcast, hair disheveled, and her dress . . . gone. Otherwise he might have been able to school his reaction.

As it was, all he could do was stare at the lush curves on display, barely concealed by her gusseted corset and snow-white petticoat. His hands tingled at the memory of those full, round hips and that nipped-in waist from when he'd tried to help her from the carriage. And seeing her with all the elegant frippery stripped away, she was a fantasy brought to life. The kind that entered a man's mind on drowsy mornings with a good stretch and tug beneath piles of warm bedclothes. Then lingered in his thoughts all day, waiting to flood his mind again that night.

Realizing his mouth was agape, he closed it with a snap and swallowed down the saliva pooling beneath his tongue. Thankfully, a sense of chivalry took over and he shrugged out of his coat as he walked to her.

He never expected her to rush into his arms either. A full-body collision of curves.

Yet when he felt her tremble, the frantic dread that had coursed through him moments ago returned tenfold. He couldn't stop himself from cinching his arms around her. And he held her so tightly that he could feel the harried beat of her heart match the conflicted rhythm of his own.

"I can't believe I was so stupid," she sobbed wetly, burying her face in his cravat. "I should never have trusted those women. I'd actually thought for a moment that members of my own sex—and strangers no less—would see me as more than a sack of money to be picked apart. Oh, I'm certain they had a grand laugh over the gullible debutante falling for their trick. And I said the day couldn't get any worse."

"You'd best not say those words in the future . . . just to be safe." He forced himself to speak with a teasing air as if they could now look back on it and laugh. As if the ordeal she suffered wasn't his fault.

But it was.

Pressing his lips to the top of her head, he drew in her berry-sweet scent before he moved apart from her. He settled his coat over her shoulders and lifted her half-tumbled hair free of the collar.

"Believe me, I won't," she said, her cheeks colored with embarrassment. Keeping her face averted, she lifted a shaky hand to wipe away the wet tracks.

"There's a handkerchief inside my coat pocket."

"Thank you," she said, reaching for it and cleaning tears and smudges from her face. "You wouldn't happen to have a dress in there, too, would you?"

"Afraid not." The corner of his mouth lifted in a grin, glad her wry humor was left unmarred by the episode.

It could have been so much worse. And the more he thought about it, the more he had the impulse to take her in his arms again.

Asher clenched his fists instead, a dark anger shuddering through him. He was tired of knowing that there were so many self-serving prigs in the world, who simply took whatever they wanted.

And yet . . . hadn't he done the same? Wasn't he just as bad as all the others?

"I managed to steal a button," she said, breaking into his thoughts. Unfolding her bare hand—clearly, they'd taken her gloves as well—she revealed smears of dirt and a small tarnished disc lying in the center of her palm. "It's all I have left of the dress I once hated, but now wish I had more than anything."

"Is that silver, by chance?"

She looked up at him, eyes brightening with understanding. "Do you think we could hire a coach with this?"

Leave it to an heiress to have no notion about the price of common services. To her a pearl necklace and a silver button were on equal footing. And Asher wondered how many people had taken advantage of her *without* her even knowing.

The thought made him angry. Both at himself and the rest of the world.

"A coachman would want at least a guinea, but that's only if we're going back to London."

She stared at him steadily. "But I'm not."

"No," he said after a breath. "We're going to your aunt's."

"*We?* Do you mean to say that you're taking me?"

"I am."

Her eyes narrowed with skepticism. "This isn't some plot to marry yourself an heiress, is it?"

He shook his head. Unable to resist the urge, he reached out and tucked a lock of bedraggled hair behind her ear. He'd already made this decision when he'd overheard the henchmen plotting.

Besides, Asher believed he'd still have time to make it back to London before the ship sailed, Wednesday next.

"No, Winn. I wouldn't do that to you. It's my fault we're in this predicament, and I'm not going to let you gad about the countryside by yourself."

She paused for a moment, scrutinizing his countenance, her head tilted at an angle.

"It's on the tip of my tongue to refuse," she said, "but even I'm not that obstinate. To tell you the truth, the thought of going alone is somewhat terrifying. As I was leaving the church, I'd imagined for an instant that either Jane or Ellie would be with me, sharing something of a grand adventure. It seems a foolish notion now."

He thought of his own plan to board a ship and sail off toward buried treasure. "I don't think it does. And you'll still have your grand adventure. I'll make sure of it."

"You're being awfully kind, considering the inconvenience my friends caused," she said sheepishly. Then she cleared her throat. "Of course, my aunt will pay you whatever monies that were . . . misplaced."

Asher arched an ironical brow at her obstinate refusal to speak the word *stolen*. She shrugged, a half grin toying with her lips.

"Then we have a bargain." He held out his hand and, without hesitation, she slipped hers into his.

A peculiar shock tunneled through him as they shook, flesh to flesh. The delicate warmth of her fingers sliding into his palm caused a visceral reaction that pooled heavily in his gut.

Instantly, he wondered if this was all a mistake. Perhaps he needed to come up with another plan.

Instead, his fingers tightened reflexively. So did hers. Then her eyes widened as if he wasn't the only one who'd felt something.

She hastily withdrew. Pressing the flat of her hand to her midriff, she cleared her throat, spots of scarlet dotting her cheeks. "And afterward, we'll end our acquaintance without anyone the wiser."

"I wouldn't have it any other way," he said, surreptitiously curling his fingers toward his empty palm.

He told himself that all he had to do was escort her to her destination. All he had to do was focus on his ultimate goal.

It would be simple . . . as long as he didn't allow anything else—like an inconvenient, passing attraction—to distract him.

Chapter 10

"I find it astonishing that a simple silver button was enough to purchase a new dress and a shawl," Winnifred said from behind a screen of shrubbery that did nothing to ward off the chill in the springtime air.

For the sake of modesty, she spread out the woolen shawl high on the spindly hazel branches. The coarse fabric was the color of her father's nightly glass of port that he always drank alone in his study while reading by firelight. And thinking of that—of how she'd never be at home again—a heavy sigh escaped.

"What is it? What's happened?" Asher asked.

Was it her imagination or was there a hard edge to his voice, like a man prepared for battle?

It was almost comical how he refused to leave her side for an instant. Even earlier, when he'd gone to the kitchen entrance at the back of the tavern, he'd made her keep his handkerchief in her hand, while holding it through a hole in the cooper's shed. And when he'd returned to her, he'd practically carried her off the property and *before* she could dress, spouting some sort of nonsense about not wanting to tempt the stable lads.

She might have laughed if the circumstances were different. "I'm just tired, that's all."

He murmured a sound of agreement. "We'll have to stay off the main road for now. That should keep us from encountering anyone who might be searching for us. Once we're a safe distance away, it shouldn't be long before we encounter a passing farmer who might offer us a lift into the next vicarage."

Without any money, she didn't think there was a point in heading to a nearby village, but she held her tongue. She saved her breath to wiggle into this plain bib-front dress, a homespun green the color of unripened olives with short, gathered sleeves and an ill-fitting bodice.

Of course, it might not have fit at all if her busk hadn't snapped in two, which forced her to remove it or else have her tender skin pinched. It felt rather liberating to toss the stiff wooden pieces to the ground. Due to the thick busk's absence, her laces weren't as tight and she could move a bit more freely.

Even so, she frowned as she secured the fastenings, where milk-white swells strained the ruffled bodice trim. She looked like she was smuggling mounds of rising bread dough across the countryside.

"Are you certain there wasn't enough silver to purchase a man's suit of clothes, or to take us all the way to Yorkshire, for that matter?"

"Yes, I'm certain," he said dryly. "No one would believe you're a man. I fear that wearing breeches or trousers would only enhance the fact that you are, most definitely, a woman."

Peering above the shawl line and through the branches, she saw him scrub his hand over his face and shake his head. She imagined that, should he turn around, she would see disgust in his expression.

"Of course," she said quietly. "I hadn't thought of that."

"And besides, that isn't a new dress. The purchase had far more to do with human nature than with silver. The garment was left behind in a portmanteau after the owner's wife stole away in the middle of the night."

Winnifred felt her brow pucker in confusion. "That doesn't explain why the scullery maid would be so eager to part with it."

"Because the owner's wife left with the maid's young lover—a man who was supposed to run away with *her* instead. From the brief tale she told, the man must have been seduced out of his wits by the owner's wife."

"Really," Winnifred breathed. In rapt fascination, she smoothed her hands down her midriff. The simple design fit her waist quite well, without being tight or modified with added reinforcements. And the length went to the edge of her petticoat hem. "This dress has lived a far more thrilling life than I have done. Imagine the stories *it* could tell."

"Best not," he murmured as if to himself.

She ignored him, too caught up in the notion that someone who wasn't shaped too differently from her had had a lover. *Two*, if she counted the cuckolded husband.

"I wonder if this is what it's like to wear a disguise

at one of those illicit masquerades. I've read about those in the society column, you know. Apparently, a great number of debutantes who've attended are either quickly married afterward or sent away by their families," she said through the branches, plucking the shawl free. It was scratchy against the bare flesh of her shoulders, but it was warm and that was all that mattered. "Have you ever attended one?"

He cleared his throat. "My great-aunt Lolly once disguised herself as a boy to board a ship."

"Lolly?" she asked with a grin, not missing the way he avoided answering.

A scoundrel such as he had probably been to a great number of masquerades. Perhaps she might convince him to tell her about them. For the purpose of the primer, of course. Well, that *and* her own curiosity, which was doubtless brought on by the illicit trysts woven into the fibers of this *two-lover* frock.

"Her actual name is Liliandra, but my mother always called her Aunt Lolly. And even though I haven't had the chance to meet her, that is the moniker I use when I pen letters . . . to . . . her . . ."

His words trailed off as she stepped out from behind the makeshift screen. She had her arms raised to sink the remaining pins into the thick twisted coiffure she'd attempted without a mirror.

But when she saw the way his gaze roamed over her figure, she lowered them quickly and took hold of the pointed ends of her folded shawl.

"Frightful, I know," she said in a rush before he could. The heat of embarrassment climbed to her cheeks. "Mother always has my dresses designed with panels to conceal my plump figure, and additional fabric added to my sleeves. According to the modiste, broader shoulders give the illusion that I have a small waist. Father doesn't say much of anything, but Mr. Woodbine frequently offers not-so-subtle advice about how I should learn to decline cake when offered. In other words, I've heard plenty of opinions already."

Asher's gaze suddenly collided with hers. Beneath his dark scowl, his eyes were the color of smoldering cinders. "Mr. Woodbine is an idiot and, forgive me for saying this, but so is your mother. Winn, there isn't a single thing wrong with your figure. And believe me, I wish to hell there were."

He practically growled those last words as he turned away.

Her heart gave an excited leap at the gruff compliment. No man had ever paid her notice, or given her any indication that she was pleasing to look upon.

She was too plump. She'd been told as much for years, her wardrobe fussed over with panels and flounces so much that she nearly hated to attend balls and parties. Mr. Woodbine wouldn't dance with her, even after their betrothal was announced, and there was no line of men ready to stand in his place. So she'd lingered near the potted palms and refreshment table with her friends.

In her experience, gentlemen did not pursue fat, freckled heiresses. Because of this, Winnifred's inner voice reasoned that Asher Holt was simply trying to be kind, out of pity over the ordeal she'd suffered with those horrible women.

The buoyant feeling beneath her breast abruptly sank. After all, on her body, this two-lover frock was merely a faded green dress.

Walking beside her, Asher reached into the inner pocket of his coat and withdrew a sleeve of brown paper. He handed it to her.

Warily, she gripped the oddly shaped, somewhat cylindrical package that was heavier on one end than the other. She wasn't sure she was up for another surprise. "And this is . . . ?"

His shoulders lifted in a nonchalant shrug. "I managed to procure something else with your button as well."

Carefully, she parted the paper and a spontaneous smile erupted. "Bread and cheese! Oh, what a marvel you are with a single silver button! I'm so happy that I could . . ."

She didn't finish. Her words trailed off as she glanced over at him and saw his gaze dip to her lips. His own curled in a grin, and she remembered at once how laughably undesirable she was. A kiss from her would hardly be a reward.

"You could *what*, Winn?" he asked, amusement deepening his voice.

Refusing to give him any fodder to chuckle over, she forced herself to finish, keeping her tone purposely light. "Why, I could marry you this instant and happily give you the fortune of my dowry. In fact, if it were in my control, I'd make you rich as a king."

"And all for bread and cheese? For a flagon of wine, I could rule the world."

"Perhaps not. But I'd throw rose petals at your feet

for a hot cup of tea," she said absently, her focus on the warm, crusty bread.

She tore off a hunk. A fresh, yeasty aroma rose from the pale, lacy interior. It must have been baked just this morning. She was salivating by the time she sank her teeth into the dense loaf, tasting the salty essence of butter that clearly had been brushed on the outside. A moan escaped her.

Chewing slowly, she closed her eyes. Lost in a moment of food bliss, she imagined herself as one of the hedonists in a Bacchus painting, draped in silks and lounging on cushions while a loincloth-clad servant dangled grapes over her mouth.

When she opened her eyes, she found Asher watching her intently.

Instantly, her cheeks flooded with color. Waiting for his look of disgust, the partially masticated bread turned into a stone in her mouth and went down her throat in a painful swallow.

"My apologies," she said. "I seem to have no manners whatsoever. I normally don't eat with such un-abashed . . . um . . . enthusiasm, so to speak."

Hastily, she shoved the package back to him, the paper crinkling against the hard wall of his chest.

Taking hold of it, he blinked in confusion. "Surely you'll need more to sate your appetite."

"It's obvious that I've eaten enough bread in my life."

His dark brow dropped to a flattened line. "Eat the damned bread."

"Thank you, no," she insisted, her ire simmering.

"That one bite shall prove sufficient for the remainder of our journey."

"Then you leave me no choice but to feed it to you."

"I'll bite your fingers if you try."

And yet, he did try. He tore off another piece and lifted it to her mouth.

She wanted to snap at him. But—heaven help her—the aroma made her weak. Her salivating tongue and mewling stomach conspired against her. Even so, she hid her lips, stubbornly pressing them closed as she crossed her arms beneath her breasts.

"I know you want this. I can see the hunger darken your eyes."

She squeezed her eyes closed, too, shutting him out.

Unfortunately, he took advantage of the opportunity and skated temptation over the sensitive of her lips. Her flesh tingled.

Then he leaned in, close enough that she felt the heat releasing from his body. A pleasing aromatic mélange of the bread, the rain, the earth, and . . . *him* . . . filled her lungs, eliciting a warm shiver that fluttered low in her stomach.

"If you don't eat it," he warned, his warm breath drifting across her cheek, "I'll be forced to kiss you into submission."

Her eyes popped open. "You wouldn't da—"

He slid the bread into her mouth.

The flavor dissolved on her tongue before she could object. And a traitorous murmur of appreciation escaped her throat.

"That's better," he said smugly. "Now, some cheese."

The offering was sharp and delicious, tingling at the corners of her jaw, the firm texture turning creamy as it melted in the heat of her mouth. She chewed and swallowed, studying his expression the whole time.

He fed her another bite, and then another, not looking at all as though he were disgusted by her. Instead, he looked . . . hungry, too. Then he dragged his thumb across her bottom lip, his eyes impossibly dark under the shadows of his lashes as he followed the motion.

"Only a scoundrel would make such an outrageous threat," she said when she could catch her breath.

"No. Only a scoundrel would have made good on his *promise*."

He grinned wickedly as he put the pad of his thumb to his own lips, tasting whatever might have been lingering there. A crumb of cheese? A scrap of bread? *Her?*

Her stomach clenched at the thought, feeling full and pleasurably weighted. The sensation was foreign to her, thrumming deep inside. And when he offered more, she declined with a shake of her head, a hand resting over her midriff. She liked the feeling too much to risk lessening its effect by overindulgence.

He ate the bite himself, then ripped off a large hunk of bread and cheese before wrapping the remainder in the paper and slipping it back into his coat.

"We'll save this for later, when we stop again. Although"—he hesitated, casting a look over his shoulder—"we could walk back to London. It isn't too late."

"But it is too late. We've already spent too much time together without a chaperone. Society would imagine the worst, regardless."

"Mmm," he murmured with a contemplative nod. "They'd expect marriage."

"I'd rather be labeled a fallen woman than to marry without love. No offense to you, of course," she added quickly. "I'm certain that aside from the kidnapping and the rakish tendencies in your character, you're a fine gentleman. But I already decided that I would never marry a man who needed my dowry. Even if he claimed to love me, I couldn't be certain."

He exhaled deeply, leaving her to wonder if it was from relief or resignation. Perhaps a bit of both.

"Sometimes you must do whatever it takes to have the life you want," he said with a nod. "No matter the cost."

She was glad he understood. Until today, she'd never have thought she was capable of doing this. In truth, she was a bit shocked with this new Winnifred emerging into the world.

She contemplated this as they walked northward for a time, along a serpentine path worn through a pasture. A hidden chorus of crickets and thrushes hushed for their approach, then continued their tune after they passed. His sure and steady footfalls were muffled by the soft-packed earth. Beside him, her skirts swished against the border of damp grasses where water droplets glittered like diamonds whenever the sun peered out from behind the swift tumble of clouds overhead.

And if it weren't for the fact that she'd run away from her own wedding, severed ties with her parents, fled from blunderbuss-toting ruffians, lost any means of currency, and felt a rise of guilt over the fact that she was now being escorted to her aunt's by the very man her friends had essentially imprisoned for research, she might have considered it one of the most splendid days of her life.

She smiled at the idiocy of such a thought. Under the circumstances, it would be wrong to enjoy herself as if she were merely walking in the park with Asher Holt.

With a sideways glance, Winnifred studied her companion's profile, trying to discern his current mood. Looking off in the distance, he absently brushed back a hank of hair from his forehead. The wind ruffled the dark layers where it curled at the ends, then tapered down to rest against the top edge of his white collar and black cravat. A stubble of soot-colored whiskers accentuated the edge of his jaw and outlined the somewhat pensive appearance of his mouth. If she could hazard a guess, he appeared to be lost in thought.

Anyone would admit that he was handsome. Glorious, even. And yet, there was something more—an aloof, almost wounded quality to his manner that compelled her to look deeper. To uncover the mystery that was Asher Holt.

"What made you desperate enough to kidnap an heiress?" she asked. "Because I don't believe that it was all about having your money returned to you."

He gave her an alert glance as if assessing a potential threat.

Then he faced the path again. Bending down, he picked up a stone and threw it into the distance. The single, lithe motion parted his coat to reveal his trim torso and, far off, sent a flurry of brown speckled birds into flight.

"My father," he answered, surprising her. "The money I had collected was funding a plan to be free of the burden of his debts for the first time in my life."

She understood the desire for an unfettered life quite well. The need to remove the influence of money from every interaction. And yet, that was the true reason behind his willingness to escort her—because he would be paid at the end of the journey.

It was almost comical to think that she'd left the church this morning, only to end up in a similar situation. Everywhere she looked there was a man needing to gain a fortune through an association with her.

Winnifred expelled the deep disappointment that came from thinking overmuch about money, and turned their conversation to a less depressing topic. "Was your aunt running away, too? Was that her reason for being disguised as a boy on a ship?"

"Something far more scandalous. She wanted to have an adventure." He lifted his brows at her in accusation. Then he walked a few steps ahead to clear a long stick from their path, testing its weight against the ground before continuing onward with it.

"My great-aunt was the youngest of eight," he continued. "My grandmother, on the other hand, was the eldest, and there were sixteen years between them. So, when my grandmother married and bore a child, this left only three years separating my mother and Aunt Lolly. Consequently, the two of them grew up like sisters. Inseparable. Their temperaments, however, were vastly different. Where my mother was quiet and obedient, Lolly was wild. Left without the strict instruction of a firstborn, she was spoiled with freedom and pursued many of *her* unrestricted fancies."

"That must have been lovely," Winnifred said wistfully.

"Even so, when it came to taking a grand tour by sea, my great-grandparents refused."

Winnifred knew all too well the unfairness of having hopes for traveling abroad dashed in a heartbeat. "But Lolly didn't let that stop her."

"Indeed." He chuckled. "My mother would often laugh and say that Lolly was so accustomed to getting her way that she didn't understand the definition of the word *no*."

"Do you think your mother might have been a bit jealous of her?" Winnifred already felt envious and she'd never even met Lolly.

"Undoubtedly. In fact, I've often thought that she told me these stories so I would have it in my mind to sail off on a grand adventure."

Winnifred's eyes rounded as she looked at him, her pulse leaping excitedly at the thought. "Is that your plan?"

He nodded. "Something like that."

She waited for him to elaborate, to explain more about this grand adventure that would free him of his burdens. But he didn't. And why should he? She was a stranger to him, and nothing more than a means to an end.

She shrugged off the sting of that knowledge, and kept to the topic of his daring Aunt Lolly. "Was her boy's disguise successful?"

"According to the stories, the ship she'd boarded had actually belonged to a pirate."

"*No.*"

He nodded. "She spent three months on the ship without being discovered for a woman. During that time, she was so small that she was relegated to the less strenuous tasks of cabin boy for the bold pirate captain, called the Mad Macaw, and kept mainly to his chamber."

Winn imagined herself in such a scenario.

In her mind's eye, Asher took on the role of a swarthy, handsome pirate dressed in snug breeches, his torso scandalously bare aside from a maroon embroidered waistcoat.

Across the bow of the ship, he spotted her. Beneath a forelock of wind-ruffled dark hair, his wicked gaze roamed down her form, taking in her trousers and open-necked shirt . . .

Hmm. The vision abruptly evaporated in a fog of doubt. Glancing down at herself, she knew that there wasn't anyone who would be fooled if *she* dressed as a boy. Asher had been right in procuring a dress for her.

Walking along, Winnifred slid a skeptical glance at him. "You're saying that for *three* entire months, he never suspected?"

"So the story goes." Asher shrugged. "However, I suspect that he had to know. After all, why else would he have made someone so scrawny his own personal servant?"

Not to mention, Winnifred thought, *Lolly would have had to conceal her monthly courses.*

"Regardless," he said, "when they reached the island, the truth was revealed."

Again, she waited for him to elaborate. But he frowned and kept his attention on the path ahead.

"And?" She huffed. "Surely you're not going to incite my curiosity only to withhold the conclusion."

Didn't he realize she was living vicariously through Aunt Lolly?

Asher cleared his throat. "It's just that I've never told this story before."

"You haven't?" Her urgency suspended for a moment. The seconds ticked by as she looked at his uncharacteristically reserved expression.

It suddenly felt as if they were sharing something more than a walk across the countryside. Perhaps they were becoming friends of a sort. She'd never had a male friend before. And wouldn't it be positively wondrous to forge a connection with Asher that reached further than a mere exchange of money?

Her heartbeat quickened at the thought, feeling lighter, as if the organ were lifting off in the basket of a Montgolfier balloon.

"I just realized that I've steered the conversation down a salacious avenue. Again," he said, absently grazing a hand along his stubbled jaw, his brow furrowed in contemplation. "Under the circumstances, it would be best to avoid the topics that would naturally lead to flirtations."

All at once, her little balloon of hope and friendship erupted in a ball of flame and crashed to the earth.

"Fear not," she said tightly, batting away a few stray curls caught by the cool breeze. "I am under no delusion that you have any interest in my person whatsoever. Therefore, you are welcome to tell me what happened next."

He eyed her with patent curiosity. "Winn, do you know when a man is flirting with you?"

"Of course," she said with a flippant wave of her hand. "And a scoundrel simply flirts for the sake of flirting. Scandalous words flow as naturally from your lips as honey from a hive. I understand this and think nothing of it. I'll merely consider this aspect of your nature as part of my research. I'm making a mental note of it now."

A rather convincing lie, if she did say so herself. But she wasn't about to admit that no man had ever bothered to flirt with her. In her entire life.

"Very well, then. I'll not try so hard to subdue my nature."

A slow roguish grin curled at the corners of his mouth as if she'd just handed him the key to her bedchamber door. Her breath hitched in a warm rush that spread over the surface of her skin.

"For the moment, however," he said with a wink, "I'll stay with the lesser of two evils and continue Aunt Lolly's story."

She swallowed, wondering if she'd been too hasty in inviting him to essentially say anything he liked. And yet . . . it would be good for her research.

"They'd just reached the island," she reminded.

Asher nodded, prodding the ground with his long stick. "The Mad Macaw had been to the island many times in his travels. So often, in fact, that he'd built a veritable palace at the foot of a mountain. He had elaborate gardens of tropical trees and wild birds, a stream that led into a cave, and a warm spring at the foot of the mountain. And, on the first night of his return, he told his cabin boy to bathe in that pool."

"Well, that seems sensible. After all, they'd been aboard a ship for—"

"Alongside him."

Winnifred tripped. Her misstep caused her to stagger off the path, but he captured her elbow, steadying her.

Perhaps this was a rather salacious topic of conversation to be having with a man. Even so, she couldn't stop herself from asking, "Well? Did she?"

Asher Holt's eyes glinted with a devil's charm, his fingertips skimming the sensitive inner curve of her elbow. "What would you have done, Winn?"

"I suppose," she hemmed, biting down on her lip as she tried to ignore the way her pulse skittered beneath his touch and seemingly everywhere else, "after three months on a ship, I'd long for a bath."

"That isn't an answer."

"Of course it is." She slipped free of his grasp and started on the path again.

"No," he said from behind her. "You told me what you'd like, not if you would have the courage to act on it."

She thought for a moment and came up with the perfect response. Grinning, she lifted her finger and said, "I would get into the pool, but I would keep my clothes on. That way, everyone is satisfied."

"That's what Lolly thought, too," he said, then paused long enough to draw out a few erratic heartbeats, leaving her in breathless suspense. "But she was wrong."

"She . . . she was?"

Beside her again, he nodded slowly. Sagely. "He wasn't satisfied until they were both completely . . . and thoroughly . . ."

"I understand now. You don't have to say more."

"Nude," he said anyway. "In the buff. Without a stitch. Naked as Adam and Eve."

"You're a wicked man."

"I appreciate that you fully accept this part of my nature."

When he flashed a grin, she rolled her eyes.

Yet as they walked on for a time, that story was still soaking in a steamy bath in the center of her brain. And getting prunier by the minute.

When she simply couldn't stand it any longer, she finally asked, "And then what happened? I mean, obviously the Mad Macaw didn't have her killed for her deception if she's still alive."

"No. He certainly didn't kill her." He laughed, then cleared his throat. "He did, however, keep her as his cabin boy for years afterward."

She gasped in outrage. "You mean to say that he *enslaved* her?"

Poor Lolly!

"Not exactly. It was more of a . . . mutual understanding," he said. "He wanted her all to himself. So he kept her as his cabin boy whenever they sailed, but spent most of his life on the island with her."

"Oh," she said, her lips curving in a dreamy smile. "That turned into a lovely story. Please tell me that Aunt Lolly is well."

"She is," he said, a softer smile on his lips, too. He

reached out and playfully tugged a stray lock of her hair. "She writes to me often with more stories of her adventures."

"Oh, what it must be like to travel to far off places."

"You're traveling now, Winn."

"I suppose I am." She inhaled deeply, absorbing the moment. Her gaze flitted over him and the view of the rolling hills behind him as the wind buffeted his coat and mussed his hair. And she thought of how astonishing it was that the pinnacle of her life's adventures should happen with him.

"And there will be other adventures," he added with certainty.

She shook her head. "Aunt Myrtle suffered an injury to her leg years ago and she never leaves Avemore Abbey. But she keeps her spirits high, nonetheless. In her letters to me, she refers to her home as Old Crow Abbey, writing that she may as well name it after herself and the other inhabitants that keep her company."

"How long has it been since you've visited her?"

"More than ten years." A sudden chill swept over her as the clouds began to gather overhead. "That was when my father cut her out of his life for refusing to marry a gentleman who was—as my father put it—her best prospect. And that is also the reason I know he will never welcome me home again."

⁂

JULIAN HUMPHRIES, Viscount Waldenfield, paced his study, fuming at the ormolu clock on the mantel. Where was that bloody investigator? He should have returned with a full report by now. It had been two hours since Winnifred had gone. Two damnable hours!

He stared down at the wrinkled page in his fist, the words already seared into his cornea.

Dear Father,

    I cannot marry Mr. Woodbine today, or ever. And while I know this will disappoint and anger you, I would rather be cut out of your life entirely than to exist solely to do your bidding and then my husband's from this day forward.

    I am my own person. I have my own mind and my own beating heart that cannot be owned by you or any man. I deserve more than to be handed over like a sack of money. So I must away for my own sake.

    In case we never see each other again, please be kind to Mother.

Winnifred

He still couldn't believe she'd actually run away, and after all that he'd done, arranging everything so that she could be a duchess one day.

He crumpled her note again. He'd done so a dozen times, then smoothed it out just as often. Now the paper was too soft, too like crushing a handkerchief. There was no satisfaction in the act. Even so, he could still shake it at his wife, which he did the instant he heard her return to the study. They'd both been pacing in their own parts of the house.

"Perhaps if *you* had spent more time preparing our daughter on what was expected of her, then this wouldn't have happened," he said, voice rising, his blood heating like steam in a locomotive.

Too used to his outbursts, Imogene merely regarded him with cool blue eyes. "Ever since you announced her betrothal to that bumptious peacock—and without speaking to me, I might add—I've done nothing but prepare her for the bitter disappointments of marriage."

"Well, one of us had to act on her behalf, and I was tired of waiting for you to clear your social calendar to have a moment of your time. If you're not shopping, then you're attending dinners at the Duke of Tuttlesby's until the wee hours of the morning."

"Don't give me that look," she warned, lips tight, stubborn chin notching higher. "You're the one who aligned our houses with the betrothal. And because of you, Winnifred had to face an abysmal life with a man who's already in love with someone else. At least *I* was trying to make her stronger so that she wouldn't have to bear heartache as I have done."

He scoffed, flattening out the page over the desk blotter. "What are you even talking about?"

"*Ha.* Are your affections for the countess so inconstant that I must remind you of her? Likely not, since you still carry the snuffbox that she gave you."

"You're being preposterous."

And yet, he could feel the weight of the object in his pocket, pressing against his chest. He always kept it close.

"I've seen the engraving," she sneered, smoothing her hands down her skirts, where—only now—did he notice the wrinkles. She must have gripped the fabric, a habit she did whenever she was too worried to think about appearances. *"For Julian, and the love that was lost but can always be rekindled . . . if you but speak the word. Your countess."*

"My friendship with the countess has no bearing on this situation," he said absently, still distracted by the motion of her hands, the flawless ivory skin, and the faint tremor that revealed her fears.

Lifting his gaze, he noticed the barest tinge of redness beneath a light dusting of fresh powder on her cheeks and nose. She'd been crying. And it shocked him how much he wanted to walk up to her and take her in his arms.

But it had been years and years since he'd had the liberty to do so.

"You're absolutely right," she said, a slight catch in her voice as she turned to fuss with a pillow. "Winnifred is what matters. She's all we have left."

Memories flashed in his mind, one after the other, of Imogene's lovely face shredded in tears and their stillborn sons in her arms.

A profound pain throbbed in the center of his chest. It was the kind of ache that never healed. It surrounded emptiness where there had once been so much hope and so much love that he thought he couldn't bear it.

But he'd been wrong. It was the loss of it that kept tearing him apart, day by day.

Before he was aware of it, he took two steps to cross the room to her. But then the butler appeared, the investigator close behind.

Julian pivoted on his heel and dismissed the butler

with an agitated wave of his hand. Then he glowered at the investigator, already impatient. *"Well?"*

"You were correct, Lord Waldenfield," the investigator said. "Your daughter was not alone in the carriage. There was a gentleman with her."

Imogene gasped. "No! It isn't possible."

But Julian, on the other hand, wasn't surprised. He'd only been waiting for confirmation. In fact, he already knew the blackguard's name.

Holt.

Chapter 11

Asher adjusted the tail of his shirtsleeves and re-fastened his fall front as he waited for Winn on the opposite side of the tree line. They'd both required a moment of privacy to see to *necessary matters* on their lengthy trek northward.

Thus far, keeping to the side roads had not resulted in the happenstance of a farmer or anyone offering them a trip into the next vicarage. Instead of conveyances, they'd encountered varieties of flora and fauna, the animal life including cows, sheep, and a cantankerous groundskeeper who had threatened to beat them both with a stick if they didn't *get off the master's land*.

The episode had warned Asher to be even more cautious. If he were recognized and seen in the company of a runaway heiress, then whatever future plans either of them had would incinerate into curls of smoke. Any debutante's family would demand they marry for the sake of her reputation.

Then again, Winn seemed to believe that her father was unforgiving and apt to completely cut her out of his life. Having met the blustering Waldenfield only once, Asher couldn't be certain. Not that it mattered, however. Shettlemane would ensure their marriage, by any means necessary.

He frowned, absently looking skyward at the dark clouds gathering overhead. "Winn, it's time we're on our way again."

She didn't answer.

With his father's despicable nature lingering in his thoughts, Asher's mind flashed to an image of Winn's face, pale and terror-stricken, as they'd fled from the henchmen in London. That hollow stare was something he'd never forget.

Instantly, the pulse at his throat jolted, beating faster. But he shook his head and muttered, "Don't be a fool, Holt. Only little old ladies fret over triflings."

The most likely reason Winn hadn't responded was because she'd moved farther down the hedgerow for more privacy. Women were often shy about these matters.

Therefore, like a man who understood the nature of things, he patiently waited another five minutes—though, in reality, it might have been only a few seconds—then called her name louder this time.

Surely she should be finished by now.

Still there was no answer.

She couldn't have gotten far. Certainly not so far away that she couldn't hear the sound of his voice. Not unless . . . someone had taken her. After all, she was a veritable magnet for disaster.

A lance of unease sent his pulse galloping, regardless of his efforts to the contrary.

Bollocks. Asher didn't wait another instant. He

pushed through the spindly branches and broke free on the other side. And his fears were confirmed.

She wasn't there. His cravat seemed to close around his neck, his breath coming in short, strangled bursts.

Scanning the landscape, he noticed a long strip of flattened grass leading away from the hedges and up, over the low hill. He broke into a run, racing as fast as his legs would carry him. "Winn!"

It wasn't until he crested the hill that he saw her.

She was standing on a wooden stile, holding a bouquet of violet-tipped clover under the nose of a glossy-coated, sorrel horse. And she dared to look over her shoulder and laugh, the impish melody carried on the breeze.

"You're huffing harder than a chimney sweep," she called out to him. "I should think a scoundrel—and one who's likely run away from many a furious husband—would have better stamina."

Asher's brow flattened into a line, his lungs burning. A stream of reprimands crowded on his tongue. But then her face lit with a sudden radiant smile, and he forgot what he was going to say.

He blinked, dumbstruck as she absently brushed aside wind-buffeted curls from her cheeks and shoulders. This couldn't be the same woman he'd met this morning. There was nothing stiff or scared in her manner. In fact, she was fairly glowing. And gone, too, was the grumpy caterpillar in the voluminous, scratchy dress.

Wearing that simple homespun frock, she'd transformed into a new being—a lush creature who lived at her leisure, existing somewhere between wild meadows and shade trees. And he was filled with a sudden and strange desire to live in that world with her.

"I heard whickering," she explained at his approach, stroking a hand along the stallion's velvety neck. "I just knew there was a horse nearby. And look! Isn't he lovely?"

The horse snuffled her other hand, searching for more clover. And when she bent down and liberated additional flowers that were just beyond the edge of the fence, he nudged her affectionately with his long head.

Asher's pulse was still rioting, his lungs tight, but from a new brand of panic that he refused to name. It made him testy. Uncomfortable in his own skin.

"Winn, you can't go scampering off into the unknown just because you think there might be a horse nearby. What if the horse were carrying a rider who saw you and decided to—"

"To *whot*? To kidnap me?" She rolled her eyes. "It may surprise you to learn this, but you have been the only man inspired to run off with me in my entire life. And it's solely because you need money."

He highly doubted that any man seeing her in this moment would ever be able to leave her. She had an appealing, freshly tumbled look about her, all flushed and inviting.

Asher cleared his throat and cast his gaze skyward, stuffing those dangerous thoughts behind the darkening clouds. "We should go before the weather turns. The next village cannot be far now."

"Or . . ." she hedged, biting her bottom lip. "We

could get much farther if we borrowed him for a day or two."

"I see that your friends aren't the only ones who believe they can take what doesn't belong to them, whenever fancy strikes."

"Jane and Ellie didn't steal from you. They merely wanted you for our research. And besides, who's to say that you had any money of your own in the first place? After all, you're not particularly flush at the moment."

He stiffened his shoulders, offended. "I won every last farthing through my own efforts."

"Gambling?" She scoffed. "A twin to thievery, if you ask me. A man wouldn't gamble at all unless he knew he could win. No man would choose to beggar himself."

"Then you'd be surprised how often it happens."

"What I meant to say is that every man who gambles is essentially hoping to take what doesn't belong to him. Therefore, the money you claim to have been stolen wasn't even yours to begin with."

"Listen here, Miss *I-can-buy-the-world-with-a-silver-button*," he said, speaking over her huff of indignance. "When a man sits down at a gaming table, he knows the risk. He's just hoping that his cards are better than his opponent's, or that he can make him think they are."

She set her hands on her hips. "Now you're admitting to employing deceptive means to take what doesn't belong to you. Yet when it comes to borrowing this horse, you're struck with a sudden bout of scruples."

"In case you aren't aware, the cost for horse thievery is rather high." His hand lifted to encircle his cravat in an automatic gesture.

"We won't get caught. Victor will make sure of it."

"And who is Victor?"

She scratched the horse's nose. "Isn't it obvious? He looks very much like a Victor—a champion of the downtrodden that will race toward victory no matter the cost. Won't you, my dear boy?"

"A pampered heiress wouldn't even know how to ride without a saddle."

"*You* know nothing of me," she said with a sniff, her eyes dancing with mischievous light. "When I was younger, I started slipping out of my bedchamber at dawn, stealing down to the stables of our country house to visit the horses. Some of them looked so lonely, so in need of the wind in their faces, that I could not help myself.

"Admittedly, my initial equestrian escapade was terrifying. I fell four times before even leaving the stall. But Henrietta was patient with me, and soon we were off, racing over the meadow and away from the sun cresting over the house."

Asher wouldn't have believed it of the woman he'd first met. But now, he could picture it clearly—her wild hair whipping in the wind, lilting laughter bubbling from her throat as she tried to outrace the rising of every new day.

He understood that feeling. That yearning for freedom.

He used to sneak away at dawn as well, wanting more than anything to leave the chaos his father created. However, invariably, the thought of abandoning his mother to face the obsessive spending and gambling episodes alone had always brought him back.

Winn gazed at him with beseeching hazel eyes. "If

there was another way, I wouldn't even think of it. But as it stands, if we remain on foot, I fear it will take weeks for us to arrive at my aunt's, and I"—she hesitated, lifting one shoulder in an uncertain shrug—"I couldn't bear it if you missed the opportunity of a lifetime all because of me."

Stunned, he stared back at her, mute as the buttons on his waistcoat.

Had she come up with this plan to steal a horse because she was worried about *him*? This was a first. Aside from his few close friends, he'd grown accustomed to finding selfishness at the core of most people he met.

He didn't quite know how to form a response. Had they truly been strangers just this morning? It didn't seem possible. Even in such a short time, they already shared a similar understanding of the ways of the world, both of them living under the shadow of their parents' choices. Both of them wanting more than anything to escape.

And she wasn't like any of the other heiresses he'd met either. She wasn't vain or spoiled, or expecting all to be handed to her on a silver platter. She'd even been grateful for the simple garment he'd procured. She hadn't whined about walking, or lamented about her feet and her back aching. No, she bore it all with her own sort of grace.

And she was clever, too. Whenever she needed to pause to catch her breath, she did so by pointing at a flower, an insect or a bird and stating its Latin name. *My goodness, could that possibly be a* Fringilla coelebs?

Never letting on that he suspected she was tired, he would stop on the path to offer his full attention. *With such a bright blue cap, you could almost mistake him for a* Cyanistes caeruleus *if not for his red feathered drawers.*

You seem to look for undergarments in every creature you encounter.

Only the ones with the brightest plumage.

Thinking about it, he almost grinned. All in all, Winnifred Humphries was quite a revelation.

Be that as it may, she still wanted to steal a horse, and her proposal turned his thoughts back to their current dilemma.

By now, those two henchmen would have discovered that Asher and Winn didn't return to London. And since the men had wagered on London or Gretna Green, Asher knew they'd make a beeline northward. Odds were, they'd cross paths at some point . . . unless Asher and Winn could get ahead of them.

"Very well," he said, resigned.

Winn issued a squeal of delight that made his skin tingle warmly. With the way her eyes were dancing, he expected her to leap off the stile and directly into his arms. His muscles reacted with a jolt of anticipation and he exhaled, preparing his lungs for his next breath to be filled with her sweet scent.

But instead, she wrapped her arms around *Victor's* neck and gave *him* an exuberant kiss. "Did you hear that? We're going on an outing together."

Asher frowned, refusing to be jealous of a horse. And yet . . . was it his imagination, or did Victor just cast an arrogant wink his way? Stranger still, his whickering sounded like a knowing chuckle.

Winn straightened, giving him a final pat. The horse

angled his head to Asher and tossed his mane in a shake, clearly all too pleased with himself.

"There's no need to glower," Winn said to Asher, misunderstanding. Stepping down from the stile, she slipped her soft hand into his. "You won't be sorry. It's the perfect plan. Nothing can possibly go wr—"

She didn't have a chance to finish.

A roar of thunder interrupted. Then a crack of lightning broke through the sky, startling Victor. He reared back on his hind legs and took off like a shot toward the hill as the clouds opened.

Through a curtain of fat, dousing raindrops, Asher lifted the shawl above Winn's head. Then he shrugged out of his tailored coat and held it over both of them.

"I know. I know. You don't have to say anything," she said with a roll of her eyes.

He was struck by a dangerous impulse to kiss those pouting lips, and not for the first time. With circumstances forcing them in such close proximity, was it any wonder he was tempted?

And yet, he wasn't going to cross that line. It would only complicate the bargain, which was already far more complicated than even she understood.

"Come on, Winn. Let's follow the horse and wait out the storm."

WINNIFRED WAS shivering to her toes in the stable loft. A row of loose boards creaked beneath her feet, with prickly strips of straw falling between the uneven spaces to the empty stall below. But at least they were out of the rain.

Victor had known precisely where to go. He'd raced up the hill toward this rickety old barn with a peaked roof and crooked red-stained wooden door. With a turn of his long head, he looked back as if to make certain they followed, then nudged the door open. It tilted inward on a slant, rusty hinges groaning with effort. Inside, he trotted over to his stall, clearly quite used to his solitary afternoon escapades across the meadow.

Even so, it felt strange to trespass here with a thatched cottage not too far in the distance and curls of smoke rising from the stone chimney.

"Winn, this isn't the time to be shy," Asher said from the base of the ladder. "Toss down your dress."

She blushed to the roots of her hair. Unfortunately, even turning crimson wasn't enough to warm her frozen fingers and stop her teeth from chattering.

"I'm n-not b-being shy," she stammered, fumbling with the fastenings. "Y-you've already s-seen me w-without the dress."

"You're quite right. Therefore, there's no reason to stand upon ceremony."

Before she could ask what he meant by that, the top of his head emerged over the edge of the loft. She might have gasped at his audacity, but then the rest of him came into view and her mind whirred to a sudden stop.

Asher Holt was naked.

Well, mostly. His bare, broad shoulders and sinewy arms appeared first, muscles shifting and bunching beneath his skin as he navigated the final rungs—and far more adeptly than she had done. Then he unfolded from a crouch, and stood.

Her greedy eyes skimmed the length of him, taking in every . . . blessed . . . inch.

Dark hair lightly furred his chest, accentuating the fascinatingly hard lines and ridges of his lean torso, then tapered down from the shadow of his navel and into the waist of his breeches. The doeskin hung splendidly low on his hips, clinging to the outline of solid thighs where the fabric was still damp and darker. And beneath the bottom cuffs—buttoned at the knee—dark hair dusted wide, muscular calves and the tops of his sizeable feet.

"With the way the wind is howling through the wood slats, our clothes will be dry in no time at all," he said, dragging her attention to his face as he stood in front of her. "I'm afraid I can't say the same for the bread."

She blinked and saw his gaze fixed on hers. Dimly she felt a tug, the drag of one sleeve, then the other. "P-pardon?"

His lips quirked in a grin. "I said, we lost the bread."

"Oh, that's dreadful. I was looking forward to it." Her voice sounded faraway to her own ears, as if in a dream.

"Lift your arms over your head. That's it," he said, and she moved without putting much thought into her actions. Her gaze drifted again over his magnificently bare throat, arms and chest until they were briefly blocked by a quick blur of green. "And don't worry. We still have a bit of cheese, and I found a few carrots in a pail. I'm sure Victor won't mind sharing."

"You're not wearing your shirtsleeves," she said inanely. "This is far better than a tour of a museum."

He chuckled, settling a coarse brown blanket around her shoulders. "The Elgin marbles or the Egyptian sarcophagus?"

"Both. Although I'll never remember the marbles quite the same. Zeus will be very much alive."

"As long as you aren't comparing me to Aphrodite I won't take offense," he said with a wink before turning away to skillfully navigate the rungs once more. From below, he called out, "We'll eat first, have a rest, and leave while there's still daylight to guide our way."

She looked down at herself. The vague fog of the last few moments cleared away with sudden, scalding clarity.

She wasn't wearing a dress. And when she saw her toes peeking out from beneath her hem, she realized she wasn't wearing stockings either. *Oh wait*, she thought, recalling that she had removed those first, draping the mud-crusted silk over the side to dry.

Even so, Asher was alarmingly good at removing a lady's garments. She made a mental note of this for the primer.

Yet he'd done so with such practiced, impersonal efficiency that he'd kept her from feeling she needed to worry at all about improper advances. In fact, other than his rakish words and a few errant touches, he'd been an absolute gentleman.

Drat it all.

Was it too much to ask if, for once in her life, she'd incite a man's carnal interest? That would make a far more interesting chapter.

Asher returned to her a moment later, the frayed rope of a wooden pail clenched between his teeth until he breached the last rung. Then he dangled it from the crook of his finger as he sketched a bow. "Your feast, my lady."

Surreptitiously, her gaze roamed over his form again. A pang of hunger clenched tight in her midriff. "Thank you, I'm ravenous."

"I can see that," he said with a low, wicked laugh that made her blush. Perhaps her ogling wasn't as furtive as she'd hoped. Wearing nothing more than breeches and a grin, he brushed his hand against hers and tugged on her fingertips. "Come and eat your fill."

Was it her imagination, or was every word he spoke salacious?

The terrible part was, she wanted to keep gawking. Looking at him was the only thing that warmed her. Though out of a sense of decency, she forced herself to stop and sat with him near the edge of the loft, dangling her feet.

"It's kind of you to agree to my scheme," she said as she broke the wedge of cheese and handed him the larger portion. An unwelcome rise of guilt twisted in her stomach. Looking around her, it was plain to see that the farmer couldn't afford much. "But I'm beginning to wonder if borrowing Victor is a good plan, after all."

Asher chewed thoughtfully for a moment, studying her with an intensity that made her wonder what he saw.

After a day of walking until she was exhausted, aching, hair in a mass of tangles, she was a complete wreck. And somewhere along the way, the sole of her left shoe had broken and the ball of her foot felt bruised. Yet while she could do nothing about her appearance, she refused to make matters worse by whining. What would be the point? After all, they were both in this together. And there was something comforting in that.

"You're not what I expected," he said, handing her a carrot after he wiped it clean on his pantleg. "When I first heard your voice and the way you chided your friends for their escapade, I thought you'd be prim and stuffy, with pursed lips and hair cinched in a tight coiffure."

"Believe me, my mother would praise the heavens if my hair ever stayed in any sort of arrangement *and* if my freckles suddenly disappeared. Though, after today, I've likely sprouted a dozen new ones."

He took her chin, tilting her head in the warm grasp of his thumb and forefinger to scrutinize her nose and cheeks. Then he nodded and released her while a grin played on his lips. "Just one more. You started out with seven and now there are eight."

She frowned, averting her face to rub her fingertips over her nose, and wishing for porcelain skin.

"I like your freckles."

Marginally wounded by his teasing, she groused. "There's little I can do about it. I've tried lemon juice and dusting powders to no avail. You will just have to suffer with my appearance for a short while longer."

Once more, he took gentle possession of her chin and held her gaze. "I *like* your freckles, Winn. And I don't ever want you to think of bleaching them with lemon or concealing them with powder. They're quite lovely just the way they are."

She frowned, confused as to why he would say such things. Freckles were dreadful. Everyone knew it.

Though, clearly, he thought she'd been seeking some sort of pacification. "Well, then you can have them."

His gaze turned warmer, lingering on those imperfections as if he actually wanted them. As if he were laying claim to each one.

She tried to look away but there was some reckless part of her that simply couldn't. All at once, her throat felt impossibly dry and her tongue darted out to wet her lips. That small, insignificant action seemed to cause his pupils to expand like spills of elderberry syrup on linen, and his nostrils flared. Then his thumb skimmed over the crest of her chin, sliding into the tender valley beneath her bottom lip and releasing a shower of tingles inside her that tightened her lungs. He made her breathless. And worse, he filled her thoughts with the preposterous notion that he might kiss her.

"They turn darker when you blush," he said, his low, drowsy tone fluttering inside her stomach. "Those tiny flecks of amber turn to burnished bronze right before my eyes."

Her cheeks caught fire and he grinned.

"You keep trying to make them seem appealing, but it isn't w-working," she said, an unexpected shiver stealing over her.

Asher instantly curved his palms over her arms and proceeded to winnow away every chill with sure, measured strokes. Dimly, she wondered if he was this familiar with every woman he met.

"That's enough talking about freckles for now," he said. "It's time to rest for a minute or two. We've a long evening ahead of us. Now, let's get you warm, hmm?"

She nodded and dropped her uneaten carrot into the

pail. Setting it off to the side, he stood and went about making a bed out of straw.

A single bed of straw.

"And where are you going to lie down?" she asked.

He pointed to the pile he'd just forked.

"Then, if you take all the straw for yourself, I suppose I'll have to stay with Victor."

At the call of his name, the horse whinnied below in a way that almost sounded like a laugh.

Asher cast a dark glare down through the floor. "I'm sure he'd enjoy that, but I'm afraid I intend to keep you to myself."

"I think not." She swallowed, rising to her feet. It was one thing to ignore propriety when he was soothing her inside a carriage, or rescuing her from a cooper's shed, or warming her inside a barn, but . . . this?

He tossed down the hayfork and chafed his hands together. "Winn, we are both cold. You're shivering and there's a bluish tinge to your lips. And, in case you haven't noticed, the wind howling around us has turned bitter and frostbitten."

She clutched the blanket tighter on another shiver and looked over at the . . . *bed*. A rise of maidenly fears set her heart on a hard patter. After all, she was in her underclothes, while he was practically— *blessedly*—naked. "Yes, but isn't this a bit too intimate to be respectable?"

"In matters of survival, keeping a respectable distance will only harm us both." To prove it, he came to her and rubbed his hands up and down her arms again, tempting her with warmth.

She couldn't stop herself from inching closer. "A scoundrel would say something like that."

"True," he admitted, but soberly. "Though you and I, for lack of a better term, have a business arrangement. I'd hardly be honoring my part of the bargain by proving myself an untrustworthy escort. Thus far, have I made any untoward advances?"

"Other than believing I was a harlot when we first met?"

His tempting mouth curled rakishly. "Yes, other than that."

She paused as if she were giving it thought, even though she already knew the answer. Sadly, it was, "No, you have not made any advances."

"There you have it," he said with an easy shrug.

The matter settled, he guided her to the center of the straw and gave special care to bundling the blanket tightly around her. Then, he must have been uncertain of her warmth because he proceeded to put a blockade's worth of straw between them.

When he lowered down beside her, he cleared his throat, his Adam's apple bobbing as he swallowed. If she didn't know better, she might think he was nervous. Perhaps he thought she was going to attempt to seduce him?

So, to ease his mind on the account, she said, "I will refrain from making any untoward advances as well."

She only hoped she didn't have another dream of a statue coming to life and accidentally put her hands all over his bare flesh. Oh, but what a lovely dream that would make! Nevertheless, she turned on her side and faced away from him, using her hair as a cushion against the straw.

"Besides," he said, shifting to lie behind her, "this would only be intimate if there were kissing involved. And certainly, with this barrier to keep us apart, you needn't worry about an eminent seduction."

Of course not. Only pretty girls would have need to worry. Girls like her, on the other hand, were taught how to politely decline plum cake, *not* roguish advances. And she was suddenly worried that she'd have no material for the primer at all.

"Although . . ." he added with a sardonic edge to his voice, "I suspect you'll believe I'm a veritable devil if I offer to untie your laces to make you more comfortable."

She almost laughed. "My laces are just fine as they are, thank you."

"If you change your mind, you need only ask."

As Winnifred let her eyes drift closed, she wondered what his response would be if she did.

Chapter 12

Asher didn't want to leave this dream.

For years, he'd awoken in a cold sweat from the nightmare of being crushed by a mountain of his father's debts. Slowly suffocating to death.

But this morning was different. In this dream, he felt the warmth of sunlight on his face while lounging on a bed of sweetly scented strawberries. Better still, there was a soft woman in his arms, her lush bottom pushing back against his ready cock in invitation.

Helpless against the enticement, he cinched an arm around her waist and rocked forward.

"Asher," the woman whispered on a slumberous sigh.

He buried his face in her hair, breathing in deeply. Such a delectable fragrance. A somewhat familiar fragrance that prodded the edges of his waking mind. It was almost as if he'd had this dream before, but he was nearly sure he hadn't. This felt too new and unexplored and altogether decadent.

"Hmm . . . ?" he murmured.

She yawned, her back arching in a stretch. "You left the hayfork in the straw. Be a dear and move the handle out of the way. I want to sleep for just a bit longer."

Asher frowned and pulled her closer, still trying to cling to the dream. Yet reality started to intrude, reminding him of a drenching rain shower, a loft, a pile of straw, and a tooth-chattering heiress . . .

"That's not the hayfork, lass."

This was Asher's thought. But it was *not* his voice.

Opening his eyes in confusion, he saw sunlight bleeding in through a wall of warped planks, felt a cushion of soft, springy hair beneath his cheek, and heard a scrape and creak of wood behind him.

He blinked into wakefulness, feeling a sense of being watched prickle the back of his neck. More alert now, he looked over his shoulder toward the ladder, startled to find a man standing over them.

"*This* is the hayfork," the man said, holding the object in question. He wasn't brandishing it like a weapon, but held it as if it were a long rifle at rest, with the stock on the floorboards and his hand around the neck. And yet, it was clear by the hard look in his lean, weathered face that he wouldn't hesitate to use it with lethal intent, if need be. "Mind tellin' me what you're doin' in my barn?"

Fully alert, Asher sat up. Reflexively, he leaned over to shield Winn. Though with his current state of morning arousal, his movements were stiff and stilted. Apparently, the straw he'd so carefully packed between them had dispersed and his loins had been nestled perfectly against the firm globes of her bottom.

The sun glinting on the sharp tines of the hayfork, however, demanded more of his attention at the moment. "We came in out of the rain. That's all. We mean you no ill will."

"The rain ended yesterday, and well before twilight," the farmer said.

Yesterday? That would mean that the light slanting in through the warped slats was the dawn. And they'd lost half a day's travel.

"Yet, here you are . . . still," the farmer continued. "Mayhap you're thinkin' to take what isn't yours." With a turn of his grizzled head, he pointed his aquiline nose and blunt chin toward the pail of leftover carrot tops.

Asher felt contrite at once. It was obvious by the tumbledown condition of the barn and the age-worn brown shirt and trousers that this man couldn't afford much. Not even the loss of a few carrots. "My sincerest apologies. Please know that I intend to make reparations for the—"

"*Whot* was that about yesterday?" Winn asked, stirring groggily beside him.

Rolling over, she splayed her hand across his abdomen, stirring his blood and forcing him to realize that it would have been more prudent if he'd slept with Victor. How in the world was he ever going to forget what it was like to lie beside Winn?

Her fingertips flexed experimentally. Slowly, she blinked up at him and her eyes curved into crescent moons on a sleepy smile. Then, abruptly, they went wide and round. A bright blush bloomed on her cheeks as she snatched her hand away.

"Good morning, sweets. It appears as though we've overstayed our welcome"—he paused, motioning with a subtle backward tilt of his head—"in this fine gentleman's loft."

Clutching the blanket to her magnificent, barely contained breasts, she lifted up on an elbow to peek over his shoulder. Then she squeaked and dropped back down.

With a look of distress, she mouthed, "Did you tell him about Victor?"

Asher flattened his brow, mouthing back, "I'm not an idiot."

Winn rose up again, hitching the blanket higher and lifted her pleading hazel eyes to the farmer. "Kind sir, you have every right to be angry. Though I hope you will be lenient when you've heard the very distressing news I must impart. You see, this man—"

In a flash, the warmth in Asher's veins turned to ice.

He realized that now would be the ideal time for her to unleash a sad tale about having been kidnapped from her own wedding. Stolen out of London. Barely escaping from a pair of henchmen out for blood.

In fact, if she played her cards right, she could garner sympathy enough for this farmer to drive her all the way to her aunt's and see that Asher was put in irons for the rest of his life.

It wouldn't be the first time someone had used him to gain what they wanted.

"This man," Winn repeated after she cleared her throat and swallowed, "and I are traveling troubadours who were set upon by thieves. They robbed us of our instruments, along with the satchel of our few worldly belongings and small scraps of food. After our ordeal, we met with a drenching downpour and took shelter in your barn to dry our clothes. I'm afraid time escaped us. And we have taken advantage of your hospitality. Please, sir, if there is a way that we can make amends, let it be known and we will gladly do it."

The farmer didn't answer directly and Asher was temporarily tongue-tied as he gazed down at her.

Winn's hair was in complete disarray with yellow shoots of straw sticking out here and there. Sleep crusted her lower lashes and a bit of dried drool sat in the corner of her mouth. And he couldn't account for it but that overwhelming, foolhardy impulse to kiss her returned.

She hadn't betrayed him. It would have been so simple for her to do so.

He should probably say something to corroborate her story. Instead, he reached out to remove bits of straw from her hair, distracted and feeling a grin warming the corners of his mouth.

In response, she batted his hand away and slanted him a perturbed glance.

Clearly, he needed to focus. He turned to the farmer to add more to the story, only to see hard gray eyes narrowed in suspicion.

"A fine tale, to be sure," the farmer said. "I imagine you're either a pair of young lovers padding off to Gretna Green, or simply using my property for an illicit encounter. Either way, I'll not have any part of it. The magistrate will—"

"We're married!" Winn announced, wrapping her arms around Asher and holding to him like a shield. Her soft curves molded invitingly against his side. And her actions wreaked havoc on his ability to form a coherent thought.

The farmer arched a brow. "Married to each other, I trust?"

"Of course, to each other," Winn said with an affronted gasp. "Otherwise we would never have . . . Well, not to say that we did engage in any sort of . . . activities last night . . . other than sleeping, of course. I certainly wouldn't have . . . um . . ." She swatted Asher's arm. "Crumpet, be a dear and introduce us."

Crumpet? Was that supposed to be him?

Asher felt a grin tug at his mouth. He winked at her, watching as her cheeks flushed the same hue as a strawberry, her freckles the seeds.

"Yes, indeed, we're Mr. and Mrs. *Strawb*"—he stopped and quickly amended with a name that sounded more credible—"Strewsbury. Perhaps you've heard of us? The Strewsbury Quartet."

Winn stabbed his side with a piece of straw. He could almost hear her unspoken diatribe: *Quartet? What possessed you to tell him that we are part of a quartet? He'll only wonder where the others have gone.*

"Can't say that I have," the farmer murmured, eyes still narrowed with marked skepticism. "But if you're a quartet, then where are the others?"

"We were separated," Winn said in a rush.

"Murdered by highwaymen," Asher said at the same time.

Damn, he'd done it again. In trying to recover from a poorly executed fib, he only made matters worse. Though it would help if she would stop being so soft and warm and distracting.

To keep from being impaled for his error, however, he reached down to strip the dried blade from her fingers.

"What my husband means," she began with a laugh, tightening her grip on the straw, "is that we were separated when we were all accosted by the, presumably, murdering sort of highwaymen."

The farmer kept his gaze leveled on them and his hand gripping the hayfork. "And just what sort of instruments do you play . . . the ones that were stolen by these *supposed* highwaymen?"

Surreptitiously, she yanked one end of their prize toward her. "I sing and I'm also a flutist. My husband plays . . ."

Her words trailed off as their tug-of-war drew his hand beneath the folds of the blanket. Inadvertently, the knuckle of his thumb dragged lightly along the underside of her corset's gusseted cups, the space warm and supple and inviting. His better intentions were being tested to their limits.

"Have you forgotten, Mrs. Strewsbury?" the farmer asked with an edge to his tone, seemingly one lie away from having them put in stocks and irons for trespassing.

Asher slid his finger over hers as he released his hold on the straw and withdrew. "It's just that she becomes shy every time she thinks of how nimble her husband's fingers are . . . on the lute strings."

It was ideal that Winn's cheeks reddened before she tucked her face behind his back. Then she pinched him, for good measure.

"Haven't been married long, I see," the farmer said with amusement in his tone. The small grin that creased his countenance suggested that he believed their story. "My own wife blushed for the whole first year. Ah, but those were the best of days. Hold on to them while you can."

She lifted her head, avoiding Asher's gaze to look at the farmer. "And where is your wife, sir?"

"Visiting her sister, a couple of hamlets north of here. I'll be surprising her with a visit today. You see, I just bought that young stallion down there for her. Claims that I never buy her anything."

"He's a fine horse," Asher said and Winn murmured her agreement, though with a trace of regret that only he would understand. "Your wife is quite fortunate, Mister . . ."

"Champion." The farmer grinned proudly, rocking back on the heels of his muddy boots. "Been married seven years now and there isn't anything I wouldn't turn inside out for my Gwyneth. And, I imagine, that horse there will pull a smart little gig as well as a cart and a plow."

"You're traveling north?" she asked, a hopeful glimmer in her gaze. "It just so happens that we are, as well."

"Seems to me that London is where you'd make your fortune."

"And we would, surely, but there are so many of us in town already."

Mr. Champion's narrow-eyed skepticism returned and he grunted. "I suppose I could lend a hand to a pair of down-on-your-luck troubadours. That is . . . if you help me by mucking out the stalls and milking the cow."

"Cow?" Winn asked uncertainly. "I didn't see a cow yesterday."

"The neighbor and I share old Betsy between us. I brought her back this morning. Then caught you lot in the loft, and an empty pail of carrots."

"I would absolutely love to milk your cow," she said with a nervous smile. "It will bring back all the days of my childhood . . . on my parents' tenant farm."

The farmer's mouth remained stern. "And what about you, lad?"

Asher didn't miss the ultimatum. "I can muck a stall better than it's been mucked before, sir."

With that, the fate of their next few hours was sealed. And would, he trusted, hold temptation at bay for a while longer.

WINNIFRED FELT the glare of a pair of big brown eyes on her.

If the puffed grunt and flare of her nostrils was any indication, Betsy was getting irritated. And what, precisely, would a large milk cow do when being squeezed for minutes on end by a person who obviously knew nothing about milking? Would she retaliate by squashing said person?

"Nice Betsy," Winn said with another skittish clasp. "Lovely Betsy. I imagine with your buttery brown coat and not a single freckle, you've turned quite a few heads from the gentlemen cows—or bulls, rather."

Betsy turned her attention back to the bundle of hay in front of her and Winn felt as if she'd been given a stay of execution.

She'd already wasted too much time in her futile efforts. When Asher had asked her earlier if she even knew how to milk a cow, she'd confidently—and perhaps stubbornly—told him that she did.

After all, he'd been wearing a disbelieving smirk at the time. And, in her own defense, she *wanted* to milk the cow. Part of her—and she couldn't quite put her finger on the reason—needed to prove to Asher that she was more than an heiress. More than a person whose daily existence was recorded in her father's accounting ledger.

Unfortunately, she and Betsy were getting nowhere. And Winn knew that she needed to hurry along or they wouldn't be able to arrive at her aunt's in time, and Asher would miss his grand opportunity.

Swallowing her pride, she strolled over to the stall where Asher was working. The instant she saw him, however, she forgot what she was going to ask him.

He was shirtless still. And even more glorious than before—if such a thing were possible. His bare back glistened with sweat, muscles bunching and flexing sinuously as he plied the hayfork, in and over. *In and over.*

Her greedy gaze descended to where his breeches rode low on his narrow hips. Beneath the superbly snug buckskin, she spied the clearly discernable outline of his taut, sculpted buttocks. His tailor and valet should be shot for covering this sublime perfection with clothes. And to think, this man—whom she was now ogling with near eye-socket-spraining intensity— had lain next to her all night long. *Her!* Undesirable Winnifred Humphries.

Breathless and weak from watching his exertion, she sighed and leaned against the stall door.

Until it shifted . . .

Without warning, the door swung wide on a groan. And with her usual, terrible luck, Asher turned around in time to see her at her most awkward, shuffling and stumbling sideways in a pantomime of poorly executed dance steps.

Then her shoulder connected smartly with the heavy wood. She winced. All over again, she felt enormous and ungainly.

What business did someone like her have thinking about being in the arms of a man like Asher Holt?

"Here," he said in a low voice, coming to her. Cupping her shoulder, he proceeded to rub her tender wound in soothing circles with the heat of his hand. Other than his mouth hitching up at one corner, he didn't mention her clumsiness. "How are you faring with Betsy?"

Winn couldn't bear to look into his eyes to see laughter. So she kept her focus directly ahead, to the dark whiskers on his jaw and the corded muscles of his throat. This, of course, opened a pathway for her eyes to wander over the broad expanse of his shoulders and the damp springy curls—glossy with perspiration—on his chest.

Instead of the sight repelling her, she wanted to reach out and touch him like she had this morning before she was fully awake enough to appreciate it. Or perhaps to lean in and dry him off with her own body . . .

She drew in a steadying breath, ripe with the odors of the barn. But underneath, she caught his scent. The raw, salty essence of his sweat combined with his own appealingly earthy fragrance. His was the aroma of supple saddle leather and sweet rain. Of untethered twilight rides and fresh dew on the meadow grass. Of warm straw beds and strong arms.

She wanted to lick him.

Shocked by her own thoughts, she cleared her throat and pointed toward the cow's stall. "Betsy is refusing to cooperate. Though, admittedly, when I said that I knew how to milk a cow, I might have been exaggerating a bit. I don't suppose . . ."

"That among my innumerable rakish talents, I also possess the ability to coax milk from a cow?" he asked with the flash of a disarming grin.

Her mind was still considering his *innumerable rakish talents* and she failed to respond. *Oh, what a chapter that would make!*

"Let's see, shall we?" He took her hand and, reflexively, her fingers twined with his as he led her back to Betsy's stall. Then before he released her, he gave her pinky a playful tug.

The gesture seemed unconscious and familiar, as if they were two people who'd known each other all their lives instead of being practically strangers. Then again, they *had* spent a night in the straw together.

Winnifred smiled to herself, still feeling his touch tingling on her skin. But when he motioned for her to resume her place on the miniature three-legged stool, she tilted her head in confusion. "I thought you were going to show me."

"I am. Just trust me."

Skeptical of his method, she gradually lowered down onto the stool, keeping her legs together and angled to the side like before.

He chuckled. "You're going to have to spread your knees, Winn."

"You make everything sound so wicked."

"Just another of my talents," he whispered in her ear, his hot breath sliding wantonly into the whorls and spiraling deep into her middle.

Then he reached around her, skimming his hands down her thighs to the inside of her knees, nudging them apart. Obediently, she opened for him and was surely blushing to the soles of her feet.

"Yes, like that," he rasped, seeming to exert more effort now than when plying the hayfork. "Move the pail between them, and tuck your skirts out of the way."

She did, and glimpsed the lace of her drawers peeking out from beneath her hem, just above her stockings and silver garter ribbons. *Positively scandalous!*

If he noticed, he made no comment. His hands coasted over her arms, the calluses on his fingertips rousing gooseflesh as he encircled her wrists in the best sort of manacle. "Lift your hands to pet her with me. Reassure her in long, slow strokes."

Winn could hardly breathe, but this time it had nothing to do with her corset. It was all because of him. He made the air in her lungs too hot. Her eyelids too slumberous to hold open. Her head too heavy. So she rested back against the solid support of his shoulder, feeling the silken cow hide beneath her hands and the sure strength of his hands over hers. She was a fool for waiting so long to ask for his assistance.

He nudged closer still, guiding her lower to the warmer, taut flesh of the udder.

"That's it, Winn. You're just letting her know it's time to let down her milk. And now, all you need to do is take hold of her like this"—he paused to situate the inner curve of her thumb and forefinger at the base of the swollen teat—"and squeeze."

Together they gripped Betsy and a short blast of milk came forth, startling Winn so much she sat forward and nearly kicked over the pail.

She gasped. "We did it!"

"Not quite, but we're getting there," he said, a smile curling his voice. "Now, take hold of another and create a rhythm."

She did as instructed and was rewarded by another spurt. Then the next time, more milk erupted until she was pulling warm silken liquid in long streams that hissed into the pail. She was so focused on her task that she didn't even realize she was doing it all on her own.

Asher stood off to the side, observing. Out of the corner of her eye, she saw him use his forearm to wipe sweat from his brow.

"Where did you learn to milk cows?" she asked.

He was out of breath when he answered. "Consider it one of the many mysteries in my arsenal."

"Oh, don't be shy about it. You can tell me."

"Very well, if you must know," he said warily, as if he knew something she didn't. Then he cleared his throat. "I was nearing my fifteenth year when I met this dairy maid in the village. She was young and pretty and eager to show me all of her—"

"Never mind," Winnifred said in a rush, suddenly hating every dairy maid in England. "I believe I can imagine the rest."

His laugh was positively hedonistic as he strolled back to finish mucking out the stalls.

LATER THAT morning, Asher scraped the last of the whiskers and shaving soap from underneath his chin. He took a hard look in the oval washstand mirror in Mr. Champion's chamber.

"You have to keep your hands to yourself from this point forward," he said to his reflection.

This was a business arrangement, nothing more. He always kept money matters separate from life's pleasures. And until now, he'd never been so tempted to merge the two.

Then again, it wasn't as if he could keep his distance, not with henchmen chasing them out of London, or his driver abandoning them on the side of the road, or nearly losing her at the Spotted Hen. It was clear he'd had no other choice but to keep Winn at his side.

At least . . . that's what he told himself.

So why had he claimed that sleeping beside her was essential to their survival? There'd been plenty of straw and a blanket, after all. Though, in his own defense, he had tried to construct a barrier between them. Could *he* take the blame if his unconscious mind ordered his body to pull her flush against him?

Mulling it over, he picked up his black cravat from the back of a spindle chair and found his answer. He had to resist her at all cost. His father's compulsions and her father's money made that fact patently clear. The two combined were flint and steel, ready to send

Asher's plans for a life free of his father's schemes up in flames.

He couldn't risk it, no matter how much he was drawn to Winn.

Keeping that thought in mind, he finished donning his wrinkled clothes and went in search of his host.

Mr. Champion was so appreciative of their work that he invited Asher and Winn to break their fasts with him. They sat in the kitchen for a meal of porridge and strong black tea, simple but satisfying. Afterward, the farmer hooked up a short, two-wheeled hay cart to the horse and sat up in the narrow perch, a driver's whip in hand. He cast a nod over his shoulder and offered them a place on the back.

Winn, who'd been mulish with Asher ever since he'd told her about the milkmaid, still didn't speak to him. Not even to ask for his help. Instead, she struggled to climb up on her own. And there was an imprudent part of Asher that was glad she made little progress, because that gave him the excuse to come to her assistance.

He strode over and settled his hands on her waist. Turning her to face him, he caught the scent of soap from her morning ablutions, her cheeks scrubbed pink. She refused to meet his gaze. She didn't speak a word either, but kept her lips pursed. Even so, she rested her hands on the sleeves of his coat, offering a nod of acquiescence.

Was that *all* she was going to give him?

It wasn't enough. He wanted to see the fire in those hazel eyes. So he lifted her, holding her aloft until they were nose-to-nose. Those eyes flashed, widening in surprised outrage.

"*Whot* are you doing?"

A smug grin tugged at his mouth. "Waiting for you to look at me."

"Well, your foolish ploy worked. Now put me down before you hurt yourself."

"Do you know what I've just realized?" he asked, in no hurry to release her, even as her feet skated in the air, seeking purchase. "Your freckles grow darker when you're jealous, too."

"I'm not the least bit—"

Suddenly, the farmer snapped the reins and their two-wheeled conveyance started to trot away. Asher was forced to cut off her scathing speech by tossing her onto the small bed of the straw-flecked farm cart.

Laughing, he leapt up beside her, their legs dangling over the edge, the box seat close at their backs. Winn gripped one of the supporting wooden dowels nearest her and pressed the other on the bed between them as the cart rumbled down the lane. Stubborn in her ire, she kept her face averted.

"The pair of you squabble like it's been six years instead of six months," Mr. Champion called over his shoulder with a wry chuckle. "Did you know each other a good spell before you married?"

"Feels like little more than a day," Asher said with a nudge of his shoulder against hers and a wink when Winn finally glanced his way. "And the instant I saw her, I just knew she'd bring pandemonium to my life."

She rolled her eyes and went back to studying the scenery.

"Aye," the farmer said. "The best ones always do, lad. That's the way it was with my Gwyneth when we met not seven years past. She was so young and bright, had a bonnet full of suitors, and wanted the world in the palm of her hand. Ah, but old as I am, I only wanted her."

"That's lovely," Winn said with a sigh. "Mrs. Champion is fortunate to have such a devoted husband."

Asher recalled Winn saying that she wanted to marry for love or not at all. So it must have crushed her spirit to have been betrothed to a man who was having a well-known and longstanding love affair with another woman. But devotion was a rare commodity. Especially for those who married to exchange wealth for a title.

Even so, Asher understood the appeal of the notion. It was what he wanted, too. In fact, if he was given the chance to strip away all the obsession, manipulation, and greed from his life and be left with only loyalty and devotion . . . Well, he couldn't imagine anything better.

"A' course the years haven't been all that grand," the farmer continued. "Mine's just a small farm, after all. Last summer's heat made for poor crops, and this spring's rain hasn't made it any better. But I've done what I could to make her happy, saved what little I had to keep her in fancy hats and dresses, never make a fuss when she wants to take the mail coach to her sister's"—he cleared his throat and tossed a pointed glance in Asher's direction—"and I don't ever try to make her jealous or fill her head with any doubts."

Asher responded obligingly with a contrite, "Yes, sir."

This time, it was Winn's turn to smile smugly at

him, her brows arching. Reaching into the scant space between them, he gave her little finger a tug in retaliation. Then he settled his hand close beside hers on the edge of the cart bed, almost like two pieces of a puzzle waiting to be fit together.

Asher abruptly shook his head to clear away that thought. It only reminded him of how well they'd fit together in the loft this morning. Best to keep such memories at arm's length.

"Being set upon by *murderous highwaymen* was unfortunate, indeed," Champion said with a timely interruption. Yet, as he continued, marked suspicion edged his tone, setting off the din of a warning bell in the back of Asher's skull. "I know that if such a terrible thing had occurred to my wife, she wouldn't be nearly as quiet about it as Mrs. Strewsbury seems to be. No." He clucked his tongue. "My Gwyneth would be in an uproar, telling every living soul about her ordeal for weeks to come."

A weighted pause followed. Asher and Winn exchanged a glance.

It was clear that the shrewd Mr. Champion had only pretended to believe their story earlier in order to garner help with the morning chores. The retribution was fair under the circumstances. Yet it was also apparent that they were about to be kicked to the side of the road unless they figured out how to earn their passage. And while walking wouldn't be the worst thing for him to endure, he knew that Winn's shoe was broken, which had to pain her whenever she stepped on a stone or stray stick.

A man has to pay for everything in this life, one way

*or the other. You may as well learn this when you're
young*, Asher's father had often said to him. A lesson
he would never forget.

"My wife is saving her voice," Asher explained, as-
suming that singing and playing the flute were also lies
she'd fabricated on the spur of the moment, much like
his fatal *highwaymen* outburst. "After all, without any
instruments in our possession, she'll have to sing for
our supper."

Winn nodded to him in approval, then angled
toward the farmer and affected a laugh. "Otherwise,
you would hear me speak of our misfortune so much
that you would wish to stuff straw in your ears."

"Well, as traveling musicians, perhaps you might
sing me a tale of woe. T'would help to pass the time.
After all, you passed away many an hour in my loft.
Eating my carrots."

Why, the crafty old codger. Ladling on guilt after
everything they'd done.

Then again, they had been planning to steal his
horse, so Asher couldn't be mad at him. He shrugged
to Winn, ready to take her hand and hop off the edge to
save them the humiliation of being booted out for their
deception.

But in the next instant, he realized that Winn wasn't
finished surprising him.

She cleared her throat, took in a deep breath and
started to sing.

He'd heard the ballad "Peaceful Slumb'ring on the
Ocean" a number of times in music rooms and par-
lors after dinner parties. Hell, he'd even flirted while
turning the pages for debutantes as they delighted an

audience. But never before had he been transported by it, taken to balmy seas where ships swayed gently over moonlight-rippled waters. He'd never heard a voice so clear, so open that he felt the warmth seep into his soul with every word.

When the final note drifted off on the breeze, the only sound he was left with was the sure, steady thumping of his own heart.

"Winn, that was . . ." Asher trailed off when he realized there were no words to describe the way the music was still lingering inside his head and rushing through his veins. The way his pulse quickened just now as her eyes met his. Or the way the surface of his skin tingled as if he were newly formed from clay and the breath that brought him to life was somewhere in her song.

But he couldn't say any of those things. They would all seem like purple prose and purely fabricated.

So he kept it simple instead.

He took her face in his hands and kissed her.

Chapter 13

Winnifred Humphries had never really been kissed.

When she was fourteen, she'd suffered a soggy pass of bulbous lips from the son of her father's former steward after he'd imbibed in Scotch whisky stolen from her father's study. Directly following, he'd cast up his accounts down the front of her apricot muslin.

When she was fifteen, she'd fallen into the arms of her ruggedly handsome riding master with her boot tangled in the stirrup of the dreadful sidesaddle. He didn't kiss her. However, she had imagined the press of his mouth to hers so vividly that it was like it had occurred nonetheless.

From the age of sixteen to one-and-twenty, she'd heard so many subtle criticisms over how her figure differed from her mother's—who was a renowned beauty—that she hadn't wanted to see anyone. She'd avoided assemblies and parties as often as she could. Until Mother insisted on a Season.

At two-and-twenty, after dining on calf's brains at supper, she'd endured a single peck from Bertram Woodbine. His lips were cold and thin and dry like two haricots verts left forgotten on the vine. When he'd finished, he'd wiped away her kiss with a handkerchief almost in the same instant. Hadn't even bothered to turn away.

And, up until a minute ago, Winnifred would have confessed to having been kissed three times. But that was no longer the truth.

Her first real kiss was happening now, in the back of a farmer's cart and with Asher Holt's warm mouth coasting over her own with slow, tender possession. Though he couldn't know it, he was stripping away every other *not-kiss* and awakening something new— the sensation of being desired.

Asher Holt wasn't drunk, taken off guard or driven by obligation to kiss her. Apparently, the scoundrel was kissing her because he wanted to. *Huh*.

Winnifred was sure that a laugh wasn't appropriate under the circumstances. But there was so much joy rising inside her that it hummed in her throat. He answered with a low murmur as he angled her mouth beneath his, his fingertips stealing into her freshly pinned hair.

Letting go of the side of the cart, she cupped her hand over his cheek, where this morning's shave had left his skin smooth and taut and fresh as sun-warmed spices. She was so enthralled by this wondrous occurrence, she completely forgot that neither of them was holding on.

Then a bump in the road bounced them up into the air.

With a blink of surprise, Asher snaked a hand around her waist, securing her against him the instant before they smacked down on the cart again. If they'd been traveling any faster, they likely would have landed in the dirt. Or worse, in the water. Because now she saw that they'd crossed a narrow bridge.

"Careful." Mr. Champion's chuckle of amusement suggested that he'd known what they were doing. "The Welland bridge is a mite bumpy."

Blushing, she made herself busy by securing her hold on the railing and brushing off her skirts. She waited until the last possible moment to look at Asher, hoping she wouldn't see him wipe off her kiss or his complexion turn the color of pea soup.

Garnering her courage, she glanced at Asher as he cast a perturbed glare at the farmer's back. Then he shifted his gaze to her and his expression softened.

Reaching up, he tenderly brushed her newly disheveled hair out of her face, sending her pulse tripping through her body. Her fluttering heart might not survive the day.

"Are you hurt?" he asked.

"A little shocked, perhaps," she said with all honesty, her gaze drifting to his mouth. "That was—"

"A fine lullaby for the hoity-toity, to be sure," Mr. Champion chimed in. "But in these parts, you'll need a tune that's lively. What the folk around here want to hear at night, when the long day's work is finally done, is somethin' they can tap their foot to or even dance to, if the spirit takes them."

An understandable request. She had professed to being a traveling musician, after all. An entertainer. Yet with her head still spinning from Asher Holt's kiss, she could hardly think.

"My parents preferred more sedate tunes." Her music training had been to impress guests of her parents with round tones and crystal-clear notes. It was only her love for singing that had made each lesson a delight instead of a chore. "I could sing something like 'Of Plighted Faith.' The melody is quite lovely."

"That melancholy drivel? What about 'The Joys of Country' or 'Two Maidens Went A-Milking'?"

"I've never practiced either of those."

"Practice," he muttered with a scoff. "Just put your heart in it, lass."

Then, much to her astonishment, the farmer cleared his throat and began to sing in a deep, robust baritone. She'd heard the energetic tune performed at the less stuffy gatherings she typically attended with her friends. Recalling it easily, she sang the second chorus with him and hummed along with the verses. But blushed at some of the bawdy lyrics.

Asher grinned as he watched the road they left behind, his long fingers drumming on the grayed wood between them, and she wondered if he was thinking of their kiss, too. Then again, considering the number of eager lips he'd likely encountered in his life, this might have been nothing more than an impulse. As quickly forgotten as scratching an itch.

Doubtless, he was merely thinking of how they were making better time now. Truth be told, they were traveling at a fine clip. The livelier the tune, the faster the farmer drove the cart.

And perhaps, Asher was also thinking about the money he would gain at the end of the journey.

The thought poked a sore spot inside her, but she quickly shrugged it off. After all, he had plans for his life, so why shouldn't he be thinking of them? It was positively ludicrous to imagine that one kiss would change anything.

All that really mattered was that he had kissed her because he'd wanted to. For now, she would keep that as a bandage over an old wound.

With all things considered, it was still going to be a fine day.

Peering up to the sky, she saw a smattering of fluffy white clouds, floating on a cerulean sea. The roads were relatively fine. And best of all, there weren't any blunderbuss-toting ruffians after them.

Though she wouldn't dare say the words aloud, it seemed like nothing was standing in their way.

"Oy," Mr. Lum said, "give over the reins, Jamey. My grannie could drive faster than you and she's been six feet under for more than twenty years."

"I have to slow down to turn off the main road, don't I? Holt is likely taking nothing but side roads to avoid us catching him."

"At this speed, if Holt were walking, he'd be apt to pass us." Lum tried to snatch the reins, but his wiry cohort switched hands and kept them just out of his reach.

"I've been thinking," Jamey began, squinting as if the process caused him pain. "Holt might know we're on to him and, if that's the case, then he'd keep to the main road to make better time. Wouldn't he?"

Lum rolled his eyes skyward. "Here I sit, trapped on a snail beside a man who's coddling his own brains."

"Well, I ask you, have we seen hide or hair of him, or have we not?"

"Just move it along. Turn down your bloody road—
Watch it, idiot!"

Suddenly, a posh white-glazed chariot charged out
from a narrow road cut between the trees. Lum's warning came just in time to miss a collision by an inch.
The horses shifted, straining against their rigging and
pawing the ground.

The woman holding the leads merely laughed to
her man, who was standing so close that a single
hair couldn't fit between them. "Naughty man! Just
look what you almost made me do. And now I've
frightened these men because you can't stop stealing
kisses."

"My apologies, gentlemen," the man said. "I should
have known better than to let Gwyneth take hold of the
reins." He tweaked one of the blue-and-white ribbons
on her hat. And when she wiggled back against him, he
issued a pained laugh, cinching an arm tighter around
her waist. "Be still now or we'll be gone so long that
she'll wonder why I don't return with any fish from my
outing to the lake."

Her low, taunting reply drifted over on the breeze
as if neither of them realized they weren't alone. "I'll
simply tell her that you were helping me deliver alms
to the poor."

"We've been making the poor wealthy as Croesus
of late."

Perking up at the mention of money, Lum sat up
straighter. Never one to miss an opportunity, he said,
"See here, you could've cost me my horses and a gig.
Not only that, but my addlepated brother will likely
suffer fits of skittishness 'cause of this."

As luck would have it, Jamey tilted his head and blinked in blank confusion.

The man in the chariot dragged his attention away from his wriggling armful and looked to Lum with impatience. Reaching into the slender pocket of his waistcoat, he tossed a gold guinea with a flick of his thumb.

"For your trouble," he said. "They pour a fine pint at the Grinning Boar coaching inn in the village."

Lum snatched it out of the air and tested its worth between his teeth. Then he tipped his hat. The man resumed his hold on the woman and they set off with a jerk, the swift propulsion whipping her thin hat ribbons like cavalry banners at full charge.

"You have an addlepated brother?" Jamey asked when they'd gone.

Lum took the reins. "Just get the brake, Jamey. We've got to make time now and we're keeping to the main road."

"But what if he's taking the side roads? We could miss him altogether."

"Then we'll be waiting for him at Gretna Green, waiting to stuff him and his heiress in the boot," Lum muttered.

"Well then, since we're already ahead of schedule, stopping at the Grinning Boar wouldn't hurt. I could certainly use a pint."

Lum opened his mouth to argue, but he had a powerful weakness for a well-poured ale. "Very well. But only one."

"You said that the last time we went to the pub.

Then you ended up passed out over the table." Jamey guffawed. "Remember that?"

"Shut up, idiot."

✧◦✧◦✧

LEAVE IT to Asher to complicate a perfectly good plan.

All he had to do was take a runaway heiress to her aunt's. Simple enough.

He'd been schooled to keep money matters from becoming personal. If he hadn't been, then selling off his mother's things when he was just a boy in order to pay his father's debts would have killed him.

As Asher grew older, it became second nature to keep a barrier in place between business dealings and pleasure. He never crossed the line. Hell, he'd once had a pretty matchmaker throw herself at him, when all he'd wanted was to hire her to find him a wife.

That was when he'd given up on the notion of marrying an heiress. The process was more trouble than it was worth.

But with Winn it was proving impossible to keep his distance.

Damn it all. Whatever happened to his vow—just this morning—to resist temptation at all cost? And yet, he'd kissed her.

In fact, he could still feel the soft welcome of her flesh and the tingling vibration from her hum of pleasure. And they'd only been getting started, too. Imagine how it might have been if they hadn't been interrupted . . .

No. Best not, he thought. It was better if he kept his mind on the plan instead.

"You're a quick study, lass, and have a fine ear for music," Champion said after teaching her a half-dozen tunes. "I must confess that, for a time, I thought you'd made up your entire story about being down-on-your-luck troubadours. And I'm even more ashamed to say that I thought you might have been out to steal my horse."

Winn's eyes widened with comic alarm as she looked at Asher.

Sunlight gilded her burnished, half-tumbled hair and the tips of her lashes. And there was a guilty, impish smile on those perfect pink lips that begged to be kissed. "It would be positively criminal to take advantage of your hospitality in such a way."

"*Criminal*, indeed," Asher muttered with one last glance at her mouth.

The farmer chuckled good-naturedly. "I've a mind to take the pair of you to the Grinning Boar. It's just up a ways. They've a fine lamb stew, and patrons enough to share a bit of coin for a proper tune from a pair of troubadours. Though it's a pity you don't have your lute, lad. If you're good enough to inspire Mrs. Strewsbury to blush at the mere mention, then I should've liked to hear you play."

Winn's gaze collided with Asher's. In her flushed cheeks, he could see the shared memory of their bodies nestled close in the straw, and he felt that pull again.

Instead of giving in, he gripped the side rail of the cart as if he were shackling himself to it and forced himself to look away. This was not a complication he needed.

On edge now, he turned his attention to the road behind them and caught sight of a conveyance rushing up fast in the distance. Instant alarm sprinted through him, and he wondered if the henchmen had found them.

Reflexively, he took Winn's hand, ready to flee into the trees that bordered either side of the road. Then he saw streamers of bright blue-and-white ribbons waving from a bonnet.

Asher relaxed. It wasn't anything more than a pair of lovebirds on an outing. Nothing to worry about.

His gaze rested on Winn as she happily hummed a tune. Her hazel eyes brightened as the chariot approached, as if she were imagining herself holding the ribbons, pealing with laughter, the wind in her face.

He could tell from her talk of visiting far-off places that she had an adventurous spirit. Perhaps that was the reason she hadn't complained over any hardship they'd suffered. She was born for escapades like this. And he might very well be losing his marbles, but he was enjoying himself, too.

At the moment, his only possessions were a ripe suit of clothes and a pearl-handled knife inside a pair of mud-and-shite-encrusted boots. Though, strangely enough, he couldn't remember a time in his life when he felt such unfettered contentment. Perhaps all he'd needed was distance to distract him from his father's constant plague upon his life.

While pondering that, he realized that he was still holding Winn's hand, their fingers threaded together, his thumb coasting over her soft skin. And it felt so pleasant that he was reluctant to let her go. So he didn't. There was no point in worrying over every simple gesture, after all.

The pair of approaching lovers drew his attention again. The way they held tight to each other and to the reins would have raised a brow in certain circles, even with the glint of a gold wedding band on the woman's finger. But they were obviously married and simply enjoying an afternoon of play. Nothing wrong with that, in Asher's opinion. In fact, if he ever took a wife . . .

He shrugged himself free of the wayward thought and released Winn's hand.

Distracted, he watched as the chariot began to swerve around them, recklessly skirting the slope of the road, and he heard the man call out with a laugh, "I warn you, Gwyneth. Slow down or you'll lose your hat."

"My hat be damned!" the dark-haired woman called out as she untied her ribbons and flung her hat into the breeze. "Drive me into the village tomorrow. You can take me to get a new hat, and then you can take me as well!"

The lovers were so lost in the moment, they never noticed that the cart they'd passed had slowed and turned onto a shaded lane before coming to a stop.

Mr. Champion stared at the narrow road ahead for a long while, the reins lying loosely in his hands. All at once, he appeared aged and weather-beaten in a way he hadn't when they'd set off. His shoulders slumped forward as if the years of his life had suddenly plummeted down on him.

A curricle followed swiftly on the road without slowing, and above it a jaunty little bonnet hung from an elm tree, caught mockingly by blue-and-white ribbons twined around a branch like streamers on a maypole.

"That was my Gwyneth," Champion said after the thunder of hooves faded in the distance. "And her sister's husband."

Both Winn and Asher shared a look. In the silence that followed, the air grew heavy, thick with the cloying scent of last autumn's leaves decaying on the forest floor.

The farmer expelled a heavy breath. "Now I understand her eagerness to have her own conveyance to visit her . . . sister."

"I'm sorry," Winn said quietly and laid a gentle hand on his shoulder.

He nodded and patted her hand in return. "Much appreciated, lass. And I'm sorry, too. I suppose you know I'll be heading back to the farm now. No sense in going on."

Having anticipated what was to come, Asher was already standing on the road, ready to assist Winn.

Apparently, she wasn't through. "But aren't you going to follow them? Tell her that you love her?"

Without turning around, Champion shook his head. "Words like those belong in songs. Once a body gets to be my age, well, we learn that a person's actions always reveal their natures, and whether or not they truly care for and respect you."

"Which is why *you* should go after *her.*"

"No, lass. There isn't a thing I can do that'd be good, for either of us."

"But she's your—"

"Winn," Asher interrupted with a stern shake of his head, his voice low. "Leave it alone."

She opened her mouth to object, but then nodded. Resigned, she laid her hands on his shoulders and he helped her down. Then Asher walked to the front of the cart to shake the farmer's hand.

After they'd bid their final farewell and awkward wishes for the best of luck, they parted ways.

Beside Asher, Winn slipped her small hand in his. "Do you think he'll change his mind and fight for her?"

He shook his head. From what he'd observed of the farmer, it seemed his life had centered on attempts to make his wife happy. And if Asher could hazard a guess, he'd wager that Champion had suspected the affair for a while. "Sometimes the obstacles are too great to overcome and the best thing a man can do is to walk away and keep his distance."

"Not if he truly loves her."

"I imagine that Champion loves her so much that he still can't bear the thought of all the pain she'll face when—or *if*—he confronts her."

"No. I refuse to believe he could simply let her go," Winn said, adamant. She released his hand and proceeded to violently rearrange the pins in her hair. "I mean, honestly. Would you leave your wife if you truly loved her?"

Asher thought about what would happen if he'd ever fall in love with . . . well . . . an heiress like Winn, for example. And then he thought about his father's obsession.

It took only a second for him to answer. "Yes, I would."

Her hands stilled. Mutely, she stared into his face, her head tilted at an angle as if she were attempting to pry open his skull and sift through the contents. In the silence, he stepped forward to help with her pins.

It would be so easy to kiss her now. To simply lower his head and press his lips to hers. To watch her guileless hazel eyes drift closed. To feel her soft surrender . . .

"But how would she ever know?" she asked, sinking the pins he handed to her.

He shook his head, trying to remember what they were talking about. "Know what?"

"If you didn't fight for her, then how would she ever know that you truly loved her?"

"Because I would tell this purely fictional creature in a million different ways, every single day." He took a step back from Winn before he did something foolish. "There. Your hair is pinned—at least for the next five minutes—and we can be on our way."

He was more than half tempted to offer his hand or proffer his arm as they set about walking but, once again, he decided it was better to keep his distance. There was no point in tempting fate.

"Thank you," she began, glancing up at him through burnished lashes, "for not allowing me to steal his horse. Though, in the end, I know you wouldn't have gone through with it."

"I'm not too certain about that," he said ruefully. "I've discovered that you're a terrible influence on me."

Winn smiled as if he were teasing. He only wished he was.

Chapter 14

~~~~~

They walked for a time, keeping to the narrow road until it curved around the bend, where they'd last seen Mr. Champion's wife and her lover.

"I feel as though I've witnessed what my own life might have become," Winnifred said, unable to shake the despair she'd seen in the farmer's face.

Asher frowned but didn't add his own thoughts. Instead, he led her through a break in the trees toward a meadow of verdant grasses. Reaching out with a guiding hand, he assisted her over a fallen branch—a touch at her elbow, another at the small of her back—and then he withdrew, keeping an unfamiliar distance between them.

Peculiarly, she'd grown accustomed to his unprecedented boldness, and this sudden, unexplained absence left her feeling unmoored.

After a few minutes of silence, he asked, "Did you love Mr. Woodbine, then?"

"Not even a little." She glimpsed his nod in response out of the corner of her eye. "That was the reason I ran from the church. I needed to be more than numbers in an accounting ledger. After all, if marriage must be a transaction, then the two parties should do so out of an obligation to their hearts, not to their coffers. I should like— No," she amended, stepping up on a small outcropping of white rock protruding from the earth, "I *demand* to be desired for all that I am. It may sound terribly naive, but I want to be the love that a man cannot live without."

Again, Asher did not reply, his gaze pensive as he set his hands on her waist and lowered her from her rock pulpit.

They continued walking, yet it was as if they were strangers to each other in a way that they hadn't been even at the beginning. As if they'd never lain together in the straw at night. As if they'd never kissed in the back of a farmer's cart.

She wondered if he thought about it at all. Or was he merely musing over the firm quality of the ground beneath his steps, and the coolness of the morning that had given way to the sudden humid warmth of the afternoon?

Why had he kissed her? After all, she wasn't the type of woman who tempted men to act without reason. There was always a reason. And the reason was always money.

However, Asher didn't need to kiss her in order for her aunt to pay him. Affection was not required for their arrangement.

Now it was her turn to frown. Her gaze drifted down to the path and the gradient accumulation of dirt climbing the hem of her drab green dress. A pebble had worked its way into the crack at the bottom of her shoe. A bur pricked through her stocking. And a terrible, discomfiting quiet settled in between the muted plod of their footsteps.

All at once she couldn't take the turn of her own thoughts a moment longer.

"You kissed me." Her blurted words startled a rabbit from the grass. It hopped off in a zigzagged panic toward a stream up ahead that wended its way through the landscape like a fallen ribbon.

"I did, indeed."

He didn't elaborate further, leaving her wanting.

She huffed with impatience, forced to prod him. "You said there wouldn't be any kissing."

"The moment seemed to call for it," he said on a slow breath as if the topic had already exhausted him. He tilted his head back to the cottony clouds overhead and she caught sight of a rueful smirk curling the corner of his mouth.

Was he *laughing* at her?

His reaction abraded the bruised pulp of her ego in a place that was already too raw.

"Rather convenient timing, considering we had an audience," she said. "You don't seem to suffer the same impulse without one."

"And what are you implying?" He turned a dark, warning gaze on her.

She merely lifted her shoulders in an inconsequential shrug. "Nothing more than the fact that having a witness might have aided you in your quest for a fortune. Doubtless, arriving in the village with Mr. Champion to prove your intimate acquaintance with an heiress would force a marriage between us."

"I don't want *your* fortune, Winn. I want one of my own," he said, his voice firm. Adamant. "I want to be unencumbered and free to forge my own life. And if I were despicable enough to force a marriage between us, then I wouldn't need to kiss you. Audience or not. Our first night together compromised us, which we both knew from the outset."

She felt ashamed and chastened for her presumption. And yet, she still couldn't stop herself from asking again, "Then why *did* you kiss me?"

Asher raked an agitated hand through his hair. "Because every ounce of sense I possess abandoned me."

She winced. "*Lovely* sentiment."

"It isn't my intention to wound you," he said, his voice softening. He tried to take her hand but she snatched it away and held her chin high.

She walked along the edge of the stream, searching for a place to cross. And the farther away from him the better. Thankfully, up ahead, there was a serpentine path of flat stones, the largest one on the bank nearest her.

"Winn," he called from just behind her. "I wasn't thinking about the farmer being too near. I wasn't thinking about your dowry."

"Splendid. We needn't speak of it again."

"Damn it all! I wasn't thinking about anything . . . other than a purely carnal need to feel your lips against mine."

She stopped at once. All the air fell out of her lungs like an anchor dropping to her feet, pinioning her in place. Had she actually heard him correctly?

He stepped in front of her, reaching up to brush a dozen wayward locks from her cheek. His fingers skimmed lightly along her jaw, stroking the tender underside of her chin. "You have every right to rail at me."

"To rail at . . ." she repeated in breathless bemusement. Then a stunned laugh bubbled out of her, light as the water tripping over the rocks. "If you expect me to be angry, then you executed the kiss incorrectly."

A scoundrel's smirk toyed with the corner of his mouth, sending a thrill through her. "Is that so?"

Winn nodded. "I think, perhaps . . . you should try it again."

His warm gaze drifted from her eyes to her lips, but slowly he shook his head. "I think we should remove that pebble from your shoe, then walk to the village before the next disaster strikes."

"But there isn't going to be—"

Abruptly, he set his long finger over her lips and flashed a grin. "Don't even finish the thought, Winn. You're a veritable weathervane awaiting the next bolt of lightning."

She was tempted to argue against the likelihood of a stray thunderstorm on such a fine day, but didn't want to tempt the Fates. Just in case. After all, he seemed to know about the pebble in her shoe. And she thought her efforts of walking without the barest limp had been successful.

"I'm sure I can work it free," she said, scraping the bottom against the dirt. "There isn't any need to fuss."

"Winn, there's no point in arguing with me. You'll only wedge it deeper," he said in the same instant that she hissed from the sharp stab in the tender ball of her foot. "See?"

Hating that he was right, she hobbled over to the flat marbled stone perched on the bank's edge.

He knelt to assist her, and reaching under her skirt, his hand gently enclosed her ankle. At the innocent touch, a flood of warmth swelled upward along the inner seam of her legs. Pulses flicked along the way, shocking a gasp out of her.

"You're rather sure of yourself . . ." she said in an airy rush as she shifted on the rock and pressed her knees together to quell the sensation. All this, and he hadn't even removed her shoe!

He looked up at her burning cheeks and his eyes suddenly turned to smoldering cinders. Then, like a *Professor of the Wayward Pulse*, his fingertips lightly grazed the susceptible flesh just above her ankle and seemed to watch the pulse rove the same path up her limbs. Her breath quickened. And he held her gaze as he slipped the shoe from her foot.

Winn didn't know why this seemed even more intimate than waking up in his arms. But perhaps she'd been too bewildered by the fog of sleep to enjoy it properly.

"Actually," she said, panting, "it's the . . . other shoe."

He stared at her for a moment, his thick, sooty lashes lowered to half mast. Then he chuckled wryly. "You've made me realize that I'd have been a lecher as a cobbler's apprentice."

"Do you fancy my muddy shoes, then?"

He grinned but did not answer. Instead, he encircled her other ankle and slipped the shoe free, eliciting the same thrill up her leg and stealing her breath. He even took a moment to rub his thumb into the vulnerable arch. *Dear sweet heavens, that's lovely . . .*

She wished she had more feet.

At least, she did until she glanced down at the filth-striped silk. "Oh drat. I've ruined my stockings."

"Your shoe isn't faring much better. Seeing this crack in the bottom makes me sorry I'm not a cobbler's apprentice." His brows lifted ruefully. "I'm afraid all I can do is tie a handkerchief around it."

"That's very kind," she said, distracted. "I can't even see my mother's silver embroidery, and the shells were so lovely, too."

"A bridal gift?"

"It had more to do with the moment we shared," she said. "In those few fleeting seconds I'd felt connected to her. And if you knew anything about my mother and me, you would know how rare that is." A weary sigh escaped her lungs. "It doesn't matter, I suppose. Perhaps I could sell the silver thread in the village. That should gain us some distance toward my aunt's."

"No," he said firmly. "You've sacrificed enough already. Just let me take care of you the rest of the way, hmm?"

Without warning, her heart lifted off in a Montgolfier balloon again, beating lighter and warmer than before. This time, she hoped it wouldn't crash to the ground.

Dimly, she wondered if Mr. Woodbine had ever said something similar to Lady Stanton, or if Father had ever said as much to Mother.

She didn't think so. It took a selfless man to put another person's needs above his own. And she felt it was an absolute atrocity that she was an heiress and Asher was a man in need of a fortune.

Was it truly only yesterday that they'd met? It seemed like a lifetime ago.

Then again, it was. She'd met him when she was still her former self in her former life. Now she was caught somewhere between who she was and who she would become during the upcoming years of living in solitude with her aunt.

He held out his hand. "Hand over your stockings and I'll give them a good scrub."

She laughed softly, touched. But she shook her head. "I'll wash them out myself, as well as the morning's dirt from the hem of my dress so that I don't look the part of a vagabond when we arrive in the village."

"Very well. A short rest will do us both good. And I could use a cool drink before you muddy the water," he added with a wink. Laying her shoes aside, he stood and walked to the edge of the stream to lift a palmful of water to his lips, wiping away the residue with the back of his hand.

Winn followed, leaning down to do the same. But being stocking-footed, her feet slid down the wet embankment.

"Careful, now," he said, reaching out a hand for her.

Unfortunately, she tilted sideways, losing her balance. Her fingertips slipped from his grasp. She started to fall backward toward the water, flailing her arms, and fully aware that Asher was witnessing yet another clumsy episode.

She prayed to hit her head on a rock hard enough to forget all about it.

But then, he lunged forward and captured her about the waist. Only, this time, he lost *his* footing. And the next thing she knew, they were both spluttering in icy, waist-high water, and wiping it from their eyes.

"Don't even say it," she warned, her teeth chattering as she tried to stand.

And he didn't, but *I-told-you-so* dripped from his expression. *Weathervane, indeed.*

Bending down, he hauled Winnifred to her feet. Then he went further and lifted her into the cradle of his arms, ignoring her startled gasp. "I cannot have you muddying your feet after all that effort."

When he lowered her to stand on a thick carpet of cool grass, he immediately stepped aside and started to shrug out of his coat, but the sodden garment adhered to his arms. So she moved behind him, stripping it inside out in a spray of water droplets. Untying his black cravat, he jerked it loose and dropped it to the ground with a soggy splat.

Looking down at it, he started to laugh. "Will we ever spend an entirely dry day together?"

As she began to absently unbutton his waistcoat, the ridiculousness of the moment caught hold of her, too. He was soaked through. So was she. A hiccupped laugh slipped out and then something deeper and joyful erupted, until tears gathered in the corners of her eyes.

She shook her head, parting his waistcoat. "Well, there's always tomorrow."

They laughed at that, too. But the sound faded as their gazes collided.

His chest rose and fell underneath her splayed hands. Through the wet linen, she could feel his warmth. Feel his heart beating fast. They both knew there wouldn't be a tomorrow. Not if they made it to Avemore Abbey by nightfall.

Soon they'd part ways forever.

Winnifred already missed him. "When does your ship sail?"

"Wednesday," he answered, his gaze drifting to her lips.

Yes. Now would be the perfect time to kiss me, she thought. *We don't have much time.*

But just as quickly, Asher turned away and bent to pick up his fallen clothes. He cleared his throat and said, "With the sun and the breeze, these shouldn't take too long to dry. Then we'll be on our way."

Surreptitiously, she blinked away the wetness gathering on her lashes.

"Hand over your stockings," he said without looking her way. "I'll take care of them and then come back to wring out your dress. You can cover yourself with the shawl for now."

She issued a noncommittal murmur as she bent to lift her dripping hem, untie her garter ribbons and slip out of her stockings. Walking up to him, she laid her hand on his shoulder, waiting for him to look at her. To say something more. But he merely opened his palm for the stockings. And after she gave them to him, he strode back to the stream.

She fought a shiver and began to work the buttons and hook enclosures. It seemed to take an eternity to remove her dress. Once she was without it, she threw the wet homespun in his direction, then tended to her task.

Clad only in her underclothes, she was still terribly wet, the pink hue of her flesh displayed beneath the clinging, transparent fabric. Hating the chafing feel of the drawers between her legs, she shimmied out of them. And after twisting out as much water as she could, she laid the lace-trimmed garment on a nearby shrub to dry in the sunlight.

Not able to remove her petticoat, she decided to flap the fabric to and fro to catch the breeze. Bending over, she fanned the ruffled hem.

"I managed to remove most of the—"

Hearing Asher's voice, Winnifred stood up with a start. He'd returned quicker than she anticipated.

Feeling the fabric clinging to her bottom and knowing how transparent it was, she turned to face him. Yet, now that she thought about it—and saw the way his gaze darkened as it raked down her form—she realized this wasn't any better.

Shyly, she crossed her hands over her sex.

"You're supposed to be wearing that shawl," Asher said, his voice too low to be chiding.

She looked down to the wool beneath her feet, but saw that she'd inadvertently pushed her breasts together. Two rosy pink crescents rose above the ruffled edge of her bodice and gusseted cups of her corset. She should probably cover those, as well . . .

Her gaze returned to him for confirmation. It was only then that she noticed and truly appreciated his partially dampened shirtsleeves, the cambric even more transparent than her own. His breeches were damp, too. And there, she spied an intriguing outline angled behind his fall front.

Recalling the statues in the museum, she wondered why there seemed to be so much more of him. And like a novice sculptor, her fingertips tingled with the need to touch him. To learn. To explore.

"Winn, stop looking at me like that," he warned, his drawl tunneling directly to her middle on a heavy flutter.

"Like what?"

"The same way I'm looking at you."

Her gaze darted up to his face, noticing the high color slanting over the crests of his cheeks and the bridge of his nose. His eyes were black, practically feral beneath the shadow of his inky lashes.

"And how are you looking at me?" she asked, breathless.

"With imprudent carnal hunger."

A jolt of pure, glorious shock raced through her, leaving her giddy. Asher Holt did not see a plump, freckled and flawed heiress. He saw a desirable woman.

Driven by a wondrous new feeling, she moved toward him.

He shook his head, but there was little conviction in his heated gaze.

She dared to slide her hands to his broad shoulders, his muscles taut and poised beneath her palms. "Are you truly looking at *me* with 'carnal hunger'?"

His hands gripped the curve of her hips, pulled her flush. "I'm ravenous."

Then he closed his mouth over hers.

Chapter 15

Asher was barely hanging on to the last shred of his control when Winn stepped into his arms. But when she slipped her hands into his hair and pressed her lush body against the full length of him, he lost it completely.

The first touch of her lips was pure decadence. The sumptuous give. The inviting pull. She brought out the hedonist in him. He needed to taste every soft sound that hummed in her throat, touch all the places veiled behind the damp cambric. He couldn't remember ever wanting a woman so much.

His hands shook as they slid down her corset lacings to the small of her back and over the firm mounds of her bottom. Damn, but she was a tempting handful, lush and curvaceous. Utterly irresistible.

"This is a mistake," he said, even as he nudged her lips apart with his own.

She melted against him on a sigh of unabashed surrender, her soft breath spilling into his mouth, teasing his tongue with the promise of sweetness. "No, this is an adventure in wantonness."

He growled, stealing past her lips to brush his

tongue along hers. And if not for her shy retreat, he might have forgotten this was new to her. He withdrew, wanting to take his time, to taste her in slow sips before delving into the dewy shallows of her mouth. But then she issued this seductive purr in her throat, welcoming him with an ardent, untutored urgency, and all his better intentions turned to plundering instead.

Winn was passionate and playful, tugging on his bottom lip with a grin. And when she gently raked his flesh through her teeth, the ring around her hazel eyes smoldered with unbanked fires.

All at once, every drop of heated blood in his body descended in thick pulses to his cock. He tilted her hips against his and . . . *Damn.*

His head fell back on a groan. He was hot and hungry. Every part of her tempted him beyond reason—her voice, *those lips*, her laugh, *those curves*. His fingers flexed possessively, and he knew he could gorge himself on her and still want more.

"Is it acceptable to kiss you here?" she asked, her mouth grazing along his jaw, trailing kisses down his throat. Experimentally, she laved the hollow niche beneath his Adam's apple, inviting him to imagine what it would be like if she consumed him completely. "Mmm . . . you taste delightfully of salt and your skin is so very warm. I feel like I want to climb inside you. Is that a strange notion to have?"

He rasped inarticulate sounds of acquiescence, wanting the same. Unable to form words, he answered with a searing kiss instead, then lowered her onto the bed of wildflowers.

Her red-gold hair spilled out in untamed waves, her cheeks flushed, and her eyes glazed with passion. He felt himself slipping irresistibly into their depths as he stretched out alongside her and took her lips once more.

She was a feast for his senses. Breathing her in, he pulled her closer, his hands roaming over the lush curve of her hips, the dip of her waist, and up to the enticing heat emanating from the underside of her breast. His thumb traced the bottom seam of the gusseted silk, then drifted higher. Barely hidden behind transparent cambric, the button of flesh puckered at the first touch. He spurred the tip with the pad of his thumb and her soft gasp filled his mouth.

Ravenous, he swallowed it down and cupped her flesh. The ripe swell spilled to the very edge of his splayed fingers and he muttered an oath of appreciation. He loved how she arched into each touch, her fingernails rasping against his shoulders, drawing him closer.

"You're driving me completely mad," he said, burning a path of kisses down her throat and feeling the vibrations of her purrs of pleasure against his lips. Her responses only intensified his craving. "I have to taste you."

With a quick tug, he exposed the milky flesh to the sunlight. A perfect pink berry awaited his kiss, and he closed his mouth over her ruched flesh, tasting her silken sweetness on his tongue.

She clutched his head and cried out, her voice raw and desperate. *"Asher."*

Her hips rolled forward, her body bowing to meet

his, seeking more with innocent welcome. Lifting his mouth from her breast, he hooked his hand beneath her knee, dragged her leg higher, and rolled his hips against her sex. The friction was so keen, so pleasurable, that they both groaned.

She fit him perfectly. Somehow, he'd known she would. They matched each other in so many ways—both of them stubborn and cynical, determined and driven. And their passion was explosive.

She lifted her hand to his cheek in a tender caress, breathless wonderment in her expression. "Is this what it's like to be desired? To be seen as a woman and nothing else?"

"I could kiss you for days," he said in answer.

Taking her mouth again, he reveled in the plush give of her lips beneath his. He could spend eternity right here, feeling her every heartbeat rise up to meet his own, their low, heavy pulses seamlessly aligned. For further proof, he rocked against her.

She gasped and pulled away marginally, her breaths short. "But that isn't an answer. Even Mr. Woodbine has kissed me. Though, of course"—she blushed—"not nearly as wickedly as you have done."

Frowning, he pressed his mouth to hers again. He had a peculiar need to make her forget all about Mr. Woodbine's kiss. Obliterate that name—and any other—from her lips.

Woodbine never deserved her, anyway. The man was an arse, and only a complete fool would plan to keep a mistress when he might have had this warm, lush woman in his bed every night.

Asher kissed Winn deeper still, and felt triumphant

when she hitched against him. If she were his, he'd pamper her in whatever way he could. Give her ten thousand drugging kisses. Awaken her body to shuddering ecstasy. Tell her in a myriad of ways just how desirable and priceless she was. And he would do these things, and more, every day for the rest of his life . . .

Asher broke from the kiss. Panting, he looked down at her, jolted and confused by the intensity of his thoughts.

On a sigh, she twined her arms around his neck and looked up at him through her lashes. "Kiss me like that again."

Instead, he rolled to his back and scrubbed a hand over his face. He needed to catch his breath. Needed to remind himself that she wasn't his. He was only delivering her to her aunt's.

"Winn, if I kiss you like that again, I'm likely to take your innocence here on the grass. And only a scoundrel would use your delightful body to sate his lust, all the while knowing that you'd never see him again after tomorrow."

"Are *you* not a scoundrel?"

"Not as much as I would like to be," he muttered with a regretful exhale, his body still pulsing and eager.

"Oh," she whispered and surreptitiously reached down to cover her breasts. "I understand. I suppose I forgot who I am for a moment."

He rose up on his elbow and gazed down at her flushed cheeks. "You're a beautiful, desirable woman."

Unable to resist, he pressed one more kiss to her lips, wanting to drink down another of her sweet sighs as if he were a drunkard and she was the last dram of whisky in the bottle.

But she didn't kiss him back.

"You don't have to tell me falsehoods, Asher. I know what I am. And fear not, you'll still get your money."

Asher cringed inwardly, trying to shut out a painful truth. "I wish we'd met under different circumstances, but that doesn't alter the fact that you *are* beautiful and desirable." And when she rolled her eyes in disbelief, he took hold of her chin and held her gaze. "Not like a sketch from a ladies' magazine, all tied up in the latest trappings. And you're not like those willowy, porcelain-skinned debutantes that all the matrons fawn over each Season."

"Thank you *ever so* much."

"Damn, I'm making a muck of this. What I'm trying to say is that none of those other creatures have what you possess."

"Legs like tree trunks and—"

He brushed his thumb over her frown, silencing her. "Your legs are lithe and strong. I've been admiring them—*and* the sway of your hips—for many a mile. And I don't know any other woman who would set a course for adventure and be capable of walking the entire journey."

She stared stubbornly back at him. "For a well-bred young woman, that quality ranks about as high in society as being plump."

She hiked her chin and pressed a hand to her bosom as if daring him to deny it. He didn't bother to. Instead, he laid his hand over hers, guiding her to cover one magnificent swell.

"Feel how exquisitely formed you are," he said, urging her to squeeze her own flesh. And when she did, her breath stuttered past her lips. As he spoke, he rose up on his elbow and drew her hand over to her other breast, then down the soft rise of her stomach and to the shadow of her sex. "Your beauty is like a flame, Winn. Warm and beguiling. Untamed and uninhibited. Every part of you, from your fire-kissed hair to every delectable inch of your divine figure, is dangerously irresistible."

He withdrew his hand, watching passion simmer in her gaze as she lingered, unmoving, in that heated nook. She stared at him without blinking, as if he'd stunned her.

Good, he thought. It was about time she started appreciating herself.

Asher sifted his fingers through her tumbled hair, removing stray pieces of straw and a few flower petals. "And the sounds you make when we kiss could very well lead to your ruin."

He leaned down to press his lips to hers once more. This time, she sighed and wrapped her arms around his neck. A smile bloomed on her face, radiating such rapture that he felt the blast of it pound inside his chest.

All at once, the beats of his heart thudded in quick, heavy succession. Unprepared, his breath came up short.

What was happening to him? He felt as though he were in the grip of some new form of panic, a thousand times worse than being chased by henchmen. Five hundred times worse than losing her at the Spotted Hen. And thinking of that, remembering all she'd been through, his conscience reared up again.

"And you deserve more." Disentangling himself, he rolled onto his back again and pressed a fist to his aching sternum.

"Mmm . . . I think I'd like more," she murmured against the side of his throat, kissing him with tender suction that made him forget his own name.

He gripped the grass at his side, trying to resist.

She draped her leg over his, pressing the enticing weight of her breasts to his chest. Nudging his fist aside, her delicate fingers trailed over him, slipping beneath the open neck of his shirtfront. And the scoundrel in him didn't stop her. He loved feeling her hands on him, even though the pleasure in her touch was nearly unbearable.

Boldly, she splayed her hands to explore every inch of his chest, pausing to study the flat discs of his nipples. He'd never been particularly sensitive there and yet her tentative exploration sent spears of urgency to his engorged shaft. Then, parting the fabric, she kissed him there, too.

At the first kitten flick of her tongue, he hissed, his hips arching reflexively. He was staggered by the force of his response to everything she did. Unable to rein in this teeming passion, his hands wove into her burnished tresses, lifting her for a deep, searching kiss.

Her hips tilted toward his. Her knee rose higher,

dragging over the turgid length of him with such exquisite, searing slowness that he nearly begged her to do it again.

On his groan, she broke away. Her attention veered to the thick form straining against the fall front.

Curiosity flared in her desire-darkened eyes. Then she nearly unmanned him with another, though more tentative, glide of her knee.

"Not the handle of a hayfork at all," she whispered in astonishment, her gaze darting up to his.

A guilty chuckle left him. He shrugged, casting all the blame to her. "You're a tempting armful."

Another puffed exhale of disbelief left her, bemusement in her expression.

Her brazen fingers coasted lower on his abdomen and his muscles rippled in anticipation, tightening. But a lingering shred of his conscience bade him to gently stay her.

He laid his hand over hers. "If we go on, your book *will* have a chapter you never bargained for."

She swallowed. Then her fingertips curled ever so slightly toward her palm, and he lifted it for a kiss.

Winn settled down on the grass beside him, resting her head just beneath his shoulder, where there seemed to be a cozy spot designed solely for her.

She absently brushed her soft fingertips in the springy dark hair at the center of his chest. "Jane, Ellie and I believe that our friend Prue may have been swept away by passion. In a garden and during a party, no less. Her parents sent her away. She wasn't there the night that Jane and Ellie . . . um . . ."

"Tied me to a chair? Put a sack over my head?" He laughed, squeezing her closer.

"Purely by accident."

"I should hate to know what your friends do on purpose."

She grinned and sketched a ticklish design over his heart. "Yes, you would. It's simply terrifying to think of all the plots we can concoct when we're together. Though Jane is typically the one who sees them through."

"Until now."

"Until now," she repeated on a shaky breath, her hand lying still. "I understand how easy it is to be overcome."

He murmured his agreement, pressing a kiss to her hair.

"I'm a bit stunned that I've run away from my life, too. Though, at the same time I'm glad that I've chosen my own path. It's empowering."

"It is." He was glad that she'd found the inner resolve to run away from her wedding. A prig like Woodbine didn't deserve her. He'd have smothered this wildness out of her, suffocated her spirit.

"It's also a bit . . . frightening."

He reached out and lifted her chin, scrutinizing her wide eyes. She shook her head and turned slightly to press her lips to his inner wrist. He felt his pulse respond with a kick, rising to meet her. "Are you afraid?"

"Not now. Not when I'm with you." She paused on a breath, drawing his hand away from her face and lacing her fingers with his, palm to palm. "Although, I imagine I will be when you leave."

"You'll be glad to be rid of me."

And yet, he was conflicted over how much he wanted it not to be true. How much he wanted her to miss him, to think of him.

"But what if I lose this new part of myself when you're gone? After all, I'm going to be secluded for the rest of my life in Avemore Abbey."

Asher's conscience flooded back, full force. Dropping his head down to the grass, his breath rushed out of his lungs until he felt empty.

"You won't lose any part of yourself, Winn," he said, wishing for it to be true. But his throat constricted on a lump of guilt as he thought of the bargain that he'd struck with her father.

The day before her wedding, he'd met with Lord Waldenfield and told him everything he'd overheard while tied to a chair, including her plan to run away in a waiting carriage. Then Asher had agreed to deliver Winn back to her father.

Yet, when circumstances had forced them to flee London, he'd sent a missive from the Spotted Hen, informing Waldenfield that he fully intended to adhere to their agreement, albeit with a slight alteration. He would have to deliver her to Avemore Abbey instead.

At the time, Asher had meant every word. Now things were more complicated.

Out of all the underhanded deals he'd ever made, this might be the one he regretted the most.

⚜⚜⚜

"THIS MAKES no sense at all, Julian," Imogene said from across the carriage. Beyond the window, the sun hung low on the horizon, gilding the worry lines on her finely sloped brow as she studied the scrawled missive in her grasp. "It's difficult for me to believe that Winnifred ran away, but it's simply *unfathomable* that you hired this Lord Holt fellow to wait outside the church."

"As I explained before, Holt approached me with information," he said in defense, recalling the dark-haired young man in a black cravat introducing himself just as he'd been about to enter White's. "At first, I refused to grant him an audience. After all, his reputation as an excessive gambler preceded him."

"Oh, yes! Now I recall the name. Gambling is a sickness in that family." She skewered him with a hard stare. "And you trusted *him* with our Winnifred?"

Julian straightened his shoulders, hackles rising. "You weren't there. When he explained that our daughter planned to run away from her own wedding, there was something compelling about his sense of urgency. Not only that, but he was patently embarrassed about being hoodwinked by a pair of debutantes and left with empty pockets."

"Winnifred would never have stolen money from Lord Holt. Whatever would she do with such a paltry sum? She doesn't even enjoy shopping." She scoffed, brushing her hands over her skirts in irritated swipes.

"I wouldn't put it past those friends of hers. If you ask me, Jane Pickerington and Elodie Parrish have either too many brains between them or not nearly enough. And, quite frankly, it was far too easy to believe that they'd concocted the ludicrous scheme he relayed to me."

"But what if this . . . *miscreant* thinks he'll gain a great deal more money by kidnapping our daughter and taking her to Gretna Green?"

Eyes glistening, Imogene looked at him the way she used to years ago, imploring him to allay her fears. He wanted to reach out and take her hand, to console and reassure her. Yet there were many obstacles between them—so many times he'd failed her—that no simple gesture could overcome their past. And his empty fist remained at his side.

"I made it perfectly clear to Holt that he wouldn't see a farthing unless he returned Winnifred to me wholly unspoiled. I've known too many opportunists in my day to take the chance," Julian said with a firm resolve that belied his own worry.

He looked down to the missive. The rain had blurred the address, delaying its delivery until late last evening. Upon reading it, he shuddered to think of what may have happened to drive them out of London. Holt had not elaborated, and the hired investigator was still piecing it together. But Julian was damned certain he would have an answer as soon as he caught up with them.

He'd been prepared to leave at once. Then Imogene insisted on coming along. Which was understandable, of course. But having her here made him anxious. Not only because he wasn't sure what they would find once they arrived in Yorkshire, but also because it was difficult to be in such close proximity.

He wanted to take a breath that wasn't filled with her alluring rosewater perfume. To stop noticing the sapphire pendant resting in the hollow niche at the base of her throat. To stop remembering that he'd bought the necklace for her on their honeymoon and how she'd spent days in bed with him wearing no other adornment.

"I do wish the driver would make haste," she said on a sigh, staring out the window.

Julian shifted on the bench, irritated by the course of his thoughts. "The roads are not as dry as one would prefer. Not to mention, our carriage is weighed down by *three* trunks for this short trip."

Imogene huffed, crossing her arms beneath her breasts. "Well, you said that my maid couldn't come along, so I had Bertha press a week's worth of dresses, just in case. The third trunk is for Winnifred. I'm sure she will want the comfort of her clothes. *Men!* You simply don't have an inkling of how difficult it is to look one's best at all times."

"You've never had any trouble with that," he grumbled.

She looked sharply at him. "Why, Julian. Was that a compliment? I didn't think you even noticed me half the time."

He didn't respond. Thankfully, the driver tapped on the hood, requiring his attention.

"Beg pardon, my lord. It looks as though one of the horses has caught a stone. We're going to have to stop for the night. Don't worry, there's a nice coaching inn up a pace. The Grinning Boar will have a cozy room for you and your lady."

Julian and Imogene exchanged a glance, then quickly looked out opposite windows.

At home, there was typically an entire house to

separate them, each keeping to their own floors and to their own wings. Over the years, he'd found a sense of peace in their distance, and a way to forget the past. Yet now he felt as if the scab of an old wound were being scraped open, demanding attention.

Even so, there was no reason to think that one night with his wife would alter anything between them.

Chapter 16

It was late in the afternoon, the air turning cooler with the sun resting behind the trees. Their stolen moment in the grass had lasted longer than Winnifred had realized.

She made a mental note for the primer about how passion was capable of stealing time. Not to mention, whatever else she might have lost. And she'd have given him all without hesitation.

Yet this *scoundrel* had chosen the gentleman's path instead. Had he not stopped, then by tomorrow when they bade farewell to each other, she may have been filled with regret.

It already saddened her to think of never seeing him again. She could only imagine how much worse that feeling would be if she'd lain with him completely. Especially since it seemed as though he was withdrawing from her.

He wasn't cold exactly, just . . . different. She couldn't quite put her finger on it.

Then again, perhaps he was merely preoccupied and thinking about the rest of their journey. After all, she was curious about that as well, wondering how they would ever find the money to hire a coach to take them to her aunt's.

Well, one thing was for certain: they would never make it to the village if she didn't find the rest of her clothes.

"Drat." Barefoot, she searched the patch of grass that was still flat from where they'd lain. "I've lost both of my garter ribbons. My stockings will never stay up without them."

Buttoning his waistcoat, he came to her side and searched, too, swiping his boot over the blades in quick, impatient sweeps. "Let's see, thus far you've lost your dress, half your hairpins, and both your garter ribbons. I'm beginning to think you'd have been better off by absconding with a maidservant."

"Likely so. Though traveling with you has had other benefits."

His perusal shifted to her, roving in a single simmering sweep. With her dress still damp, she could feel the bodice cling to her breasts, her nipples taut and sensitive beneath her layers. She knew what it was like to feel his lips on her. The skillful flick of his tongue. The warm inner recesses of his mouth . . .

"Winn," he warned with a quick shake of his head. And she knew he was telling her not to look at him with *imprudent carnal hunger.*

She blamed him for making it so difficult.

"A maidservant," she clarified, her voice raspy, "would have found a way to repair that horrid busk, and I'd have been dreadfully uncomfortable. At least with you I can breathe."

Her statement might have been more convincing if she actually were breathing at the moment. But thinking about all the things he'd done and said made her want to run back into his arms.

And drag him down to the grass.

A low growl rose from his throat. Then, with a jerk of his hand, he untied his black cravat. Her pulse gave an excited—and somewhat trepidatious—leap. Was she about to be ravished?

Unfortunately not.

In the next instant, he bent down and retrieved an ivory-handled knife from inside his boot and proceeded to cut a long sliver from the silk.

She frowned. "*Whot* are you doing?"

"I'm making garter ribbons for you so that we can leave and put ourselves farther away from temptation. You're making all this damnably difficult, I'll have you know," he muttered crossly.

Staring down in astonishment at his bent head, she felt her lips curve in a smile and a warmth blooming inside her chest. "Am I?"

He grunted in response, cutting the black sliver in thirds. Then he stood and handed them to her with a querulous set to his jaw. "Two for your stockings. One for your hair. There's no need to bother with the pins when you look lovely with it down. I'll keep what's left of them in my pocket."

Winnifred was glowing. She was sure of it. As she stood there with silken black ribbons dangling from her grasp, her heart radiated so much heat that she knew it would burst open at any moment. "Asher?"

He slanted her a tense look that kept her from telling him how sweet he was.

Instead, she pointed to the ivory-handled knife in his grasp. "That looks rather old. Is it a family heirloom?"

He offered a curt nod and dropped down to his knee to slide it back into his boot. "It's the last thing I have left from my mother. Everything else has been sold over the years because of my father's gambling obsession. Nothing was precious. Nothing safe from his greed or the next object to catch his fancy."

Her brow knitted in a frown, and she wished he'd never suffered a day in his life. "Has it always been that way?"

"Long enough," he said as he stood and began to fold the rough edge of the cravat so that it lay in the center of the garment. "I was ten years old when I first met the jeweler, Mr. Windle. He purchased my mother's ruby brooch so that I could buy back the horses and carriage that my father had lost at cards the night before, while my mother lay dying of fever. Then two days later I had to sell something else to pay the undertaker. But not because father had lost again. No, he'd gained a king's ransom that night, but decided to shower his friends with lavish gifts, purchase six high-stepping grays, and order a gleaming new carriage until every last farthing was spent."

"Oh, Asher," she said, her heart breaking for him. "That must have been awful. You should have been free to be a child, to mourn her loss, and to be nurtured by family and friends."

He shook his head. "My father alienated all his family and my mother's as well. Whatever friends he had were just like him—loyal only to the gaming table.

Living for the thrill of the moment. The rise and fall of fortunes, like kings of sandcastles unconcerned with the next wave."

She watched as he began to tie the wrinkled cloth around his neck with rough, impatient movements. "You mentioned before that he's the reason you wear a black cravat. Though, admittedly, I'd heard tales of it before we'd ever met."

"I'd never intended for this to become a notorious garment. It was an act of rebellion, a physical demonstration of finality. I was done with him and I'd wanted him to know it."

A chill rippled through her as she thought how similar that was to her father's way of cutting people from his life. And since Asher had become distant without warning, directly following their interlude, she had to wonder if that had been a *demonstration of finality* as well.

No, she told herself. It was because he was still tempted. Hadn't he said as much?

She chafed her hands over her arms and chose to believe the better option. Then, sitting down upon the flat rock by the stream, she picked up her stockings and weighed them in her hand. "When did you start wearing it?"

"Years ago, when I was still at university," he said. "I'd had a terrible row with him. We'd exchanged our share of insults and honesty, the latter hitting like cannon fire. When the smoke had cleared, it had felt as if we'd waged a battle that neither side could ever win. And yet"—he drew in a deep breath—"for a time afterward, Shettlemane had ceased his reckless spending. On holiday, we'd actually spent time together, hunting and riding through the countryside. A regular father and son." His mouth twisted ruefully, jaw clenching on a tight exhale. "It didn't last, of course. Like a drunkard's thirst, his need to gamble and spend returned, stronger than ever before.

"We'd been attending a dinner party, with a standard friendly game of cards afterward," Asher continued, a hard, unforgiving edge in his voice. "All at once, he'd turned crazed and fever-eyed, willing to lay down the jewels worn by every marchioness—including my mother—for the past hundred years. After losing, he'd merely shrugged and told me that he was sure the next hand would have won it back for him. All he'd needed was to borrow a few more pounds. But it didn't make a difference. They were gone, and their new owner— Lord Seabrooke—remains too smart to ever wager with them."

To her ears, it sounded as though Asher had tried to win them back a time or two. How frustrating it must have been to have so much family history stripped from his grasp. "Surely, when you came of age, you knew you could walk away from this compulsiveness."

"When I came of age, the marquess started borrowing against my name, further trapping me in this madness." He held her gaze. "Those men at the jeweler's weren't after you, Winn. They were after me."

She nodded. "I suspected as much. My father is likely angry, but he wouldn't send men to kill me. For that to happen, I would have to matter to him. No, it's far more likely that he has already disowned me. He's even more stubborn than I am, and far too proud." A breath of hurt and resignation gathered tightly in her lungs. But when she saw Asher's frown, she subdued it, not wanting him to think that all she cared about was her own future. "It doesn't ease my mind to know that they were after you instead. Is there any chance that they will stop their pursuit?"

"None at all," he answered distractedly. "I've dealt with them, and dozens like them, before."

"And yet you gamble as well. I should think you would hate the practice."

"I do. I even hate that I'm good at it." He expelled an exhausted breath. Finishing his knot, he turned away to pick up his coat where it was drying over the edge of a branch. "Yet I always return to the practice that was taught to me since infancy. My mother used to say that my father could see the shadows surrounding other people's souls and charm their desperation into the open. I suppose I'm more like him than I wish to be."

Finished with her knots as well, she settled her skirts in place and moved toward him. "But you're not. You've proven that you don't use people." She glanced to the patch of grass and blushed. "And I'd wager that, when you meet your friends for cards, you don't use them either."

He shrugged into his coat, studying her. With the light at that particular angle, the coldness was gone from his eyes and now they looked as soft as mink fur.

"Over the years, I have adopted a few tells—a lift of the brow, a clearing of the throat—in order to give them a fair chance." A wry grin toyed with one corner of his mouth. "It took an age for Ellery to catch on. In fact, if it wasn't for his wife, I think I'd still feel guilty each time we played. But Gemma is a keen observer of people and found me out straightaway. Then again, the reason is likely because she has a dark history similar to mine. Though at least she escaped hers."

With those words, his grin fell, flattening into a grim line, and a shadow crossed his gaze.

Winnifred lifted her hand to rest it against the contours of his cheek. "You will, too. I have complete faith in your determination."

Something pained flashed across his features, and slowly he dragged her hand away. "You don't even know me or what I'm capable of. And if I told you the despicable things I've done, I'm afraid that—"

"Have you ever tried any other means to gain your fortune?" she interrupted, dismissing his claim. She knew him better than he thought. "Perhaps you should think about investing."

"I've made many investment attempts. Some have been thwarted due to a sudden drain in my own accounts. And others have become lucrative enough that the earnings put the scent of money underneath my father's nose."

"And you had an opportunity to change all that, but my friends interfered," Winn said, feeling guilty for her part. She fidgeted with the ends of the last ribbon before lifting it to her hair, doing her best to gather it into a tight queue.

"When we reach my aunt's," she continued, "I'm going to see that you are paid more than what you initially lost."

Asher shook his head and turned her around. Slipping the ribbon from her grasp, he tied the queue himself. "No, Winn. Let's stop talking about the money, hmm? I don't want anything from your aunt."

"But we made a bargain," she said, confused as she pivoted to face him. And seeing regret and resignation in his expression, she felt a jolt of panic. "Surely, because of our kiss in the grass, you wouldn't leave me to make the rest of the journey alone."

"No. No, of course not," he said earnestly and set his hands on her shoulders, soothing her with up and down sweeps. "I was never going to take payment from your aunt."

"You weren't?"

"It wouldn't be right. My bargain"—he swallowed and lowered his hands—"was never with her."

He looked away, and Winnifred thought it might be out of shyness. A rise of tender emotion filled her heart and lungs and stomach. So big and buoyant, it was like a vast island—Asherland, where all the natives lounged together on soft patches of grass and kissed endlessly. "Why didn't you tell me from the beginning?"

"You'd have hardly accepted my escort if I'd told you the truth. You're so stubborn, you would have gone alone. I refused to risk it. And I certainly wouldn't toss you to the wolves now."

Winnifred leapt into his arms, rewarded by his reflexive response, pulling her flush. Her heart pounded hard in her chest, the heavy beats so intense that her eyes prickled with tears as her mind reeled.

And to think, all this time, the journey had nothing to do with money.

"Then what will you do?" she asked, lifting a worried gaze.

He rested his forehead against hers and closed his eyes. "All that I care about at the moment is taking you to your destination."

She could hardly believe it. While part of her felt guilty, most of her was too happy and slipping dangerously close to Asherland's windswept cliffs that overlooked Lake Head-Over-Heels.

"That sounds suspiciously like you're prepared to change your name and roam the countryside at your leisure after this is over," she teased, wanting to dispel any remnants of the pall that had cast a momentary shadow over a most wondrous afternoon.

It worked. A grin curled his lips as he straightened and took her hands in his. "The notion of living life with nothing more than the clothes on my back is more appealing than I ever could have imagined."

"You'd make an excellent Mr. Strewsbury."

He inclined his head, keeping her beside him as they began to walk toward the village. "Founder of the renown Strewsbury Quartet, if I recall."

"Indeed. Famous in hamlets across the whole of England."

Smiling, she could easily imagine such a life. Every day would be a new adventure. At least, as long as she was with Asher.

"Though it is a pity what happened to the others."

She laughed. "I cannot believe your first impulse was to say they'd been murdered by highwaymen. Well, one thing is for certain—we're going to need a better story before we arrive at the village if I'm going to have the chance to sing for our supper."

"You won't need to, Winn. Like I said, I'll take care of things and find a way to your aunt's."

She slid a glance to his profile, to the set of his jaw. "You plan to gamble."

"It's what I know."

"But—" Winn stopped herself before she argued her point.

It would be useless. She already knew he was going to be stubborn about this. So instead of ruining what had been a lovely interlude, she decided to save her breath and simply show him that there was always another way.

Chapter 17

What was Winn doing to him?

For the better part of their journey, Asher had started thinking of this as an unplanned adventure instead of a business arrangement. He blamed her entirely. She made it far too easy to forget the constant manipulations that had driven him here in the first place.

Instead, he'd thought about her laugh and whether or not it would alter over the years ahead, deepening with old age, or if it would remain light and musical. He'd also wondered how many freckles she'd gain over the course of her life and if she would still steal away at dawn for bareback rides across the countryside.

Yet when reality intruded, he knew he'd never have the answers. The bargain he'd made with Waldenfield ensured that. It loomed overhead like a storm cloud, and the guilt he felt nearly choked him.

He caught himself wishing that all the things Winn had told him about her father disowning her were true. Not for her sake, but for his own. If she was correct, Waldenfield wouldn't be waiting at Avemore Abbey, and there would be no chance to recuperate the stolen money.

Strangely, that possibility was almost a relief. He must be going mad.

After all, opportunities like the Hollanders' expedition didn't come twice in a man's lifetime. And Asher still planned to sail away in just a handful of days.

There wasn't any time for more complications, or adventures, or . . . earth-shattering kisses in the grass. He needed to focus on getting to Avemore Abbey, then figure out a way to earn his passage.

In the meantime, Winn was still his responsibility. His to keep safe. His for only one more day.

"Stay close to my side," he said, curling his hand tighter around hers.

The Grinning Boar was not directly along the well-traveled route of the Great North Road, but it was near enough to make Asher wary.

Night had just fallen over the sleepy village square, the oil lanterns gradually being brought to life. A handful of shop front windows were dark as mirror glass, their doorways enveloped in shadows. A stout man lingered near the long carriage house, his back pressed against the outer wall as he stared up at the stars through the rings of smoke he puffed from his pipe. On the other side, a woman laughed near the blacksmith's hut as a tall, broad-shouldered man in a long leather apron leaned in to steal a kiss. And in the center, by the village well, a drunkard lay on the cobblestones with his head on his hat.

Winn's melodic laugh warmed the chilly stillness, and she whispered conspiratorially, "Are you afraid the lamplighter will use his ladder for nefarious purposes?"

"This is no teasing matter," Asher said sternly, wondering how he was going to gamble and watch over her at the same time. "Your eyes simply aren't accustomed to seeing potential threats. The quaint fieldstone facade of the inn may look safe—even cozy—to the average passerby. However, behind the golden glow emanating from the windows, I see the shadows of a dozen or more men who may be deep in their cups and eager for a brawl. Unfortunately, that is precisely where I will have the best luck in finding a game of cards, and to win enough to provide us a night's lodging as well as coaching fare for tomorrow morning."

She wrinkled her nose at him. "In just a few short miles, you've turned into a veritable curmudgeon. And you also seem to be wearing horse blinders. Has it occurred to you that there's always another choice to be made? Or that *I* might have a better idea?"

"Since your previous helpful suggestion was stealing a horse, I have a fairly good notion your plan would entail something that would land us both in irons."

"That was only one idea. All the others I have are perfectly legal."

She set her hands on her hips, the bodice of her dress straining to contain her magnificent breasts. One glance at her pouting lips and he was sorely tempted to kiss her. But he had to resist. He suspected that this runaway heiress posed the biggest threat to his future that he'd ever faced before.

"*All* of them?" he asked, dubious.

She shrugged, her shawl slipping down her shoulders. "Since you have no need for my assistance and want to continue running your solitary life the way you've always done, there's hardly a point in telling you."

He bundled the shawl around her. "Such a stubborn creature, you are. Simply hate it when you don't get your way."

She opened her mouth to protest. He leaned down and stole a quick kiss. Couldn't resist, *damn it all*.

"Just let me take care of things, Winn."

Her hazel eyes narrowed and glinted impishly in the lamplight, but she gave no further argument.

A moment later, they stepped into the Grinning Boar. The air was thick with the scent of pipe smoke and the sweet, yeasty aroma of ale. A stout, bald-pated man stood behind a weathered bar. Through an oak-beamed archway, Asher spied several tables, each occupied by men either snoring or half-asleep over their pints.

Not exactly the crowd of rabble-rousers Asher had anticipated. He'd have a difficult time finding a game of any sort.

"Well, you were right about one thing," Winn said cheekily. "They *are* deep in their cups. Perhaps you can wager on who will stay asleep the longest."

He slanted her a look and muttered, "I'll come up with something."

The man behind the bar approached, pausing to call over his shoulder, "Wife, we've another pair of weary travelers."

"If they're anything like those two maggots who spent the whole day drinking only to pay up with brass farthings, then send them away," a shrill voice called back from beyond the slanted door on the far wall.

The man shook his head and flashed a broad grin. "Pay no mind to that woman. I ken you need a place to rest your feet a spell, and we've a nice warm fire just there." Draping a bit of toweling over his shoulder, he extended a meaty hand toward Asher. "Me name's Oslo, and you'll be pleased to know that me wife makes the finest lamb stew and shepherd's pie in the land. Just don't tell her I said so. It goes to her head."

Yet he spoke the words loud enough to be heard in the next county. An instant later, a tall, reedlike brunette emerged from the slanted doorway, carrying a tray so overladen with covered dishes that it might have weighed more than she did.

"Sure enough," she said, her words as clipped as her steps as she crossed the stone floor. "And I bake an apple tart that's brought more than one man to his knees, begging for my hand in marriage."

"Modest as a butterfly, me wife," Oslo added with a murmur and a wink.

"And all it gets us is a fine reputation for letting the locals fall asleep at our tables."

"After a long, hard day and so much rain—not to mention those blasted threshers—to worry the farmers, this is a fine place to rest a weary mind."

"So is the dirt beneath the churchyard," the wife said with a sniff. "If I've said it once, I've said it a thousand times, we need something to liven the place up and *not* any of your grand ideas about opening a gaming parlor. That would only attract more maggots."

Bollocks. The news didn't bode well for Asher's plans at all.

Oslo looked to them as if to defend himself. "Not

true. Why just today, we've even got a fine gentleman and lady in our rooms upstairs."

"And not a single enticement to draw them down," his wife added.

Asher felt a chill slide through him at the news that there were a lord and lady upstairs. He didn't want to linger. There was too much of a chance that it might be someone he knew, or who knew of him.

"You're all the enticement anyone needs, me lovely," Oslo said, pinching his wife's cheek.

She narrowed her eyes. "Always with the sweet talk when I've a point to make. All I know is that if I get more of their kind"—she lifted her gaze to the ceiling—"through our doors, then perhaps our rooms'd be filled every night."

"And why would you want that? Nearly broke my back carrying up pails of water because Lady Hoity-Toity demanded a bath after the lads had lugged three trunks upstairs already. Then borrowed your best scullery maid for the night to"—he paused to lift his little finger and bat his eyelashes—"*assist* with her *toilet*."

She huffed and looked directly at Winn, shifting the tray in her grasp. "Men! I hope your husband doesn't give you half as much trouble."

"Sadly, he does. Mr. Strewsbury tends to believe he knows best in all things. Simply cannot take a single suggestion," Winn said, sliding him a haughty glance.

He tucked her hand in the crook of his arm, ready to depart and come up with another plan. "A man has more experience and knows the ways of the world."

This got him another grin and a nod from Oslo.

"Perhaps in certain circumstances," Winn added,

that impish light flickering in her eyes again. "How-ever, if we had traveled in the direction that *I* had sug-gested, we never would have been robbed by a pair of highwaymen."

"No!" the owner's wife gasped.

Asher gritted his teeth and gave her hand a gentle but prodding tug. "Crumpet, there's no need to tell that story again. After all, as the man said, they don't have any rooms and it's growing late."

He would have to try his luck in the morning. For now, they needed to find a place to rest for the night.

"Well, I've been up in arms for days," she continued doggedly and patted his sleeve. "They took everything we had, even our instruments."

"Instruments?" The wife's eyebrows arched high on her forehead. "Are you musicians?"

In that instant, Asher knew he'd lost the battle. Winn was going to have her way no matter what. He could feel it in the stubborn, steady beats of the pulse at her wrist, and see it on the faces of her rapt audience.

Winn affected a bashful grin. "We do well enough at festivals, I suppose. And we have been on the stage a time or two, or a few dozen, but who keeps count of these things?"

"Oslo, dear," the wife said sweetly. "We could cer-tainly spare a pint and a bit of dinner for a song or two, don't you think?"

Winn coyly looked up at Asher and batted her lashes. *The little gloater.* He nearly laughed. A man certainly had to admire such a wealth of tenacity.

And the next thing he knew, Oslo was holding the tray while his wife announced—to a mostly slumbering audience—that they were about to be delighted by the *world-famous* Mrs. Strewsbury.

In the meantime, as if donning a costume, Winn slipped the shawl from her shoulders, folded it on the bias and tied it around her waist. It had the unfortunate effect of emphasizing her delectable curves. Pleased with herself, she straightened her shoulders and looked up at him.

Asher couldn't take his eyes off her. He doubted any other man with a pulse would be able to either. And it was this thought that had him ready to drag her out.

As if reading his mind, she wagged her finger and murmured, "If you take a single step into that taproom, it had better be to perform and for no other reason."

Gauntlet dropped, she sashayed to the hearth at the far wall and began to sing. And with the very first notes of the lively melody she'd learned from Mr. Champion earlier, the room came to life. Heads lifted from their pints, men scrubbing the gauze of sleep from their faces, while feet began to tap beneath the tables.

Asher felt a helpless grin tug at the corners of his mouth as she flashed a triumphant smile. A mixture of pride, awe, and something he didn't dare name stirred within his chest.

"She's a treasure, that one," Oslo said after the first chorus, thrumming his fingers against the side of the tray.

"Indeed, she is."

"Like me wife said, I can offer you food and drink, but we've no room. Well, unless you'd want the little loft above the boiling house out back. 'Tisn't very big, but it'll be yours for the night if you want it."

"Thank you. That's very kind," Asher agreed with a nod, knowing that staying in the loft would put them beneath the notice of any lord and lady traveling. Not only that, but he knew that Winn would be appreciative for a place to lay her head, regardless of where it was.

He still marveled at how she was different from anything he might have expected. Or from any other woman he'd ever known. He genuinely liked her. Too much, perhaps.

It wouldn't be easy to let her go.

But he refused to think about that right now. Instead, he turned to Oslo. "You wouldn't happen to have a lute, would you?"

HOURS LATER, and after many more songs, they were finally settling down for the night on a pallet in the tiny loft of the boiling house, a pair of empty copper stills beneath them.

Winnifred stretched out against his side. There wasn't any need to bother with the pretense of putting a barrier between them, especially since there wasn't any room. The two of them took up every inch of this cozy space.

"I don't think I've ever been so tired in my life," she said on a yawn.

He tucked her closer against him. "You were an absolute wonder. I never imagined such bawdy lyrics spilling from your lips. I'm quite scandalized."

"It would take far more than a few songs to scandalize you."

"Perhaps," he said, yawning, too. "But I imagine more than half the men in the room fell irrevocably in love with you. They'll be pining for Mrs. Strewsbury for the rest of their days."

She smiled into his shirtsleeves, her hand resting over the warm, steady throbbing of his heart. "At first, I was positively terrified to step in front of them. Then I looked at you and—"

"And you wanted to put me in my place."

"Well, yes." She laughed lightly. "I also noticed a keen change in myself. For most of my life I'd felt like I was wearing the wrong skin, and had the wrong hair, and needed to do something to change it all. Yet, when I was standing there and looked across at you, I felt like I'd been in the right skin all along. It's peculiar, isn't it? But it seems that I had to step away from everything I knew in order to appreciate the person I really am."

He was quiet for a minute, then lifted her hand to press a kiss to her palm before settling it back over his heart again. Other than that, he gave no response, but it didn't matter. She was quite content.

"And you were exceptional on the lute, Mr. Strewsbury. You surprised me."

"I know," he said drowsily, a grin curling his voice. "And I've been wanting to crow all night about how you didn't believe me . . . but now I'm too tired. You'll have to deal with my overinflated ego in the morning."

There was such comforting assurance in the words *in the morning* while lying in his arms. It was a promise that he would be here for her, as well as an expectation that she would be here for him.

Her parents' marriage had never taught her about the sublime joy of spending each day with someone she cared for. And she cared for Asher far more than she ever thought possible in such a short span of time.

A voice in the back of her mind warned her not to jump off the cliffs in Asherland and fall head over heels in love with him, but she was too exhausted to listen.

"Why didn't you ever marry an heiress?" she asked, her eyes drifting closed. "I'm certain you've had the opportunity."

"Are you offering, Winn?" he teased, brushing his hand soothingly down her back.

"No." She kept a wistful sigh to herself. "Simply curious."

"It's difficult to say. All I know is that I could always find a reason not to."

"Mmm," she murmured.

Yet right before she drifted to sleep, she could have sworn she felt a kiss on her forehead and heard him whisper, "Though the real reason might be that . . . none of them were you."

Then again, she may have already been dreaming.

Chapter 18

Asher felt the delicate glide of fingers through his hair. A soft press of lips to his temple. And when he drew in a breath, it smelled of strawberries.

He smiled and pulled the warm body next to him closer. "Good morning."

"Careful," Winn said with a light laugh. "You'll spill our tea. And after all the pains I went through to carry it up the ladder, you are required to appreciate every single drop."

At that, he opened his eyes, a frown knitting his brow. "You left the loft on your own? Without waking me first?"

Blinking, he saw her sitting up, the handle of an earthenware pint in her hand, and his arm wrapped around her shapely legs.

"I did wake you. Several times, in fact," she said, tsking him for not remembering. "We even had a conversation where you argued that you were fully conscious *and* that your eyes were open. They were not. Though you have surprisingly lucid conversations when you are still asleep."

"My valet has mentioned something to this effect before," he said absently as he rose up to his elbow.

Taking the cup, he drank down a good portion of the tepid—but thankfully strong—brew. "Did I say anything else?"

"Hmm . . . nothing of import. You did, however, refer to me as Mrs. Strewsbury and scolded me for not waking my husband with a kiss. You said it was quite rude to badger you when you were clearly awake, and clearly in need of kissing."

Asher couldn't recall ever blushing in his life, yet the sudden swell of heat prickling his cheeks indicated it may very well have been happening in that instant.

Embarrassed, he cleared his throat. Then, sitting up, he averted his face and carefully studied the construction of the cup and the dark liquid down in its depths. "Thank you for the tea."

"I brought a muffin, too," she said, producing a brown cake within a folded cloth, which he took with gratitude, inclining his head. "Although I am sorry that the kitchen didn't have any strawberries yet this season. You indicated that you enjoy them more than any other berry you've ever tasted."

Asher coughed on his first bite. Her hand descended to his back, patting him between the shoulder blades, and he took another long swallow of tea. He wished his sleep self wasn't so bloody transparent.

Deciding it was time for a change of topic, he said, "Did you sing like a lark again this morning, or did you venture on a sunrise raid through the kitchen?"

"Neither," she said with a shrug. "I just . . . thought you'd be hungry."

The hesitancy in her tone gained his full attention.

As always, she was lovely, with her hair tied back in a black ribbon and wayward ringlets brushing her temples and cheeks. However, she was a terrible liar. She blinked owl-eyed at him and pulled her bottom lip between her teeth.

Suspicious, he set his tea and bread aside. His gaze traveled the length of her green dress, all the way down to the shawl draped over the bottom half of her legs and feet. And when he peeled the russet wool away, she immediately tucked her slippers beneath her.

"Winn, lift your skirts."

She splayed her hand over her knees and scooted over an inch. "Such a scoundrel. But we should really be on our way. In fact, I'll climb down the ladder first and then *yoooш*—"

He snagged her about the waist and drew up her hem to see her shoes—one with his handkerchief tied in a neat bow on top—and her calves.

Her lovely, *bare* calves.

"Where are your stockings?" Yet he already knew. "You sold them, didn't you?"

Only Winn would sacrifice the last thing of value she possessed. Only Winn would do something so impulsive, so maddening, so utterly . . . selfless.

And only Winn would come into his life at the worst possible time.

She sighed and turned to press her forehead to his. "We're running out of time, Asher. You need to be back in London in a few days. So I had this notion that, if we had the money, we could catch the next mail coach to my aunt's. Then you'd be able to—"

He kissed her, sinking headlong into those lush,

welcoming lips. *Damn it all*. Why did she have to be an heiress? It would be so easy to fall in love with her.

Sliding a hand to her nape, he angled his mouth over hers, punishing both of them by deepening the kiss, tasting her sweet surrender. Falling in love with Winn was a terrible idea. Marriage would only trap them in the same chaos he'd endured all his life. He couldn't bear the thought of inflicting that hell on her. And yet . . .

He wanted her to be his. In fact, he'd never wanted anything or anyone so much. He ached from wanting her. To see her face every morning. To lie beside her every night. To hear her voice and to make her laugh. And if the circumstances were different, he'd give himself over to this love that was burning like an ember inside his chest. He'd let the flames consume him.

He'd beg her forgiveness for the deal he'd made with her father, and do whatever it took to win her heart and marry her. And he wanted it so much that he could hardly breathe.

Asher broke the kiss, panting as if he'd just tried to scale a mountain but couldn't reach the summit. He pulled her close and realized all his thoughts were selfish ones.

His circumstances weren't different. If he didn't find a way to earn enough money *and* make it back to London in time, they might never be.

"Don't be angry with me," she said.

"I'm not. I just wish that you weren't so . . ."

"Foolish?"

He took her face in his hands and shook his head. "Remarkable, in every conceivable way."

Tears suddenly gathered in her eyes. "You will not think so when I tell you that the next mail coach will not come until tomorrow. And by then, I fear it will be too late."

He pressed a kiss to her lashes, her nose and her lips once more, the surrounding skin reddened by his whiskers. "I should have taken better care with your soft skin and shaved before I kissed you."

"You are rather prickly, but I don't mind," she said, lightly brushing her fingertips over his jaw and making him want to be petted by her all day long.

But they didn't have all day.

"How much coin do you have?"

Reaching behind her, she produced the coins, resting on the flat of her palm. It wasn't much, but with a little ingenuity it might end up being enough.

He laid his hand over hers, the copper and silver growing warm between them. "Winn, if I ask you to wait for me, would you?"

She searched his gaze and, in the quiet moment that followed, neither one of them drew a breath. "Do you mean . . . here, in the loft?"

To be honest, he wasn't sure what he meant. His thoughts were a jumble of *if*s—if he could get her to her aunt's in time . . . if he could return to London in time . . . if he could make the fortune he thought he would . . . if he could free himself . . . if she forgave him . . . if everything went to plan . . .

But the vision of the future was opaque and uncertain. So of course, he wasn't asking her to wait for him forever.

Was he?

"Stay here for a few minutes," he said at last. "I'll return shortly. And please, whatever you do, don't say that thing you always say before disaster strikes."

She smiled and tipped forward to press her lips to his once more. "I'll be right here."

❦❦❦

ASHER SHAVED his morning's beard with his boot knife and the water Winn had left in a pitcher at the bottom of the ladder. Staring at his warped reflection in the copper still, those *if*s swirled inside his head, the future more uncertain than ever.

But he was determined to change that.

He left the boiling house and crossed the yard behind the Grinning Boar. Heading toward the street, he was trying to figure out a way to procure a coach and driver, one willing to take them the rest of the way to Yorkshire for less than a crown.

With an absent glance out at the town square, it appeared far different than it had last night, almost idyllic. In the gleaming light of morning, the cobblestones teemed with men and women tilting their hats in welcome, milling about the shops, toting baskets, driving carts. There were even children playing by the well. In such a setting, he doubted he'd successfully rouse a game.

Distracted by his thoughts, he nearly ran headlong into Mr. Lum, staggering down the pavement beside his laughing, gangly cohort.

Asher's boots skidded to a full stop before he had the presence of mind to retreat around the corner. He pressed his back against the shingled wall, his pulse racing.

"Shut it, Jamey," came Lum's gravelly voice. "You're giving me a bleedin' headache."

"You're just grogshot. A fine cup of tea will set you right again. And you'll be glad to know that, while you were dead to the world, I made inquiries. Seems as though there haven't been any mail coaches who stopped by here with anyone like Holt or his heiress. So they can't be ahead of us, can they?"

"Of course they aren't ahead of us. That little gig can fly. Mark my words, we'll find Holt and his heiress before they can reach Gretna Green. Then, with both of them tied up, we'll send a letter to Waldenfield offering him first claim on getting his daughter back. For a price, of course."

"But . . ." Jamey hesitated. "I thought we were supposed to take the heiress back with us, too. So the marquess can do the extorting to Waldenfield."

Asher's blood went cold, listening with dread. So that was the plan his father had hatched—to ransom Winn to her father?

"Oy! And who says we won't?" Lum shouted, then lowered his voice, speaking in singsong as if to a child. "But first we're going to play nice and friendly with the man who has all the money. That's the way we'll get some for ourselves."

"Ah."

"*Idiot.* Come on, then. Let's get our gig. The blighter who runs the carriage house made me pay him up front like I wasn't good for the money, and I don't want to be around when he realizes that the coin's *newly minted*, if you ken my meaning."

"But I been waiting all mornin' for ham steaks and soft eggs, and you've still got that guinea from the bloke yesterday."

"I'm not about to spend good coin if I don't have to. If these country folks are too stupid to mistake a brass farthing for the genuine article, then they get what they deserve." Lum sighed. "Though I could use a cup of tea, and considering you inhale as fast as you eat, I don't expect it'll matter much. Besides, we know where they're going. We'll either catch them in Gretna Green or somewhere along the way."

Asher frowned and heard the door to the inn close. He thought Shettlemane had already sunk as low as a man could go—stealing from his own son and sending henchmen after him. Apparently, he was wrong.

This changed things considerably. It was one thing to have Lum after him, but after Winn, too? No! Asher wouldn't allow her to be in harm's way.

Icy fury and desperation surged through him. It had the peculiar effect of centering all his thoughts. Now, with his mind clear, he realized he only had one option.

He had to steal Lum's curricle.

Chapter 19

Finally, the Fates were smiling on Asher. Outside the carriage house, the pair of horses were harnessed, and Lum's ready gig merely tied to a hitch. All he had to do was climb in and—

"*And* just who might you be?" asked a grizzled man in a flat felt cap and brown coat who stepped out from in front of the horse. He had a pipe clenched in his teeth and a whip at his side.

Asher offered a smile. "Well, this is my curricle."

The man smiled back and approached him in a genial fashion, but then clamped a hard hand over his shoulder. "Nah. You see, I remember the large fellow who tossed me this false coin, and you aren't him. But we get our share of thieves around here and we know how to deal with them. Got a set of irons next door at the smithy's."

Thinking fast, Asher shrugged free and took a step back with his hands raised in innocence. "As you say, the fellow who left this gig was intending to rob you, but I have coin."

Reaching into his pocket, he withdrew the money from Winn selling her stockings.

The man took it without delay. Then he jerked his

head in a nod toward the square. "That settles up with what he owes me from last night. Now be on your way before I fetch those irons."

Bloody hell. Asher felt robbed. Then again, that was what he'd been intending to do . . .

"What about striking a wager?" he asked, desperate.

"Not the wagering sort."

"A fair trade, then?" Glancing down, he knew his coat wouldn't fit the man's burly physique. "What do you think of these top boots? They're made with the finest calf leather."

"Don't need fancy boots."

Asher suddenly felt the weight of the pearl-handled knife tucked inside his boot.

To have any hope for a future, for a life he could be proud of—that didn't include robbery, or bartering, or demeaning himself—he knew what he had to do.

On a heavy exhale, he reached down. As he stood, he gripped the knife that had been his companion for two decades, then turned the handle toward the man so that it wouldn't appear threatening. "What about this? As you can see, it's a fine blade. And that's genuine gold filigree in the pearl handle."

The man's black-beetle eyes roved over it with interest. But then, another man—an older gentleman in a broad-brimmed hat and silver mustachios—strolled over, scrutinizing the knife.

He seemed familiar to Asher. He had a regal bearing and a finely tailored suit of clothes, like any wealthy gentleman who might stay in London for politics and gaming. Yet it was clear he kept to the country and preferred outdoor sporting, for his skin was tan, and his blue eyes were so pale and clear they appeared sun-bleached. "Pardon me, but have we met before?"

"Not as of yet," the man articulated in a rough growl of a voice as if he were used to calling out to his dogs on a hunt.

The carriage house stablemaster handed back the knife. "Don't need a fancy blade either. Got anything else?"

"May I?" asked the older gentleman, holding out a swarthy hand. Not having anything else to lose, Asher handed it over. And after studying it for a moment, he said, "This knife is quite rare, actually. Do you see this insignia here? Well, that indicates it was once part of a royal house. It's worth a great deal of money."

To Asher it was priceless.

The stablemaster scoffed. "See here, are you lot working together?"

Asher answered with an absent shake of his head, his focus on the gentleman. "Are you a collector?"

"Mmm . . . Something of that nature," he said with a slow grin that curled his mustachios. "How much would you like for it?"

This was it. His only chance. Asher turned to the stablemaster. "How much to take this curricle?"

The man shrugged. "Five pounds for my trouble."

Asher looked to the man with the mustachios. "Five pounds, then."

"For a treasure like this, you could purchase this entire village square."

"Perhaps, but if I don't take this gig immediately,

then the treasure I hold most dear will be lost." He held out his hand. "Do we have a bargain, then?"

The man shook, his grip solid, his gaze inquisitive. Then, without delay, he delivered the coins to the other man and Asher stepped up into the bench and picked up the ribbons.

Just as he released the brake, the gentleman came up beside the gig and lifted the brim of his wide hat with the tip of the blade. "It has been a pleasure, Lord Holt."

By the time it registered that he'd never given the man his name, Asher already had two in hand and was driving away. But in the next instant, it didn't matter, because he saw Mr. Lum and his associate crossing the village square.

In fact, they were running from an angry Oslo, who burst out of the Grinning Boar after them. "Stop! Thief!"

Then Lum spotted Asher and all hell broke loose. His eyes gleamed with triumph as he mouthed, "Holt," and a cruel smile split his face.

"Stop! Thief!" Lum shouted, pointing to Asher.

The villagers wore confused expressions but started to crowd toward the carriage.

Recalling many of the faces from the tavern last night, Asher was forced to slow the horse to keep from injuring anyone.

"Thief! Thief!"

This time, the shout came from a lilting feminine voice he knew quite well.

And when he looked across the square, there was Winn beside Oslo's wife, pointing at Lum and Jamey. "Those are the highwaymen who robbed my husband and me. Stop them! Please, stop them!"

Those same villagers who'd been about to corral Asher suddenly turned their glaring attention to the henchmen.

They both stopped and Lum stripped off his hat, placing it over his heart. "We're the innocent ones. The chit's lying! That's our gig. Just ask the man from the carriage house."

The stablemaster pulled his pipe from his teeth and Asher held his breath.

"The lady's right. Them's the two thieves."

Oslo came up behind Lum and Jamey and clamped hands on their shoulders. "Been paying with brass far-things, they have. Where's the smithy?"

Relief rushed through Asher, but he knew they weren't out of danger yet. Without wasting time, he drove the horses around the blockade and toward Winn.

"You promised to wait," he said with a grin as she took his hand and climbed up to the curricle's black-painted bench situated beneath the curved hood.

She blinked innocently, holding the shawl on her lap. "I was waiting in the general vicinity. Someone had to watch over you, after all."

He was so busy grinning like a fool that he almost didn't see Lum and Jamey break free from the jeering crowd. Out of the corner of his eye, he witnessed them push an old man aside and appropriate his horse cart.

"Hold on, crumpet," Asher said and snapped the reins, spurring the horses forward and jolting them both back against the hard bench.

The henchmen were rounding the well, kicking at the villagers who tried to stop them.

"*Did* you steal it?" Winn asked in a scandalized

stage whisper laced liberally with excitement. Someday he would have to chide his little heiress for her
criminal predilections.

"Not exactly."

"Don't tell me you gambled this morning."

"I didn't gamble," he said absently, trying to focus
on finding a path out of the square.

The sun was bright, cresting the trees just enough
to blind him. Squinting, he turned through a shaded
opening that he thought was the way to the main road.

It wasn't.

Instead, he found himself in a small grassy paddock, charging toward an open gate on the other side.
Beyond that was a cottage with a yard full of chickens
and a woman bent over a tub, scrubbing clothes beside
a wash line tied between two trees.

Winn swatted his arm. "Well? How did you acquire
this curricle, then?"

"You could say that I . . . bartered for it."

"With only the few coins that I—" She gasped, covering her mouth. "Oh, Asher, not your knife."

He swallowed. "There was no other way."

With a glance, he saw her eyes flood with tears, her
bottom lip trembling. Then she buried her face against
his shoulder and cried. "This is all my fault."

"Of course it isn't," he crooned, turning his head
to press a kiss to the top of hers. "Waiting outside the
church to kidnap you has been the best—"

The rest of his words were drowned out by a bucket
of dirty water that slapped him in the face. He sputtered and spat, wishing he would have been paying
closer attention as he passed the washer woman.

Coughing, his mouth filled with the bitter taste of potash and . . . well . . . he didn't want to think about the rest. His eyes stung, too, and he squeezed them closed to stop them from burning. But that was a mistake.

Squinting at the narrow path between the cottage and the paddock fence, he barely caught sight of another woman, and this one was shaking out a rug from the first-floor window. All the dust and filth fell on him, sticking to his skin and eyelashes.

He couldn't see a thing.

He sneezed and coughed again, slowing the horses.

"Why are we . . ." Her question trailed off as she lifted her head and began to pat his coat. "Whatever did you drive us through? A storm cloud and an ash heap? You're positively filthy! And half of my dress is speckled and dirty."

"Winn, are there men still chasing us in a horse cart?" Using one hand, he began to untie his cravat since his handkerchief was tied around her shoe. "Because if they are, perhaps we can talk about this later."

"Then let me drive," she said with impatience.

"Do you know how to drive?"

She was already taking the reins from him as he slid the cravat from his collar. "Of course. After all, how difficult could it be?"

Alarm jolted through him at the same time she spurred the horses, catching Asher off balance. He nearly lost his seat.

"Apologies," she said in singsong, giving the lead another flick and spurring the horses faster. "You'd best hold on tightly."

"Why is that?"

"Well, there's a narrow turn up ahead. But I think I see the road."

"What do you mean, *you think*—"

All at once he felt, rather than saw, the curricle lifting onto one wheel as they made the turn.

When it slammed back down on two wheels, Winn laughed with pure, throaty joy. "I love driving!"

He was terrified but caught himself smiling like a fool as he wiped filth from his eyes. Looking at her and seeing her so free and uninhibited, he couldn't help but marvel at her. She had such zest for adventure. For life.

Was it any wonder that he'd fallen irrevocably in love with her?

"Apparently, we missed quite the show this morning, Lord Waldenfield. I just finished tying up the trunks when I heard all about a pair of thieves who went on a rampage through the square. Half the village has gone after them."

As his driver spoke, Julian scanned the cobblestone square with a more critical eye, glad it was Imogene's habit to take an age to ready her toilet in the mornings. Even when they were in a rush. "Any other news to report?"

"Well, my lord," he said, lowering his voice. "I kept a keen ear out and dropped Holt's name a few times in conversation, but no one's heard of him."

"Very good, Bastion."

The driver cleared his throat and shifted from one

foot to the other. "There's news of high waters in a few places along our route, my lord."

"And?"

"Well, with all the additional weight from the trunks . . ."

"Yes, yes." Lifting his gaze to the luggage, Julian knew he should have refused Imogene's demand to take *all* of them. But this cumbersome mountain was a clear representation of how he was unable to refuse her. "Just drive us there as quickly as possible."

Inside the inn once again, he mounted the stairs to the rooms, passing a maid in the hall who'd left Imogene's door ajar. He had no intention to invade her privacy, but she caught him watching her tie a heathered gray ribbon beneath her chin. And like him, she let her gaze skim over his form with familiarity.

"Did you have someone brush out your coat?" she asked, stepping into the corridor.

He looked down, inspecting the green wool for a flaw. "I managed it on my own, but a boy came by this morning to polish my boots."

"You do quite well for a gentleman traveling without a valet."

He inclined his head casually to accept the compliment, concealing the fact that his pulse quickened. It was one of the most intimate exchanges they'd had in ages. And the saddest part was that he'd specifically worn the green coat for the journey because, years ago, she'd told him how much she liked the color on him. "Did you manage to sleep last night?"

"Some," she said. "It was kind of you to have a tray

of milk and brandy sent up. I didn't think you'd have remembered."

She averted her gaze to fuss with her gloves, but there was a distinct tinge of color rising to her cheeks.

"You always had trouble sleeping in a strange place. I hope the revelry belowstairs into the wee hours didn't bother you."

She glanced up at him with a quizzical smile. "Peculiarly, I found comfort in the quaint country music. I even thought that the girl's tone had a similar quality to our Winnifred's. Though I suppose that was simply brought on by missing her. If not for the exuberant performance to serve as a distraction, I might have lingered all night in the quiet over my thoughts and worries."

Seeing the strained fragility in her gaze, he wanted to reach out to her, to offer his hand in something other than assistance into or out of a carriage.

"Imogene, I hope you know that—"

The maid appeared again, interrupting to tell them that the carriage was waiting out front.

Once she was gone, Imogene asked, "What were you about to say just then?"

He was going to tell her that she never needed to worry alone. That he'd never deny any request of hers, no matter what state their marriage was in at the time.

The sentiment seemed far too flowery now that he thought about it.

So Julian merely swallowed and shook his head. "It's not important. Shall we?"

He proffered his arm, and they walked downstairs and out to the pavement. But at the carriage door, she stopped and lifted a troubled gaze to him.

"Julian, what if we don't find her waiting at your sister's?"

"Then we'll go to Gretna Green."

"And if she isn't there?"

"I'll find her, Imogene," he said. "I promise."

Out of the corner of his eye, he noticed a handsome, mustachioed man looking their way with suspicious interest. Reflexively, he crowded closer to Imogene and handed her into the carriage.

Once safely inside, she cast a curious gaze over his shoulder and then back to him. "I know you will. You have always been a fine protector."

For an instant, he felt a stirring of hope that, perhaps, they could start again and reclaim what they'd lost so long ago.

Yet as he felt her fingertips slip from his own, he thought to himself, *Not always.*

Chapter 20

⁓

After the first hour of her introduction to driving, Winnifred let Asher take the reins. He'd become rather insistent directly following a near-fatal collision. Not for them but for an entire gaggle of slow-waddling geese.

So she'd settled back, finding a sense of peace and comfort riding beside him. They'd passed through a few rain showers, rested the horses while Asher told her another story of Lolly's adventures, and then the sun came out again and they were on their way.

She wanted their journey to last for hours longer, but time was fading out of her control. And by early evening, they'd arrived.

The sun rested over a copse of trees like a candied orange in a sweetmeat dish. Standing tall at the end of a long weather-worn drive behind an open iron gate, Avemore Abbey looked like a molded pudding dusted with white sugar and dotted with spires. Cut into the pale stone, rows of recessed mullioned windows shone like mirrors, and at the base, one half of a broad oaken door opened at their approach.

Winnifred glanced again at the sun's position above the trees, wanting some magic to hold it in place. Once it fell, it would end their final day together. An emptiness gnawed at her and she knew her heart would feel it even more, come morning.

Asher slowed the curricle. "It'll be dark soon."

"Mmm-hmm."

"The horses are tired," he said. "They'll need to rest."

Her gaze swerved to Asher. "And to be brushed and fed."

"True." He nodded, his throat constricting on a swallow. "Do you think your aunt might invite me to linger until morning?"

"She'll insist upon it."

"Then we'll have a few more hours," he said quietly, reading her thoughts.

Just then, a woman emerged through the doorway, her long plait of silvery russet hair draped over the gray shawl on her gently rounded shoulders. Leaning on a cane, she shielded her eyes, scrutinizing the trespassers in the curricle.

"Winnifred?" she asked in startled disbelief. "Is that you, my dear girl?"

In answer, she waved and smiled and felt tears sting her eyes all at the same time. This was the beginning of a new life for her, a new chapter. And yet she couldn't conjure any happiness, not when she was still clinging to the last page of this one.

Unable to help herself, she laid her hand over Asher's on the reins and squeezed.

"It is I, Aunt," she said, clearing away the emotion clogging her throat. "Though how could you possibly recognize me? I was just a girl when I was last here."

Not only that, but she must look a fright in her

mud-speckled dress, with the ribbon barely clinging to her hair.

"You've grown into the very portrait of my own mother and she was the most beautiful woman who ever lived. I knew the instant I clapped eyes on you," her aunt said, walking with an abbreviated step toward the curricle. "Well, don't dawdle. Come here, girl, and greet me properly."

As soon as Asher lifted the brake, Winnifred scrambled down. Her aunt summarily crushed her in a fierce embrace, scented with the comforting fragrances of cedar, lavender and old books.

Clinging gratefully to her, she asked quietly, "Am I welcome, then, Aunt?"

"Of course you are. For as long as you wish," she said, her eyes wet as she brushed a soft hand over Winnifred's cheek. Then, after Asher stepped down, she turned her attention to him. "Surely this isn't the man you wrote to me about. Your Mr. Woodbine? Why, he doesn't appear to be odious and unpleasant at all."

She laughed at her aunt's audacity. "If he were Mr. Woodbine, he would be insulted indeed."

"Though I can assure you," Asher said, standing beside Winnifred, "Mr. Woodbine is those things, in addition to being a braggart and a complete buffoon. He let Winn slip out of his fingers, after all."

"You see, I . . ." she hemmed. "I left him at the church and ran away from my wedding."

Her aunt cackled with laughter and took Winnifred by the arm, leading her inside. "Goodness me! I should have loved to see the look on my brother's face. That makes two marriages he's arranged, and both with the same results. When will your father learn not to interfere in matters of the heart?"

"My heart wasn't involved in the least."

"Ah." Her aunt's green eyes twinkled. "But that brings us back to the question of who this young man is."

"Aunt, this is Viscount Holt," she said as they stopped in the vaulted stone foyer, surrounded by niches of marble statuettes. "Asher, this is my most exceptional aunt, Miss Myrtle Humphries."

"At your service, madam," he said with a bow.

Aunt Myrtle turned narrowed eyes on him. "Holt, you say? It's been a number of years since I've been in society, but I recall the family name."

Reaching out, he took her fingers and lifted them to his lips. "Then I offer my humblest apologies."

"Effusive charm will earn you no favors."

Winnifred laid her hand on his sleeve. "Oh, that's just the way he is. Incorrigible flirt."

Her aunt harrumphed. "All I want to know is if you are anything like your father."

Asher straightened, jaw clenched to twitch. "If I were, I would beg you to shoot me here and now."

After a moment of further scrutiny, she nodded and began to walk down a long corridor, bidding them to follow. "I liked your mother, Lord Holt. You have her eyes, you know."

"Thank you, my lady." Those eyes grew soft, a tender smile on his lips. He whispered to Winnifred, "I like your aunt."

"I heard that, flatterer," she called back over her shoulder. "I also notice you're wearing a black cravat. Are you in mourning for your father, by chance?"

"Eventually, I trust."

"What I mean to ask is whether or not mourning is the reason you haven't married my niece yet?"

Embarrassed, Winnifred's cheeks heated to scalding. "He isn't going to marry me."

Aunt Myrtle stopped with a firm clack of her cane and faced them. Her brow arched with the same superior skepticism that her father often employed. "No?"

"No," she answered, ignoring the sudden piercing pain in the vicinity of her heart. "He has other obligations and he'll be leaving for London in the morning. That is . . . if he is welcome to stay the night?"

She pursed her lips and lifted one shoulder. "As long as he likes. Though I think a trip to Gretna Green at first light would serve the two of you far better."

"Aunt!" Winnifred gasped. "I . . . or rather, the two of us . . . aren't even interested in marriage."

Her aunt eyed them, one after the other. Then her gaze dropped purposefully to the space between them.

Both Winnifred and Asher looked down at the same time, then jolted. They were holding hands, fingers twined, palms flush. Neither of them moved quickly to separate either, but did so only after a reluctant squeeze.

Meanwhile, her aunt cackled with glee, the sound echoing as she walked up a recessed stone staircase. "Seems to me the pair of you could use a good scrubbing and a meal. Perhaps, at dinner, you can tell me about your grand adventure from London."

"How do you know it wasn't one disaster after another from the very start?" she asked, smiling when Asher reached out to tug on her little finger.

"Because I've had my share of them and I can see

the effects in your eyes. It's clear to me that you're quite in love . . ."

"Aunt!" Winn nearly tripped up the risers.

". . . *with* having adventures, of course," she added cheekily, her teasing words tumbling down the stairs, one after the other.

Winnifred slid a glance to Asher. But he was staring straight ahead and frowning.

Frowning?

Instantly, her mind provided an answer—he didn't want her to love him. Not her. Not plump, freckled—

No. She stopped herself, knowing that those thoughts came from her predisposition to take another's opinions and let them burrow under her skin.

Perhaps she was plump. But that didn't mean she couldn't also like the way she filled out this dress or secretly thrill over the admiring gazes she'd recently begun to notice.

She may not possess her mother's willowy grace and ethereal beauty that complemented many a parlor and ballroom. But she had never really liked stuffy assemblies anyway. She'd always preferred open, breathable spaces and was thankful to have strong limbs, well-suited for a trek across the countryside. And the truth was, she'd always liked her hair. She'd often thought of it as the rebellious part of her, refusing to be managed or constricted.

Winnifred wanted to like her terrible freckles, but perhaps that would take more time.

Though most of all, she liked the way it felt to be with Asher. To be free to explore and to discover. To touch and to tempt. To laugh and to fall in love.

Somewhere along the way—in between that first shouting match beside the carriage and the quiet moments lying in his arms—she'd fallen in love with him. And she would have bet her life on the fact that he was feeling the same way.

At least, until he frowned just now.

Then again, she didn't know much about scoundrels and knew even less about falling in love. Her future contribution to the primer was suddenly looking rather confusing and pathetic.

Through diamond panes of window glass, she saw the fading light of sunset, the orange tinged with a veil of lavender that threatened the close of day. Seeking a semblance of reassurance, she reached out just enough to let her fingers brush against his.

Asher surprised her by catching her hand and holding it tightly. He didn't let go until they reached the top of the stairs. But he was still pensive, and she still didn't understand the reason.

Then, greeted by a maid and a footman, they both went their separate ways.

ALL THE *if*s that had been spinning in Asher's head earlier finally came to a full stop. His last encounter with Mr. Lum had made everything blindingly clear. A future with Winn would never be possible unless he could protect her from his father.

He refused to put her at risk again. Therefore, he had to get on that ship and return with a fortune large enough to keep his father from causing any more chaos. It was the only way.

But how was he going to make it happen?

For more than an hour, Asher paced the length of his room and tried to find an answer, though there was hardly enough floor in the room to pace. This used to be an abbey, after all. The rooms held only a bed, wardrobe and washstand. And beyond the high, narrow window, a long seldom-traveled driveway pointed toward an uncertain future.

Looking out, he felt as though he were already in a cell, rotting away in Fleet, alone and unable to pay the debts his father had accrued in his name.

Lungs tight, he rubbed a fist over his chest. The air tasted musty and stale like the thoughts haunting him. He couldn't breathe in here.

Striding out into the corridor, he startled a maid bustling about her duties. His methodical steps echoed down a long, constricted passageway. When he'd nearly reached the end, a familiar sound drew his footfalls around a bend and down the evening-darkened archway. Like a moth seeking a source of light, he found it in the lilting melody of a bawdy tune.

A smile tugged at his lips. *Winn.* All it took was the sound of her voice and everything became clearer at once. There was only one thing that truly mattered—a chance at a new life. With her.

Asher reached the door and listened to her song, letting each note burrow inside him. He braced his hands on either side of the frame and pressed his forehead against the wood, breathing in the polish of turpentine and beeswax, and wishing their obstacles were simpler.

But they weren't.

She was still an heiress and he was still a man without a farthing to his name.

She was going to live here and he would be away for months, even years, trying to amass a fortune great enough to withstand his father's obsession.

And in addition to all that, she might not forgive him for making a bargain with her father. Even without Waldenfield here to collect his daughter, Asher needed to tell her the true reason he'd been waiting at the church that day. There was no room for deception or manipulation in the future he wanted.

During the drive, he'd rehearsed a speech in his mind a thousand times. But the words were still all wrong and he feared he would lose her. It was a gamble he couldn't risk.

So for now, he turned around and walked away.

❦❦❦

AT DINNER that evening, Winnifred wore one of Aunt Myrtle's dresses from years ago before the accident that injured her leg, when she'd still ventured into London. It was a lovely rose-colored muslin with wide gold piping around the sleeves, a low-cut bodice and a gold sash beneath her breasts.

Having grown accustomed to wearing the newer fashions, she felt practically naked in this thin gown with only a chemise and bust bodice beneath.

The servants had also laundered and pressed Asher's clothes and polished his boots. He was never more handsome, with a fresh shave that accentuated the sculpted lines of his countenance.

Sitting across the linen-draped table from him, it

was difficult not to blush at the memory of his eyes widening when he'd first seen her this evening, and then how they darkened. She knew what that hungry look meant now, and felt a corresponding flutter in her midriff.

Drawing her away from those thoughts, Aunt Myrtle asked to hear all about their adventure. Winn recounted most of it from the very beginning, leaving out the more salacious parts, of course. And her aunt cleverly avoided any question of how they'd slept during their nights together, or what they did when their clothes were wet from rain.

Winn decided not to mention the stream at all, or the loft in the boiling house. There were certain memories too precious to share.

In the warm glow of the flickering chandelier overhead, her aunt eased into the straight-backed armchair at the head of the table and turned her attention to Asher. "You must be in dire straits to have been desperate enough to resort to kidnapping. And yet, here you have an heiress so conveniently at your disposal."

Winnifred rolled her eyes. "Lord Holt would not use me in such a manner. All he ever wanted was the money he lost in order to embark on a grand opportunity, which is perfectly understandable." Especially considering what she knew about his father.

Asher stared into the wineglass in his grasp, then cleared his throat. For most of dinner and before, he'd remained pensive and withdrawn, and Winnifred worried that his journey was weighing on his mind.

Aunt Myrtle slid a glance to Asher. "And will this grand opportunity take you far away?"

"It will, indeed, madam," he said, looking from her to Winnifred. "And for how long, I cannot be certain."

"The passage of time is a burden we all must endure," Aunt Myrtle added with a flit of her fingers. "However, the pain that comes from absence can always be lessened if there is a plan in place for your return. Some men, so I'm told, would list *taking a wife* as a priority. Would you, Lord Holt?"

Winnifred might have chided her aunt for delving too deeply into personal matters. Instead, she found herself holding her tongue *and* her breath.

He set his glass down and pushed away from the table. Then, standing, he bowed. "Madam, I wonder if you would permit me to escort your niece for a walk about the grounds."

Aunt Myrtle's lips curved in a small, knowing smile. "Of course you may. I imagine you have a great deal to discuss. And since the two of you are far beyond my chaperonage at this point, I would not intrude by offering my escort. However, I should warn you that my limbs feel the approach of rain not far off and, should you venture into the singing garden where all my songbirds like to visit, mind the latch on the gate. It tends to stick."

"I should not think we'll stray far from the house," he said, then looked to Winnifred. "Miss Humphries, will you take the air with me?"

She frowned, utterly perplexed by this sudden stiff decorum.

But then a little voice in the back of her mind whispered that, perhaps, *some* conversations required a degree of formality. Speaking to the members of the royal family, for example. Or a servant about missing silver. A steward regarding the accounts. Or even . . . a gentleman who planned to ask for a woman's hand in marriage?

Her heart gave an excited leap.

Her mind warned her that the thought was far too outlandish.

Hmm . . . Whatever the reason, she was never going to discover it while sitting here at the table.

Holding his gaze, she said, "Yes, of course, my lord."

Chapter 21

Madam Humphries did not adhere to many formalities, and yet being in her company reminded Asher of society's expectations.

It was one thing to pretend to be Mr. and Mrs. Strewsbury among strangers. Yet with a member of Winn's family, it was quite a different matter.

He'd been traveling alone with Winn for three days. Her Aunt Myrtle doubtless expected a proposal of marriage to save Winn's reputation. And he found himself wishing that his life was that simple—find a girl, fall in love, obey the obligation to one's heart and marry her, then spend eternity in utter bliss raising a dozen freckled children.

He expelled a tense breath as they walked side by side past the orangery. The white stone walls gleamed in the slivers of moonlight that strained through the slender celestial paths between gathering clusters of clouds.

"I do not know how long I'll be away," he said after a lengthy silence. "It could be months, or longer."

"How much longer, do you think?"

"If the weather is optimal, the voyage there will take a month." He didn't elaborate further. In her bleak expression, he could see that she understood what might happen if the weather wasn't optimal, or if they encountered other dangers along the way.

She breathed in the cool night air, then let it slip out slowly. "This is something you must do. It has been your plan all along. And if I were to tell you that I wish you had sailed away to gain your fortune years ago instead of now, it would be terribly selfish of me."

"Then I'm glad you did not tell me," he said with a wry chuckle. "And I will not tell you that I have the same wish."

She tilted her head back to gaze heavenward and whispered, "Then why didn't you?"

He nearly smiled at the soft, petulant demand for an answer. "Aside from the fact that this opportunity had yet to present itself?"

"Yes, aside from that. After all, there must have been others."

"Likely so," he mused, thinking over the core reason he'd stayed for so long. "It may sound strange, but I never pursued any other prospect with such fervor because I was trying to honor my mother. You see, when she was still alive, she told me how men prove themselves through their loyalty and that I was on my way to becoming a fine man in that regard. I was nine and this conversation happened to coincide with the advent of a packed satchel hidden beneath my bed. You see, I'd planned to escape my father that very night after he'd wagered on, then lost, my horse in a card game."

"Do you think she knew?"

"I do," he said, remembering her fondly. "I've tried

to stay loyal to her memory for all these years. I've tolerated Father's madness. Cleaned up one catastrophe after another. And whenever I believe I've reached my breaking point and refuse to comply, he will threaten to sell something of hers, something that I'd thought was safe from his greed. Then I always find myself sinking to a new low."

She squeezed his hand and he looked down, almost startled by the contact.

Since the moment they'd stepped out into the garden, Asher and Winn had been walking at a respectable distance apart—his hands clasped behind, hers in front.

Yet without thinking at all, they'd merged closer. Their hands were now twined tightly, fingers laced, neither of them wearing gloves. And if it weren't for the manicured setting, her aunt only a length of grass and a window away, he might allow himself to imagine they were alone again, wandering the countryside and thinking of nothing more than where they would sleep curled up beside each other.

"Perhaps," Winn began, "your mother was stating that you'd already proven your loyalty. I imagine she would have wanted you to be loyal to yourself as well."

He said nothing, but let the comment drift down into his heart. She seemed to always have the words that were like a balm over a raw wound, letting him know that his course was the right one. And yet, every moment spent with her made him long for things beyond his reach.

He wished he could take her with him. Wished the

obstacles between them weren't as insurmountable as they felt.

At the end of the promenade, they turned down a narrow footpath, and Asher knew it was now or never. "Winn, there's something I have to tell you."

But his statement was drowned out by the chirrup of birdsong rising over the ivy-enshrouded wall beside them.

"The singing garden," Winn said with a pleased gasp and tugged on his hand. "Come inside for a minute? There are so many lovely trees that the birds have always come here to roost, larks and nightingales and dozens of others. I could even list their Latin names if you like, and this time it won't be because I'm out of breath." She grinned as if they were sharing a secret, and drew him farther down the path. "You'll love it in here. It sounds like a cathedral with all their calls ringing out at once. In fact, when I was just a girl visiting my aunt, I used to steal out of my bedchamber in the middle of the night and pretend this was a church, with a little altar bench situated beneath an arch of night-blooming jasmine."

"And did you leave offerings at this altar?" he asked, imagining little Winn with her wild hair and taste for adventure.

She nodded. "Ribbons and strings for the birds to weave into their nests."

"Then perhaps we should leave something before we go."

"I have part of your silk cravat tied in my hair. I think that's the only reason the combs have managed to keep my coiffure tidy for this long." She lifted her shoulders in a delicate shrug that drew his appreciation—and not for the first time—to the creamy skin and supple swells on display, taunting him.

How was a man supposed to focus on what he needed to say when his thoughts kept careening off course?

He knew the softness of her skin beneath his touch. The texture of her flesh on his tongue. The sounds she made when he drew her into his mouth.

And all at once he wasn't thinking about what he intended to say. Instead he was thinking about how good it felt to have her close to him.

The gate creaked when they crossed the threshold into the singing garden. Then, for a moment after that, there was no sound at all, just a palpable alertness from the unseen avian occupants in the trees that flanked the perimeter.

Winn held a finger to her lips, her eyes dancing as she drew him deeper inside. The air was sweetly perfumed with the array of dew-speckled flowers along the path. Most of them were slumbering with drowsy stalks, heavy-budded in clusters of dark green shadows. At the far end on a small hillock of grass sat a bench—her little altar—beneath an untamed and unmanicured arch of moon-white blossoms.

She stopped walking and slid her arms around his neck, tilting her face up for a kiss. It felt perfectly natural to pull her into his embrace, to breathe in the scent of her hair. And when he gazed down at her, standing in her girlhood chapel, he saw a clear vision of what he wanted for the rest of his life.

And yet, along with this certainty came a sense of panic, thudding in his chest, reminding him of what he stood to lose.

His hands flexed, gripping muslin, holding fast to her while the strain of the restless quiet suddenly closed in on him. Then he reached up and withdrew her hands from around his neck.

Her brow knitted in confusion and, perhaps, even hurt. "Do you not want to kiss me?"

For all the days of my life, he thought. But it would have been unfair to speak those words. They sounded too much like a promise.

"Winn, you need to understand that my father's compulsions destroyed my mother. He didn't just take her fortune when he married her. He took her soul, too. He is like a leech that senses one last drop of blood in his victim. Once he catches the scent of money, nothing is safe or too precious. Ultimately, he would destroy your life through me."

She chafed her hands over her arms. "Why are you telling me this?"

"You know why."

"If we both know, then say the words."

Frustrated, he raked a hand through his hair and turned away from the altar. "I have nothing to offer you."

"If that's true, then I want all of it. Every single ounce. Because I'm fairly certain there's love hiding inside this . . . *nothing*," she said stubbornly. "Do you deny it?"

How could he deny something that covered him like a suit of clothes, visible to everyone? Only with this, every stitch penetrated his skin, the needle digging through to the marrow of his bones. This ill-fated love was already a permanent part of him.

He faced her again, his words sharp with futility. "If I had all the bloody money in the world, I'd steal you away to Gretna Green this instant. But I don't. And I won't marry you until I do. So it's useless to imagine anything between us. You have to understand that!"

Her eyes flooded. Pale green pools stared at him in mute agony before she rushed past him and to the gate.

She jerked on the iron bars, the latch frozen just as her aunt had warned. Yet that didn't stop her. She shook them until they rattled.

He came up behind her, gripping the gate above her hands, sheltering her. She stilled, but the stuttered sounds of her anguish wrenched his heart and he rested his forehead on her shoulder. "Winn . . . please don't cry. I hate this as much as you do."

"I highly doubt your level of loathing surpasses mine," she cried, sniffing wetly. "After all, I'm trapped in the garden with a man who gives me glimpses of a wondrous future, only to strip it all away in the same breath."

"Believe me, it isn't all biscuits and cakes to be the man who cannot marry the woman he loves."

She sucked in a startled hiccup and a tremor tumbled from her body into his. "But you've been thinking about it—a life with me?"

"There are so many parts of my plan that can go awry, it wouldn't be fair to ask—"

She turned suddenly and pressed her finger to his

lips, her lashes clustered into spiky thorns from her tears. "If nothing goes to plan . . . if everything turns to chaos . . . if we both end up poor as church mice . . . I'll wait for you, Asher. I'll wait for you until the end of my days."

He held her tightly and they sagged like the stems on the path, bowing toward each other in the shadows. They belonged together. No one had ever burrowed so deeply, so completely, into his soul. He didn't even care that she was turning all his plans inside out.

Yet there was still one thing he regretted, and he had to confess it before it was too late to undo the wrong. "Winn, there's something else I need to tell you."

"Whatever it might be, it doesn't matter," she said, smiling up at him. "I love you and nothing will ever change that fact."

He kissed her lashes, tasting her salt on his tongue. Her steadfast certainty tunneled through him, filling him with hope and he eased his mouth over hers, sinking headlong into the promise of a future with her. She would be his someday. And, knowing that, he cinched his arms around her.

She clung to him, a sense of urgency in the press of their lips, the nips of their teeth, and the hungry sinuous slide of their tongues. Frantic seconds, minutes, eons passed without concern that they were leaving no air in the garden or in themselves. Even with their lungs burning and empty, they still couldn't stop. Both of them knew he would be gone tomorrow.

He drew her body flush with his, length to length, wishing that he could take her with him. He couldn't imagine being separated from her for a single day. And he didn't know if it was because he was light-headed and not thinking clearly, or if everything suddenly became clear, but a new plan started to form in his mind. Perhaps there was a way . . .

But before he could finish the thought, it began to rain. Again.

Chapter 22

$\overbrace{\qquad\qquad}$

Winnifred tipped back her head and squinted wryly at the dark sky overhead. "You were right. We will never spend a dry day together."

Asher laughed and took her hand, escaping to the shelter of the arch. Shrugging out of his coat, he settled it over her shoulders, the residual warmth inside the wool chasing out an involuntary shiver.

"Come here," he said, tugging her closer by his lapels and back into his embrace.

Even in the shadows, his body was achingly familiar, every sculpted line imprinted on her brain. His scent permeated the space around her, his skin, his shaving soap, his heat. It all made her knees quiver like a pair of isinglass jellies carried on a platter.

He shored her securely against him, his lips brushing away the tiny droplets of rain that clung to her lashes and skin, trailing down until her waiting lips were under the searing pressure of his.

She loved the way he kissed. He told her a story in those deep, tender pulls, the almost frantic growls that revealed how much he was holding back. It was the story of how they met and how they'd fallen in love with a certainty that was frightening. And how this unexpected love would link them forever, no matter if they were worlds apart.

With the rain falling around them, hitting wet leaves with the rhythm of a clock wound too tightly, too fast, she whimpered into his mouth. Time was speeding out of their control. Her aunt could send a footman to check the gate at any minute. Morning would come. He would leave.

She clung to him like the last petal on a flower. "I don't want this day to end."

He held her closer still, his hands gripping, roving down her back and over her hips in a near-desperate caress. He pulled her against him, aligning their bodies. And through the thin layers of her clothes, she could feel his hard length and her reflexive tilt to cradle him. Hear his breath hitch.

A sense of expectation filled her at the sound. She knew what it was like to be held by him, to have his body poised above hers. She wanted that again, his weight, his warmth, those deep, otherworldly kisses. She wanted his hands on her.

Reading her thoughts, his caress shifted course, moving up along the curve of her hip, the cage of her ribs, and then—*ah*—he cupped her breasts. Her nipples hardened instantly, her flesh drawing tight beneath the coaxing heat of his hand, her hips cambering with welcome, with need. He flexed, surrounding her, then grazed his thumb over the tip, drawing out a needy mewl from her throat that lifted off into the vines above them.

He did it again, a tender pinch through the damp muslin. She closed her eyes on the sweet ache that roused a heavy pulse, low in her body. And she pressed her legs together to keep it right there, nestled to his insistent thickness. But Asher had other ideas.

He lifted her in his arms and took her to the narrow bench, draping her legs over one side of his lap. She twisted to find his mouth as his hands teased down her body—waist, hips, knees and lower. Then he encircled her ankle and she squirmed, restless, searching for something to ease that throbbing ache.

Devouring her impatient, needy whimpers with his probing kiss, his hand slipped beneath her hem to follow the line of her borrowed stockings, up to those black garter ribbons, and higher, skimming over the bare flesh of her thigh. He groaned. "So soft on the outside. So strong beneath."

"And you like that, yes?" she asked on a sigh as his lips skimmed down her neck, laving the rain from her skin with the heat of his tongue.

He murmured against the swells of her breasts, just above the edge of her bodice as his hand roamed higher, over her hip and under to cup her bottom, kneading her flesh. "My mind is filled with wicked thoughts, Winn. These thighs, your stamina, bareback rides at dawn . . . for hours."

She had a sense that he wasn't talking about *horseback* riding when she felt a tremor course through him, quivering into her. A picture formed in her mind, but it dissolved away when she felt his hand coast over her hip again to her inner thigh, chasing tingles all the way to that throbbing pulse. She knew he was going to touch her. She wanted him to. But that didn't stop her shy gasp at the first tender cupping over her sex.

"Shh . . . let me touch you," he whispered against her lips and she acquiesced with a nod, seeking the pressure of his mouth, the taste of him.

He gave it to her, his tongue entering her mouth as his fingers skimmed through tawny curls, finding the seam of her sex, where she felt swollen and tender and wet. He growled, a deep, possessive sound that told her he liked this, too. And that she was his.

Her body agreed, hips slanting toward the heat of his hand, needing pressure against the insistent throb of her pulse. There were no maidenly fears that made her cautious, that wanted to demur. *"Please."*

"So impatient. So stubborn." He grinned against her mouth, chiding her with a nip. Yet even with this tender reprimand, he gave in to her demands, nudging closer, coasting over the furled flesh. "So wet."

She bucked against the slide of his finger and she turned her head, seeking his lips, taking his tongue inside her mouth as his finger centered in tight swirls, chasing the pulse. Then he entered her. A slow glide of his finger into the damp heat. A choked, desperate sound tore from his throat and he rocked against the curve of her hip.

Winnifred felt the hardness of him, the heat through his breeches. She wanted to touch him, take his flesh in her grasp while his finger plunged with sure, authoritative strokes, his palm pressing against that pulse.

She groped between them blindly as her body clenched around him, her kisses frantic.

Then he turned her at once. Now she was straddling him, hem riding high. One of his hands lifted to her nape, fusing their mouths, and the other tore at the fall front fastenings beneath her fumbling fingers. And then she felt the heat of him.

The thick, heavy jut of flesh was in her untutored, though eager, grip with him guiding her motions. Up and down. Down and up to the slick droplet resting on the full mushroomed tip like a bead of dew. Fascinated, she ran her thumb over the slickness and his breath fractured on her downward stroke.

His hands moved to her hips, to her breasts, and he tugged at her bodice, revealing her to the night, to the rain that now seemed to fall warmly on her skin. She arched back on a gasp as he took her nipples simultaneously, one in a slow roll between his thumb and forefinger and the other in his mouth, suckling and swirling.

The throbbing of her sex demanded attention, urging her to roll her hips against the broad shaft. She found the answer to ease this ache. All she had to do was this—*yes, like that*—and grind against him. Her body drew taut all over, like a corset about to erupt.

Asher lifted her and her hands flew to his shoulders for purchase. He pressed his cheek against hers, his breath hot in her ear. "Winn, put your feet on the ground. I want you in control. I don't want to hurt you. *Damn.* I'm bloody shaking again."

When she did, she felt the hard, insistent head poised at the entrance of her sex, his voice crooning, "Slowly now. Yes. Let me inside."

Now she felt a nudge, the stretch, the heat, the burn of her flesh as she sank inch by inch, encouraged by the helpless, guttural sounds he made, the almost desperate grip on her hips.

"So bloody tight, Winn." He arched his neck on a hiss, jaw clenched as he lifted her again. And on a low oath, he drove her down onto him, his hips thrusting up into the wet constriction, impaling her.

She cried out from the swift invasion, the terrible fullness, the unbearable grip of her flesh pulsing around his. And she was ready to thrash him, but it was Asher who admonished her instead. Resting his damp forehead against hers, eyes screwed shut as if in pain, he let out a series of staggered, panting breaths, and told her that she felt too good and it wasn't fair that he was so close already.

Close to what?

But he kissed her again before she could ask, his lips easing over hers in a tender caress. He was speaking to her again without words, his monologue promising love and patience. And after a moment, when she sighed and melted against him, his tongue delved into her mouth and promised rapture to her body as he began languid rotations of his hips beneath her, slick and slow.

The ache faded, but the clenching remained. Only now she welcomed the sensation, the grip, the slide. The friction brought back her throbbing pulse, more potent than before. Deep and insistent. Her body yielded to his, her hips seeking to match his gentle rocking canter.

The frenzy quickly came over her again as she clung to him, her nails biting through his shirtsleeves to his shoulders, the pebbled peaks of her breasts brushing against his waistcoat. She wanted this to go on forever. Tingles spread out beneath her skin like an unexpected storm brewing inside her.

She tugged his lip into her mouth, raking it with her teeth, and his rhythm broke on a hungry growl, his thrust driving deeper, a bump that made her gasp on a sweet lightning bolt of sensation.

He grinned against her lips on a *hmm*, then angled her hips to nudge that spot again and again, sending fierce jolts of pleasure through her. They seemed to build into one massive thundercloud. Then her breath came out on a keening cry, her fingers rending the seams of his shirt. The storm broke on an endless rain shower of warm, cascading tremors.

She hunched against him, quaking, head bowed, scalp tight, toes curling in her slippers. And then he jerked inside her and lifted her suddenly.

Taking her hand, he guided her to grip the slick heat of him, his flesh surging beneath her palm as he pumped and shuddered, silken ribbons pulsing from his body in arcs toward the grass.

He fell back onto the bench on a final, spent breath, tugging her down to drape across him. He pressed a kiss to her head, his hands roving over her back, her arms, her sides, as they listened to the birdsong fall around them.

&ploplop&

ASHER AND Winn entered the house through the back doors, holding hands and laughing at how they never spent a dry day together. When they passed the dining room, it was dark, the dishes cleared away. Even so, Myrtle Humphries was not too far, the shuffle and punctuated step of her cane echoing in the corridor.

At their approach, the sound paused and she turned

her keen gaze on their wrinkled and rain-speckled clothes.

"You were right about the gate," Winn said with a nervous laugh and a shrug.

Her aunt pinioned him in place with a knowing arch of her brows. "I trust every matter has been settled, Lord Holt?"

Absolutely and irrevocably, he thought, pressing Winn's hand closer against his palm. He'd decided with the first touch of her lips that he could never endure months, or even years, apart from her. And though he didn't yet know how he'd manage it, he was going to take her with him on that ship and marry her.

When he inclined his head, Myrtle nodded and turned again to walk away. But she called over her shoulder, "And I was right about the rain, too."

Chapter 23

Later that evening, a maid brought Winnifred a clean nightdress and helped to plait her hair. Shortly after her departure, Asher rapped on her door for a final kiss goodnight and to bid her sweet dreams.

And that was all. He'd even proved his intentions were perfectly innocent by leaving her room. Her intentions, on the other hand, hadn't been quite as pure.

She'd followed him into the corridor, dragged him back to her room—though with little resistance from her captive—and then kissed him senseless against the door.

This morning, Winnifred awakened to the press of his lips on her bare shoulder, the apricot light of approaching dawn sifting in through the open window. She smiled and rolled sleepily onto her back, thinking that their night together had been nothing like traveling in a crowded coach. At least, not one *she'd* ever hired.

Asher stole around her waist and drew her flush against the heat and hardness of him. While he nuzzled her neck, his hand drifted upward to cup her breast.

"The servants will be awake soon," she said with a giggle.

He pressed a kiss to her nose, to the place where he'd professed—last night by lamplight—to having a favorite freckle. His lips brushed hers before browsing his way down to the exposed nipple he spurred to a ripe peak. "All the more reason to make haste."

She arched back on a gasp as he drew her flesh into his mouth, the gentle suction sending a quickening straight to her womb. "Haven't you had enough of me?"

"Not possible. I need to hear you say my name once more before I start my day."

"Asher," she offered, pretending that she misunderstood. The truth was, she hadn't had enough of him either.

He shook his head, his eyes meltingly dark with sinful promise. "You have to say it properly."

"We barely slept at all and I'm"—she hesitated, blushing even after all their shared intimacies—"a little sore."

"I know," he crooned, trailing kisses over the soft rise of her middle, scandalously dipping his tongue into the hollow of her navel. "And I'm aiming to make amends straightaway. You see, there's really only one way to soothe such tender flesh. Now, just close your eyes and rest a bit, while I feast on you."

He slipped smoothly beneath the coverlet like a dark seal in water, and she felt the rasp of his morning whiskers against her inner thigh as he nudged her legs apart. She wanted him to touch her again. Her body was already taut with eager tension, like a spear of whalebone nearly bent to breaking. But what she felt over her sex was not his hand or his fingers.

It was his mouth.

She gasped, her knees jolting upward, her hands in his hair, tugging him. "You can't."

"Mmm . . ." he murmured against her with a slow lick. He wasn't budging. In fact, he splayed his hands over her bottom, cinching her higher as if she were a wedge of ripe fruit.

She was wide open to him as his tongue fanned out over her, bathing the entire length of her sex. Then he nipped her gently and narrowed his focus to the willing throb, circling with clear intent. And her fingers threaded into his hair, holding him there—*yes, there*—and he chuckled knowingly against her. The wicked man.

Winnifred never knew anything could feel like this. The warmth of his mouth. The deep, searching kiss. The slow, languid lick . . . a swirl . . . a flick . . .

Oh. Her hips hitched, a spiral of sensation rippling over her in the quickening of approaching cataclysm. And then it broke over her, her back bowing off the mattress, neck arching on his name. And she no longer cared about the servants, or the clock ticking, or even if the world were about to end. She just needed this.

She just needed him. Always.

❧❧❧

BEFORE THE servants could catch them together, Asher slipped back into his chamber. He tried to sleep, but his thoughts were too restless, still too uncertain. The only things stopping him from marrying Winn were his father and hers. And the only way to escape his own was to be completely free of her dowry.

He needed to ensure that Waldenfield would rescind it.

Dressing for the day, Asher went downstairs to write a letter. The open windows he passed carried in a cool, damp breeze of early morning and dew. From far off, he could hear the plod of horse hooves and the jangle of rigging, likely a farmer bringing milk to the abbey at this hour. And down the hall, he could hear the swish of a broom and the soft murmur of servants' voices as they began their duties.

Otherwise, all was quiet and he was glad to have a few moments more to gather his thoughts. But when he crossed the threshold of the paneled study, he stopped short.

Myrtle was waiting for him.

In the soft glow of the sunrise sifting in through the window, the older woman sitting behind the desk didn't appear menacing. Yet, there was shrewd certainty in her gaze *and* in the hand resting on the cane across the blotter.

"I thought I'd find you in need of ink and paper, Lord Holt. The early morning hours often bring clarity that is easier to spill onto a page, rather than speak face-to-face."

Understanding her meaning, he straightened. "I'm not here to write a letter to Winn and then leave her behind. I would not do that to her. She holds my heart and every last shred of my soul."

Myrtle sniffed, unconvinced. "A genuine love is proved by honorable actions."

Her matter-of-fact statement reminded him of Mr.

Champion, and Asher wondered if she, too, had experienced a love that had not been reciprocated.

"I have every intention of marrying your niece," he assured, his words punctuated by the distant rapping of the door knocker.

"Then why is there marked hesitation in your gaze that I did not see last night *after* the two of you came in from the rain, hmm?"

He shifted from one foot to the other, uncomfortable with having this conversation when he'd just left Winn's bed. *Before* everything was settled between them. "It has to do with her dowry."

In that instant, Myrtle's eyes flashed and she stood, her hand gripping the hilt of the cane.

"You misunderstand my meaning," Asher continued with haste. "The reason I came downstairs this morning is to ensure that she has absolutely no dowry to speak of. She must be fully free from the burden of her fortune. The letter I plan to write is to your brother, Lord Walden—"

A hand clamped down on his shoulder from behind and he whirled around with a start.

And there stood Lord Waldenfield in the flesh.

Chapter 24

Winnifred was still in a place of pure contentment when she drifted down the stairs later that morning, her hair tied in a queue with Asher's black cravat ribbon. Hearing his voice, she hurried her step.

The last thing she expected to find was Asher standing in the hall with her aunt *and* her father and mother.

Even from this distance, she could see thunder in her father's expression, hear raised voices.

"It wasn't my intention to deceive you—" Asher began, but Father cut him off.

"Don't take me for a fool! You've already proven your intent."

Aunt Myrtle tapped the tip of her cane on the floor. "You're not giving the boy a chance to explain."

"There is nothing to explain. I made a bargain with Viscount Holt to deliver my daughter back to me if she did, indeed, flee from her wedding. Instead this insolent, disreputable knave took her away. His reasons are patently clear."

Winnifred's steps slowed as she looked from her father's high color to Asher's sudden pallor the instant he glimpsed her approach.

"What do you mean, you *made a bargain* with him?" she asked.

Mother gasped and rushed forward to embrace her. "Oh, my dear, you had us so worried. And that note you sent . . ." She pulled back just enough to put Winnifred's face in her hands, her own eyes tired, drawn and glistening with unshed tears. "I never want to read a letter like that again. And what have you done with your hair? You look positively wild."

"I've lost most of the pins," she said absently, looking beyond her mother's shoulder. "Father?"

"Lord Holt came to me the day before your wedding to tell me about a plan he'd overheard when your friends . . ."

A cold chill sank deep into her bones as he spoke. She recalled conversations with Asher about his need to escape his own father, and of him telling her that he was ashamed of the things he'd done.

I always find myself sinking to a new low.

". . . and I trusted," her father continued darkly, "that we'd struck a gentleman's agreement. Though, in the case that I was wrong, I had an investigator close at hand. Not close enough, however."

Hands shaking, Winnifred looked to Asher. "Tell me it's not true."

But she read the answer in his hesitation, in the guilty exhale that followed.

"Winn, I didn't know you then. I only wanted to get my money back and to start a new life. I told you this much."

This much . . .

Those two words instantly made her wonder about

the rest that he hadn't told her. "And what about taking me to the jeweler?"

"After hearing your story about the necklace, I thought it wouldn't hurt to help you a little."

So he'd felt sorry for her? Strangely, his *pity* didn't make her feel any better.

"Mother, please, not now," she said as she felt the tug of her hair being plaited. Looking at Asher, she asked, "And were you still planning to deliver me to my father, then, too?"

"I was," he admitted gravely, and with a look of contrition she'd seen him employ when they'd been in the back of Mr. Champion's cart, like a mask he wore whenever the occasion suited him. "At least, until those henchmen arrived. And later, after I heard them talking at the Spotted Hen, I knew I couldn't take you home without putting you in danger."

"Which is, I presume, the moment you sent this missive," her father said as he reached into his coat pocket and withdrew a water-stained letter.

She stepped forward and took it from his grasp, skimming the contents with dismay.

Lord Waldenfield,

I regret to inform you that unforeseen circumstances have forced my errand out of London. Rest assured, however, that I will adhere to every letter of our bargain and bring the delivery safely to your sister's in Yorkshire.

Sincerely,
Holt

"*My errand . . . the delivery . . .* You wrote about me as if I were a parcel and not a person."

"I didn't want to damage your reputation by using your name should the letter fall into the wrong hands."

"Whyever should you worry? A ruined heiress would be a windfall for you after all your efforts. A ready fortune tied up with ribbons. Though I don't imagine you bargained for the journey to take so long, or the added ordeal of pretending to be my . . . friend."

"Winn, you know better. Everything has changed." He took a step forward. But her father held out an arm in front of him and Asher stayed where he was.

Standing between them, her father eyed them shrewdly. "And I said I would only pay you *if* you returned her wholly unspoiled."

Dimly, she wondered if Asher had thought of this moment. Of how he would suddenly confess that they'd been intimate in order to cement a marriage with an heiress.

Sometimes you must do whatever it takes to have the life you want, he'd once said to her. *No matter the cost.*

Her cheeks heated with hurt and fury. But her blush was likely misconstrued as maidenly shyness. "Which I am, of course. After all, what man would look at me and see anything more than a means to an end?"

"If that is the case," Father said with a nod, "then Mr. Woodbine informed me that he would still have you. But in a quiet ceremony and without a wedding breakfast. There would be no need to bring attention to the situation, after all."

"Not now, Julian," Mother said, her brow knitted with worry lines as she looked at Winnifred and tucked a curl behind her ear. When their gazes met, it was as if she could see the truth, but she didn't say anything.

Asher clenched his jaw, a muscle ticking in the corner. "Winn, I need to speak with you. In the garden."

She knew what he would say. Or rather, what he might say. He could so easily manipulate her into believing . . . well, just about anything, apparently.

And because she loved him, she wanted to give him one more chance to prove who he truly was—the Asher Holt she thought she fell in love with, or the Marquess of Shettlemane's son.

"Father, so that we can have this matter settled and out of the way, might you pay Lord Holt first? I should like to retrieve a shawl from upstairs before I go into the garden." Then she turned to Asher with almost too much hope stinging the corners of her eyes. "I'll meet you there in a moment."

She watched as his fingers curled around the thick roll of pound notes thrust into his hand before he strode outside.

While Mother and Father lingered in the foyer, arguing in hushed tones, Winnifred walked upstairs. She heard the abbreviated step of her aunt close behind.

"Your father's at it again. He did the same with me, finding a man who was willing to take pity on me after my accident but turned into a veritable scoundrel." She expelled a weighty huff. "Don't let my brother put doubt in your mind. Go out to the garden and settle this matter before it stews too long between you. Get it all out in the open. Tell him how you feel. How he has hurt you by not revealing the truth to you. Then, hear him out. There are always two sides to a coin, my dear."

Winnifred agreed with a reluctant nod and put a borrowed shawl over her shoulders.

She told herself not to despair. After all, Asher couldn't touch her the way he did, or look at her with such tender affection, if he didn't love her. Right?

Avoiding another encounter with her parents, she went down the servants' stairs and out the back way.

Yet when she walked to the garden, Asher was nowhere to be found.

She called his name, but there was no answer. She even walked to the singing garden. He wasn't there either.

Frantic, she ran back to the empty promenade, then around to the front of the house, and nearly collided with a gardener, who was picking up broken shards of a clay pot.

"Oh, forgive me," she said, her voice quavering. "Did you happen to see Lord Holt venture this way?"

"Apologies, miss, but I don't know anything about Lord Holt."

Then, she supposed, it was possible that he was still inside. Perhaps he'd been waiting for her at the bottom of the main stairs . . .

"Although I can tell you," the gardener called out as Winnifred started to walk away, "I saw a curricle heading back down the drive just a few minutes ago."

She stopped in place, weighted with dread.

All the blood and warmth drained from her in one icy deluge. And in that moment, she had the answer she never wanted.

Asher Holt was only a scoundrel, after all.

Chapter 25

Asher groaned, his head splitting. He reached up to soothe the raw, throbbing ache at the back of his skull, only to realize his hands were tied. So were his arms and legs.

Not this again.

He squinted at the cranium-shattering sunlight streaming in beneath a familiar curved black hood. The trees beside the speeding curricle were nothing but a passing green blur.

The last thing he remembered was storming toward the garden. He'd been distracted by the weight of the money in his pocket and wishing he hadn't taken it. He should have shoved it back into Waldenfield's hand. But just as he'd been about to march back inside to do that, he'd heard the crunch of steps behind him.

Caught movement out of the corner of his eye . . .

The next thing he knew, he was here on this hard, black-painted bench.

He sat up clumsily as a pair of geldings plodded the earth beneath its hooves with a deafening rumble. They might as well have been stomping directly on his skull.

What had they hit him with?

"He's awake again, Lum," a voice said from over his shoulder, riding on the boot. "But he seems a mite punch-drunk. I don't think you should've knobbed him with that clay pot. He's been in and out for hours."

Hours? Winn would believe that he'd abandoned her.

"Ah, he doesn't mind, do you, Holt? We've been down this road a time or two before," Lum said with a gravelly chuckle. Asher started to bite at the knots on his wrists. Damn, the bloody things were tight. If he managed to break free and leap out of the speeding gig without killing himself, he'd have to cut the bonds loose.

Then he remembered, he didn't have his knife anymore.

There were so many things he didn't have anymore, like his dignity. But he refused to lose Winn, too.

"Oy! Stop straining against those binds. You're only going to get yourself killed and we won't get paid."

"Then take me back to Avemore Abbey."

Behind him, the other one added, "Well, if we did go back, then we can grab the heiress, too."

"Shut it, Jamey. The marquess said that if we couldn't nab the heiress, then he'd think of another way to extort Waldenfield." Lum reached out and shoved a burly arm hard against Asher's throat. "I'm warning you one last time to stop your wriggling. We're only a couple hours away from Seabrooke's hunting lodge, where Shettlemane is waitin', and he doesn't want your face bloodied."

Asher dragged in a breath as Lum lowered his arm. He hated to imagine what his father would try next.

"Then again," Lum said with a cruel grin, "I might well tell him that I had no choice in the matter."

The last sound Asher remembered for quite a while after that was the way Lum's knuckles cracked when he made a fist.

By the time he awoke, he was no longer inside a rocking curricle, but lying on the floor in front of a blazing fire in a broad stone hearth.

Unfortunately, he was still restrained. The rope digging into the flesh of his wrists was on a short tether to the ropes around his lower legs, and he wasn't able to stand or stretch out. He could sit, at least, but his head spun with the attempt.

Even so, he wasn't too dizzy to notice the darkness of late evening enshrouding the room, the shift of the polished Hessians next to him, and the signet ring that caught the firelight as a hand thrummed lazily on the arm of the chair.

"You've sunk to a new low, Father. Surely you didn't find it necessary to accost *and* restrain me," he said, cringing at the volume of his own voice and the popping of his sore jaw, courtesy of Lum.

"You put the men on a merry chase," the marquess said with a dismissive shrug. "And commandeered their curricle. I honestly didn't know what you might do if I'd simply asked you to join me."

"I'd have told you to rot in hell."

His father's gaze dipped to the black cravat—which was admittedly a little tattered, a little *less* than before, but still served its purpose—and he sneered. "Soon enough, I'm sure. In the meantime, I plan to live in a manner fit for a man of my station. And you may just prove to be worth all the trouble you've brought me of late."

"And what about the trouble you've—"

Asher stopped himself before wasting his breath. He understood the workings of his father's mind enough to realize that he'd likely concocted a fantasy where he had all of Waldenfield's money and it was going to buy him everything he never knew he wanted until now.

"Take me back to Avemore Abbey," he said. "We'll get all this settled before you garner any grand ideas about me marrying an heiress. It isn't going to happen."

Because if Winn would even hear him out . . . *if* she forgave him . . . and *if* she agreed to marry him, then he'd beg Waldenfield to make certain that she was no longer an heiress.

A flash of irritation lit his father's eyes. "Waldenfield won't want a scandal and, with you disappearing from the abbey, he'll already start wondering whether or not you can be trusted to keep quiet. His accounts will be ripe for the plucking by the time he returns to London."

"You don't believe you have the power to blackmail a man with Lord Waldenfield's money, do you? He can pay people to keep things quiet, or even to invent an entirely different story."

"Perhaps, but that's why I plan to visit him. On your behalf, of course." With a tilt of his head and a condescending teacher-to-pupil nod, the marquess flashed a grin. "I'll offer him a bargain for keeping silent about the possibility of a child."

"That's a lie."

Those lips curved again, eyes flashing with cunning delight. Then he clucked his tongue. "Have I taught you nothing about letting your emotions get the better of you? I'm ashamed. Thought you'd tamed that *tell* when you were just a lad."

Asher schooled his features. It was like lowering an old blind over a window. Even so, it was too late.

"But you'd have been careful, I'm sure," Shettlemane continued. "Wouldn't want to take the risk of her thinking that you'd trapped her into marriage, after all. No, you'd have wanted it to *seem* like marriage was her choice."

He despised the way his father twisted everything to sound so tawdry and underhanded. "I'm not like you."

"And yet *you* were the one who kidnapped the girl in the first place. Brilliant plan. Not even I have ever ventured so low."

"Who told you I kidnapped her?" But even as he asked, he already knew the answer. *Portman.*

Asher swallowed down a rise of bile and guilt burning the back of his throat. Every decision he'd made since the beginning fell under his own moral scrutiny. And he hated himself.

"When your driver returned to London without you inside that old carriage, I had the men ask him a few questions."

In other words, they beat it out of him. "What happened to Portman?"

Shettlemane scoffed. "He'll live. But I had to sack him, of course."

"He isn't in your employ."

"Oh, but he is. In fact, your driver and all your servants are paid through the monies earned on Ashbrook Cottage land. And you happen to be looking at the new deed-holder. You see, the trustees and I recently came to a mutual understanding."

"You finally found a way to manipulate them to do your bidding," Asher accused. "What was it—a wager, a threat, or something more despicable?"

He chuckled. "It wasn't anything *I've* done. This was all your doing. When they saw the threadbare state of Ashbrook Cottage, most of the furnishings gone"—he dared to cluck his tongue—"they agreed that you're no longer fit to live there."

"They know very well who sold the furnishings. Now, what is the truth, if you even know how to speak such a foreign tongue."

"Whispers, my dear boy, about you absconding with a rich debutante, whose father has yet to invest his money in their bank. And since we're all about to be family, I said that I could scratch their backs if they scratched mine."

Asher had known what his father was capable of and yet this still came as a shocking blow. He'd thought the trustees were above reproach. That when he sailed off, Ashbrook Cottage would be waiting for his return.

But even they had a price, apparently.

Would he ever be free of Shettlemane's manipulations? Even as a child he'd known this was a never-ending struggle.

He wanted to howl with rage, curse the heavens for handing him such a worthless father. But what would that solve? Nothing. He'd tried for so long to honor his mother's memory, to be the man she'd wanted him to be. But it only kept him locked in a prison of his father's making.

. . . your mother would have wanted you to be loyal to yourself as well.

Winn's whispered words filled his mind, soothing him and taking him back to their moments in the garden. She made him see possibilities where he'd been blinded by obstacles.

She also made him realize that nothing should hold him back from the life he wanted.

"Be warned. When we get to London, I'm severing ties with you," Asher said with the cold certainty of a man who had reached the absolute limit. "Permanently. There's nothing to keep me there, or in England for that matter."

"Hollow threats." The marquess patted his pocket. "The last time you said the same to me, you were so incensed that you neglected to realize the money clip, with the winnings from your wager with Lord Berryhill, had slipped from your sleeve. I must say, this hatred of yours has been quite lucrative for me."

Stunned with pure animosity, Asher went numb, blood lumbering icily through his veins. He should have guessed it from the first moment. Should have known that his own father was more capable of robbing him than a pair of debutantes.

But now there was no escaping the damning truth. Everything terrible that had happened to Winn had been all his own fault. And Asher was going to make it right, no matter what.

Chapter 26

It was Monday morning by the time Winnifred and her parents arrived in London. Aching from the two-day journey, all she wanted to do was curl up on her bed and sleep for a year. But she'd been home for less than a quarter hour when she heard raised voices and arguing below.

An agonizingly familiar drawl rose up the stairs. "Lord Waldenfield, I implore you not to believe a word my father says."

Even though Winnifred's mind was through with Asher, her heart beat excitedly. He was here!

No, she thought, holding firm to her resolve to forget about him. He'd abandoned her. Had proven that he'd only wanted the money, after all. Not her.

And yet, that foolish organ beneath her breast wanted her to give him just one more chance. Perhaps—the *bu-bump bu-bump* suggested—he had a good reason for leaving.

Her mind harrumphed, not so willing to forgive. *Without a word? Not even a missive scrawled on a scrap of paper?*

Very true, Winnifred thought, her hand white-knuckled on the railing. She'd walked halfway down the stairs without even realizing it.

"As far as I'm concerned," her father bellowed, his voice ringing out from the direction of his study, "both of you are encouraged to leave."

"Lord Waldenfield, it is hardly in your best interest not to hear me out," another man intoned. He had the voice of a practiced actor on the stage—the kind of character who appeared effusively charming while hiding a dagger behind his back.

The marquess, she thought. After all she'd heard of him, it was as if she knew him already.

"I do not see how any matter of mine concerns you, Lord Shettlemane."

Her father usually spoke more diplomatically. However, he'd been cross for the entire duration of the journey home, glaring out the window at the country-side.

Winn had tried to keep her tears silently to herself, but they rolled down her cheeks and she'd been unable to stop them. Father had gruffly given her his handkerchief. This only made her cry in earnest because she thought about Asher's handkerchief, still tied around her shoe and hidden at the bottom of the trunk that Mother had brought to Yorkshire.

"Lord Waldenfield is correct, Father. You needn't spend another minute here," Asher said tightly. "You've taken enough already."

Lord Shettlemane chuckled. "That is precisely why I am here. To see that amends are made for what has been . . . taken."

Winnifred held her breath, the intimation clear in the sly inflection. Had Asher told his father—

No. Asher hated his father, and he would never confide in him.

"As I said to you at Avemore Abbey, I have kept to the terms of our bargain," Asher said quickly. "Your daughter is unharmed."

Unharmed? Ha! Tell that to her shredded heart. She'd been nothing more to him than a parcel to be delivered in exchange for payment.

"I fear my son is playing the gentleman for your sake." Lord Shettlemane tutted. "But you and I were once young men in our prime. And while it may be difficult for you to imagine your daughter in the hands of a renowned scoundrel, I'm afraid it will not be difficult for most of society."

"Father—"

"It only takes a whisper," Lord Shettlemane continued, ignoring the icy warning from his son. "The news of Lord Waldenfield's heiress disappearing the morning of her wedding in Viscount Holt's unfortunately identifiable carriage will link the two of them, no matter what has or has not transpired on their sojourn together."

So Shettlemane came to blackmail her father, did he? She felt the hair on the back of her neck rise and she gritted her teeth.

Wasn't it enough that she was heartbroken? No, indeed. Now she had to endure the threat of public humiliation over what she'd thought at the time had been *love*. In fact, she couldn't even bear the thought of living with her aunt any longer. Memories of her moments with Asher in the garden and in the abbey would haunt her for the rest of her life.

Her father growled. "Are you threatening to 'whisper' into the ton's ear about my daughter?"

"My lord, you've misunderstood. I am here as an ally. As such, it behooves me to tell you that, if there was a wedding announcement between them, it would help to keep society quiet, I'm sure. And a grand wedding would show everyone that your family name has no mark of disgrace upon it at all, not even in nine months' time."

A breath escaped her. Reflexively, her hand covered her middle. And yet Asher had been careful not to spill inside her. At the time, she'd assumed it was because he didn't want to bring shame on her for carrying his child before he returned from his journey and they would marry.

She never imagined he'd intended to abandon her altogether.

He'd played her for a fool. And it hurt to know that she was like so many debutantes who had fallen for a scoundrel's sweet words and passionate embraces only to be left with nothing in the end.

"And Lord Holt," her father said in an even tone that was usually accompanied by the lowering of his brows into a battle line, "is that also the reason you have come here?"

"Absolutely not!" Asher growled. "I have no desire whatsoever to marry your daughter in order to—"

"Good," she heard herself say as her foot left the bottom tread. Standing in the open doorway, she faced the man to whom she'd given her only true possessions—her heart and her body. It was a painful realization that they had not been enough for him. "I wouldn't marry you either. Not even if you paid me."

"Winn, let me finish."

"I am marrying Mr. Woodbine," she said, shocking herself if no one else. Her unexpected declaration felt like a cistern of cold water had been poured over her head. She felt the iciness of it in one swift deluge, seeping into her bones. Her teeth nearly chattered as she continued. "I've had t-time to reconsider my f-feelings and I would prefer a life with him more than anyone else."

After all, it was obvious that she was going to be manipulated into some sort of marriage, so it might as well be to Mr. Woodbine. At least with him, her heart would never suffer again because he would never possess it.

Not only that, but she could keep disgrace from her family, and immerse herself in a life so full of managing her own house and social obligations that she wouldn't have a minute to think about Asher Holt.

"No. You want to marry for love, or not at all," Asher said quietly and had the audacity to reach for her hand.

She drew back.

Her fingers trembled, prickling and aching to be in his grasp just once more. And as her gaze roved over his features, she thought she saw a bruise on his jaw. She wanted to reach out, to cup his face . . .

But those were thoughts of the woman who'd loved him, and who'd thought he'd loved her in return.

She straightened, holding on to her resolve. "I would rather be with someone who is honest about what he expects from the beginning." Then, to her father, she

added, "Running away was a mistake. I wasn't thinking or behaving like myself. *All* of my actions only fill
me with regret."

Her father stared back at her. His brow furrowed
quizzically like a man addressing a stranger who
seemed familiar but he couldn't quite recall the name.
Then, all at once, those lines eased into their usual
horizontal slashes, and he nodded succinctly.

She knew he would call upon Mr. Woodbine this
very day and make the arrangements. He would likely
add more to her dowry, as well. And she didn't care if
he did.

Winnifred was numb to everything now. She had
nothing left of herself to give.

Asher stepped in front of her, his dark gaze inviting
her to remember every moment they'd spent together.
"You're only saying this because you don't understand.
I have a plan, Winn."

"A scoundrel's plan which hinged on a payment
from my father. There is no need to pretend otherwise.
And while I appreciate your escort to my aunt's estate,
I would rather forget the entire ordeal."

"Come with me," he said, the entreaty so low that
she almost didn't believe she'd heard it. But then he
said it again, this time edged with desperation.

Her heart twisted, cracking through a layer of ice,
trying to believe that she was all he really wanted.

Her mind, however, recalled standing alone at Avemore Abbey while he drove away with a fistful of her
father's money. And her heart gave up the fight.

Without a word in response, she turned around and
walked away.

Chapter 27

"**W**inn!" Asher couldn't let her go. He had to explain everything, and without Shettlemane nearby to make it all sound so sordid and tawdry. He took to the stairs after her. "It isn't what it—"

"You've tried my patience enough," Lord Waldenfield growled as he gripped Asher's coat and dragged him back.

Still not fully recovered from Lum's blows to his head or from being tied up for the better part of two days until this morning, he struggled to find his footing and staggered.

"You're *foxed*," Waldenfield accused with disgust.

Asher shook his head in denial, ready to defend himself, but all at once, his empty stomach roiled with nausea. Gripping the bannister, he drew in a slow breath. The last thing he wanted was to keck in front of Winn's father.

Shettlemane stepped forward with his saccharine grin. "Surely you can see the proof of my words now, my lord. We can settle this matter smoothly enough, I should think."

Waldenfield was seething, a vein pulsing in his neck. "If you leave my house this instant, without another word falling from your conniving lips, then I'll send a messenger to your townhouse with £500 this very day. Take it or leave it." Then he advanced, looming over Shettlemane and forcing him to shuffle back against the wall. "However, if I hear the slightest whisper about my daughter's recent journey to Yorkshire involving anything or *anyone* other than a mere visit with her aunt, I will see that you are ruined so thoroughly that not even the lowest dregs of society will invite you to tea."

Asher didn't want to leave, but he was hardly in a position to argue his case at the moment. And Shettlemane, never one to miss an opportunity for quick money, left without another word. He even drove off, forgetting to order Mr. Lum to strong-arm Asher into the carriage as he'd done earlier.

The sleek black landau and four grays—which the marquess had purchased under Asher's name just last week—trundled away, leaving Asher alone on the pavement. Apparently, his incarceration was over. He'd served his usefulness.

Doubtless, his father was still plotting a diabolical scheme. Or perhaps, Shettlemane was simply waiting for him to cause a scandal by cajoling his way inside by any means necessary. And Asher wanted to. Humiliating her and her family, however, would hardly prove his love.

But he believed he knew a way that he could.

Turning, he cast one more look over the townhouse, hoping to spy a glimpse of Winn's face from a window. Instead, he saw Waldenfield's visage behind a parted drape, glaring murderously. A prickle of warning raced down Asher's spine.

He knew that if he stood there any longer, his chances of winning Waldenfield's favor would dwindle into dust. So he inclined his head and walked away, heading toward the Hollander twins' townhouse to put the plan he'd formed at Avemore Abbey into motion.

His friends lived a mere two streets over and around a corner. Regrettably, when Asher arrived, he was forced to demean himself once more by explaining that he didn't have the money for their voyage on Wednesday.

As he suspected, they offered to pay his passage.

"I am in your debt," he said humbly to Avery and Bates in their study. "However, I may have one more person boarding with me. That is . . . if she'll consent."

And forgive me, he thought.

"She?" Two said with a nudge to his brother. "Is this a light-o'-love who's taken your fancy?"

Asher's gaze darkened. "I am hoping to make her my wife, so mind what you say and how you say it."

One's eyes widened. "A wife? We didn't even know you were courting any prospects." Then he reached out and took Asher's hand, pumping it up and down while clapping him on the shoulder. "A wife! Surely this calls for a celebration. Ring for the housekeeper, brother. Have her see that—"

Asher pried free of the grip. "Save your congratulations until I have her hand in mine. Until then, I don't want to risk startling the Fates. I haven't asked her yet. At least, not properly."

"Well . . . tell us about her, then," Two egged on with a broad grin, chucking him in the shoulder.

But Asher shook his head, wanting to keep Winn and his hope to himself for the moment.

"What I need now is a good deal of paper and ink," he said. "I have a book to write, or part of one at least."

If Winn and her friends were writing a primer on *The Marriage Habits of the Native Aristocrat*, then perhaps offering her pages of "How a Scoundrel Falls in Love" might reclaim her heart.

One went behind the desk and stacked an entire drawerful of paper on top. "We'll assist in whatever you need. Won't we, brother?"

"It goes without saying," Two offered with a grin. Then, abruptly, his face fell. "Oh, blimey! I just thought of something."

"Thought I smelled smoke," One teased.

But Bates remained serious. "The captain's superstitious. He might not allow a woman on the ship. It's supposed to be bad luck, after all."

That was a problem. How was he supposed to take Winn with him if the captain refused to sail with . . . women . . .

Aunt Lolly, he thought at once.

Asher looked to his friends with expectation. "Fellows, might either of you have the costumes you wore to the last masquerade?"

"Do you mean the ones where we were both dressed as friars?"

"The ones with the long beards and robes?"

Asher grinned. "Precisely."

WHILE HIS friends were searching for the costumes in the garret, Asher wrote furiously. He sent off part one—"When a Scoundrel Meets His Match: And Why Drinking an Entire Pint of Rum Isn't Always a Terrible Thing"—within an hour to Winn.

By afternoon tea, he'd sent her parts two and three—"How to Tempt a Scoundrel: And Twelve Reasons a Debutante Should Never Hide Her Freckles"; and "When Mother Nature Conspires Against a Scoundrel: Wet Again."

Shortly following, he'd had a brown paper parcel containing the friar costume, a loaf of crusty bread, a wedge of cheese, and a carrot delivered to her. He hoped the first would pique her curiosity and the others would elicit fond memories, as they did for him.

Asher was in the midst of writing part four—"Confessions of a Scoundrel in Love: And Why Every Household Should Have a Singing Garden"—when a messenger arrived in the early evening.

Along with the parcel and every letter. Unopened.

There was, however, a folded missive with two words written in an elegant hand.

No more.

W. H.

Standing there, as the Hollander twins quietly shooed the messenger out the door, Asher read it a dozen or more times. But the words never altered as he hoped they would.

"Merely a bout of cold feet," Avery said with a pat on his shoulder. "She'll come around."

Bates hissed an uncertain breath between his teeth.

"Well, I hope it's a quick *bout*, because we sail the day after tomorrow. What? Why are you glaring at me, brother? It's the truth, isn't it?"

"Holt, pay no heed to that mistake at birth. All you need to do is find a way to get through to her. If only we knew her friends. What did you say their names were?"

Asher lifted his head and tucked the missive in his pocket. Winn had spoken of her friends a handful of times on their walk, but she'd always referred to them by their first names—Jane, Ellie and Prue.

He started to think back to the day he'd been hailed on the street by a pair of debutantes. "Jane," he said, and then remembered her cousin and the surname came to him. "Jane Pickerington."

"See here," Bates said, his face scrunched with thought. "I know that name. I think I even went to her home for tea one time. And it was complete madness. I never went back."

"Holt isn't asking for you to pay a call, dunderpoll. Just tell us where she lives."

A SHRED of hope carried Asher across the threshold of the large house in Paddington. The grave butler inclined his bejowled head as if Asher had been expected and escorted him to a solarium.

The air was humid inside the windowed space, a variety of potted plants in urns crowding the stone floor, and budding trees stretched to the domed ceiling overhead.

A plain, slender young woman with brown hair—whom he vaguely recognized from that evening on the pavement—stepped out from behind an array of ferns. In her gloved hands, she carried a letter and a small brown vial of indeterminate contents.

"Lord Holt, I believe we are acquainted and so we shall skip the formalities. I know why you are here."

"Forgive me, but I must disagree," he said, imagining that she thought his visit pertained to her abduction of his person, and her apology. "I am here because of—"

"Winnie," she interrupted succinctly. "I know you were the one who stole her away instead of my cousin. He was at the wrong church at the time. Nevertheless, I have vowed to despise you for whatever you have done to my dear friend. Her letter"—she paused to wave the page in her hand—"does not go into detail. However, she assured me that you are a scoundrel, a skilled manipulator, and not to be trusted. Now, because of you, she is determined to marry that dreadful Mr. Woodbine and the date has been set. And if you so much as contact her at any time before that day or even decades into the future, I will use this."

She held up the vial and he eyed it with wary suspicion.

"And what is *that*, exactly?"

"It is a mixture of all the poisons I have in my collection, along with a small amount of my experimental gunpowder, and"—she shrugged—"lavender to improve the odor."

He took in the fact that she never once twitched but stared at him fixedly. If he were playing cards against her, he could believe that she had a winning hand, and the thought sent a shudder through him.

Looking at the vial again to ensure the stopper was in place, he cleared his throat. "I understand; however, it is vital that I speak with Winn this very day. Everything depends upon it."

"Absolutely not."

Tucked underneath his arm, he carried every unopened chapter he'd sent. Now he held them out for her to take, advancing a step. "All I'm asking is for you to give these to her. Read them first if you don't trust my intentions. I love her. Every moment we're apart is airless and void. I'm suffocating without her. Please, Miss Pickerington. *Jane.* I'm begging you."

Miss Pickerington issued an exhausted sigh and lowered the vial. "You are far more cunning than she let on. There's an earnestness in your countenance and speech that invites future study into the behavior of scoundrels."

For an instant, he thought she might relent.

But then she drew in another breath and emitted a shrill whistle between an infinitesimal gap in her front teeth. "Boys! Come and play barbarians and marauders with our guest, Lord Holt."

And before Asher could even blink, he heard the stampede of at least a dozen feet. Then turning, he saw an army of boys of various heights and hair colors, all brandishing weapons from wooden swords to wooden battle axes. And they charged toward him with a war cry and—as he would soon learn—a taste for destruction.

They stripped the letters from his hands, growling

like animals, biting and ripping each page. After a quarter hour of trying to defend himself from the brood and gather the torn pieces, he gave up and limped out of the house.

There was nothing more he could do here, and he still had one last dire visit to pay tomorrow.

Chapter 28

By the following morning, Winnifred was still numb. She stared blankly at the ribbon patterns on the blue silk wallpaper in her bedchamber as Abigail cinched her laces.

Tomorrow Asher's ship would set sail. And Winnifred realized, with a small degree of surprise, that knowing he would soon be gone didn't make the emptiness inside her grow any larger. It remained the same.

Heartache wouldn't swallow her up. It would simply remain a cold, vast void inside her. For the rest of her life.

And since there was no point in delaying the inevitable marriage to Mr. Woodbine, she'd even asked her father to hurry things along. The sooner it was done, the better. And so, in two more days, she would become Mrs. Bertram Woodbine.

She was so numb that it no longer made her shudder with revulsion. Marriage to Mr. Woodbine wouldn't be the end of the world. Her world had already ended, every continent submerged in a great flood.

Winnifred's throat constricted on that thought,

and when the last button of her horrid chrome-yellow dress was fastened, she whispered, "That will be all, Abigail. Thank you."

She needed a moment alone. Unfortunately, her mother breezed in just as a meager breath shuddered out of her.

"Good morning, dear," she said with a smile that abruptly tilted downward. "Are you unwell? Are your laces too tight?"

"They are fine," she said quickly, suspecting that they were the only things holding her together. And that, perhaps, she was fooling herself for believing the void couldn't grow any larger. "Jane and Ellie are coming for tea tomorrow afternoon. Therefore, I have ample time for a shopping excursion, if you like."

Winnifred wanted to keep herself as busy as possible for the next two days. And for the rest of her life.

"I would like that very much," Mother said, coming up to her to fluff her sleeves, eyeing her critically. She pursed her lips. "After seeing you in that dress of your aunt's, I have a mind to alter a few of yours. The sleeves should not be nearly as broad, I think. As for these additional reinforcements, they are superfluous when you already have a narrow waist."

Winnifred waited a beat, anticipating a less flattering remark. When that moment passed, however, she was forced to add her own. "A waist that only *appears* narrow on a figure as plump as mine, you mean."

Mother blinked as if clueless. "Whyever would you say that?"

"Well, that is how your comments usually arrive—

something nice, followed by a harsh reality," she said wryly. "On my wedding day, for example, you gave me those lovely stockings, like your mother had given you. Then remarked on how you made certain to embroider in vertical lines for a slimming effect."

"*I* wear vertical stripes as well, for the same purpose," she said in self-defense and cupped her daughter's cheek. "You're my daughter, Winnifred. Of course I think you are lovely."

She stepped back. "I've never had that impression."

Her mother's eyes misted over and she abruptly walked to the brocaded drapes, fussing with the silver tassel tiebacks. She cleared her throat and stared out the window. "I've always been weak when it comes to criticism. When faced with my own failings, I tend to retreat and distance myself. So I suppose I thought that I was helping to build your strength, where I've never been strong. I wanted you to be braver than I have been."

"And *I* wanted to be loved for who I am."

Mother turned with a start, her face bleached white.

"But you *are* loved, and more than any child could—" Her voice broke, blue eyes flooding with tears. "I have been a terrible mother. You are my only child and I've failed in letting you know the most important thing."

Crossing the room, she clasped Winnifred's hand and whispered hoarsely, "You are loved, my dearest."

Then she rushed out of the bedchamber.

By this time, tears were stinging Winnifred's own eyes. She fought hard to blink them away, fearing that the dam inside her would break. So she concentrated on the sentiment behind her mother's speech. She let the words seep into her lungs on a stuttered breath and absorbed the truth in them.

Until now, she'd believed that Imogene Humphries wanted her daughter to be an exact replica, perfect in every way. It was astonishing to realize that she didn't see herself as perfect at all. She saw herself as flawed and weak.

Even so, Winnifred had always supposed Mother loved her, in her own way. She'd just never fully believed it until now.

"You aren't a terrible mother," she whispered to the empty room, incapable of keeping it bottled up. There was only so much these laces could hold, after all.

ON TUESDAY morning, Asher borrowed a horse from Avery Hollander and rode an hour west of London to Ashbrook Cottage.

It was time to bid farewell.

Now that Shettlemane held the deed, his first act of retaliation—once he learned Asher had actually gone away on a ship—would doubtless be to sell this house. The marquess might even believe it would bring him back.

It wouldn't. Not this time.

Before going into the house, however, Asher walked through the untamed garden his mother had so loved. She'd frequently sat beneath the old ash tree, marking the seasons from the weathered bench that still rested against the trunk.

The gray branches overhead only hosted clusters of dark buds. But soon they would burst with vibrant purple flowers, followed by a canopy of silver-green leaves that rustled in soft summer winds, turning crisp and red-gold in autumn. Then, in late winter and early spring, the ash-keys would litter the path.

Picking up one of the winged seeds at his feet, he held it in his hand, recalling the laughing moments when they'd collected them like coins from a treasure chest, before tossing them into the wind.

She'd once told him that she'd been sitting in this very spot, with a hand splayed over her swollen womb, when she heard the tree tell her that her child's name should be Asher.

He sat there now and lingered on the cold stone for most of the morning, remembering the soft sound of her voice and the way her brown hair had always smelled of tea with milk and honey.

"Goodbye, Mother," he whispered, his throat constricting as he let the ash-key fall.

A breeze ruffled his hair and chilled the moisture gathering in his eyes. Then he stood and left the garden without looking back.

Heavyhearted, he entered the white stone cottage. Aware that he intended to leave for an extended time, the servants had already covered the few remaining furnishings and chandeliers in sheets.

He gathered the small staff in the kitchen and told them that his father had finally schemed the deed from the trustees and Asher would no longer be able to guarantee their positions. As expected, there was weeping and railing, especially from those who'd lived here during his mother's time. He promised fine letters of reference. Then, after sharing tea and bread with each of them, he went upstairs to his bedchamber.

A short time later, Asher cinched the worn leather straps closed on a pair of aged valises, before shaking his valet's hand. "Mr. Lejeune, I'm grateful for all your years of service, but I hope you know you've been more than a valet to me. I remember every scolding you ever gave me when I'd come home from university, full of piss and vinegar. And to tell you the truth, I don't think I'd be half the man I am if not for you."

The older man's droopy basset hound eyes watered and he sniffed. "My lord, it has been a great pleasure watching you grow from a lad. Most of us have only stayed on to watch over you. And with that said"—he walked over to the console by the door and withdrew a parcel—"the rest of us have put a few things together to take with you on your journey. Mrs. Flemming embroidered fresh handkerchiefs. Mrs. Hervey baked your favorite biscuits. And Mr. Wey and I put together a few coins. It isn't much, but we all wanted to send your lordship off properly."

Touched and mildly embarrassed, Asher felt tears prickle the corners of his eyes as he weighed the package thoughtfully. "It should be I who gives a gift to each of you."

"We know that your lordship has done his best for us, more than anyone else would have done under the circumstances. And if it isn't too much to ask, we'd be much obliged if your lordship would write to us every now and again."

"I'll write you so often that you'll be sick to death of hearing about my travels across the sea."

With another sniff, the valet mopped at his considerable nose with an embroidered handkerchief and then managed a smile and nod. "I should like that, my lord."

"What's all this blubbering?" his father asked, making a sudden—but not wholly unexpected—appearance. He'd likely come to gloat and threaten.

"I already told you, Father," Asher answered as Mr. Lejeune slipped out the door. "I'm cutting you out of my life. I'm leaving. And this time, you won't be able to send any henchmen after me to clean up your messes."

Without turning around, he carefully packed the parcel inside one valise. There was nothing else in this room that truly belonged to him, or that wouldn't be sold during another obsessive episode.

The only thing he wished to have was the certainty that Winn would wait for him. And that, no matter what happened—whether he found the treasure or only sand—he would have a life with her.

But because of his father's interference, that dream was now over, too.

"You're not going to leave," the marquess said with a laugh. "Then I'd have no choice but to sell this cottage." When that earned no response, he went on, firing off threats one after the other. "But before I do, I'll have that old tree in the garden cut down. Oh, those logs will make a grand fire, too. And then I'll sack all the servants. Most of them are too decrepit to find another post. And it'll all be your fault, my boy. Every bit of it."

Asher expelled a weary breath, his shoulders heavy as a yoke. Taking hold of both valises, he turned and walked past Shettlemane without another word. He was finally done with it all.

There was nothing left for his father to take.

Chapter 29

B y evening, Asher was determined to leave London behind and forge ahead with a new life. At least, that's what he told the Hollander twins.

In the forefront of his mind, however, he could only think about Winn. Those infernal *if*s had been swirling inside his skull and leaving him with the lingering thought that, should he go to her one last time, it might make a difference.

Picking up his hat, he passed the twins on the way out.

"Well done, Holt. We've just come to fetch you for a proper send-off celebration," Bates said with a waggle of his brows in the lamplight. "A night of merriment awaits us in the fine company of a few opera dancers."

Avery, on the other hand, said, "I don't think he's leaving with us," and released a lengthy sigh. "You're going to her again, aren't you?"

"I'm likely beating my own head against a rock, but I have to try." And without another word, Asher sprinted away, leaving them to celebrate without him.

He was out of breath by the time he reached Winn's house. After a robust rap on the knocker, the butler opened the door and eyed him warily.

"Lord Holt, I cannot allow you admittance."

"Is it that blasted Holt, again?" Waldenfield barked from within, then marched across the foyer and filled the doorway like a blockade. To the butler, he said, "I'll handle this."

Then he stepped outside, closed the door behind him and crossed his arms. "Let us be done with this once and for all. I'll even hear you out, if you like. So, tell me, what are your intentions toward my daughter?"

Asher straightened and offered the complete truth without varnish. "I want to marry her, my lord. I want you to rescind her dowry. And I want to take her away with me on a ship that sails tomorrow morning."

His wiry red brows arched in amusement. "Is that all?"

"It is not a jest. I am in earnest."

"Very well, then," he said wryly. "What are you offering my daughter, a life of uncertainty? A promise of flitting off whenever a whim takes your fancy?"

He thought about the coin in his pocket from the servants. "At the moment, I have next to nothing. At least, nothing more than love to offer her, and a promise to give her the happiest life she could imagine."

Waldenfield's mouth tightened. "Did it ever occur to you that my daughter *wants* to marry Mr. Woodbine? He will make her a duchess one day, after all. And she will have a fine house and a life that will allow her to hold her head high in society."

"A life from which she ran away. She never cared about becoming a duchess. All Winn wanted was to please you and her mother, and try to live up to impossible standards."

"Mind the ground where you tread, young man," Waldenfield warned darkly.

"Forgive me, my lord. It's just that I know how difficult it is to live in the shadow of a parent who constantly demands more than any person can be expected to give." Asher stood tall, straightening his shoulders, and looked him in the eye. "Winn deserves to be loved for who she is and I can give her that."

Waldenfield scoffed, studying him with hard scrutiny. "You're one of those romantics, with your head full of poetic delusions. Permit me to be crystal clear, Lord Holt. My daughter is not pining for you. In fact, she is so eager to marry Mr. Woodbine that she insisted the wedding be done with utmost haste. The date is set for the day after tomorrow."

Asher winced as though he'd been struck. He certainly felt the sting of the blow.

But Waldenfield wasn't through delivering his beating. "My daughter hasn't mentioned your name once since you left. And in case you aren't aware, it was her decision to have your letters returned at the door, not mine."

This, Asher knew too well, had been his last chance.

Swallowing down the bitter truth, he inclined his head. "I am grateful for your candor, my lord. I shall be away for an indeterminate amount of time, and so I wish you and your family all the felicities that one can possess in life. I will not trespass again."

❧❦❧

THAT EVENING after dinner, Winnifred stopped by her father's study to bid him good-night.

When she pressed a kiss to his cheek, he looked at the clock on the mantel and frowned. "So early? It's not quite eleven."

"Merely tired from a long day. I don't have mother's stamina for shopping," she said, offering him the same excuse she'd given to Mother when she'd left the parlor a moment ago.

Though, in all honesty, the excursion had only been a jaunt to the milliner's, where her mother had spent far too much time praising how well Winnifred wore a hat—without once mentioning that it effectively hid her unruly curls—and then to the draper's to discuss the importance of the perfectly upholstered chair.

She turned to leave, when her father suddenly spoke, stopping her.

"You don't sing any longer."

"I will, if you like," she said reflexively but secretly hoped he would not ask it of her.

The very thought of singing made her lungs feel tight, close to suffocation. She pressed a hand to her middle and drew in a breath before she faced him, forcing a smile in place. At least, she hoped it was a smile. Contentment was a disguise that fit about as comfortably as a steel corset with an iron busk.

Thankfully, he shook his head. "I used to hear you humming to yourself or singing oftentimes throughout the day. I suppose I noticed how quiet it has been these past days."

"Perhaps you need to send Mother on an excursion for a music box."

"Perhaps," he said with a sardonic curl to his lips. Then he looked at her intently, his mouth in a grim line. "This wedding business is on my mind, as it is doubtless on yours."

She offered a nod but said nothing.

"I want what's best for you, Winnifred. I hope you know that."

"I do," she said, and meant it. She understood better now that her parents were flawed creatures, just like everyone else. And she appreciated that they tried to do the best they could. "You'll be glad to know that there won't be any running away this time. I've come to terms with my marriage to Mr. Woodbine. With him there will be nothing to speculate over. No unwelcome surprises waiting to spring out at any moment. I know precisely what I am to him and he will never be capable of fooling me into believing otherwise."

His frown deepened. "Is that what Holt—"

"Please, Father, don't say his name," she said in a rush.

She tried to smile afterward, to stand tall. But she was suddenly too exhausted, and especially tired of how her parents were always looking at her as if she were about to dissolve into a puddle at any moment.

She said nothing more as she excused herself from the room. But in the corridor, she pressed her back against the wall and tried to catch her breath.

Then, when she was alone in her bedchamber, she let her false smile fall. She was fairly certain no one knew that part of her died a little more every day. No one knew she clutched her pillow to bury the desperate sobs choking her.

She tried not to think of Asher Holt, or how she'd once felt priceless and beautiful in his arms. She tried to ignore the suffocating agony of losing a love that she never truly had in the first place.

But every night, her pillow and her heart knew the truth.

It had all been a lie.

⋘⋙

IMOGENE WALKED into his study that evening, charging forward in a rustle of silvery-blue taffeta, and stopped on the other side of Julian's desk. She set her hands on the graceful flare of her hips and expelled a huff to gain his attention.

As if she imagined he wasn't aware of her every moment of every day.

"Well, Julian? Did you see Winnifred at dinner?"

He casually lifted the first page from the wedding contract and turned it upside down beside the stack. "Of course, we were all at the same table."

"You're so stubborn and single-minded that you never see what's truly important. But surely, even *you* have to realize that she's in love with Viscount Holt."

Yes, he did. He'd seen it in her face with such stark clarity that it was almost as if he'd been looking into a mirror. He wanted to save her from the pain that would come from loving someone too much. After all, he knew too well that love was like a plague on some hearts, slowly devouring and destroying.

When Holt had come here this evening and boldly told him that he could offer Winnifred nothing but love, Julian feared that her fate would be similar to his own. After all, he'd once married for love.

He would rather see his daughter strong and self-assured in her position in society than be crippled by a romantic heart.

Julian stood and straightened his waistcoat, walking around his desk to face the wife who'd unknowingly brought him to his knees too many times to count.

"Imogene, our daughter is going to be a duchess. As her father, it is up to me to ensure that she has everything. Winnifred deserves . . ." He cleared his throat and said, "All the things I never had the chance to give our other children."

They grew still, staring at each other, the air quiet aside from the barest crackle of embers from the hearth. The faint tick of the clock on the mantel.

"This isn't about her becoming a duchess, is it?"

"Winnifred is all I have."

Imogene flinched. Lines drew taut above the bridge of her delicate nose, breaking through the typically flawless perfection of her face. "Don't forget about your countess."

"She is a friend, a dear friend, and nothing more. After you and I lost our last son"—he paused when her breath hitched, feeling the tightness of it in his own lungs—"you withdrew from me. You didn't even look at me, let alone speak to me, and I needed someone to confide in."

"I needed someone, too. I was in agony."

"I know," he said quietly. "And I blamed myself for it every single moment of every day."

She stared at him in confusion, eyes wide. "But I thought . . . you blamed me. That I had failed you as a wife."

He shook his head and took a step toward the barrier

between them. "I was certain it was my fault. It was as though the Fates had decided that one man could not have it all. That he had to endure unendurable pain to deserve what he'd already been given. And because of my selfish desire to have wealth, happiness, *and* a house filled with our children, I might have lost everything."

Imogene took a step forward, too, anger and anguish in the flash of her eyes. "You could have told me your fears instead of distancing yourself from me. *I* am your wife, after all. The countess is not." She poked him in the pocket. "'For Julian, and the love that was lost but can always be rekindled . . . if you but speak the word. Your countess.' Explain that!"

"Don't you understand? That engraving is about you and I. Yet, I knew that if we had consoled each other, you'd have been carrying my child again before your body and heart had healed. I couldn't risk it. I couldn't risk losing you." On the admission, he uncurled the fists at his sides and reached out for her, cupping his hands over the slender curve of her shoulders and feeling a tremor roll through her. "I'd rather there be coldness between us as we pass in the halls than never pass you in the hall again."

"You stupid, stubborn man," she said, swatting at his chest, tears glistening in her eyes. "I hate you."

He dared to draw her into his arms. A rush of pure joy shuddered through him when her body yielded against his in an achingly familiar embrace. "I know."

Her cheek rested above the hopeful beating of his heart. "'. . . if you but speak the word.' What *is* that word, Julian?"

"Genie," he said softly. It was the name he'd called her so long ago, back when pulling her into his embrace hadn't been such a hard-fought battle.

A sudden sob wracked her body. She clung to him, crying in his arms as he pressed kisses over her hair, her temple, her cheeks.

Then finally, after so many years of wanting, he eased his mouth over hers.

Chapter 30

Before dawn the following morning, Winnifred jolted awake, gasping for air. She'd had a terrible nightmare of being suffocated by a stack of one hundred thousand coin-filled pillows that reached to the clouds, and Mr. Woodbine sitting on the very top with Lady Stanton.

She couldn't breathe, even without wearing a corset. Standing, she crossed her bedchamber to open the sash, but the cool air did nothing to ease her tremors and anxiety. Her wedding was tomorrow and every time she thought of it, she felt ill.

Usually, she could calm herself with the knowledge that this wouldn't be a typical marriage. Mr. Woodbine wanted nothing to do with her. She would be free to live her life, unmolested by her husband.

At least, *after* the first obligatory night.

She gripped the sill and put her head outside, taking in big gulps of fetid air. Here she was on the precipice of selling herself in marriage to a man she did not—and would not ever—love, and she didn't even know how much the odious man stood to gain.

How many holidays would he take with Lady Stanton? How many jewels would he buy her with Winnifred's dowry?

She told herself that it didn't matter. This wedding would happen regardless. And yet . . . she had a pressing need to know how much she was worth.

There was one way to find out.

After another steadying inhale of the dewy morning air, she snatched her dressing gown from the foot of the bed and swept downstairs to her father's study.

She didn't know precisely where she would find her wedding contract, but she knew it had to be in one of his desk drawers. Proof of that seemed to be in the scrawled note resting on his blotter: *Mr. Woodbine, eleven o'clock.*

Splendid. It seemed her nightmare would arrive this morning.

And this morning Asher is sailing away, her brain reminded her, needlessly. Both she and her shredded heart knew very well that he was leaving today. That she likely would never see him again unless by chance at some distant point in the future.

It would be years after his return from making his fortune. They might pass on the street without even knowing it. Sit across from each other at a dinner party as if strangers . . .

Winnifred clutched the front of her dressing gown, pressing a fist to the burning ache and emptiness threatening to spill out. Then she forced herself not to think about *that* future, but to focus on the more immediate one instead.

She rifled through one side of the desk, frantically searching. It yielded nothing, and so she moved on to the other side.

In the top drawer, she found another stack of ledgers, a handkerchief and a book of poetry. She found the last object quite peculiar, considering the desk belonged to the least romantic-minded man to ever walk the earth. Putting that incongruity aside for the moment, she replaced each item as she'd found it.

Yet when she reached for the wrinkled handkerchief, the fold slipping open in her grasp, she realized it wasn't what she thought at all.

It was her letter.

The paper had turned soft and cloth-like, the ink barely visible. The salutation and the first paragraph had all but disappeared. The second paragraph, however, was still clear as if freshly penned. Then again, she recalled feeling the words with utmost vehemence, so perhaps she'd given them additional ink.

> *I am my own person. I have my own mind and my own beating heart that cannot be owned by you or any man. I deserve more than to be handed over like a sack of money. So I must away for my own sake.*

A tear dropped from her lashes, bleeding into the page with tiny thistle-like lines. And suddenly she knew—*again*—that she could not marry Mr. Woodbine.

Yet, after insisting that she'd changed her mind and having Father make all the arrangements, she couldn't simply bow out. And she was nearly positive that there would be no way to run out on this wedding.

"You stupid, foolish creature," she said to herself. "You're in a veritable pickle now."

Winnifred laid the letter inside Father's desk and

closed the drawer. Then, slipping back upstairs, she began to pace the floor of her bedchamber.

How could a person call off a wedding without actually being the one to call it off?

Well, obviously, it would have to be Mr. Woodbine. And yet he'd proven to be all too eager for her fortune, even willing to marry *the cow*, as he'd so poetically put it.

Hmm. She thrummed her fingers together, thinking. Her stomach churned riotously, burning the underside of her heart, as if she were on the precipice of life imprisonment. Or worse . . . the gallows. She could practically feel the noose around her neck. For a stay of execution, some women had been known to plead their bellies. If only she . . .

She stopped on a gasp.

Yes! That might do the trick. After all, Woodbine would hardly want to marry a woman if she was carrying another man's child. Which she wasn't. Or, at least, she *believed* she wasn't.

She splayed her hand over her midriff, wishing she'd never fallen in love with Asher. Wishing she didn't love him still.

Pinpricks of tears stung her eyes, blurring the walls of her bedchamber. Dimly, she wondered if she would carry this heartache with her for the rest of her life, like a broken limb that had healed but was left misshapen and without function.

A maid tapped on the door and came inside to sweep the ash from the hearth and light the fire, and Winnifred rushed to the washstand to splash water on her face, pretending she wasn't crying. She knew how servants would gossip and didn't want word traveling back to her parents.

"Thank you, Millie," she said to the maid. "Would you please send Abigail up after she's breakfasted with the others? I should like to get dressed, for I am anticipating a call this morning."

"Very good, miss."

As soon as the door closed, she blotted her face with a flannel and eyed the tufted pillow on the stool in front of her vanity table. *Hmm.*

⚬⚬⚬

THAT MORNING, Asher and Avery helped Bates stagger drunkenly into the carriage waiting outside their townhouse.

"Come on, you big lump," Avery said, rolling his brother onto the tufted velvet bench.

"I think I'm in love," Bates slurred, his hat tumbling to the floor. "Prettiest opera dancer I've ever clapped eyes on. Hers were green, you know. Green and so very pretty. And she could sing like a lark. Holt, you should have joined us. Did I tell you her eyes were green?"

Asher turned away, his mind picturing peridot green surrounded by cinnamon bands, his memory hearing the voice of an angel, and his heart ripped into shreds.

He looked skyward as if for a bolt of lightning to put him out of his misery. But the sky was clear and cloudless.

The perfect day for sailing.

Yet when he thought about stepping onto the ship a few minutes from now, his stomach roiled in protest, even though he hadn't imbibed in a single drop last night. He was as sober as the grave. After leaving Waldenfield's, he'd returned here, packed his two satchels, and waited for the dawn.

He was ready to leave London behind. It couldn't happen soon enough. The last thing he needed was another reminder of Winn and all that he'd lost.

"Lord Holt!"

At the sound of his name, he turned to see the familiar face of his driver, or at least the parts that weren't covered in yellowing bruises. And he was walking with a limp, as well—Lum's handiwork, no doubt.

"Portman! I'm so glad to see you," he said honestly, striding along the pavement to shake his hand.

The driver doffed his weathered hat, eyes downcast. "I canna tell you how sorry I am for leaving you that day, my lord."

Asher felt a twinge in the center of his chest, but shook his head. "Think nothing of it."

"But that's why I'm here, my lord. It's pressing on my very soul. I need to explain what made me do it. I just canna live with myself if you sailed away thinking the worst of me."

From the carriage he heard Bates singing off-key, and then Avery leaned out the open door. "Holt, I hate to interrupt, but we mustn't delay."

Asher looked at Portman's troubled countenance and knew he couldn't leave him like this. Turning to Avery, he said, "Go on ahead. I'll take a hackney in a minute and meet you there."

The conversation didn't take long. After a handful of reassurances that he had no intention of putting

Portman in irons, Asher bade him to leave those memories in the past where they belonged.

Unfortunately, the instant before he rode away in the hackney, Portman slipped something through the open door that was more tangible than a mere memory that might dissolve away in time.

"Just so you know, I was never gonna keep it," Portman called out as the carriage jolted into motion.

Asher looked down and expelled an oath. It was Winn's missing pearl necklace. What the devil was he supposed to do with this now?

He slipped the pearls into his pocket and vowed to put them out of his mind until he could find an errand boy.

Then he arrived at the docks. Yet, he didn't expect to see the Hollander twins standing about with their trunks piled beside them. "Why have you not boarded the ship?"

"It seems that our ship"—One turned to point toward a vessel off in the distance—"set sail without us."

Asher absently patted his waistcoat for the watch he did not have. It couldn't be too late. He'd spent a mere five minutes with Portman. "Surely the captain couldn't leave without those who hired him and his crew."

"We were equally mystified," Two said, seemingly sober as he took a step toward Asher and offered an envelope. "Then we were approached by your father's driver and given this."

"My father? What does Shettlemane have to do with this?" Alarm and dread riffled through his blood in hot and cold waves as he cracked the seal and skimmed the letter. Then his shoulders slumped in defeat.

He staggered brokenly over to the trunks, sinking down on one of them.

"'My dear foolish boy,'" Asher read aloud. "'I am proud to say that you played an excellent hand. You have learned well. I never would have suspected that you could keep such a prize hidden—so well and for so long—from the man who taught you all he knows. In fact, I do believe you might have been on this very ship before I knew anything about the treasure. Which surely would have happened, if it wasn't for the drunken boasting from one of your acquaintances to Lady Clarksdale. I cannot recall which of the brothers it was"—Asher paused to spear Bates Hollander with the same look his brother was giving him—"but you should warn him about being more discreet in the future. After all, one never knows whose interested ears might not dismiss such a fable as Lady Clarksdale had done.'"

Avery thunked Bates on the back of the head. "You idiot!"

"'It was doubly fortunate for me,'" Asher continued, "'that the ship's captain you hired was an acquaintance of mine years ago when I'd served my duty in the Royal Navy. After that, it was a simple matter of bartering and coming to an agreement of how we will split the treasure. Quite the boon for me, I should say.

"'However, because of your clever deception and clear need for one more lesson from your father, I put the sale of Ashbrook Cottage in the hands of my solicitor. Think of that the next time you don one of your blasted black cravats. Additionally, I have informed my steward that if you so much as set your foot anywhere near the threshold, every servant will lose their post.' Signed with a flourish, 'The Marquess of Shettlemane. P.S., Seabrooke still expects to collect £2,000 from you.'"

Asher let the letter fall out of his hands and simply sat there, staring out toward London with the bitter, briny scent of the sea permeating every breath.

He truly had nothing left now. Not even hope.

Chapter 31

It was nearly half past ten when Winnifred was informed that she had a caller. What a day for Mr. Woodbine to be early! Her maid had only just finished dressing her hair with silver combs to match her slate-gray dress—a stark color for a desperate purpose.

"Might I have a moment, Abigail?" Winnifred asked with quiet reserve, while inside, her pulse was rabbiting. She wondered if she was going to get away with her deception. And yet, she had to. Mr. Woodbine must call off their marriage!

Resolved, she grabbed the tufted pillow as soon as her maid left and then stuffed it up her dress, nearly rending the seams at her waist in the process.

Downstairs at the parlor door, she noticed that the evidence of her *child* was sliding gradually toward her hip. She made a hasty, wriggling adjustment. Then, after drawing a calming breath, she walked into the room.

"Good day, Mr. Woo—"

She stopped, shocked to see the dark-haired figure standing across the room.

It wasn't Mr. Woodbine at all.

Asher Holt turned away from the window. But it couldn't have been him. She knew he was gone. Had sailed away and out of her life forever.

For a moment, he simply stared back at her, with those cinder-dark eyes. His hands were curled at his sides, tension in the lines of his tailored dove-gray coat.

The two of them might have been a matching set of figurines. And like a porcelain statuette, she wasn't breathing. Her heart had stopped as well.

It became quite obvious that she'd died in that moment—either from shock or heartache, she wasn't sure.

"Winn," he said in a low greeting.

Her heart started up again. She tried to take in a deep breath, but she was back to busks and tight laces. "Asher . . . or, rather . . . Lord Holt. I thought you were on a ship."

"Clearly, I am not." He didn't elaborate, but reached into his coat and withdrew a slender parcel wrapped in brown paper. "I thought you should have this."

She wondered what it could be. A gift in hopes of reconciliation?

But he didn't hand it to her. He only moved half the distance between them and laid the object on the oval table in front of the settee. "After being barred from entering these past days, I never imagined I would be ushered inside this morning. Otherwise I wouldn't have wrapped it."

The icy hardness in his tone enveloped her as she took the steps toward the table. Not here to reconcile, then. He was obviously angry, which irritated her. Of the two of them, she had far greater right to every hard-hearted emotion.

It was too easy to remember how he'd curled his fingers around her father's money.

Picking up the parcel, she unwrapped it stiffly to find the last thing she expected. A four-strand pearl necklace.

"Portman delivered that to me this morning," Asher said evenly. "He apologized profusely for abandoning us, and said he would have brought it sooner, but his wife had their child and he has been distracted and sleepless. Additionally, he also believed I was prepared to have him taken away in irons."

This necklace wasn't even on the list of her top two thousand worries, and the day it went missing seemed like a lifetime ago. "I hope you left him with peace of mind."

Asher nodded. "I told him that there was nothing to fear, and that we'd fared well enough on our own."

She averted her face to hide the warm flush rising to her cheeks. "Was it a boy or a girl?"

"A girl. Lucy."

"That's lovely," she said, their conversation falling into some strange sort of stiltedness. "And . . . she is healthy?"

Again he nodded, and glanced to the door.

A torrent of anxiety filled her, knowing that he would leave now. And she should want him to go. After all, it had only been about money for him. From the very beginning to the bitter end.

She stared down at the horrid necklace, choking it in her grip.

"And here I'd thought you'd be happy to have those," he said, his tone provoking. "Especially considering your sudden change of heart. Such a changeable thing, it is."

The stiltedness was abruptly replaced with a fresh surge of fury and hurt. How dare he pretend that his actions had nothing to do with hers!

She shook the necklace at him. "He called me a cow when he sent these. There was a card to Lady Stanton and in it he . . . referred to me as a cow."

"And yet you're marrying him."

"At least he *wants* to. I'd rather have that than a man who proclaims to my father that he has *no desire whatsoever to marry* me. Just think, you might have had a fortune within your grasp had you lied to him the way you'd done to me."

She threw the necklace at him.

And it would have been glorious . . . *if* it hadn't slammed down directly on the floor in front of her. Damnable dress, she could hardly move in it.

"For your information, I was attempting to stop my father from blackmailing yours, and from orchestrating a grand coup to tell the ton that he was about to be vulgarly rich through association. I didn't want you or your family to be used in that manner."

"Ha! That is a fine thing for you to say. Tell me, how did you spend the money my father paid you? Because I thought it was supposed to earn your passage to a life free from your father's influence. But that must have been *another* lie you told me."

"For your information, I was planning to shove that money back into your father's hand, until I was clubbed over the head near the garden. By the time I came to, I was hours away from Avemore Abbey and being driven by those henchmen to my father, who—at some point while I was unconscious—picked my pockets clean. So *ha* back to you." He raked a hand through his hair, seething. "I lost everything that day, while you gained yourself a husband, who'll grant all your little heiress wishes by making you a duchess one day."

Her heart stopped beating. Her fury evaporated on a single, winged breath. "So, you . . . didn't leave me by choice?"

"I tried to tell you but you were too stubborn to listen. I wanted to explain everything and beg you to forgive me, but now"—he shook his head—"it's too late. You are planning a grand future that I can never give you."

At once, hot tears streamed down her face in great soggy runnels. A shuddering sob broke free. And the stupid part was, she wasn't sure if she was desolate or overjoyed.

Asher came back to her on a sigh and closed the distance between them to mere inches. Withdrawing a handkerchief from the inside of his coat, he proceeded to dry her cheeks in tender passes. "Shh . . . don't cry, Winn. Your tears are cutting through your face powder and your freckles are showing."

"They aren't my freckles," she said with a sniff, drawing in his familiar scent.

A corner of his mouth curled. "Of course they're yours. They're on your face. Who else would they—"

He broke off and his eyes met hers.

"I gave them to you, remember?"

"I do," he said, using the pads of his thumbs now

instead of the handkerchief. He cupped her face, tilting it up, and his gaze drifted to her mouth . . .

But then he withdrew abruptly and paced back to the opposite side of the room. Briefly, she touched her lips, her fingers trembling. She lowered her hand before he turned to face her, the table between them once again.

"Oh, and by the by, your friends never took the money in the first place. It was Shettlemane all along."

Of course she'd known her friends weren't guilty, but had no desire to gloat over him. Not when she knew how much the discovery must have wounded him.

"It's understandable that you wanted to believe it was someone other than your father."

He shrugged. "Regardless, with ample years of proof, I should have known better. He even managed to manipulate the trustees into giving over the deed to Ashbrook Cottage. And now he's put it up for sale."

"No!" She gasped, and moved forward without thinking. "Oh, Asher, I'm so sorry."

"It was only a matter of . . . time . . ." He frowned, his gaze drifting lower over her form.

With a start, she realized the pillow was slipping. She groped for it futilely. Then it fell down to the floor. Embarrassed beyond belief, she kept it hidden beneath her skirts, standing stock-still.

"What was that?"

She was sure her cheeks would catch fire. *Drat!* "I thought you were Mr. Woodbine, and I was going to claim that I'm with child so he would call off the wedding."

Those dark eyes scalded her, his jaw clenched. Bending down, he stripped away the pillow from beneath her hem, and held it in his fist. "By pretending a pillow is *my* child? To escape a wedding that you shouldn't be having in the first place?"

"Well, the way you say it, the plan sounds rather foolish."

"Why, Winn?" He took her by the shoulders, forcing her back one step, then two, then three. "You said you wanted to marry him more than anyone else."

"I was angry at the time."

"So you were going to marry him just to hurt me? To put me in utter agony?"

"No," she said, hiking her chin with self-righteous indignation. "I was heartbroken. You're as much to blame as I."

His teeth clenched. "Then why not marry him and complete my torment?"

"Because I love *you*, damn it all!"

Asher crushed his mouth to hers, hungry and fierce. All the tension, anger and heartache gathered like a storm cloud, crackling with lightning. Then it transformed into a sudden torrent of heat and feral desperation.

She twined her arms around his neck. He lifted her against him, hands splayed over her bottom, gripping. *Yes!* An exultant sigh left her, rejoicing in their reunion.

"I never wanted your dowry," he growled, walking with her toward the parlor door, sealing them inside with a hard click of the latch. "I only wanted you."

She whimpered into his mouth, her body aching for his touch, legs snaking around his waist. These days had been the most desolate of her life. "I thought you'd left me."

"And I thought I'd lost you."

"Never. Not till the end of my days. Not even then," she promised, kissing and molding herself against him, needing more. Her hands groped over him, sliding beneath his coat, clutching at his shoulders.

He pressed her against the door with his hips, the hard length of his erection between them. She hitched reflexively, and he felt so good, so right that an unbidden mewl of longing escaped her. He reached under her skirt and . . .

Then they heard someone rap impatiently on the door knocker downstairs.

Breathless, they broke the kiss, saying in unison, "Woodbine."

Forehead pressed to hers, Asher's hand lingered at the edge of her stocking, his thumb rousing tingles and pulses beneath her skin. She held on to him tighter. Perhaps, if they were quiet, they could . . .

He shook his head as if they shared the same thought. Then, after a reluctant exhale, he gently lowered her.

"I need to speak with your father," he said, taking special care to smooth her clothes in place and leaving her jelly-kneed with every skillful pass of his hands.

She beamed with a breathless smile, leaning against the door for support.

"But I can't marry you."

Her smile fell. *"Whot?"*

He grinned and leaned in to kiss her, while situating his own clothes. "Not today. I can't go to your father without any prospects at all."

"Whatever are we going to do, then?"

"I don't know, but I will figure out something soon. I promise," he said sincerely. "And when I return—and I will do so with as much haste as I can manage—be prepared to leave with me that very minute. Have your bags packed and waiting."

"Are you going to abduct me?"

"If I have to." He winked at her and walked over to retrieve her pillow, then put it in her hands. "In the meantime, keep our child safe."

She hugged it to her bosom. "You'd asked me to come with you. Would you really have taken me aboard the ship without even marrying me first?"

"I even had a plan to disguise you as a friar. I think I would have liked you in a robe with nothing underneath." He brushed his wicked grin across her lips.

"Scoundrel."

Then he sobered and gathered her in his arms, crushing the pillow. "Though, to tell you the truth, I'm glad my father commandeered the ship."

Asher nodded. "He did. And he would absolutely hate to know that his act of subterfuge hasn't left me in unmitigated despair. Quite the contrary. I have all that my heart could ever desire, because now I'm here with you."

She sighed, glad he was here as well, but also hated that his dreams had been dashed. Lifting her hand, she smoothed the silken dark tendrils away from his forehead. "I know you had your heart set on finally being free of all his manipulations."

"And I shall still manage it, somehow. You've re-kindled hope within me. Who knows? Perhaps the

Hollander twins will have discovered another treasure map by the time I make my way to their townhouse."

"You seem so certain," she said, gazing up at him with her heart.

"Because you make everything possible. You and your—*No carriage? Then fine, we'll walk. No money? We'll sing for our supper*—taught me that no obstacle is insurmountable. At least, as long as I have you." He lowered his head for another lingering kiss, then stepped apart from her. "But before I leave, I must ask you a question."

She grinned, imagining she knew what he was about to say. "Go on, then. I'm waiting."

"Winn," he said with grave sincerity as he tilted up her chin, "would you like me to kill Mr. Woodbine on my way out, or just maim him for being so horrible to you?"

She rolled her eyes. "Just leave, and don't come back until you have the right question on your lips."

Chapter 32

Still utterly destitute, Asher now walked to the Hollanders' townhouse with a quick step, optimistic that some grand plan would start to unfold.

In order to marry Winn, he needed enough to return every farthing Lord Waldenfield had paid him. Enough to pay off his father's debt to Seabrooke, and never face his henchmen again. Additional money for the special license, a place to live . . . to start their lives . . .

Not only that, he needed to ask Waldenfield for permission *and* to withdraw Winn's dowry. He didn't want her ever to question how much he loved her. Having her was all that mattered to him.

Unfortunately, by the time he arrived at the Hollanders' townhouse, he hadn't come up with a single idea worth a shake of salt. He hoped they'd be struck by one of their farfetched, but surprisingly brilliant, ideas. In the back of his mind, however, he felt guilty for the way that his father had taken away their dreams as well, and knew they'd likely be drowning their sorrows for weeks to come.

Climbing the stairs to their study, he was surprised to hear them laughing heartily. And when he entered the drawing room, he was shocked to see who was standing with them.

"*You,*" Asher said to the man with the gray mustachios. Not only had he sold this man his knife in the village square across from the Grinning Boar, but now he recalled seeing him at Mr. Windle's jewelry shop the day they'd tried to sell Winn's pearls.

The man bowed with a flourish and in his gravelly bark of a voice said, "Sir Roderick Devine at your service."

"The privateer?" Asher asked, looking to One and Two, who were grinning like cats who'd eaten the heads and tails of all the goldfish in a bowl. And it seemed like they weren't going to tell him a thing, so he turned his attention back to Devine. "The Hollanders bought your hunting lodge."

"True enough," Devine said with a sly, amused twitch of his mustachios.

"Yet I was under the impression that—and forgive me for saying this—you'd *died* years ago."

"Privateering was a precarious walk along the plank. One minute, you're looting for the crown, but then the war ends and suddenly it's treason." He lifted his hands in a helpless shrug. "So I arranged to make it appear as though I'd perished at sea, rather than face the hangman's noose."

"As anyone would," Asher said, digesting this in slow bites.

Then he saw Bates nudge Avery with his elbow, both of them fairly bursting with laughter. The former coughed into his fist, poorly disguising his words, "Ask him about the treasure map."

Asher glanced back to Devine. "Is it real?"

"Indeed. The map is the genuine article." That sly grin returned. "The treasure, however, was unearthed years ago."

The twins guffawed, slapping each other on the back.

"And to think," One said, "we'd have sailed all that way for nothing but sea air and sand."

"Holt, your father has done us all a favor," Two added, wheezing.

Devine handed a waiting glass to Asher and poured a liberal amount of rum into it. "Just what a man like Shettlemane deserves, I should think."

Asher took the glass and scrutinized the stranger. "How is it that you knew my name in the village, and that you seem to know my father?"

Devine's winged brows rose and he looked to Asher. "I'll only say that I am acquainted with someone who knew your father long ago. Now, let us forget treasure maps for the moment and drink a toast, for I've been informed by these fine fellows that you have settled your heart on taking a wife."

Asher held up a hand. "Don't startle the Fates. I'm still unsure of how to accomplish this feat. But I must, and *before* her father decides to marry her to someone else."

"What can we do to help?" Avery asked, staggering up to tap his glass to Asher's and gulp down a hearty swallow. He was half drunk and it wasn't even noon.

"Do you know of anyone who might need a shop clerk? A cobbler looking for an apprentice?"

DIRECTLY FOLLOWING Asher's departure, Winnifred went to her father's study, prepared to call off the wedding. With her hand on the latch, she took in a deep breath to garner her courage. But when she heard Mr. Woodbine's voice beyond the door, she paused, listening.

"I think an additional five thousand pounds per annum should justify all the inconvenience I've suffered," he said.

"Or better yet," her father began, his tone dropping so low with warning that it raised gooseflesh on the back of her neck, "let us discuss a certain necklace and the note that came with it."

Realizing that she'd left the pearls in the parlor, she rushed back to retrieve them. When she returned to her father's study to hand them over, however, she opened the door to find him gripping the front of Mr. Woodbine's cravat and glaring down into his wide, terrified eyes.

"*Settlement for breach of contract?* How dare you! My daughter was always too good for the likes of you. You money-grubbing worm. If I had that necklace in my hand, I'd cram it down—"

"Thank you, Father," she said, stepping into the room, so happy she could burst. Whalebone beware!

He abruptly released her betrothed and cleared his throat. And when she laid the necklace in her father's hand, the ashen Mr. Woodbine fled the room without a backward glance, nearly bowling Mother over in the corridor.

"Julian," Mother tsked, but with a smile playing on her lips. "Did you threaten Mr. Woodbine?"

He straightened his coat. "I did, indeed."

"What a relief!" Mother said, shocking Winnifred to her heels. "I am glad we're finally rid of him. I cannot count the times I'd wanted to tweak that man's nose whenever he wrinkled it with distaste. I hope the duke and his brothers live forever and that overbearing stuffed shirt never inherits."

Father nodded in stern agreement, and looked to his dumbfounded daughter. "I only wanted what was best for you, but I refused to acknowledge what a complete arse that man is. If I'm to be honest, I was ready to beat the pulp out of him the day these arrived." He held up the pearls, then dropped them with an unceremonious clatter onto his desk. "Thankfully, you had more sense than I. Though that isn't to say I'm condoning you running away and worrying your mother sick, young lady."

"Quite true," Mother agreed, but reached out and squeezed her hand. "Even so, I have made my share of mistakes. Instead of trying to prepare you for heartache, I should have taught you to honor the demands of your heart. A marriage should have love *and* affection to see it through hardships."

Realizing her mouth was agape, Winnifred closed it with a snap. Who were these people and what had they done with her parents?

"Now, what's this I hear from the servants about Lord Holt paying a call this morning?" Mother asked, and Father's brows lowered.

Winnifred blushed under their combined scrutiny. "Well, you see . . . Lord Holt and I have something of an understanding between us. I have every confidence that he will soon request an audience with you to ask for my hand in marriage."

She relayed a few more details—though none that would compel her father to *beat the pulp* out of Asher—and explained that they'd both professed their love to each other.

Mother smiled and embraced her.

Father's brows remained low. "I'm not convinced that Holt is worthy. He's a bit too arrogant if you ask me. Stood on my very doorstep last night and tried to tell me that he knew my daughter better than I did."

"Father." Winnifred set her hands on her hips, her stubborn glower matching his own.

"Then again," he added on a resigned exhale, "I suppose it wouldn't hurt to give him another chance."

"If you'll recall, Julian," Mother said, slipping her arm beneath his, "my father wasn't terribly pleased with you either. He thought you were too full of yourself."

Father gazed down at her with a reminiscent grin. "I had you on my arm, Genie. How could I help but be a little full of myself?"

Again, Winnifred gaped at her parents. She had no idea what had transpired between them for such an alteration, but she wasn't about to question something that filled her with hope.

"I'll just leave the two of you alone then . . ." she said, backing out of the room. "I'm going to check with the kitchen about the tea I'm serving when Jane and Ellie arrive."

"Oh, that reminds me," Mother interjected, following her into the corridor. "The first few of your altered dresses arrived a moment ago. They will be simply lovely on you, I'm certain." She pursed her lips as she slid a glance to her daughter. "Don't give me that look of disbelief, and stop waiting for me to add something critical. I took your words to heart, my dear. And I am trying to make up for the years I've wasted every opportunity to fawn on you."

Winnifred rolled her eyes. "I hardly need *fawning*."

"Then at least, tell me you are eager to try on each dress, complete with hat and gloves."

"Must I be *eager* or simply willing?" she asked with a wry lift of her brows. What had she gotten herself into?

⚜⚜⚜

A SHORT while later, Asher stepped out of the Hollanders' townhouse, ready to embark on his first order of business.

"Holt," Devine called from behind him, donning his hat as he left the townhouse as well. "I know you have plans to scour London for a prospect, but I wonder if I might talk to you for a moment. Would you share my carriage, by chance?"

"I'd be honored," Asher said, climbing inside the sleek lacquered chaise. He gave the direction of his solicitor's office in Cheapside.

He'd formulated a plan of action to extricate himself from his father's grip. He knew there was little he could do about his father borrowing money against his name. There would always be disreputable money-lenders who chose to ignore proper procedures. But he could draft letters, stating that he refused to be held responsible for monies lent to anyone who falsely used his identity. This might be the only thing to help him in court over the years to come and keep him out of Fleet.

When they were on their way, Devine didn't waste any time. "I wanted to return this knife," he said, placing it on the table between them. "It wouldn't be right for me to keep it. After all, it's part of your inheritance."

Asher looked down at it with fondness. "It is all I had left of my mother's, but I cannot accept it. Our trade was a binding agreement. You helped me out of a tight spot and this is the very least I can do to repay you."

Besides, he'd been clinging to places and objects that inspired her memory long enough. His mother would always be with him, no matter if he had the knife or visited her grave at Ashbrook Cottage.

Devine stared at him quizzically. Then gradually, one side of his mustachios twitched in a grin. "You're not at all like your father. It was always Liliandra's wish that you would favor your mother's temperament."

"Liliandra?" Asher startled, sitting forward. "Do you mean my Great-Aunt Lolly?"

Devine chuckled. "As I said, this knife is part of your inheritance. Didn't your mother ever tell you about her aunt stealing away on a ship?"

"And just how would *you* know anything about that?"

"As the perished privateer that I am, my name is Sir Roderick Devine. Yet for years on the open seas, I was an infamous pirate known as the Mad Macaw. And I offered the treasure that goes along with that knife to Liliandra when I proposed. Bold as brass, she'd said she would only marry me if she could give the entire ship and the treasure in its hold to your mother. She even made me sign a contract and put the whole of it in safekeeping."

Stunned in speechless disbelief, Asher couldn't form a reply.

"Liliandra read your mother's letters to me," Devine continued. "That is how I became acquainted with your father. And she'd always wanted your mother to be able to escape."

Someday, Asher . . . Someday, the two of us are going to sail away on a treasure ship and start a whole new life, full of adventure.

"So the stories were true?"

"Knowing Liliandra and her inclination to protect your mother, she likely didn't tell the whole story."

Asher blinked. "And to think, my mother had a treasure all that time. Did she know?"

"Aye, but she wrote to Liliandra and asked that it be kept from you for a time."

"She was afraid that I would turn out like my father," Asher surmised. And thinking of Shettlemane, he felt a shiver course through him. "Once he realizes that there isn't any treasure from the map he stole—and after an entire voyage of imagining how he'd spend it—he'll be even more of a ruthless gambler than before. No. It is still best in safekeeping. Perhaps I'll leave it for my own children one day."

"I'm afraid that won't be possible," Devine said gravely. "You see, there's much more to tell you about Liliandra."

Chapter 33

Winnifred waited all morning and the early part of the afternoon for Asher to make an appearance, but he never came. Though he had sent a puzzling parcel earlier of a half-dozen black cravats and a note that read,

> *Eager for a fresh start. Do with these what you will.*
>
> *Yours irrevocably,*
> *Holt*

Thankfully, both Jane and Ellie had arrived a short time ago, to distract her.

She'd sent them the news of her broken betrothal to Mr. Woodbine and her reconciliation with Asher. Over tea, she'd given them all the thrilling details—well, *nearly* all—about how she intended to marry Asher. *If* he should ever arrive on her doorstep.

"I'm glad it's all settled between you," Jane said, fishing through her enormous paisley reticule. "Because Lord Holt did, indeed, stop by my parents' house and try to persuade me to give you some letters he'd written. Though, regrettably, I'd set my brothers on the attack before I'd bothered to look at them. Ah, here it is." She lifted a fat, wrinkly scroll tied with a red ribbon and waved it like a baton, then placed it within Winnifred's grasp across the low oval table. "But take care with how you unroll it. I didn't have all the pieces and there are some parts missing altogether—I believe my brothers ate them—but you'll soon see that they aren't letters at all. They're chapters."

Winnifred stared at her in puzzlement.

"For our primer," Jane added with a little nudge. "Go on, take a look and see for yourself."

Strangely, her hands were shaking when she untied the ribbon. Asher had written chapters for the primer?

The instant she read the scrawled words "When a Scoundrel Meets His Match: And Why Drinking an Entire Pint of Rum Isn't Always a Terrible Thing," she smiled. And scanning farther down, her eyes misted over when she saw "How to Tempt a Scoundrel: And Twelve Reasons a Debutante Should Never Hide Her Freckles."

Perhaps she was starting not to mind her freckles after all.

"You're blushing," Ellie said with a cheeky grin. "If you're going to read the whole of it now, please do so aloud. Though you may whisper the more salacious parts, if you like. Just not too quietly."

Winnifred didn't have the chance to respond. In that same moment, the butler appeared at her side, presenting her with a letter on a salver. She set the scroll aside with tender care and inspected the letter.

"It's from Prue," she said, eagerly unfolding the single page to the crisp handwriting. They hadn't heard from her for a fortnight. "'Dearest Winnie, Lord F—has found me.'"

"Dear heavens!" Ellie exclaimed. "What an ominous beginning."

"I shudder to think what will come next."

Winnifred eyed her friends over the edge of the paper. "You would surely discover the answer sooner if I may continue."

"No one is preventing you," Jane said with an impatient swirl of her hand in the air.

"'Lord F— has found me,'" she repeated for effect. "'We met by chance at an assembly and he asked me to dance. I could barely speak, let alone refuse him. And before he handed me back to my aunt, he whispered that he would pay a call on the morrow. I was nothing but nerves and jitters all day. However, instead of a call, I received a missive through my maid, explaining that my aunt and uncle barred him from entering their house, and I nearly breathed a sigh of relief. Until I read what came next. If you can believe it, he asked me to steal away at midnight so that he might speak with me. I am in such a dither that I hardly know what to do. I should not slip out of my window in the middle of the night to see him. And yet . . . how can I not? I shall write again on the morrow with more news. Your muddleheaded friend, Prudence Thorogood.'"

"Lord F— is most definitely a scoundrel. There's no question," Ellie said.

Jane nodded, her lips pursed in contemplation. "We should expand our research. Not only should we scrutinize the methods of the marriage-minded gentleman, but we should learn absolutely everything there is to know about scoundrels. I'm certain it will be of use."

Her friends nodded in commiseration, then looked to Winnifred.

She swallowed. "All I can say is that they are quite persuasive and far too easy to fall in love with."

"What's this?" a low, familiar drawl said from the doorway, causing tingles to race over her skin. "Surely you haven't fallen in love with anyone else since we last saw each other, Winn."

She grinned without turning to face Asher. "I suppose that depends on what you have to say to me."

Her friends gawked at her.

Ellie said, "But you've gone to the window a thousand times— *Ouch!*"

She stopped when Jane pinched her and held a finger to her lips.

"I have a question for you, Miss Winnifred Humphries," Asher said, sending her heart skittering beneath her breast.

Unable to bear their separation a moment longer, she stood and found herself gathered in his arms as he swung her around in a circle. She smiled, her greedy gaze roving over his dark features as if it had been years instead of hours since she'd seen him. And he looked quite splendid in a fresh white cravat.

"Are your trunks packed?"

She set her hands on his shoulders and her slippers on the ground. "That isn't the right question."

"Very well, then," he said with a rakish grin. "How would you like to set sail by week's end and visit my Great-Aunt Lolly in the south of France?"

She gasped. "Truly?"

He nodded.

But then she shook her head. "I want to say yes, but that is still not the right question." After all, she recalled how willing he was to take her on a ship without marrying her first.

"Would you like to travel till your heart's content, then live in Ashbrook Cottage—with me, of course—for the rest of your life?"

"Ashbrook Cottage? But I thought your father . . ."

He shrugged smugly. "I hold the deed now. Not only that, but a *friend* of mine and I took care of matters with Lord Seabrooke and his henchmen as well."

"That's rather mysterious."

"Would you have me any other way?"

She arched a brow and stepped apart from him. "I'm not certain I'll have you at all."

"Stubborn," he said and leaned in to steal a kiss. Then he knelt down.

Ellie gasped. Jane issued a huff of impatience. Her father cleared his throat at the door, and her mother said, "Hush," and swatted Father's arm.

"I have your father's consent, and a special license," he said softly. Then he tsked her and stood again, removing a handkerchief from his pocket. "I'll never get through this if you cry, because then I'll have to kiss you."

Her father cleared his throat again.

She blinked rapidly as if that would dry up the flood gathering along the lower rims of her lashes. "It's just that everyone I care most about in the whole world is here in this room and I'm so happy."

He dabbed away the tears that dropped as he whispered, "I fell in love with you when we were standing at the crossroads. It started to rain and it just washed over me—the feeling that my life would be empty without you by my side. Marry me, Winn? Be with me for every adventure, and for every quiet moment, and for everything in between?"

Blubbering in earnest now, she nodded. "Of course I will. Just . . . not quite yet."

Her scoundrel was leaning in to kiss her again when he stopped and blinked in confusion. Then Asher, her friends and her parents all exclaimed a simultaneous *"Whot?"*

Winnifred sniffed, taking hold of the handkerchief in his lax fingertips. "As you know, Jane, Ellie and I are writing a book. I cannot possibly abandon them. They are my dearest friends and—"

He silenced her with a gentle fingertip to her lips. "I know how important this is to you, and it is your loyalty to your friends that makes me love you all the more."

"Oh, Winnie, for heaven's sakes!" Jane declared, rising to her feet. "If you don't marry this man—"

"This instant," Ellie chimed in with watery-eyed vehemence.

"—then we'll never forgive you."

"But what about our book?"

Asher took her hand in his. "You could always write your chapters in letters to them."

"Brilliant notion, Lord Holt," Jane offered. Then, looking a bit chagrined, she shrugged. "And I apologize for threatening to poison you with a vinaigrette and for sending the *horde* after you."

"Perfectly reasonable under the circumstances." He inclined his head. Then he turned back to Winnifred, expectation in his gaze.

She didn't leave him wondering. "Yes! I'll marry you without delay."

Since it was official, she expected him to kiss her. Instead, he kneeled down again.

"There's one more thing you should know," he said, unsheathing his pearl-handled knife from his boot.

She gasped, eyes wide. "But how did you get it back?"

"Winn," he said with a grin and a lift of his dark brows, "have I got a story to tell you."

Epilogue

South of France
October

Winnifred found Asher in the garden on the bluff where they often stood together, gazing out beyond the limestone balustrade toward the vast blue of the cape. The afternoon sun was low enough in the sky to gild the breaking waves and the tops of palm tree fronds rustling in the Mediterranean breeze.

They'd been living in this paradisiacal white stone chateau as guests of Sir Roderick and Liliandra since they'd arrived in April.

Months ago, after learning the news that Sir Roderick's hunting lodge had been sold, Aunt Lolly and Sir Roderick had set sail for England from their island home. The sale had meant that the treasonous privateer, Sir Roderick Devine, had been declared dead, and it was now safe for him to return.

Yet once they reached the coast of France, Lolly had been in the grip of a malaria fever. But she was determined to meet her great-nephew at last, so Sir Roderick vowed to bring him to her.

Winnifred recalled the instant she'd first met Lolly. She couldn't believe that the slender, spirited woman with the dark eyes and shoulder-length hair the color of moonlight had ever been sick. Lolly was more full of life than anyone she'd ever met.

With a hearty embrace, she'd welcomed Asher as if he were her own son, then welcomed Winnifred with the same motherly affection. Well, *if* Mother had been a pirate.

Smiling at the thought, Winnifred grazed her fingertips over the smooth trunks of the skinned palm trees along the familiar stone path and made her way to Asher.

With his head bent and hands clasped behind his back, his attention seemed to be on the brightly colored fish in the fountain pool. As she drew closer, however, she noted the pensive furrows on his brow and wondered what was weighing on his mind.

Yet the instant he turned to see her approach, his contemplative frown disappeared into an easy grin. He held out his hand to her. "Have you finished your chapters, at last?"

"As you will note by the dreadful black stains on my fingers," she said, offering them for inspection. He took hold of her hands and tugged her into his arms, drawing in a deep breath as she melted lovingly against him. "I fear it will take days before the ink will wash away."

"All the better for me, because it appears you've given yourself a dark freckle here on your chin as well."

She grinned when he kissed her there. "That must have been when I was thinking of how to answer some of Jane's questions. She requires more information to understand just how and when I realized that you were a gentleman with honorable intent instead of a scoundrel bent on seduction. Though I suspect she has a personal reason for wanting to know. She mentioned a certain man in her letter."

"Did you give her an answer, then?"

"I didn't. I'm afraid my mind started to wander to . . . this morning."

A wicked gleam lit his gaze. "Before our sea bath or after?"

"During," she said on a low sigh as his lips grazed her earlobe and he began to nibble her neck. "You proved that the water wasn't too cold, after all."

"You kept me quite warm and snug." He went back to the mark on her chin. "This gives me ideas of how I could put freckles all over your body and pay homage to them."

"I will not have spots of ink all over my body. What will my maid think?"

"Likely that you've been frolicking *in the buff* with your husband in the broad light of day." He waggled his brows with meaning and she blushed, thinking of *after* sea bathing. She'd had sand in more places than she ever thought existed on herself.

"Enough of that talk or we'll soon be scandalizing those fish." She tsked him playfully, then turned more serious as she brushed a wind-ruffled lock from his brow. "When I'd first walked into the garden, it seemed as though something was on your mind. Would you like to tell me about it?"

"I was only thinking about a report I'd heard from one of Devine's crew. Apparently, my father has re-married."

"Oh?" Winnifred's brows lifted. "Do you suppose he fell in love?"

He shook his head. "Shettlemane can only love money. Which means that this American widow must have a great deal of it."

"Perhaps we should warn her, do you think?"

"She's a widow six times over. I'm not entirely sure that *she* is the one who needs the warning. And when you came upon me, I was contemplating whether or not to send him a letter."

Winnifred smoothed his worry lines with the soft pad of her thumb and rose up on her toes to press her lips to his. "I think you should. You can send your letter along with mine. Oh, and my aunt Myrtle wonders if we plan to return by Christmastide, as do my mother and father."

"Whenever you should like to return, you need only say the word. I am ever at your beck and call for any sort of adventure."

Gazing up at him, she wondered how she could love someone so deeply in such a short amount of time and, moreover, have him love her in return. Perhaps it was just like Asher had once said to her—that with all the rain they'd encounter something was bound to take deep root and blossom, and for them it was love. Simple as that.

It didn't seem possible, but she grew more content every day. In fact, especially today.

She was fairly bursting with the secret news she'd had on her lips since morning. One of the maids in the house was also a midwife, and she'd confirmed what Winnifred had been suspecting for the past two months.

"Then again," he said, cutting through her thoughts

with a tone of uncertainty, and drawing her attention to the way his gaze softened on hers, "perhaps we should wait until after our child is born."

"You cad!" She swatted at him as he held her, though wriggling, in his arms. "How long have you known?"

He chuckled, nipping at the frown on her bottom lip. "Winn, we haven't spent a single day or night apart. It became fairly apparent when you stopped having your courses."

"Hush!" she said, blushing to the soles of her feet, searching the garden to see if anyone was near. "You could have made known your suspicions."

"To be honest, I suspected you were going to tell me this morning before sea bathing, and I was so over-joyed by the very thought that I was swept away in the moment . . . before, during *and* after."

"Then you don't mind lingering here awhile longer?"

"I only want to be wherever I can hold you, where I can feel every beat of your heart, hear every sigh, breathe in your sweet fragrance, and taste every kiss."

"Even if there's . . . quite a bit more of me as the months go by?"

Whatever fears she may have had were put to rest as he splayed his hand in a warm caress over her middle. "I cannot imagine anything more beautiful than seeing your lush body swell with my child, and I know I will love you all the more."

And, in the end, that was all that mattered.

Don't miss the next installment in
The Mating Habits of Scoundrels, wherein
a bluestocking on a quest for information stumbles
upon the long-lost heir to an earldom . . .
in the London underworld!

MY KIND OF EARL

Fall 2020

Who will this mysterious hero be?
If you've read THE ROGUE TO RUIN,
you've met him! If not, now is your chance . . .

At Avon Books, we know your passion for romance—once you finish one of our novels, you find yourself wanting more.

May we tempt you with . . .

- **Excerpts** from our upcoming releases.

- Entertaining **extras**, including authors' personal photo albums and book lists.

- Behind-the-scenes **scoop** on your favorite characters and series.

- **Sweepstakes** for the chance to win free books, romantic getaways, and other fun prizes.

- Writing **tips** from our authors and editors.

- **Blog** with our authors and find out why they love to write romance.

- **Exclusive content** that's not contained within the pages of our novels.

Join us at
www.avonbooks.com

An Imprint of HarperCollins*Publishers*
www.avonromance.com

Available wherever books are sold or please call 1-800-331-3761 to order.

FTH 1013

*G*ive in to your Impulses!

These unforgettable stories only take a second to buy and give you hours of reading pleasure!

Go to *www.AvonImpulse.com* and see what we have to offer.

Available wherever e-books are sold.

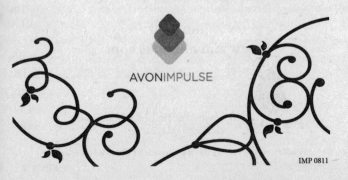

AVONIMPULSE

IMP 0811